THE WRATH OF SETH

T0151676

About the authors

Born in Switzerland, Oliver Frey a.k.a. Zack ended up in London and, after attending film school, plunged into gay art and publishing. Innumerable illustrations poured from his pen and brush for British magazines *HIM International*, *Vulcan*, *Teenage Dreams*, the *HIM Gay Library* series, and *Mister* magazine. For *HIM* he created the mold-breaking Rogue comic strip and later *The Street*, which was part of the inspiration behind cult TV series *Queer As Folk*. The Internet has spread his reputation to an enormous global fan base through many sites and blogs. Some of his comic-strip work has been published recently by Bruno Gmünder—*Bike Boy*, *Hot For Boys: the Sexy Adventures of Rogue*, and *Bike Boy Rides Again*. As Zack, Frey has taken gay erotic art and comics to new dimensions. He lives with life-long partner Roger Kean in a medieval town on the edge of Wales.

British-born author Roger Kean, who met Oliver at film school, has had careers as a movie cameraman, film editor, journalist, and magazine and book editor. As an author he has written books on historical subjects both factual and fictional, and gay fiction, including: *Felixitations*; *Thunderbolt–Torn Enemy of Rome*; *A Life Apart*; *Gregory's Story*; *What's A Boy Supposed to Do*; and for Bruno Gmünder *Boys of Vice City*, *Boys of Disco City*, *Boys of Two Cities*, *Boys of the Fast Lane*, *Boy of the West End*, *Blood and Lust*, *The Warrior's Boy*, *Deadly Circus of Desire* and *The Satyr of Capri*.

BOYS OF IMPERIAL ROME

THE WRATH OF SETH

by Zack

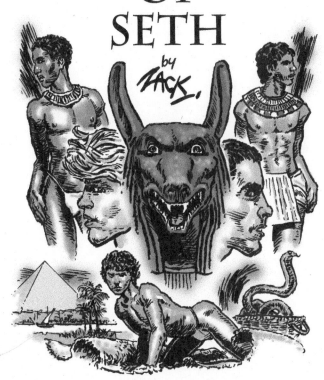

BRUNO GMÜNDER

Copyright © 2016 Bruno Gmünder GmbH
Kleiststraße 23-26, 10787 Berlin, Germany
Phone: +49 30 61 50 03-0
Fax: +49 30 61 50 03-20
info@brunogmuender.com

All text and artwork © 2016 Reckless Books-Zack/Oliver Frey & Roger Kean
www.zack-art.com

All characters depicted are 18 years of age or older.

Printed in Germany
ISBN: 978-3-95985-155-8

More information about Bruno Gmünder books and authors:
www.brunogmuender.com

To Scavola and Rick Russell for their
enthusiastic encouragement

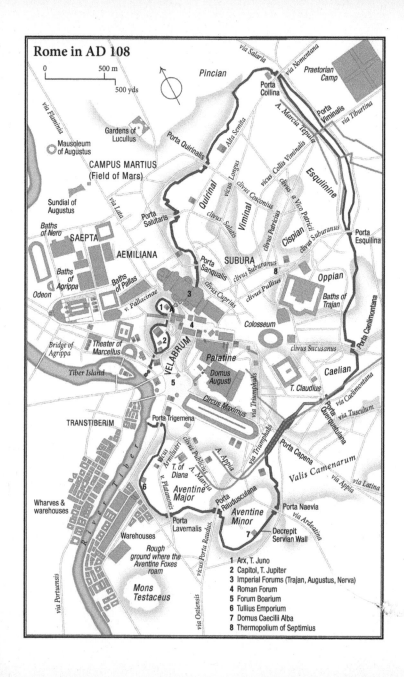

Rome in AD 108

0 — 500 m
500 yds

Pincian

via Salaria

via Nomentana

Praetorian Camp

Porta Collina

Porta Viminalis

via Tiburtina

A. Marcia Tepula

via Flaminia

Gardens of Lucullus

Mausoleum of Augustus

Porta Quirinalis

Alta Semita

CAMPUS MARTIUS
(Field of Mars)

vicus Longus

vicus Collis Viminalis

clivus Coseonius

clivus a Vico Patrici

Esquiline

Quirinal

Sundial of Augustus

via Lata

Porta Salutaris

clivus Salutis

Viminal

clivus Patricius

clivus Suburanus

Porta Esquilina

Baths of Nero

SAEPTA

AEMILIANA

Baths of Agrippa

Baths of Pallas

Baths of Pallas

Porta Sanqualis

SUBURA

clivus Suburanus

clivus Pullius

Cispian

8

Oppian

Baths of Trajan

Odeon

Porta Caelimontana

v. Pallacinae

clivus Cupris

3

Colosseum

1 A

Bridge of Agrippa

Theater of Marcellus

2

4

clivus Sucusanus

Caelian

Palatine

Domus Augusti

T. Claudius

Tiber Island

5

via Triumphalis

Circus Maximus

via Caelimontana

via Tusculum

TRANSTIBERIM

Porta Trigemena

via Triumphalis

Porta Querquetulana

vicus Armilustri

clivus Publicius

A. Appia

Porta Capena

Porta Capena

T. of Diana

v. Marcia

Valis Camenarum

via Appia

Bridge of Agrippa

River Tiber

6

Aventine Major

via Appia Latina

v. Platonius

Wharves & warehouses

Porta Lavernalis

Porta Raudusculana

Aventine Minor

7

Porta Naevia

via Ardeatina

Warehouses

Rough ground where the Aventine Foxes roam

vicus Porta Raudis.

Decrepit Servian Wall

Mons Testaceus

via Ostiensis

via Portuensis

1 Arx, T. Juno
2 Capitol, T. Jupiter
3 Imperial Forums (Trajan, Augustus, Nerva)
4 Roman Forum
5 Forum Boarium
6 Tullius Emporium
7 Domus Caecilii Alba
8 Thermopolium of Septimius

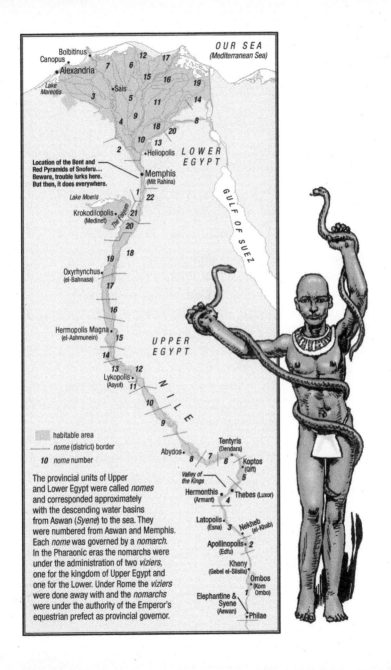

OUR SEA
(Mediterranean Sea)

Bolbitinus
Canopus
Alexandria
Lake Mareotis
Sais

7 12 17
6
15 16
3 5 11
9
4 18 20
10 13
2
Heliopolis

14
8
19

LOWER EGYPT

GULF OF SUEZ

Location of the Bent and Red Pyramids of Snoferu...
Beware, trouble lurks here.
But then, it does everywhere.

Memphis (Mit Rahina)

Lake Moeris

Krokodilopolis (Medinet)

1 22
21
20
18

The Fayum

Oxyrhynchus (el-Bahnasa)

19
17
16

Hermopolis Magna (el-Ashmunein)

15
14

UPPER EGYPT

Lykopolis (Asyut)

13 12
11
10
9

NILE

habitable area

nome (district) border

10 nome number

The provincial units of Upper
and Lower Egypt were called *nomes*
and corresponded approximately
with the descending water basins
from Aswan (*Syene*) to the sea. They
were numbered from Aswan and Memphis.
Each *nome* was governed by a *nomarch*.
In the Pharaonic eras the nomarchs were
under the administration of two *viziers*,
one for the kingdom of Upper Egypt and
one for the Lower. Under Rome the *viziers*
were done away with and the *nomarchs*
were under the authority of the Emperor's
equestrian prefect as provincial governor.

Abydos

Tentyris (Dendara)

8 7 6 Koptos (Qift)
5
Valley of the Kings

Hermonthis (Armant) 4 Thebes (Luxor)

Latopolis (Esna) 3 Nekheb (el-Khab)

Apollinopolis (Edfu) 2

Kheny (Gebel el-Silsila)

Ombos (Kom Ombo)

Elephantine & Syene (Aswan) 1

Philae

In spite of Rufio's moans of protest, Quintus Caecilius Alba, as a highly educated patrician, feels it might be useful to understand units of Roman measure. The **uncia** (**unciae**, pl.) is the Roman inch (and ounce) and is $\frac{1}{12}$ of a **pes** (**pedes**, pl.), the Roman foot (modern: 0.971 ft / 29.6 cm). 2½ *pedes* equals a **gradus** (**gradii**, pl.) or "yard" (modern: 2.427 ft / 0.75 m). 5 *pedes* (4.854 ft / 1.48 m) equals a **passus**. A **stadium** is 625 *pedes* (607 ft / 185 m) and finally it takes 5000 *pedes* to make a **mille** or *mille passus*, the Roman mile (0.919 mi / 2.22 km). But don't worry, as sensible boys they won't expect you to remember much of that…

Finally—at Rufio's insistence—as a budding poet, Quintus would like to apologize in advance to Catullus.

"Slow down a moment," Rufio said.

Quintus caught hold of Flaccus by the arm. "Go where?"

Flaccus gave both boys an exasperated look. "Don't you listen? The Emperor's off to Egypt, and you're going with him."

Quintus and Rufio exchanged startled glances, both thinking exactly the same: *There is great danger to Caesar should he venture to Egypt... and to all who might go with him.*

P·R·O·L·O·G·U·E | ANTELOGIUM

138 years earlier: Alexandria, 3rd day of Sextilis, 30 BC

A blast of wind blew the last of the desert's daytime furnace across Mareotis. The lake's brackish waters did little to dampen its hot blast, which bore a tempest of sand in its grasp. The flying grit scoured the temple's walls, walls that looked as ancient as Egypt itself though in truth it was a modern building, created barely two hundred years before by the third Ptolemy, known as Euergetes, the Benefactor. But little of benevolence existed within the twisted precincts of this far-flung adjunct of Alexandria's famous Serapeum.

Such ill boding failed to bother the handsome young man in his early thirties who approached. A peremptory hand motion signaled his friend Agrippa and the two most loyal and trusted guards of his praetorium to remain outside; the matter that had brought him to this place—dreaded by ordinary Egyptians—was one that he alone must attend to. If the blood about to be shed was indeed royal it should be on his hands alone. It seemed an appropriate location for the final act and he felt no trepidation at entering the *temenos*—the official domain of the incorporeal being to who the temple was dedicated: Seth, god of disorder, misrule, and chaos. Was he not himself the adopted son of a powerful god and was he not now the undisputed ruler of the Roman world? He had come to bring order to chaos.

Small pylons formed little more than an ordinary open gateway to a long, narrow enclosure. An intricate frieze of thin, exotic figures, godlings of the ancient culture, decorated the tall sidewalls that abated the fretful wind. At the far end a paltry, undecorated opening pierced the hewn face of rock to which the sidewalls abutted. The light of flickering torches from inside spilled out unevenly onto the ground. The temple officiates had been given strict orders and, having carried out the necessary rites, had made themselves scarce amid muttered incantations of "*O Setepenptah, O Sekhemenkhamun—*"

Gaius Julius Caesar Octavianus wanted the one who now waited for him inside to be quite alone, the one the priests called the "Chosen of Ptah" and "Living Image of Amun-Ra." He had waved aside Agrippa's fears for his safety. What danger could a boy just turned seventeen be to him? A so-called prince raised in the effete court of Cleopatra and latterly under the lax patronage of Marcus Antonius, a callow youth, and now Caesar's prisoner. Yet living, Caesarion—Little Caesar—posed a very real dynastic threat…

He ducked under the low lintel. His nailed boots scraped hollowly on the stone entry step. The holy of holies within was cramped, little more than a transverse room with two darkened side chapels at either end. Underfoot, soft sand blanketed whatever stone lay beneath its shroud. Three firebrands planted in low iron sconces threw light across the ceiling, itself festooned with all manner of strange devices. The dancing flames brought the painted walls to life, a writhing convocation of ancient deities amid incomprehensible pictographs; primitive and disturbing. But he had eyes only for the boy.

Even as he withdrew his short sword from its scabbard Octavian sucked in a breath. The rumors were true after all. The bastard son of Julius Caesar was more beautiful than any Greek sculptor could envisage. Not in the Egyptian manner as he'd expected, face-painted like a doll with eyes enlarged by the artifice of khol. This boy was all manly Roman, sturdy, defiant, and surprisingly calm, considering his impending fate. He did not appear as a captive; his very stance suggested he regarded himself as Octavian's equal. His eyes glowed in the low light, a quiet appraisal of the victor come to claim—

"I know my life is forfeit, Octavianus."

He stepped close, unafraid or—if so—keeping his fears well hidden.

Octavian stepped forward as well, until their faces were but a hand's length apart. "Address me as Imperator, whelp." The quiet command sounded mild but contained a hint of steel. "Well, well… the juvenile who claims the name of Caesar."

"Because it is mine to claim. More than you, I think, for I am the direct issue of divine Julius Caesar's loins, whereas you *claim* only adoption."

Octavian took in the features of his adversary, of his youth, his vitality, his beauty. Abruptly, he threw out a spatulate hand and clasped the back of Caesarion's neck in a hard grip.

The boy resisted the pressure. His wide eyes were unwavering as he anticipated the sharp thrust of the drawn gladius to his vitals, unwilling to give the master of the world any satisfaction. The gasp he loosed at the shocking impact was smothered as Octavian's merciless lips covered his own.

For a moment drawn out to eternity intransigence ruled, and then the boy melted, parted his warm lips and let Octavian press through the yielding portal with his urgent tongue. It was the atmosphere in this place, perhaps something thrown on the flames by the departing priests, but Octavian's loins were on fire, his reason fled before the onslaught of erotic longing.

The world reeled, garish figures revolved around his mind, with their strange, tall crowns, the form of one slender alien with a long, thin, straight-out erect penis seemed to skewer Octavian with his blank gaze, and then the floor came up to meet him. He was aware of the gladius thrown from his hand in the fall, but the sandy floor cushioned the landing, and then the boy's lithe body lay entwined in his arms. Fire met fire, lusty, urgent, a flurry of exploring hands groping between his thighs, arousing him.

All but one torch had burned down to a stub. Octavian roused himself, sat up on the temple floor, alone. Caesarion was gone and Octavian was unsure how such a thing had occurred. The boy had bewitched him, overwhelmed his senses with the lure of sex. How had it come to this? How had his icy control, his far-seeing common sense been rendered so ineffective? And yet the evidence was laid before his eyes: the disturbed body shapes etched in the sand where they had lain and fucked… and the boy's absence. There was magic afoot in this cursed place. He came to create order yet succumbed to chaos. The whispered words came back to his dazed senses. A secret tunnel from behind a panel in one of the shrine's two Rammesid side chapels, he'd said as he planted a parting kiss on Octavian's forehead. But it hadn't been love, not even affection. There was something disturbingly gloating in the action.

Octavian staggered to his feet, recovered the discarded, unused gladius and pondered on how to persuade Agrippa that the deed had been successfully carried out, that the two guards were assured the threat to their commander's supremacy removed.

As he gathered strength and walked toward the temple entrance, the last torch guttered and died. Outside, the desert air had rapidly cooled. He pulled his cloak tight about his shoulders, briefly checking to see that any signs of what had really taken place showed... no stains of unbridled lust. No one would ever discover his shameful secret: that it had been Caesarion who fucked Caesar, that a mere boy's ardency had overcome and penetrated the Imperator. Octavian shuddered briefly, and then forcibly thrust away the memory. He was an achiever and a pragmatist. What was done was done, and what could one adolescent boy with no claim do to harm the power base he'd created?

He turned his back on the Temple of Seth. A myriad stars painted the black sky like an oriental king's diadem.

Across the lake a jackal moaned at the rising moon.

O·N·E | I

"I don't feel like a boy tonight." Flaccus Caepio groaned unhappily. He leaned against the slick wooden rail and retched hoarsely in a manner his colleagues in Rome's Cohort III Vigiles Urbanae would have derided as womanly. He'd lost count of the heaves, and still the tempest worsened. "Why, oh why by Neptune's twisted balls did I agree to come on this cursed voyage?"

"At least... *ooher*... you had a choice," Junius Tullius Rufio moaned in miserable sympathy as he threw up the last of what he'd reluctantly eaten for dinner. "I did — *heave* — not."

"Venus preserve us," Quintus huffed irritably at his companions. "How many times must I tell you that if you're going to void your guts do *not* do it into the wind. And bringing up dinner like that is such a waste. I think Septimius did us proud, considering the problems aboard ship. Those Cretan snails in garlic and garum were delic—*ughnn!*"

Quintus staggered back from the assault to his midriff. Rufio's cheeks might have been a glorious shade of green in contrast to his flaming red locks, somewhat dimmed where spray from towering waves plastered tendrils like seaweed to his broad forehead, but he still retained sufficient strength to jab his pointy elbow into his friend and lover's flat stomach. "It's not fair..." Rufio began, before lurching back to the ship's rail as another wave aided his own stomach's desire to be empty.

"It's hardly my fault that you suffer the sea!" Like his brother Marcus, Quintus Caecilius Alba found little to trouble him on the briny wave. *Perhaps it's because we are patrician while those two are merely plebs.*

14

He shook away the unworthy thought and turned with a stab of envy to the real presence of Marcus aboard the Emperor's flagship—at, it had to be added, at the Emperor's insistence. Instead of being on the exposed deck supervising his marines and rowers, Marcus was tucked up cozily in Trajan's cabin, no doubt getting a good imperial seeing to by his regal namesake. The Emperor had no problems with a rough sea either. Far from it, Quintus could well imagine how Marcus Ulpius Nerva Traianus would be using the quinquereme's wayward pitching to add a corkscrewing motion to his… screwing.

He dashed the back of a hand across his brow to clear salty water from his eyes and peered out with not a little trepidation at the gathering fury. Quintus understood Rufio's barely suppressed terror after the nightmare they had shared with sexy Cassander in the Bay of Naples early in May, when a tremendous storm caught them adrift in nothing more than a small fishing skiff. Of course, they had no idea then that two months later would find them afloat again but this time at the mercy of the great Middle Sea on the way to Egypt.

Fierce gusts of wind hurled white spume from breaking wave tops. The following gale drove the big quinquereme before it. Until this leg of the voyage, the weather had been kind, as Quintus recorded in the diary of their travels Caesar commanded him to write. ("I'm surrounded by official scribes, but I want your poetic muse to put some color into what we observe on this great journey.") The flagship *Fortuna* rowed out of Trajan's new port basin near Ostia on the 14th day of June and made Messana in Sicily two days later. They sailed again for Nicopolis in Epirus and from there to Monemvasia at the southern tip of the Peloponnesus. Then came the southerly crossing to Crete. After a short sojourn at Gortyn, provincial capital of Roman Creta et Cyrenaica, the vessel had set sail from Lentas on Crete's southern coast in fine weather on the 29th day of June, but the sea rose up with great rapidity, and now it felt as though only the high stern poop prevented the mountainous waves from plunging them all to the bottom of Neptune's watery graveyard.

As night came on the storm increased in ferocity. So far the Roman officers and marines remained calm, but Quintus saw unreasoning terror strike the land-lubber cohort of Praetorian Guards huddled with the presently redundant oarsmen under the eaves of the lower deck in a vain attempt to keep dry and hide from the angry ocean. The two helmsmen at the stern kept their posts manfully and struggled with the giant sweeps to keep the bow into the waves and the wind abaft to fill the reefed sails.

The senior officers—Centurion Maximianus and *Fortuna*'s captain, Trierach Maesenius—were gathered in the small poop-deck cabin with the pilot taken on at Lentas. Quintus guessed they'd be grumbling at Optio Marcus Quartus Caecilius Alba being absent from the deck watch and gossiping about what Empress Pompeia Plotina would think about him being in the Emperor's quarters—were she on board. Plotina was tucked away on the suitably named *Vesta* with her household slaves and female companions, while Hadrian and the rest of the Palatinate court followed in a third ship, the equally well-named *Apollo*. The self-styled prince—the Rising Sun, as he sometimes liked to style himself whenever Trajan was absent—relished residing in the bosom of his *comitatus*, his adolescent companions. Trajan much

preferred the soldier's solitary life, so long as the choice of two or three husky young men were at hand to enliven his nights. As often as not of late, that would be Rufio and Quintus, but since serendipity had thrown Marcus into the melting pot at Capri their services had been less in demand.

A freak of the gale brought a snatch of conversation to Quintus's ears. He heard gloom in the pilot's voice. "Things are bad, domini. Unless this storm blows out or the wind changes quarter we'll be dashed against the coast of Cyprus." Quintus considered it wise to keep this unhappy opinion from Rufio and Flaccus, as they continued addressing the heaving sea in abandoned projectile unison.

All night the galley ran before the tempest. Half the soldiers and crew took turns bailing out water, and several times heavy seas broke over the vessel with such violence that all on deck thought their end to be at hand. When morning came the wind had shifted several points. "A blessed nor'easter," crowed the pilot, relief bubbling from his brine-soaked pores. As the sky brightened, everyone on deck stared fixedly ahead over the waste of still angry foaming water. "There!" the pilot shouted. He pointed at a bright spark on the dark horizon. "The Pharos. We are on course, great Neptune and his hand maiden Nereids be praised."

Quintus screwed his eyes half-shut to give sharper focus to the growing finger pointing at the heavens. The fabulous lighthouse, tallest building in the entire world, beckoning them to the haven of Alexandria. With the golden dawn came a sense of wellbeing that brought to mind Rufio's description of Alexandrian boys: "Glories forged from Greek libido and Egyptian sensuousness, trained in the arts of giving pleasure. Oh Quintus, my fine friend, what lovely fucks we'll be getting."

"You shouldn't believe everything other poets write," Quintus retorted, but he grinned conspiratorially nonetheless—no poetic smoke without the muse of fire. Of course, pleasure and sexual release were not the only reasons for this excursion to Trajan's personal province, which Quintus pointed out by reminding Rufio that as a representative of the Tullius Emporium of Artistic Excellence the search for fine statuary to embellish the Emperor's numerous building projects back in Rome was of at least equal importance. Irony, however, was not one of Rufio's strong suits.

At that moment several figures emerged onto the slippery deck. From one stairway came Rufio's mother Junilla, ushering her youngest before her. Tullius Cato threw Quintus an exuberant sideways grin as he ran past and then—taking full advantage of the ship's now gentle rolling—jammed both legs against the wet boards in a rigid stance. Like a street urchin sliding on a rare slick of winter ice he skidded expertly to halt foot-to-foot with his brother.

Dripping, bedraggled, and stained with his ejecta (and maybe some from Flaccus), Rufio glared down at dry, clean, warm Cato with the baleful expression of one rudely woken.

"You've been sick," the boy said in a provocatively flat delivery.

"Fuck off."

"And good morning to you too, Brother Rufio. Hail, Flaccus… oh dear," Cato trailed off. He leaned back in a theatrical pose of sorrow as he took in the equally disheveled vigilis. "I suppose as a firefighter you're more used to flames than water." Cato slapped his thighs gleefully and chortled. He ducked nimbly under Rufio's attempt to grab him by the neck in order to strangle the life from his wiry body. Cato's bright moods were mightily enhanced since he and Quintus's body slave Ashur hit it off. On one hand, this annoyed Quintus—Ashur was supposed to have dealings only with his master, his dominus—on the other the odd friendship kept the little wretch at bay. Cato had played the would-be wanton with both he and poor Flaccus (who in any case had eyes only and unrequitedly for Rufio). And meanwhile Ashur made himself useful in looking after Junilla and Cato's simple shipboard needs. He served Quintus as well, though in his capacity as bed warmer they'd had sex only twice since leaving home, such matters not so easily arranged aboard a warship.

As Junilla walked gracefully along the narrow strip of deck above the rowing stations Quintus could see that the night's violence had left her as unruffled as himself—at least he was less ruffled since it became clear that Salacia, Neptune's hand maiden of the overpowering force of water, had once again failed to clasp him in her seaweed-festooned grip.

"Leave Cato alone, pet," Junilla chided Rufio. "I'm sorry you had to face the weather out here." She managed to sound genuinely sympathetic in the wake of Cato's callow disdain. No one expected such unpleasant weather in July and the trierarch had insisted that his passengers would find it much better to live, eat, and sleep on deck, which—seeing that private cabin space was at a premium—made a necessity sound like an adventure. The two private cabins under the stern deck were given over to the Emperor and his few personal slaves, and the smaller, little better than a broom closet, to Junilla, which she allowed Cato and Ashur to share with her for sleeping.

"But why didn't you huddle below in the dry by the rowers?"

"Because, Ma," Rufio answered with commendable restraint, "you can't chuck up dinner down there—"

"Well, you can, actually," Flaccus added miserably, "but it's not advisable because the sailors tend to get violent if you puke all over them."

Junilla pouted her understanding. "Poor you. But *you* seem in fine fettle, my Little Mars." She smiled with warmth at Quintus. He wished she wouldn't use that particular adjective since he stood shoulder to shoulder with her. And come to think of it he bridled at the reference to that awful pantomime Trajan had forced him to act out in that awful entertainment for an awful barbarian prince. Quintus prided himself on his poetic sensitivity, not his skill at pretending to be the God of War. Besides, his family had been on the verge of disowning him altogether at the *horror* of a Patrician son *acting* on stage in front of an *audience*. All of Rome's upper class knew that only prostitutes of either sex performed on stage. However, since it had been at the Emperor's command, and the association of Quintus with Trajan facilitated the return of imperial favor to the Caecilii in no short measure, so his father Lucius and mother had reined in their righteous displeasure and reluctantly forgiven their youngest son his misdemeanor.

Junilla shook out her glorious mane of auburn hair. "Was the storm very bad?"

Quintus was sure Rufio was about to regurgitate some final remnant of dinner, but only a strangled gasp of indignation issued from between pallid lips.

Quintus nodded. "It was quite bad Lady— sorry, Junilla." He still had difficulty using her name, even though she sometimes called him son-in-law in recognition of his relationship with Rufio. Very little fazed the Lady Junilla Tullia Rufia, not even the Emperor, and certainly not her eldest son's sexual antics.

"I thought I felt the ship move," a deep voice boomed from the companionway that led up from the private quarters. "I thought it no more than a lively blow," said Augustus Caesar Marcus Ulpius Nerva Traianus, Conqueror of Dacia, Ruler of the World, and—

according to Junilla—all-around Good Egg. A blithe smile greeted the rising sun. He stretched healthily and then nodded to Junilla. "Good morning, my Lady, and Tullius Cato, Quintus… ah, there you are you rapscallion." He beamed at Rufio.

Quintus spotted his brother Marcus skulking behind Trajan as if, like the fabled ostrich, burying his head in the sand might render him invisible. But then the Emperor stepped forward with care past a deckhand mopping up the last of the water and walked across to clap Rufio on the shoulder. "Now where's your cook-friend Septimius. Go find him and get him to hustle up a fine breakfast before we reach Alexandria." Rufio slapped a hand to his mouth with an audible gulp and rushed for the side. As he leaned far out over the rail, Trajan looked about him in surprise. "Was it something I said?"

Quintus cast eyes to the deck boards to hide his grin, but he made a fist with the tip of his thumb poking up between the first and second fingers, the fig gesture of good luck, a private vow to make it up to Rufio as soon as his lover's feet were safely on land again.

Trajan wondered aloud what might have happened to the rest of his small fleet, but the lack of any other galleys within view didn't seem to worry him unduly. "No doubt they'll catch up with us," he said airily and swept up to the poop to engage Maesenius and Maximianus in weightier matters than seasick boys and a possibly missing Hadrian and Empress.

Quintus sidled over to where blushing Marcus shuffled uneasily. Seeing his younger brother headed his way, he tried to turn aside, but even a quinquereme was limited for space. "You've become something of a favorite, brother. How many times is that since we left Ostia?"

"You keep your filthy thoughts to yourself, you little shit. Can I help it if the Emperor finds my tales of naval derring-do fascinating?"

"More *do* than *daring*, I dare say." Quintus made a show of stifling a chuckle.

"I swear on our father's good name in the Senate… if you say anything to Primus or Secundus I will remove your testes and weeny prick and then you won't be much use to that red-headed catamite friend of yours."

Quintus had no intention of informing his two eldest brothers of the newfound sexual delights Marcus had discovered. That was his business, but… "You be nice to me and I'll keep your little secret, though it would tickle them both pink to know that you actually have some derring-do to boast of." And with that parting shot, he gave Marcus a dismissive grown-up shoulder pat and walked off to find Septimius.

That's where it had started, a month ago back on the 11th day of June, at the Thermopolium of Septimius, halfway up Clivus Suburanus on what was supposed to be a romantic evening out at the eating house Rufio insisted served the best food in all of Rome. The patron himself was about to deliver them an appetizer when a dying man rudely interrupted him. Quintus had looked up to see Septimius's eyes go wide in alarm. And then suddenly a hand shoved hard on Quintus's back as the intruder thrust between him and Rufio. The man reached out a shuddery hand to Septimius and gasped out words barely understood, his voice thickened with a horrid burbling like clotted sewage in a drain.

"Sep… Sept–imius… *uurrgh*… Isis d-dies. Desert Seth rises—"

And with that, the man fell forward and went face down into the terrine, squashing it beyond repair.

The incident not only ruined dinner, it also blew the cook's cover as a purveyor of culinary skills. He replaced the merry hail-and-well-met, mine-host jollity with a grave expression. The word "dependable in a scrap" came to Quintus's mind. "I think what I have greatly feared for years is coming to pass," he began in a quiet voice. "In Egypt… The Lion Rampant flexes his claws. There is great danger to Caesar should he venture to Egypt… and to all who might go with him."

Which had been very well, because Egypt was the other side of the Middle Sea, what Romans called "Our Sea" (and who was there to argue with the conquerors of the world?), and neither of them was ever going to Egypt. And then Flaccus found them as they strolled back toward the Forum Romanum. The vigilis often moonlighted for Junilla, helping out at the Tullius Emporium of Artistic Excellence, and she'd sent him to find the boys. Caesar Trajan had decided on an immediate trip. "Bit of a sudden decision," Flaccus said. "Needs a load of statues, urns, decorative things, apparently and wants Lady Junilla to go with him to advise, and she won't go without 'her boys,' as she said. Includes, you Quintus Caecilius Alba."

"Slow down a moment," Rufio said.

Quintus caught hold of Flaccus by the arm. "Go where?"

Flaccus gave both boys an exasperated look. "Don't you listen? The Emperor's off to Egypt, and you're going with him."

After a day of rush and bother, of gathering essential traveling supplies and clothes, of settling work matters at the Emporium to make sure Junilla's various enterprises would continue to prosper, the boys walked down the Aventine in the direction of the Circus Maximus to visit the Baths of Licinius Sura. "They're damned snooty at this new place," Rufio warned Quintus. "But as a patrician and a senator's son you'll be okay, especially with that witheringly nasal upper-crust tone of yours."

Quintus refused to rise to the bait. All the dashing about in preparation for the hasty leave-taking had drained even his normally boundless energy. As had the rushed explanation to his stuffy old father Lucius—*What? Off again? You've barely been back from that silly jaunt to Capri. When will you settle down and start to master the family's clients, and what about Vipsania Metella—?*

Mother just wept, as became a virtuous Roman matron. She produced one drop for her tear cup and then told him to make sure he wrapped up warm and didn't go near any fast and loose Alexandrian women. At least there was to be no wrench in leaving Ashur behind. His Syrian body slave had served Quintus since they were both knee high to jumping crickets. At the news that he was taking his slave with him, Rufio's reaction was less exuberant than Ashur's until Quintus promised they could share the boys' services. Rufio was never happier than when he had a new body to play with, and he kept giving Ashur exploratory glances as the three of them bounced downhill.

At least Quintus's sudden, unexpected absence from Rome meant another delay in the threatened nuptials. With Trajan's patronage of the Caecilii and the subsequent return of the Caecilii clients' to supremacy in the building materials trade, Lucius Caecilius Alba no longer had need of Vipsania Metella's extensive dowry as he had done before, but from his father's last words Quintus suspected the reprieve would not last long.

"So, as a scruffy pleb with a rusty head, how do *you* get in Licinius Sura's baths?"

Rufio flicked a troublesome curl of hair from his eyes and grinned brightly. "The door attendant wouldn't let me get anywhere near, but Ma has made it her business to ensure everyone on this side of the Aventine knows she is…" he went into editor-of-the-games public delivery, "…by patent of Augustus Caesar Traianus appointed master of imperial ceremonies and statuary. So the snobs have to humor me," he said, dropping back to normal Rufio, "or risk annoying the Emperor."

"Uncle Livy has—well, *had*—a subscription to use the baths. Joined as soon as they opened—"

"But thanks to his ever-loving nephew, Livius Dio is right out of favor."

"And funds." Quintus smiled happily at the thought of his hated uncle rendered into penury. "I suppose the water will still be clean if it's so new?"

"Not too bad. Lots better than at Agrippa."

Quintus grimaced. "No wonder Livy used his ill-gotten gains to buy his way into these baths. Last time I walked all the way across town to the Baths of Agrippa it was like swimming in liquid shit. Took Ashur a good hour to scrape the muck off me with a strigil—" He shuddered at the memory.

"And then I had to struggle back and forth with buckets of water drawn from the nymphaeum to wash you down," Ashur said helpfully, with a firm nod. "You really did stink, which is not what you expect after bathing."

"Shut up," Quintus growled. "If I want your opinion I'll ask you for it. And you can't say the Baths of Titus are any better," he said to Rufio. "Oh, this looks very smart," he added as they arrived at the grand portico entrance to the bathhouse built by the wealthy senator-consul and close friend of Trajan.

They left Ashur guarding their clothes in the apodyterium against theft by one of the casparii—even in privately owned bathing establishments the dressing room slaves were notorious thieves. Following a sweat in the sudatorium and relaxing in the caldarium baths, the boys found an unoccupied bench in a private niche of the tepidarium. Ashur found them there, their discarded loincloths, belts, footwear, and tunics gathered up in his arms. And he'd included his own clothes in the bundle. "I looked out of place coming through here all dressed up, dominus," he reasoned with a cheeky grin.

That Ashur didn't address him by his name, which he did whenever they were private, pleased Quintus. It wouldn't do to let patrician standards slip in front of Rufio. But pretty much everything else slipped the instant Rufio extended a languid hand and fondled Ashur between his silky thighs.

"Lovely tight globes of Eros," he commented.

Quintus raised a dark eyebrow.

"What can I say? Your poetic influence rubs off on me."

"Pish! That'll be the day. And who said you could lay hands on my property?"

"You did. You said we could share."

Ashur sniffed. "I know I have no say in it, but I'm not at all sure about being shared," he said with a look of naked lust directed at Rufio. The lie of his statement became immediately visible as his cock sprang erect in Rufio's palm.

"Oops… sorry." This was not addressed to Ashur but as far as Quintus could see Rufio didn't look in the least apologetic, and before Quintus could reply Rufio pulled the slave down between them on the warm bench.

"I meant when we're away from Rome, not here in public," Quintus hissed in alarm. The short time they had known each other was too little for Rufio's carefree attitude to life to have rubbed away Quintus's inherited patrician horror of public display, whether it be emotion of any kind or getting naked and engaging in sex.

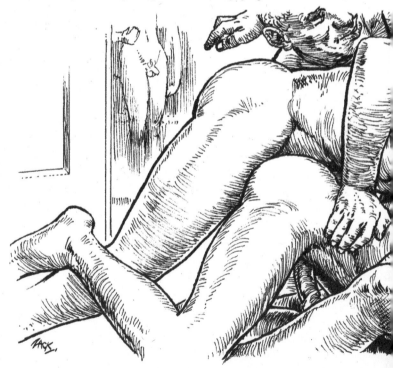

The lustful glance Rufio threw at Quintus from the valley between Ashur's brazenly upthrust buttocks caught Quintus in his loins. He dragged his gaze from the sight of his lover eating out his body slave's ass. Across the way in the tepidarium's tasteful gloom, on a bench a mirror to the one they occupied, a handsome, dark, curly-headed slave busily massaged a man stretched out on his back. With one hand the masseur worked his customer's big cock while twisting and squeezing his balls with the other. The man's face was hidden beneath a linen cloth, which rose and fell with every pent-up breath. Convulsive body movements betrayed his proximity to the precipice of climax, confirmed by low growls in his heaving throat.

Quintus watched in distracted fascination—Ashur's questing hand had found his own erection—as the burly masseur increased

the ferocity of his masturbation. With a last drawn-out groan of pleasure, the prone man exploded, first a small eruption and then a veritable fountain. At the crucial moment of the third ejaculation the expert bath attendant dropped his mouth over the muzzle of the cock and sucked down hard. On the bench, his customer arched his back as if he were in agony.

In an exquisite echo, Quintus felt his own throbbing cock slide between Ashur's lips, felt his practiced tongue flick wetly over the piss-and-cum-slit, and then take in his whole length. The slave sucked him at the same furious pace Rufio now fucked Ashur's stretched ass.

A movement in the dim light of distant clerestory windows caught his attention and Quintus looked up to see they had an audience. The man from over the way and the masseur stood over them. Quintus felt helpless, flushed with shame at being seen like this and at the same time deluged in lust. Glazed vision barely took in Ashur's lithe, olive colored body, pressed up on all fours, spine stretched between Quintus's thighs and Rufio's insistent pummeling.

Beside the writhing threesome, their neighbor—arms wrapped around his masseur's waist—worked the bath attendant's foreskin back and forth until the husky young man could no longer bear the torture and unloaded a copious spray of cum over Ashur's straining back. In his exertion, Rufio almost fell headlong into the spreading pool. He locked eyes with Quintus with that heart-stopping yearning they, only they, shared, and with that connection together they filled Ashur at both ends.

T·W·O | II

The Aventine, Rome, 13th day of June

"You never met my Aunty Tullia Velabria."

Quintus nodded his agreement. "You have mentioned Antonia, but I didn't know you also had an Aunty Velabria."

"We try not to talk of her... that is me and Cato. She's my Ma's evil twin. I think she's a year or two older in fact, but they might as well be twins from appearance. But if you think Ma is a tough walnut, well..." Rufio looked skyward for inspiration. "...Ma's a shrinking maiden beside Aunty Velabria's *myrmillo*."

Quintus tried imagining Junilla shrinking from anything, but that seemed as absurd as her sister fighting other gladiators in the arena, wearing a helmet styled like a rearing fish, with arm guard, loincloth, and thick belt, her naked breasts jutting forward like the twin prows of a war galley, a thick gaiter covering the right leg and instep, and wielding the *myrmillo*'s gladius and tall, oblong legionary's shield. He tried to imagine it, and failed.

Clean, if a little exhausted from the afternoon's pleasant bathhouse experience, the boys and Ashur were dragging their feet back up the hillside through several narrow streets toward the western edge of the Aventine hill and the Tullius Emporium of Artistic Excellence.

"Does she have the same hair color?" Quintus had decided to ignore Rufio's hyperbole. "Keep up, Ashur. The slope's not that extreme."

Ashur muttered rebelliously that he was exhausted from his bathhouse exertions, but the other two took no notice.

"Aunty Velabria's voluminous head of hair defines the color of Hades."

"So she's not a Rufia to your Rufio. Talking of Rufia-Rufio, when did you last see Woof-Woof?"

At the mention of sexy young Felix Ostiensus (he liked taking it on all-fours, doggie-style, hence the nickname), Rufio gave Quintus one of his shit-eating grins. "Are you jealous?"

At the suddenly interesting turn of the conversation Ashur caught up swiftly so he could earwig.

Quintus squared his shoulders in patrician disdain. "Of course I'm not. Besides, we shared him."

"You did? How?" the slave squeaked.

"Quiet, Ashur!"

"But *I* had him first," Rufio pointed out lightly.

It was a classic sigh of long suffering. "*You* have had *everyone* first."

"Who's this Felix?" Ashur would not be put down so easily.

"Son of the western Aventine Crossroads Club boss, Clivius Ostiensus Lignum Orientum, and he's as terrifying as his name sounds," Rufio explained. "You don't fuck with a Crossroads shrine boss."

"Just his son?"

Quintus clipped his cheeky body slave about the ear.

"Exactly," Rufio said. "In fact, Quintus, my little Mars-pet, I saw him briefly this morning when I carried a message for Ma to Clivius. You know how they like to know the comings and goings of those under their protection… though the gods only know how he'll cope with Aunty Velabria. If he tries to up the monthly shrine donation," he said, referring to the protection racket money that each trader had to pay the local Crossroads Club unless they wished to find their premises razed, or worse, penises erased, "she could break him you know."

"And Felix?"

"Heartbroken, of course." The laconic head toss made Rufio's abundant fiery locks fly about his face like a burning halo catching the late afternoon sun. "And that was just at *your* going away." He broke into happy chortles and fled from Quintus's grasp, through the broad gateway into the Emporium's wide forecourt, surrounded on three sides by warehouses, workshops, and opposite the entrance to the rambling house.

Dodging between slaves and paid "expert" laborers dusting off bronze busts, crating up or unloading goods, covering over repairs to marble statues, polishing ornate tripods to grace the town houses of the wealthy, the three lads made for the less than imposing front porch. A strong smell of lye greeted twitching nostrils.

"Aunty Velabria arrived yet?" Rufio called out cheerfully as he burst through the door into what the family called the *tablinum*, though it was more of a cosily chaotic family area than an office.

Junilla straightened up from behind one of the large, lime-scrubbed tables, source of the clinical stink. She waved aside a kitchen girl. "Go scrub the other one, Aella. And be thorough this time. I'm not going away for the gods know how long leaving dirty eating tables behind." She turned on the arrivals with a sharp expression. Quintus noted with relief that this was aimed at her son. "About time, too. How long does it take to get clean, huh? Oh, wait, silly me. You dallied on the warm benches for a bit of roll-me-over and how's-your-father." She looked accusingly at Ashur, whose blush instantly gave him away. "To the kitchen with you."

He looked to Quintus.

"Do as you're told."

Junilla relented. "You look half starved, boy, and you'll find something to eat out there."

Ashur brightened at the prospect and almost ran into the bony elbow of Damianus on his way to the kitchen. The family and business secretary was seated in a corner scratching away at tablet and almost hidden behind Junilla where she was finishing the packing of a large chest of clothes. Quintus stepped forward to help her.

Junilla smiled warmly and squeezed his shoulder. "You are so kind. I'm sure your mother must love you, dear Quintus." The look she threw at Rufio suggested she loved him a lot less, but Quintus knew it was all put on. *If Mother loves me, she has a funny way of showing it.*

Rufio took no notice of the implied criticism. "A Caecilius in the hand is worth two of me, Ma." He fired off a cheeky wink at Quintus. "You know I'm all fingers and thumbs when it comes to folding things neatly. The Battle Axe not here yet?" he said, returning to the subject of Aunty Velabria, and raised an alarmed eye at Junilla's sudden expression of warning.

Quintus smirked, and bent to the task to avoid seeing the carnage, though the crack of heavy object colliding with unaware head rang out loudly, accompanied by an un-Rufio-like squawk. *Ooh, that must have hurt!*

"Lovely to see you again, Nephew." The woman's follow-through swing took the leather carryall bag right back over her shoulder.

Just like a myrmillo's opening feint!

Rufio scuttled to his feet, half under the nearest table. "Aunty, how nice—"

"Shut it, pipsqueak. Greetings, Junilla. I see your boy's attitude hasn't improved since my last visit."

Aunty Velabria—Quintus knew with certainty it was she—advanced into the room, stepping over her felled nephew. She was Junilla's mirror image, only... larger in every sense. Having witnessed the blow she'd delivered, he gave some credit to Rufio's absurd notion that she'd even terrify the Aventine Crossroads boss Clivius Ostiensus. Rufio stood, ruefully rubbing the side of his head. He grinned a bit goofily at Quintus as Velabria and Junilla embraced briefly like a clash of Titans, one goddess of fire, the other of the night.

"I met this lump outside." Velabria waved imperiously at Flaccus, who waited uncertainly in the porch, framed in the doorway. "He claims he's going with you. I can't believe you're taking him along on this crazy jaunt. I'd have thought you could have hired better protection than a mere fire watcher."

From behind her bulk, Flaccus opened and shut his mouth like an indignant fish on a hook.

Junilla stuck a hand on one hip and glared back at Velabria. "The Emperor himself commanded his presence on this trip and—"

"That's a blessing from Bona Dea. I wouldn't want him under foot here."

Quintus closed the lid of the chest and ran into Velabria's fierce gaze as he straightened up. "My... aren't you a handsome hunk." Her eyes swiveled between Rufio and his mother. "Are you his squeeze or hers?"

Junilla gathered him up. "Quintus Caecilius Alba, scion of the great Caecilii, is a very good friend to Rufio."

"I see," Velabria grated, evidently seeing all too well (and clearly ignoring her sister's patrician name-dropping).

Quintus blushed a brighter shade than Rufio's hair. He tried a little duck of his head. "Lady, I am delighted to meet you—"

"Stuff it, pretty boy. You've no doubt heard all about me from my egregious nephew. Now, Junilla, let's get down to business. You're leaving me Damianus I trust?"

At hearing his name the secretary shrank deeper into his shadowy recess. His look of sheer terror told Quintus that Damianus knew his mistress's sister very well.

"Of course, dear. You'd find the Emporium falling apart without Dammy's help."

Velabria sniffed dismissively.

"You will give Velabria all the help she asks for, won't you Damianus. Otherwise—"

"—guts torn out and minced up for a terrine, Mistress. I know," he muttered miserably before bending his head back over whatever he was writing.

"I've dictated a stack of notes, so once you settle your slaves in the quarters, get together with Damianus. He'll bring you up to speed—"

"As a snail."

"—and we can get ourselves ready for Trajan's escort. Wagons, carriers and a half cohort of Praetorians are due by the sixth hour, otherwise we won't make Ostia before nightfall."

Quintus expected Velabria to express awe at her sister's association with the Emperor, but her apparent lack of interest disappointed him.

"I wish you good fortune on your travels, sister."

"Why, thank you."

Midnight curls tossed as Velabria shook her head airily. "After all, I want you back. I can't spend my life here hawking trinkets to noble numbnuts."

"Aren't we sailing from Portus?" Rufio interrupted before his aunt and mother could set about each other.

"Of course, pet, but the best overnight accommodation is in old Ostia. Athenos—the new Palatine chamberlain," she said, aiming a sly venom at Velabria, "has reserved us rooms at the House of Diana and commandeered an insula of luxury apartments along the same street for the imperial court. And I want you on your best behavior," she added for Rufio's benefit, "and you!" she snapped at Cato, who had just come in from his last day at school, taken one look at Velabria, and turned tail. Eutychus, the tutor Junilla had hired for the duration of the trip to ensure her youngest continued with his education foiled his escape and ushered the boy forward to greet his aunt. Brave, cocky, cock-of-the-walk Little Aventine Fox, destroyer of traitorous imperial secretary and assassin Acacus, nemesis of Kaeso Casca Malpensa (a.k.a. the wicked Satyr of Capri), quailed as he stepped close for Velabria to lay a palm on the top of his head in blessing. Aunty Velabria was indeed a termagant.

The sudden arrival of another presence rescued Cato from almost certain death by asphyxiation. "And who's this?" Velabria demanded, now well into the role of Emporium boss.

As one, Rufio and Quintus said, "Septimius!"

The cookshop owner acknowledged Junilla. "Lady, I'm commanded to meet here with the contingent of guards on their way to escort your party to Ostia."

"And you are?"

"He's this cook—" Rufio began.

"And who *commanded* you?"

"Has a place in the Subura—"

"I am Gnaeus Septimius Corbulo, Lady."

Quintus stepped forward, eyes bright with enthusiastic curiosity. "I say, you're not related to the great General Corbulo are you?"

Septimius smiled and inclined his head modestly. "He was my great grandfather's brother."

"He fell foul of Nero's jealousy," Quintus informed everyone, "and fell on his sword when commanded to do so by the tyrant. A truly honorable man!"

"And a very dead one," Rufio noted drily.

Quintus bridled instantly. "That's an insult to a great man's shade, as well as…" he indicated Septimius.

"I take no offense. It was all before I was born."

Junilla was still regarding Septimius with some puzzlement. "I left the Emperor's presence not two hours before and he made no mention of your accompanying us, Corbulo."

"He can't have heard of your culinary skills," Rufio began, "so why *are* you coming along?"

Septimius offered a grim smile in contrast to his usual cookshop geniality. "If I told you, I'd have to kill you." And then he grinned into the shocked silence. "I'm on a need-to-know basis in my capacity as a former *frumentarius*. Lady Junilla, if I may have a word with you… in private?"

Junilla suggested they take a walk around the yard. As soon as Velabria, torn between harassing Damianus or following her sister and the mysterious man outside to find out what was going on, turned her back momentarily Rufio signaled Quintus to follow him to his bedroom. Alone at last, Quintus rolled sideways shoulder-to-shoulder with Rufio and buried fingers amid his lover's luxuriant golden locks. The action sent a thrill of ownership through him, a sense of belonging that he always found odd, since their backgrounds were so different. At times Rufio's attitude roused irritation in his breast, even anger, and Rufio knew he could do so and played on it. *Just as well I'm such a tolerant person.*

With a long-limbed stretch, Rufio sat forward. "I suppose I'd better get some kit together. I suppose you did all your packing in a trice when you spoke to your father about our going?"

"Of course."

"You mean you thrashed Ashur and made him pack everything."

"Naturally. You should have a body slave to take care of you."

"I've got you to take care of me." He made a fist and pumped it over the bulge in his tunic.

"Har, har..." Quintus glanced sideways. Leaning back against the wall, he couldn't see Rufio's expression but from the sudden set of his broad shoulders he could tell darker thoughts were wandering through his head. "An *as* for your thoughts?"

"They're worth lots more than a tenth of a denarius, thank you," Rufio reproached Quintus automatically. He twisted around. "What was all that crap that man spouted about Isis and Seth? And what about Septimius, huh? 'The Lion rampant flexing claws, great danger to Caesar,' and so on. What was all that about?"

Quintus shrugged. "I don't know, but something's obvious. Your cook friend may be a wiz with a saddle of wild Umbrian boar roasted with chunks of turnip, celery, carrot and rosemary, basted with a heavy-bodied Ligurian red wine and served with savory pulse fragranced with a garum sauce from Calvus of Whereeveritwas but he's been a lot more than a chef in his time. He told Junilla he'd been a frumentarius once."

"What's a frumenty-whatsit?"

"You really know nothing about the military, do you?"

"You haven't a clue about culture."

"Take that back, you brazen gutter scum!" Scandalized, Quintus shot forward and raised his right fist to his breast, as though gripping a formal toga. "I – am - a - poet," he declared in oratorical tones.

"Great furniture, statuary, and monuments are culture. Poetry's just a jumble of words." Rufio broke into a falsetto, singsong voice. "Now he goes down the shadowy road from which they say no one returns. Now let evil be yours, evil shadows of Orcus, that devour everything of beauty: you've stolen lovely sparrow from me, now my eyes are swollen and red with weeping—"

Wonder lit Quintus's dark eyes. "Rufio! You remember some of my lines."

"Must be hanging about with you, Doggerel Boy. The shit's rubbing off on me. What's all that nonsense about anyway?"

Quintus drew a deep breath. "It's an ode to the death of my pet sparrow—that's when I was pretty small—and the evil god of the Underworld snatched him from me, evil Orcus, who punishes the breakers of oaths—"

"And your sparrow had broken a promise?"

"No… it's… oh you wouldn't understand."

"I rather more enjoy that one… how does it go? Ah yes." Rufio gave Quintus a dirty grin. "I don't speak to boys, but to hairy ones who can't move their stiff loins. You, who read all these thousand kisses, I'll fuck you, and I'll bugger you—"

"Vulcan's brass balls, you do remember, and ahh…"

Rufio's lips silenced Quintus. His hand wormed under his rucked up tunic and under the windings of his loincloth. In moments Quintus was naked and vulnerable, half laughing, almost choking, on his back, legs forced apart, and with a casual spit on his fingers, Rufio worked them into his lover's ass. "I'll fuck you, I'll bugger you, and find heaven in your Orcus opening, Poetry Boy."

Quintus felt the familiar weight of Rufio's big cock slide

inside him and through creased-closed lashes was aware of a face peering through the open door—Cato, mouth open in a wide *O*, but a knowing glint in his eyes. And then the apparition vanished and Quintus melted into the hard fucking Rufio was giving him.

"So where were we?"

They were still sprawled on Rufio's bed, languorous after the unanticipated sex. Quintus had noted that he should write more poetry with a sex theme if a reading ended up like that.

"You wanted to know what frumentarii do."

"Grain collectors, I know what it means."

"In the army they combine their quartermaster's function with acting as informers for the legion commanders. After all, they get to know everything that's going on in the province they work, so a frumentarius makes an ideal spy."

"And that's what Septimius was doing?"

"I imagine in Egypt, where he must have become party to some conspiracy or something, and now it's rising up again."

"And we're headed right into the lion's jaws. Who's Seth, by the way?"

Quintus wasn't entirely sure, but he was spared exposing his ignorance by a clamor from within the house and Junilla's raised voice calling for them.

"It's barely been two weeks since we battled Malpensa's gladiators and stared certain death in the face," Rufio grumbled. "Hardly time to recover breath and off we rush again. Well, this is it." He jumped up, grabbed any clothing he could lay hands on, and willy-nilly stuffed the items into a leather satchel. "There. I'm packed and ready."

Quintus shook his head sadly and drew his arched brows together into a straight line, an expression of mock resignation at his friend's imperturbable response to urgency. "Let's go, then. Into the great Ptolemaic unknown populated by strange people, vicious creatures, the evil Blemmyae, men with horns thrusting from their foreheads, and incanting priests weaving magic spells above their mummies."

"Leave my mother out if it." Rufio grabbed Quintus by the wrist and dragged him off bodily.

T·H·R·E·E | III

Alexandria, early on the 7th day of July, AD 108

Fortuna's rearing prow blocked out rising Apollo's chariot as three hundred oarsmen's regular strokes propelled the vessel toward the dun-colored strip of land. The city showed itself as a necklace of fine buildings, which sparkled like distant jewels in the dawn sunlight.

Flaccus tilted his head far back to gaze at the Pharos. "Damn, but that thing's big enough to imagine fabled Zeus sitting and spinning on it."

Rufio's startled laugh went off with the light breeze. "If he did he'd have been shafting himself." He rounded on Quintus. "Isn't the great statue on top an image of the Greeks' Father God?"

"I thought you were the expert on statuary," Quintus said grumpily.

"I am, but this is historical and cultural. That's your department."

"It *is* supposed to represent Zeus."

"Thank you. You see, Flaccus, my little fire-starter, there's no accounting for taste, and for all I know a Greek god may well enjoy pleasuring himself on… well, himself. I can't wait to see what statues and urns and monumental stones await us," Rufio said, peering at the curved, low-lying islands that protected the massive harbor of Alexandria. The worst effects of the tossing sea seemed to be diminished now the quinquereme had reached calmer waters. To the left, where the obviously man-made mole curved toward land, his eyes lit on the towering bastions of the imperial precincts, glowing a warm yellow in the low sunlight. "The palace must be stacked to the rafters with magnificent objects."

Quintus followed his gaze. "I wonder whether we'll find a bust of Caesarion."

"Who's he?"

"Don't you know anything of the recent history of your adopted home?"

"If I can't sell it, I'm not interested."

Rufio's smart retort drew a snort of contempt from Quintus. "Well, you *ought* know the background before we dock," he said in a lofty tone.

A low growl rumbled in Rufio's throat. "I have a bad feeling you're going to tell me."

The vessel's rocking in the low swell only aided Quintus as he adopted the classic rhetorician's stance, feet set slightly apart, right arm crooked to grasp his tunic at the breast. Although he looked faintly absurd, Rufio always found the pose made his groin tingle for some reason. Perhaps he just fancied fucking the ponce out of the patrician.

Quintus cleared his throat. "Once upon a time the successful general Gaius Julius Caesar—"

"I know him. He's a god and the Roman cunny who threw my mother's forbears into chains and dragged them all the way—"

"—who became Dictator of Rome as the result of a civil war against Pompey the Pompous. Pompey fled to Egypt, where the treacherous lackeys of adolescent King Ptolemy, the unlucky thirteenth of his name, had Pompey murdered. He was married to his elder sister, Cleopatra, no less than the seventh of her name and—"

"Pompey was married to Cleopatra?"

"No! Ptolemy."

"To his sister!" Rufio waggled his eyebrows. "Did they... you know, do the business?"

"Of course not. For one thing at that age I doubt Ptolemy could even get it up. Anyway, that's not the point. Don't interrupt."

"No, don't interrupt," said Flaccus, his eyes alight with interest at the tale.

"So... Julius Caesar swept in and took over everything in Alexandria, booted the child off his throne in retribution for slaying noble Pompey—"

"He was pompous a moment ago."

"Pompey was *nobly* pompous, and anyway it's not for barbarian semi-Greeks to go around assassinating Roman commanders, even defeated ones. Sooo... Caesar took Cleopatra for his concubine and got her with child even though he'd just married her off to her other brother Ptolemy, the fourteenth of his name."

"By Jupiter's bouncing balls, that was damned quick."

"Caesar sojourned in Alexandria for quite a while, fought off a siege of Ptolemaic malcontents, burned a library or two—that was by accident, though," he added hastily. "Look, the thing is, she gave him a son—"

"Ptolemy, the fifteenth of his name, I presume?"

"Exactly, but also called Caesarion. And that was the problem for Julius Caesar's adopted son Octavius—who became Octavianus Caesar on his adoption—when he went to war against Marcus Antonius, who had abandoned his wife Octavia—she was Octavian's sister—and taken Cleopatra as his new wife and called himself King of Egypt and the East."

"Wait, wait! I got lost there. Why was this Octavianus warring against Antonius?"

Flaccus startled both boys with a sudden gust of superior laughter. "Oh, Rufio, you know even I know all about the civil war."

"Another civil war?"

"A civil war between the triumvirs for control of the Republic," Flaccus said in a surprisingly school teacher's voice. "Though Antony and Octavian had already kicked dear old Lepidus out—he was the third triumvir, you see—which is when Antony seized the East and threatened to hold it against Octavian in the West, and—"

"Are you done?" Quintus demanded, hot spots showing on his cheeks. "Who's telling this tale?"

"I just wish you'd get to the end," Rufio said. "Look, we're almost under the Pharos."

They all looked up at the mighty tower with its three tapering sections rearing high enough for Zeus to snag the occasional cloud passing overhead.

"Octavian's fleet defeated that of Antony and Cleopatra at the Battle of Actium, and chased his enemies back to Alexandria, where he cornered them in the palace," Quintus continued when he had their attention again. "As he prepared to defend himself against the might of Octavian, Antony heard that Cleopatra had taken her own life rather than become the concubine of her lover's enemy—"

"Which enemy?"

"Octavian, of course. The concubine of her lover's enemy and her previous lover's son—"

"The previous lover…?" Rufio looked completely confused.

Exasperated, Quintus snapped. "I told you, Julius Caesar. Pay attention for Jupiter's sake. Look, I know, it's complicated, but these Egyptian Greeks are not to be compared to us virtuous Romans. So… noble Antony fell on his sword in despair. As it happened the message was ill given, for Cleopatra was still manning the defenses, but when she heard of Antony's suicide, she fell on an asp—"

"A what?"

"It's a serpent," Flaccus said.

Quintus gave Flaccus his icy who-are-you-pleb? look. "Thank you."

"It's just I thought you said she'd fallen on her—"

"I know what you thought. So... they were both dead, and Octavian annexed Egypt as his own province. That was in the month of Sextilis, which the Senate later renamed August in honor of Octavian who they renamed Augustus. Got it? But Octavian who wasn't yet Augustus had a problem with Caesarion, who the Greeks had proclaimed a god, son of a god, and King of Kings. At the advice of his counsellors and the Alexandrian philosopher Arius Didymus, the conqueror had the boy Caesarion put to the sword and his body secretly buried."

"How old was he?"

"What? I don't know... seventeen, eighteen, something like that."

"What a waste." Rufio fluttered his eyelids. "I'd have bent him to my will and made him my bed slave—"

"The gods of the Firmament preserve us!"

"There was no 'happily ever after,' then?"

"No," Quintus snapped. "Not for poor Caesarion. However, Octavian went on to become Princeps, our first Emperor, and ruler of the world."

A naughty light dawned in Rufio's eyes. "Ah... *that* Augustus. The divine one?" He grinned broadly and the faint scattering of freckles danced across his cheeks.

For a moment a dangerous glint of suspicion entered Quintus's narrowed eyes. "You knew all of it, didn't you?"

"Well— ah no... No, no Quintus! Remember your patrician dignit—!" Rufio jinked away, ducked under Quintus's arm, but failed to escape his grip. They grappled, flashing-wild red and close-cropped black heads banged together, and then both boys were shaking with laughter.

Flaccus stroked his chin and looked on with envy at the way Quintus's arms encircled Rufio's slim waist. "I hope the harbor whores are up to the mark," he muttered. "I don't think I'll be getting much action in the palace somehow."

"After the warrens of Rome you will find the great palace of Alexandria bewildering," Prefect Crispus assured Quintus grandly. He was completely ignoring Rufio, who could see the insufferable man even thought conversing with Quintus as being several levels beneath his dignity. Rufio didn't much care. As he'd whispered to Quintus while they followed in the governor's haughty second-in-command's brisk steps, "Anyone who insists on being always addressed as Lucius Junius Quintus Vibius Crispus can't possibly be efficient. Surely three names is sufficient?"

"It's very exotic," Quintus said, trying not to look everywhere like some country bumpkin tourist.

"It is very *grand*," Lucius Junius Quintus Vibius Crispus contradicted. "Expanded over the centuries by generations of Ptolemies, it is far more elaborate than the Palatine."

Rufio felt aggrieved on behalf of Quintus. As he'd learned in another interminable lecture Egypt did not have a proconsular governor, a senator who was awarded a province to govern after he'd been a consul. Egypt was too vital to the Emperor's interests, for it was where Rome's essential grain came from. The risk of some disgruntled patrician holding Rome to ransom by withholding the grain for making the bread that kept the mob happy was too much for Augustus to risk and so Egypt remained the Emperor's personal province. To administer the country, the Emperor appointed an equestrian prefect, a man of far lower rank than any senator, as his personal legate. This meant—as Rufio knew—that pompous Lucius Junius Quintus Vibius Crispus wasn't even a prefect, and as a mere equestrian several social levels beneath Quintus. Of course, he was an old curmudgeon, at least in his mid-twenties, so he was playing the superior age card. *Condescending cunny.* He nudged Quintus. "Didn't you tell me pompous pricks get murdered here?" he muttered, just loudly enough that Crispus should hear him.

Before their guide could respond, another flunky swept around a corner, as gaudy in his apparel as Crispus, and halted abruptly on seeing them. "Prefect Lucius Junius Quintus Vibius Crispus," he gushed obsequiously.

"Ah," Crispus intoned nasally. He glanced at Quintus. "This is my notarius, Lucius Pomponius Bassus Cascus Scribonianus."

Rufio sighed.

"Good Lucius, my time is in short supply, so I should be pleased that you take over the responsibility of showing the Emperor's guest and his… er, companion, the general amenities of the palace, the Library, Mouseion, and of course the Soma and the tomb of Alexander the Great. I shall see you again this evening at the banquet the Legate has arranged."

Quintus lowered his head in polite acknowledgment. Rufio gave the departing prefect who wasn't really a prefect a broad smile and sent him on his busy way with the universal gesture of self-abuse. Quintus engaged the florid notarius in conversation, while Rufio wondered how Cato—sent off for an "educational" walk with his tutor and Flaccus along the Canopus Way—was getting on. And then a movement in the corridor ahead caught his attention and in a trice his eyes were glued to an extraordinary sight. Passing along the same hallway down which Pompous Crispus had taken but in the other direction were two extraordinary young men. Dressed identically in Greek-style gymnasium tunics so short that the *meandros* key-design-edged hems rode on the bulges in their loincloths, they possessed an unearthly beauty. Leggy youths, firm in calf and thigh, skin tone lightly bronzed from careful exposure to the Egyptian sun, they strolled along the passage, heads held high

on long necks, like gods in possession of their realm. Dressed the same, they were also identical in looks and, more astonishing, two striking, ebony-hued slaves followed them, whose fulsome figures promised many delights that Rufio could easily imagine. He recalled the two delicious Nubian boys he'd had at Lucretia's Lupanar after the Lupercalia festival the day he first set eyes on Quintus watching with his family in the Forum… and lashed him with his goatskin whip. Like their masters, the slaves were also identical twins.

Scribonianus saw the object of his interest. "That is Aufidius and Aulus, sons of Legate Servius Sulpicius Similis."

"Will they be at tonight's banquet?" Rufio wanted to know. He winked at Quintus.

"Oh, most certainly. The Legate is most anxious to present them to Caesar."

Quintus flinched in amused irritation when Rufio elbowed him in the ribs. "Then we'd better get in quick before Tra— er, before he does."

"You can't have everything you set eyes on," Quintus hissed.

"Want to bet?" Rufio grinned evilly. "Faint heart never fair lad won."

"Once you've seen one library, you've seen them all, I say." Rufio tugged at Quintus. "Come on, it's just a pile of scrolls. Like the rubbish you scribble down."

"Hundreds of scrolls, thousands, perhaps millions, a storehouse of the entire knowledge of the world…"

Rufio found the contents of the Mouseion of more interest, and would have spent time examining some of the metalsmiths' work in an annex if it hadn't been for the draw of the famous Soma, which contained the tomb of Alexander. On reaching the Soma quite a crowd had gathered, including Hadrian and a gaggle of his youthful cronies. He and the Empress had survived the tempest and made landfall within two hours of the *Fortuna*. Ever the tourist, Hadrian had joined them for the excursion.

"Follow me please people and keep together." The guide's voice echoed in the vaulted chamber at the heart of the Soma. "We now come to the tomb of Alexander the Great. His body became the subject of wrangling between his generals as to where it should rest—Babylon where he died or Siwa Oasis where the gods of Egypt anointed his head. Vergina in Macedon where lay his father Philip was the final decision, yet only our founder, Ptolemy the Savior had been given Alexander's instruction, and he brought the hero's mortal remains to Egypt."

"Ptolemy's men ambushed the cortege and stole the corpse," Quintus whispered to Rufio.

"Do spread out so everyone can have a good view. The remains were interred at Memphis and later transferred here to the city he founded, to be encased in a form-fitting gold coffin in the manner of the ancient pharaohs. A little under two hundred years ago, Ptolemy the tenth of the name decided the people of the city should venerate Alexander's body and removed the gold coffin to replace it with the beautiful crystal sarcophagus you see before you now."

"He means Ptolemy Alexander—who had the nerve to use the revered name—was so short of cash he had the gold melted down," Hadrian murmured to one of his companions.

"He's as cynical as you," Rufio told Quintus as he peered with professional fascination at the well-preserved corpse, its face serene above the original tunic, belt, soldiers' greaves… "There's no breastplate," he observed.

"It was looted on the orders of Caligula so he could wear it when he crossed the bay of Baiae." Quintus quietly informed.

"Why's he got a silver nose?"

Having caught the question, Hadrian looked over at the boys, nodded a distant recognition. "It's said that Augustus accidentally knocked it off when he bent to kiss the corpse."

Rufio nodded his thanks at the answer and leaned close to Quintus. "It's also said that Alexander liked fucking his best friend Hephaestion."

"You really do know how to lower the tone."

"And now if there are any questions?" the guide asked, passing between his audience with a small purse opened for donations.

Rufio and Quintus were strolling back through the Mouseion precincts when a short, stout fellow clad in a dirty smock popped out from a doorway and accosted them. A bright chortle of greeting issued from a mouth almost entirely hidden in a great bushy beard and mustache. After instantly recoiling, Rufio found himself drawn in by the jolly-wicked twinkle in the man's eyes, almost equally obscured by thick gray brows that resembled a pair of marmosets set sideways above his lashes. "Oooor, yes. Yes!" He clapped stubby fingers together in apparent glee and then wrung his hands happily. "What a pair of beauteous Roman boys." He gurgled and shuddered as if he were about to orgasm. "Come this way, yes, yes. I can see at a glance that you are men of the world, and I, Epigonus of Tralles, will cast you in silver as heroic figures."

"Excuse me—" Quintus began.

Epigonus halted and turned half way back to look at Quintus. "You are not shy?"

"Shy? Of what?"

"Of posing nude for me, of course. Have you not heard the name and fame of Epigonus of Tralles?"

It was Rufio who broke the sudden silence. "Of course. Maestro, your work is famed throughout the Imperium." His face was wreathed in surprise mixed with what Quintus recognized as excitement—the sort of excitement Rufio expressed when he was about to get an erection. "You really mean, you want us to pose for one of your pieces?" Now there was wonder in his eyes. Quintus began to get worried.

"I do! I do! I do, oh yes, lovely lads. Let's go through to my workshop and see what you're like under all those official looking tunics and whatnot."

"Rufio, please tell me… what's this about?" Quintus tried to hold Rufio back but ended up being dragged in after him.

"Epigonus is the foremost silversmith in erotic stemware."

"Erotic… *stem*ware?"

"He specializes in boys fucking in different positions on the most lovely goblets you've ever seen. No, of course, you're a stuck up patrician so you won't have ever come across one, and believe me, coming is what you want to do when you do see one. I had no idea he was working here in Alexandria. This is a chance to be immortalized."

"Having sex?"

"What's wrong with that?"

"Well…" For once, Quintus was lost for words.

* * *

On the wide spaces of the magnificent Canopus Way the crowds
parted to flow around a strange tableau, two men who appeared to
be in the throes of panic, one clearly a big bad Roman, the other a
real Greek (as against an Alexandrian Greek).

"I thought you had your eyes on him, Eutychus," Flaccus bellowed
at the distraught tutor.

"You are supposed to be the vigilant one, are you not? Isn't that
your job title? Oh gods above, the Lady Junilla will have my guts for
her garters."

"You don't know how nearly true that is," Flaccus muttered
darkly. "Look, we have to be sensible about this and apply logic to
the problem."

Eutychus glared at the big vigilis in mock astonishment. "Logic?
You're a night watchman. What can you know of logic? The boy
has escaped our clutches. Even now some nasty Egyptian priest is
probably raping him. Subjecting the poor innocent to disgusting
pharaonic rites involving hybrid human-animals with long penises,
and—"

"Shut it, you paedagogue. Inventing horrors won't get him back. If I know Cato, he's more likely to be subjecting some poor priest to horrors with that staff sling he insists on tucking under his belt than the other way around. Let's split up. He can't get far. I'll go this way, you go that way."

Cato was having the time of his young life, footloose in a strange and exciting city, assailed on all sides by bright color, bustling people dressed in all manner of weird garb, from the Jews with their dark, voluminous shirts that fell from shoulder to scrape on the paving stones, Nabataean types, darker of skin than the Jews, heads wrapped in long winding cloths, the occasional Roman merchant in lightweight toga, accompanied by burly slaves to clear an imperial path, and everywhere the nattering Greeks dressed in anything from almost nonexistent tunics to brilliant syntheses as gaudy as anything seen in Rome on festival days. But here in Alexandria, it seemed like every day was a festival.

After giving boring Eutychus the slip and disappearing into the market crowds before Flaccus could spot him, Cato weaved a happily aimless route through a market packed with every conceivable commodity. He wondered what his comrades in the Aventine Foxes would think to see him prowling through this forest of stalls and shops set into the exterior walls of the Museum place—Mouseion, as Quintus insisted on pronouncing it. He wished he'd paid more attention to his Greek studies. It was one thing reading the written word, quite another to understand the gibberish. As Woof-Woof Felix was fond of saying, "It's all Greek to me."

Roman money spoke Greek, though. When his tummy rumbled Cato remembered he hadn't eaten anything since the breakfast that Septimius fellow whisked up on the flagship, and that hadn't been more than a selection of fruit brought from Crete, and inevitably tasting of salt. The delicious aroma of meat grilling on charcoal drew him to a rickety looking stall where a slovenly individual turned chunks of lamb over sizzling flames. With long, stringy hair covering the face and slumped under a shapeless smock of sacking Cato couldn't tell if the vendor was a man or a woman.

A shake of the head was the only answer when he tried asking for a skewer, that and a stream of harsh gibberish. Cato produced a sestertius, one of three his mother had given him. A pale claw struck out. There was the sense of nails raking flesh and the coin vanished in a flash to be replaced by a red-hot skewer of meat.

"Ouch!"

He walked on, licking his lips, switching the hot skewer from hand to hand, chewing happily and hardly noticing where he was going until walls closed in on either side. The noise of the market dimmed behind him. He was alone…

F·O·U·R | IV

Alexandria, later on the 7th day of July, AD 108

"It is only civilized of you, as you know me, to tell me your names," Epigonus wheezed as he showed them into a large, untidy chamber. A large tripod bearing a sketching board stood facing a long couch of scattered cushions and an arrangement of silken ropes dangling from hooks in the ceiling. Two of the walls bore shelves packed with all manner of metalwork in bronze, gold, and silver.

Quintus went blank in his head for a moment, aware of the folly of telling this gnomic Greek their names.

"I am Gnaeus Fabius and my friend is Titus Valerius," Rufio spoke up, giving Quintus a hard look.

Of course. Clever Rufio. The names they'd used that time they first met Malpensa, though at the Mansio at the Sign of the Ibis in Sinuessa the monster had introduced himself as Kaeso Sempronius Caprarius: goat by name and goat by nature, as he and his henchmen proceeded to drug them and then fuck them to buggery.

"Who likes to go on top?" Epigonus asked, uncomfortably close to Quintus's wayward thoughts. The artist busied himself setting up the tripod and arranging the board at an angle on it. He clipped a sheaf of expensive looking papyrus to the board and picked up a stub of charcoal from a tray on another small table. He peered at them. "Ah… you Romans, with your virtuous natures. But wait! You, with the red hair…Gnaeus. I think you are from Gaul?"

Rufio shrugged his shoulders in acknowledgment. "So what?"

"Your friend, who is so assiduously examining some of my cups over there—"

Quintus straightened up with a guilty jerk from where, open-mouthed, he'd been looking at the beautifully detailed coiled bodies of men, boys, women, in all kinds of carnal positions.

"—is clearly of noble standing, and I know Romans don't like to take the effeminate position, though Athena knows why when good Greek boys love a good buggering. But you, my fiery friend, may do as you please. Or rather, as I please."

Rufio flared up. "Are you calling me a barbarian—"

Epigonus thrust a scrap of papyrus in his face. "Nonsense. See! I have a rough drawing of the position you boys will take. Show him."

Quintus stepped over to look at the drawing in Rufio's hand. His mouth snapped shut.

"Looks like you get to be on top," Rufio murmured. He sucked in one cheek so his mouth twisted into a naughty S-shape and, with one eyebrow raised, he resembled one of the priapic satyrs on an Epigonus goblet.

"As you see," the maestro broke in, "top is a relative term. Now strip off those clothes and take your positions on the couch. I trust to your youth to be capable of rousing yourselves and keeping that way for the time I need to capture your essence, though there is no need to actually expend your essence, if you know what I mean." It seemed clear they did. "And here, place this on your head." He handed a flaky laurel wreath to Quintus. It felt as if it were made from some insubstantial metal.

"Oh. The last time I wore one of these I was playing Mars, God of War."

"That must have been magnificent, my boy. Just so erotic."

"I was fully clothed."

"Such a shame." Epigonus licked his lips as before his bulging eyes both boys revealed their naked glory, at least that's what Quintus thought he was doing, since the exuberant beard hid all but a flickering red tip of tongue. He sat on a low stool behind his drawing board with an appreciative puff of breath.

In spite of his misgivings and feeling of shy awkwardness, Quintus felt his loins tingle and his cock thicken in anticipation. He decided to ignore the gurgle of appreciation from behind the drawing board. He slipped from his loincloth and lay on the couch, his upper back supported on a fat cushion, as Rufio stretched languorously above him like a wild animal sensing a coming chase. He climbed across prone Quintus, checking the sketch in his hand as he did so. He let it go so he could give Quintus a friendly squeeze. The paper fluttered to the floor and with his freed hand Rufio reached up to hang onto one of the overhead ropes for support before settling his angled haunch on Quintus's thigh and raised hip.

"Yesss…" Epigonus began scratching away with his charcoal. "Gnaeus Fabius, tuck your legs up to the back of the couch and present your beauteous ass to me. There… aaah, so voluptuous, yet taut with fine muscle. Guide in your lovely hard weapon now, Titus my boy. Grip him firmly above the hip to give yourself more leverage for the entry. Ooh yess, yes, yes, magnificent."

Quintus took a breath and then with a now well-practiced flick of his hips, slipped easily into Rufio's presented hole. Rufio gave a deep grunt and rolled very slightly back onto the penetration.

"Fuck him for me, and you, Gnaeus, respond with all your body. Look half around at me… give me that look, you know it, lips parted in ecstasy, you are so, so, so, urgent for your friend's cock ripping into you. Titus, drop your left leg, foot on the floor so you can thrust up more violently. Now slide that hand from his hip over the top and reach for his hardness. Oh… beautiful."

The maestro's insistent instructions faded in Quintus's ears as he lost himself in the mounting pleasure of fucking up into Rufio, who responded by pressing down, then rising up to push down again. With head twisted sideways, Quintus felt Rufio's ridged spine digging into his cheek and as they moved in coital rhythm it slid against the sweaty back. Overhead, the rope onto which Rufio clung creaked in its fixing and merged with the different speed of the artist's screeching charcoal.

"Rufio… I– I'm going to come."

"Rub me harder, faster!"

"Oh my!" Epigonus gushed.

Into the sudden absence of scratching charcoal on papyrus, Rufio groaned and loosed a great arc of semen, to be joined a moment later by a strangled gasp against his shuddering back as Quintus gave into necessity and shot his own cum deep into his lover, astonished that he'd managed under the weird circumstances.

The Greek put down his drawing and stood, panting as heavily as if he had taken part in the sex, which the prominent convexity in the front of his smock made it look as if he'd wanted to. "You look such a delightful picture of spoiled innocence," he told Quintus. "The wreath slipped askance over one eye, like a little Pan… so delectable. Now, it's time for Gnaeus to wear the crown."

"What?" they both said.

Epigonus frowned in a schoolmasterly manner. "It may have escaped your slender attention spans, but any cup has two sides.

We have committed one to paper ready for me to cast and work in silver, but now I need the other side. This is where Gnaeus gets to screw Titus." He tucked his head in questioningly. "You boys do switch, don't you?"

It was not in Cato's nature to retrace steps if there were an alternative on offer. True, the narrow alleyway looked uninviting, but a few lines of clothing strung out here and there high overhead indicated some level of normal habitation, which was comforting. Two-story buildings stretched ahead to the left, matched on the right by the Museum's much taller outer wall. The way ahead wasn't straight. Projections sticking out at intervals from the Museum's wall where extra chambers had been added on at later dates obliged the buildings to the left of the alley to follow an irregular line. But even though he couldn't see far ahead, Cato reckoned he must be headed back toward the outer wall of the palace precinct. At some point there he should find a way through to the Library and so into the palace, past the guards and back to the sumptuous quarters the visitors had been given… and into a storm of trouble for slipping away from his tutor and Flaccus.

The narrow alley was unfrequented but for the occasional figure burdened by baskets on shoulders, scurrying past on their way to the market. So when he heard voices coming from a small side alley that cut into the depth of the Museum, he was surprised to recognize one of them as his brother's. Curiosity was Cato's second, third, and fourth name, but additionally there was something in the quality of Rufio's speech that hit Cato deep inside. And then he heard Quintus. This was too much to avoid! He slipped into the cutting, which was no more than an access to two doorways, the one on the left barred, the one to his right cracked open, and through which he heard a third voice.

"Now, Gnaeus, this time I want you seated on the edge of the couch, one leg on the floor, the other slipped between his legs, so that your— No, Titus. Drape yourself across Gnaeus, on your side... yesss, just like that."

Gnaeus? Titus? What's going on?

Cato shook his head in puzzlement. Surely he'd heard his brother and his handsome patrician love-bunny. When he spoke, the third man's voice sounded as if it came like water over gravel, bubbly with suppressed excitement mixed with repression and longing.

"Oh my beauties, this is going to be the finest cup I ever cast. Who shall be the buyer, who the receiver of such... such... erotic, coital wondrousness?"

Cato swallowed the last morsel of his meat skewer and dropped the sliver of wood to the floor. He tiptoed cautiously toward the doorway and by inclining his head could just peer through the gap. He almost gasped but had the cunning of mind to suppress it. His reached up and instinctively grasped the travel charm Felix had given him. The rigid winged phallus felt hot in his sweaty palm. The sight that greeted his wide-open eyes had him instinctively grabbing himself.

Both boys were still naked, Rufio seated upright on the edge of the couch, Quintus spread sideways across his lap. With his right hand gripping Quintus under his right knee, Rufio raised the leg and slid his right leg between his lover's splayed thighs. As for Quintus, he was stretched out fully along the couch's edge, left thigh trapped under the flattened meat of Rufio's right thigh. On the seat behind the boys lay the second sketch Epigonus had made. Rufio glanced over his shoulder to consult it. He slipped his left arm under Quintus to grip his breast and twisted the hard nipple until Quintus cried out and wriggled in the unrelenting grip. He pulled Quintus back hard against his upper abdomen. Quintus strained against the pressure for a moment and then relented so that Rufio bent him into a bow, which pushed his belly forward exposing his excited (but not entirely hard) cock and balls to Epigonus. It made him a wanton and perversely he relished the humiliation as mush as the feeling of Rufio's cock pushing eagerly at his exposed asshole.

"Now Gnaeus, now! I can see you are ready and your Ganymede waits, panting with lust, but also with love glimmering in his doe-eyes. Your mighty sword is poised to take what it desires, dripping with the gore of lubricious longing…"

Quintus had no idea how long the Greek would witter on in this hackneyed poetic mode, but once again he faded the man's singsong voice out as Rufio bent his head down close. Hot breath washed against his ear, and Rufio whispered, "The old goat is creaming his underwear… that's if he's wearing any."

He wanted to laugh, but his chest was too tight, and then the familiar sensation of Rufio's engorged cock head easing into him made him moan instead. He tried to suppress the shuddering exhale but when Rufio strained up off the floor and pressed deep into him, he just groaned again. The cock might be familiar, the position was not, and that strangeness brought with it a renewed excitement. His own cock sprang out—he heard Epigonus gasp—and Rufio instinctively brought his thigh-supporting hand out and around over Quintus's hip to grasp it firmly.

Quintus gave in entirely to the fucking and the stimulation of Rufio's hand stroking his shaft, and in moments both boys were going at it like a team of chariot stallions racing for the finish.

Epigonus draw feverishly, his every charcoal stroke recording the sex, first this detail, then that, a quick rubbing out, redraw, change papyrus sheet. But the instant he sensed Quintus had reached the point of climax, the moment when Rufio's neck muscles bulged like a bullock's taking the strain of a loaded plaustrum wagon and every sinew stood out like wires under his skin, Epigonus dropped everything and flung himself forward on his knees, a worshipper at the altar of the couch. He leaned in anxiously and Quintus first felt hot breath on the

oozing tip of his pumped cock, then the eager flick of tongue, and it brought him off.

A deep bass rattle sounded in his chest. Rufio lowered his head again to his ear, bit down hard on the lobe, and growled, "Gods above, but I love you Quintus." He came hard. Quintus shuddered at the thrusts and the pressure of cum jets filling him. He shouted and let fly, the mouth of Epigonus enclosing his shivered cock head as the man's hands alternately stroked and tugged on his aching balls.

Silence settled. Gradually the distant sounds of the market intruded; the shuffle of scholars' sandals on the other side of the door made themselves known. The outer door creaked, but it failed to rouse Quintus from the drained, but pleasant lethargy he felt. Rufio moved under him and he became aware that his friend's leg must be losing feeling, as indeed was his own. They untangled gingerly, blood beginning to circulate again.

"I trust you won't record this little episode in the diary?" Rufio said.

"You don't think it will entertain Trajan when he reads it?" Quintus teased, and then relented. "No, I'll skip over it."

"What are you smiling at?" Rufio asked the Greek artist. "That *is* a smile under all that fungus?"

"Hmmmm…" Epigonus got to his feet with a bit of a struggle, wiped the back of his charcoal-smeared hand across his lips. "Roman essence has its own particular taste," he said with some satisfaction. "We had a visitor."

"What?" the boys said again in unison.

"A lad, a mere lad. But you know, in spite of his hair being brown, I could swear he had the same face as you, my dear Gnaeus."

"Me?" Rufio gave Quintus an alarmed look.

"No, Ruf– er, Gnaeus, he's safe with Flaccus and that tutor fellow," Quintus assured him.

"I shall include him in my cup as the unbidden intruder, the voyeur at the door," Epigonus warbled on, unaware of their consternation. "I must begin work on it tomorrow when the light returns. It will be magnificent. Under 'Epigonus fecit' I shall inscribe it as the 'Fuck Cup of All' and sell it to some worthy Roman senator." He saw the look of fright that crossed both faces. "Oh, don't worry, my beauteous boys, your faces will not be recognizable as your own, more's the pity, for they are glorious visages. And our little visitor, he will be seen peering in at the door, an expression of curiosity and barely suppressed desire on his impish face at seeing two much bigger boys fucking."

Rufio appealed to Quintus. "Impish face…?"

"No, no it couldn't be. How would he find us here?"

* * *

"No! Absolutely not. I don't care what you say, I will not aid you in deceiving Ma."

"But you don't have to," Cato wailed.

Even Quintus could see the brat was putting on the distress.

He'd burst into the sumptuous suite of rooms given over to Junilla's family and servants. Quintus and Rufio each had separate bedchambers, but had slumped on the huge bed in Rufio's room after their artistic exertions. Out of sight behind a cascade of gauzy curtaining that hid a small personal bath the size of three farm wagons, Ashur could be heard tidying up the supply of unguents that needed no tidying.

Cato ran a hand through his bird's nest of brown curls, took a deep breath, and put on his best innocent look (never a successful one). "You can use your influence on Flaccus and persuade him not to tell on me."

"My influence?" Rufio looked baffled.

Cato gave his brother a sly jab in the ribs. "You know... he's soft on you."

Quintus felt the need to intervene and raised a lecturing forefinger. "Cato that is simply illogical. Think about it. Even were that the case, what about Eutychus, your tutor? He's not 'soft' on Rufio."

"There! You see, there's no way out of this one, my dearest Little Fox." Rufio gave Cato a consoling pat on the back, but the boy didn't seem very put out at the failure of his plan. In fact his cupid's smile turned positively evil.

"In that case, I might have to tell Ma about you and Quintus doing stuff in front of that dirty old Greek."

"It *was* you," Rufio groaned. "How much did you get to see?"

"A lot of you," Cato retorted gleefully. "And you too," he added in a softer tone. He leaned close and rubbed the side of his head in a catlike way against Quintus.

"He's a sculptor," said Quintus, pushing Cato off. "And you stop acting like a Bast—"

"I'm not a bastard!" Cato shouted with an angry leap back.

"Like a *cat*, I meant. Bast is the cat goddess of Egypt. That man is a maker of fine silver goods. We were posing for him."

"Likely story," Cato sneered. "I saw you going at it."

Rufio grabbed Cato by both shoulders and whipped him around. "And when did you start sneaking about and peeping through strange doorways?"

Cato didn't answer at first, but his smirking expression turned guilty and then defiant. "Well… I did sneak—as you put it—down the companionway on *Fortuna* one late evening and the guard on duty was snoring. I heard sounds from inside and the drape across the door was… well, a bit gapped."

"You didn't!" Rufio looked aghast at the implication.

"I did, actually. And there was the Emperor with no clothes on, and he seemed to be firmly stuck to your brother Marcus," Cato said to Quintus.

"He'll have you crucified if he finds out."

"I think not, Rufio, not after I helped save his life at that bash for the Nabatean prince and that of the Empress and all those honored guests. Anyway, who's going to tell?"

"Good point," Quintus agreed. And then curiosity got the better and he frowned. "Just how exactly was Trajan stuck to Marcus?"

The grin that split Cato's face spoke volumes. "A bit like I saw you and Rufio earlier. So," he turned on his brother, "what about Ma and dealing with Flaccus?"

Rufio sighed. "All right, you little bast-thing, I'll see what I can do, but we may have to dispose of Eutychus. I don't think he'll be as amenable. Perhaps we can slip one of those asp serpents down his back."

"That should do the trick."

"I wasn't serious. I may have to employ reason… ah, that's your department, Quintus."

"Don't look at me, I'm—"

"Oh, by the way I almost forgot," Cato broke in. "Did you bump into a strange man lurking just outside the palace grounds? You know, where you come in from the Library bit?"

Quintus looked at Rufio, shook his head. "What strange man?"

"He was dressed in a long black gown, made of some shiny fabric like it was wet and he'd just come out of a bath or something wearing his clothes, and he had long black hair, black eyes, and some sort of black stuff painted on his lips. Really strange. He stopped me and said, 'Has Rome come to Egypt?' Which I thought was an odd thing to ask. I mean, hasn't Egypt belonged to Rome since Augustus grabbed it, like you told us, Quintus?"

Rufio wasn't inclined to take it seriously. "Perhaps he was one of those reanimated Egyptian mummies the pantomimes go on about and hasn't caught up with what's taken place these last years."

"The guards at the gate there chased him away when they let me pass."

Quintus drew his brows together. "Should we tell Septimius?"

Rufio shook his head. "Can't. He disappeared the moment we

docked muttering about chasing after the Shadows of Seth, or something."

"Seth, again...?" Quintus drew his brows together. "I'm going to the Library to see if I can find out something about this Seth character."

"And I'd better go find Flaccus and Eutychus, and tell them you're safe. I'll point out just how much trouble they're in for losing you," he growled at Cato. "I'm sure they'll see the sense in keeping it quiet when I remind them that Ma will have their balls minced up for a terrine if she ever discovers how they let you get away."

Cato purred.

The tavern was a well-set establishment just off the western Canopic Way adjacent to the forum—or agora, Septimius had forgotten the Greek-Latin confusion in Alexander's city—and the temple of Poseidon and Caesar. He slipped in through the porch entrance quietly and took in the room. A large square space with two off-center pillars supported a crisscross of smoke-darkened beams carved in the style of the late Ramessid period with cartouches and other arcane symbols looking very authentic. Septimius hated theme taverns, but this one was well frequented so his meeting wouldn't stand out.

He spotted his target wearing a roughspun dishdasha of alternating brown and dark-gray stripes and a dun-colored turban of a peculiarly flat-topped shape with a tail tucked through the outer winding that slipped down over the front of his left shoulder. The man wasn't alone and shared a table with three other companions. The four were engaged in a playoff of two games of Petteia, which as a Roman Septimius called Latrunculi, or Mercenaries. The contact didn't look up at Septimius passing close by to reach the counter, but concentrated on the eight-by-eight checkered board with its colored stones. At a quick glance, it looked as though he was losing.

Septimius ordered a cup of wine and savored the rich, fruity

Egyptian liquor. It had been some time since he'd last tasted wine like it... a taste few Romans grew to like, but he'd learned to appreciate its slightly astringent flavor. A cry of delight and a groan of despair announced the conclusion of one of the games. A moment later, laughing ruefully, the man in the striped dishdasha pushed up against the counter and called to one of the servers in a boisterous voice.

"Another game lost! More wine, Abbas!" He turned fractionally toward Septimius. "They cost me so much, these men, running their dogs all over my city. Do you play, friend?"

"There was a time when I did, but after I lost eight games in a row to Agathocles of Koptos I vowed never to waste my coins again."

"I remember Agathocles well," the man replied in a lower voice. "It's good to see you again, been a long time."

"Indeed. I'm a respectable chef now. That is to say I was, but my lord insisted I return. What news?"

"None good. Seth rises. The desert hides everything, but with Rome come to Egypt I sense much is afoot. It is not safe for him. The word has gone out, the command 'Isis dies' has reached to every cell. We must not be seen together again. Beware the feast. I know not what, but I have heard of a delivery to be made."

And with that he gathered up the rough tray of cups filled with wine Abbas the serving boy banged down on the counter and strode back to the players with boastful words of how he would now slaughter his opposition.

A delivery...? Septimius suppressed a shiver. *Night is soon upon us. I must get back to the palace, but what to look out for?*

F·I·V·E | V

Alexandria, evening of the 7th day of July, AD 108

"By Minerva's munificent minge," Flaccus murmured to Rufio, "this makes the Domus Augusti banqueting hall look like a Subura cookshop." His unfavorable reference to the imperial palace's state dining rooms back in Rome was exaggerated but Rufio didn't object—his eyes were drinking in the abundance of statuary. It wasn't every day that a lowly pleb vigilis ever got through the palace vestibule entrance, let alone into the imperial precincts, but Flaccus had been swept in as a part of Junilla's team when she arranged entertainments for the visit of Obodas of Nabataea back in March.

Quintus too was quiet as he gazed around, trying hard to not look impressed. Rufio knew him well enough not to be fooled by the insouciant expression. *Of course, it doesn't do for a Roman of the senatorial class to allow a provincial public building to overawe him.* Never mind, Rufio decided to be impressed by his surroundings. The vast, double-vaulted hall presented a conflict of artistic pretension on a grand scale, as if the decorators of several unconnected cultures had competed for eminence. Some wall paintings depicted bare-chested, kilted Egyptians in a peculiar stance, as if a god had come down and put two twists in them so their feet and heads were seen in profile but the torso front on. These, painted in hot colors of sun and wheat, alternated with cooler blues and greens of typical Roman bucolic countryside scenes.

Rufio caught his mother eyeing some of the marvellous Greek marbles and bronzes of heroes, athletes, gods and goddesses disporting in deep hemicycle niches. And all around, a forest of elegant scarlet columns topped by gilt Corinthian capitals supported the two vaults, on which all the zodiacs of Roman, Greek, and presumably old Egypt glowed from the wealth of torches and lit candelabra. Musicians added tinkling airs to the atmosphere from amid a tableau of statues of young Greek boys, naked and evidently practicing wrestling at a gymnasium. The sounds of twinned tibia pipes and flutes mingled with the strains of lyre and cithara, timpani and a sweet Egyptian sistrum, "beloved of the goddess Hathor," said Quintus, showing off his recently acquired knowledge from a perusal of the Library's Egyptian section.

Along the sides were tables and chairs for the local administrative staff unused to Roman ways, while for the Romans triclinium-style groupings of sumptuous couches were arranged to provide a view of the high table. This, Trajan and the imperial entourage swiftly occupied the moment the lesser guests were settled at their places by an army of servants, which in the case of Quintus included Ashur who had refused to be parted from his master for the occasion. In accordance with ancient tradition, the three couches around the high table were graded in importance: *summus*, *medius*, and *imus*—top, middle, bottom. Each couch had space for three to dine in comfort. In pride of place Trajan reclined with the Empress Plotina to his left and the equestrian prefect of Egypt, Legate Servius Sulpicius Similis, on his right hand. Hadrian, Junilla, and Marcus occupied the median couch, facing the wife of Similis, who for some reason reclined on her own.

At a lower height, the other tables and couches were less traditional in their arrangement and accommodated senior members of the legate's comitia, including the over-named Lucius Junius Quintus Vibius Crispus and his notarius Lucius Pomponius Bassus Cascus Scribonianus. Rufio and Quintus, Flaccus, Eutychus, and Cato—Familia Tullii, as they'd nicknamed themselves—were clumped together "at a happy distance from that asshole Crispus," as Rufio put it. "I see Marcus made the top table," he said to Quintus as they were helped to an array of appetizing dishes.

"Yes, but it's a consolation prize. He is to remain with the ship, while we travel to the ends of the known world... oh, look." He nudged Rufio's thigh with his slippered heel. "The fashionably late make an entrance."

"Scribonius did say Legate Similis wanted to present his sons to Trajan, and being last to the party certainly makes them stand out."

"As are you," Rufio teased, reaching a hand over Quintus's hip to fondle his cock through his tunic.

Quintus blushed furiously and thrust Rufio's hand away before any others of Familia Tullii might see, but both gazed in open-mouthed astonishment at Aulus and Aufidius. The boys' unearthly beauty was enhanced by their choice of costume, the blindingly white stiffly pleated skirt of ancient Egyptians, their naked torsos glistening with a sheen of oil, into which was etched in sharp lines late adolescent musculature. Each twin wore a magnificent *weshket* collar, so wide it stretched from collarbone to breast, composed of golden tubes strung in five horizontal, concentric layers. The collars had an outer row of leaf-shaped pendants, stuck with all manner of costly stones: turquoise, lapis lazuli, garnets, carnelians, and glittering black obsidian. With each row of tubes varying from a rich, red gold to a pale yellow-white, the boys looked as if they might have climbed down from one of the wall paintings. Only a gold headband instead of one of the weird Egyptian headdresses set them apart as Roman.

As the twins stood facing Caesar, their identical Nubian slave boys wafting long-handled fans of ostrich and flamingo feathers over their short-cropped heads, Rufio tapped Quintus on the thigh and leant in close, though it wasn't likely anyone would hear over the general hubbub and musical accompaniment. Quintus turned to look at him and Rufio nodded his head at the twins' backs. "Those odd kilt things don't half show off their bottoms nicely. You don't get that from the paintings, do you?"

"Well I hope they don't show them off to Trajan, not while Pompeia Plotina is present."

"Was that a salacious giggle I heard?" Rufio grinned wickedly. "I claim the one on the left, but I fancy yours as well."

"How can you tell?" Quintus chuckled and dipped his chin to choke it off with a smile. "They're identical."

"Be nice to discover if there is a difference… somewhere."

"They might not approve of your kind of discovery."

"Or yours. Don't pretend indifference. Besides, dressed like that is like advertising."

"What are you going on about?" Cato, who was reclining on the other side of Rufio, wanted to know.

"Nothing for your delicate ears, boy."

"Fucking great pair of asses," Flaccus said across Cato, as Rufio slapped hands over both his brother's ears. "Oops, pardon my Gallic."

"The crocodile is an acquired taste, I have found, Caesar," said Legate Similis.

Trajan hardly knew the man, at least personally. He was well aware of the army man's record and approved both his military and civilian administrative abilities, but he liked even better the lack of equestrian ambition. Egypt needed a firm hand but one utterly loyal to the Emperor. Fortunately, there was nothing of the lean and hungry look about Similis, though his wife Terentia bore watching.

"Some say it resembles chicken, but I find it more chewy, although the way my cooks prepare it does render it edible."

Trajan chewed thoughtfully for a moment, but decided not to express his disagreement and instead reached for a baked dormouse drenched in garum. Good old-fashioned plain Roman fare was more to his taste. In fact he wasn't hungry after a tiring day spent catching up with the most immediate concerns of governing this vital province. It wasn't just the vision of the governor's two extraordinary sons reclining only a few hands' reach away that had robbed him of appetite. (Both were alternating in giving him fluttery glances, as though coordinated for maximum impact.) Far worse was the intense scrutiny to which that rapacious rascal Tullius Rufio was subjecting them. Not helped at all by seeing Quintus, beautiful, virtuous Quintus, giving the twins the eye as well. Fucking his brother Marcus had been fun, but somehow not as enjoyable as making delicious young Quintus writhe and twist and turn and squirm and moan and wriggle and…

Neither Aulus nor Aufidius was paying those two the slightest attention and yet Trajan was too well versed in the ways of attraction to miss that all four youths were anyway engaged in an erotic game. Of course, with Plotina at his side, he was on best behavior, unlike Hadrian who had barely stopped ogling the twins.

Jupiter knows what the alliterative Servius Sulpicius Similis must think… or is he pandering them to me, or to Hadrian in return for preferment? What is it he wants that he doesn't already have? Adlection to the Senate, no doubt. Perhaps more ambition burns in that fat breast than I thought.

Hadrian swallowed whatever he was eating and cleared his throat. Although he addressed Similis, his eyes never entirely left the twin visions reclining on the opposite couch. "Talking of acquired taste, you must have garnered much knowledge of this strange and exotic land."

Similis patted his red lips with a small napkin. "Oh I hardly ever have time to leave Alexandria. Of course, in my role of legate of Legion III Cyrenaica and XXII Deiotariana I do spend time at the fortress, but I'm well served by my senior tribunes and two effective camp prefects. But the detachments at Memphis and farther south along the Nile I leave to the command of tribunes who know much better than I the lie of the land."

"But are you not the least curious about the customs and peoples?" Hadrian said. "I'm sure I would find it all most fascinating. And I see none of the fabled Jewish community among the guests."

Similis rewarded Hadrian with a pitying smile. "They are troublemakers worse than those who claim ancestry with the pharaohs. You must have read of the embassy of Philo to Caligula to complain of the Jews' bad treatment at the hands of the Alexandrian Greeks. Always a pain in the fundament, the Jews. But as for the rest of this benighted province—excepting those grain-producing regions of the delta and the great oasis of Faiyum—even Philo was at a loss to categorize Egypt and its arcane traditions of politics and bureaucracy, which he described as 'intricate and diversified, hardly grasped even by those who have made a business of studying them from their earliest years.' No, my dear Hadrian, an intimate knowledge of Egypt is incidental to my record of service to great Caesar." He bowed to Trajan.

At the obsequious gesture, Trajan dipped his fingers into a golden bowl of water and rose petals offered by a slave and then dried them on a cloth presented by a second boy. "Indeed, Similis, your responsibility is to the good conduct of the province, but I wish to see the real Egypt of the great pharaohs, the necropolis of Memphis with its pyramids and mastabas, and the ancient places of Abydos and Thebes where lie by repute the kings who caused to be built the greatest of temples to their arcane gods. I wish to visit my fort at Elephantine as well as reach the southernmost island and the source of the Nile at Philae. The citizens of that far off place have beseeched me to be present at the dedication of a kiosk in my name to shelter the bark of Isis." He paused to indicate Junilla, who had until that time remained politely silent. "And we must accomplish all of our journey for my mistress of statuary to fulfil her obligation to me."

Similis inclined his head in submission. "I will have word sent to the fort to ready the honor guard. There will be transport by road and by canal barge to Sais, where awaits the great river barge to take all your family, servants, and court to the source of the Nile... and to safely return. But I must caution you to not stray from those paths and places the commander of the cohort accompanying you advises as being safe."

"What do you mean?" Hadrian said angrily. "There is danger in the province?"

"Lord," Similis insisted, "as I have said, this is a strange land, as long as the empire itself, as narrow as a snake. On either side trackless wastes hide all manner of perils, animal, mineral, and… human; or, more accurately, both less and more than human. There have been raids on Roman and some Greek settlements in the south. Messages have been left."

"What messages?" Trajan demanded.

Similis looked deeply embarrassed. "You must understand how difficult it is for the soldiers to pursue wraiths into the deserts. Tribunes commanding vexillations up and down the river at…" He searched the ceiling overhead for the places, "at Lykopolis, Muthis, Thebes, Pselchis, other forts, they tell me these monsters appear as if from the very sand itself, men perhaps, but dressed as frightening visions from the ancient Egyptian bestiary. They terrorize the villagers, pillage and burn and disappear as if they had never been present."

"And these 'messages' you mention?"

"There is some disparity, but many say it is something like 'Rome comes to Egypt.' Others say that the time is ripe for Seth to fall upon the land…" Similis held arms wide in a helpless gesture. "Whatever it means. Clearly deranged fragments of desert dwellers trying to frighten the peasants who work the lands along the river banks."

"Why 'Rome comes to Egypt'?" Hadrian wondered. "We've been here as effective rulers for more than a hundred and fifty years. And who is Seth?"

Rufio could tell there was some discussion at the high table that was exercising the legate and his imperial guests. He saw his mother speaking, though nothing said there rose above the echoing noise of a hundred or more people eating, drinking, and singing to some of the more popular tunes the musicians played. Only the Empress, Lady Terentia, and the two objects of his distant lust (and of Quintus, evidently) were taking no part in the conversation. "Tear your scrutiny from Aulus and Aufidius, whichever way around they are."

Quintus grinned guiltily at Rufio. "I was only trying to determine what they're talking about up there."

"Of course you were, but you don't need your tongue hanging out to do that. Tell me what you found out this afternoon."

"Har har. What do you want to know?"

"Who's this Seth fellow?"

"From what I read, no one you'd like to meet in an alley on a dark night… or anywhere at any time frankly. In the Egyptian mythos he commands the desert, conjures up storms, and is god of disorder, violence, and chaos. In human form he is a powerfully built man, but with the head of a monstrous jackal with a long curved snout."

"Sounds like a real charmer."

"I saw a jackal in the arena once," Flaccus butted in. "Horrible creature. Tore several criminals to shreds quicker than a virgin boy's orgas… sorry," he added for the benefit of a fascinated Cato.

"Seth was one of the original gods," Quintus continued. "His parents were the first gods, Nut the sky goddess and Geb the earth god. There were two other children, a boy and a girl, Osiris and one who should be familiar to us in Rome… Isis."

A quiet gasp escaped Rufio's lips. "'Isis d-dies. Desert Seth rises…' You remember? The words that man said with his last breath?"

Quintus regarded Rufio thoughtfully and nodded affirmatively. Then he gathered the strands of the tale again. "Osiris and Isis get married and—"

"His sister! What, just like Cleopatra and her brothers Ptolemy whatsit and Ptolemy whosit?" Rufio sounded scandalized. "No wonder the old Egyptians were crazed and they passed their madness onto the conquering Greeks."

"As I was saying, Osiris is a good god, bringer of civilization and culture, but Seth is envious of his brother for, well just for everything, so he kills him, chops up the body into forty-two bits—"

"This is starting to sound really good," Cato said.

"—and scatters them all over the world."

Rufio frowned over a curl of juicy fig. "Forty-two is very precise… And that's it?"

"No, no. Isis searches everywhere and finds all the bits of her husband's corpse. Then she reassembles Osiris and embalms him, but not before copulating with his body, and from his loins springs the seed that she bears as their son Horus. Now Horus is immediately the bitter enemy of Uncle Seth for murdering his dad—"

"They grew up quickly, then, in those days?"

"Shut it, Cato," Rufio snapped.

"It's a myth," Quintus said with dangerous patience.

"Like the Greek ones Eutychus is always going on about?"

"Yes, similar, but far more logical."

"Really?" Rufio scoffed.

"I was joking. So these two fight for supremacy over Egypt, and Seth tries to prove he's the top dog by seducing Horus—"

Cato's eyes went wide as marbles. "He fucks his nephew, *ughn!*"

The hand Rufio hastily slapped over his brother's mouth didn't quite stop him.

Quintus nodded. "Exactly, but I said 'try.' Clever Horus jams a hand between his thighs and catches Seth's cu— er, stuff in his palm and throws it in the river, which might explain why the crocodiles are so vicious. So Horus determines to get his own back, and knowing that Seth's favorite food is lettuce—"

"Ugh," said all three listeners at once.

"—he takes a leaf and works himself up and spreads his own seed over it. Soon enough, Seth comes along and eats the lettuce."

"No!"

"Like salad cream," Flaccus threw in.

"And then Seth appeals to the other gods for justice."

"I thought you said they were the first gods," Rufio pointed out.

"Well by then there were lots more. Look, I didn't write this stuff. Anyway, Seth says he dominated Horus so the gods call up Seth's semen, but it answers from the river where Horus threw it, so that rules him out. Then Horus counterclaims that it was he who dominated Seth and the gods call up the semen of Horus and of course it answers from inside Seth, so they make Horus ruler of all Egypt and banish Seth to the desert."

"That's a bit hard," Flaccus offered. "Just because he swallowed a load of Horus's—"

"Eeww, they must've been a funny lot," Cato said. "Who'd want to do a thing like that?"

"And that's the end?"

"Not really," Quintus answered Rufio, "but after that the Greek interpretations become terribly confused. Still, when the abacus is fully drawn Seth is not a pleasant creature. So just as well he's long been banished." A sudden commotion interrupted any further discussion.

"What in Hades' name!" Rufio gasped in a horrified voice.

Quintus was on his feet an instant after Rufio. Even before they could make a move the shrill screams of Plotina and Terentia rent the air, underlined by Hadrian's unmistakable parade-ground bellow.

Rufio could hardly believe what his eyes told him. The lid of a woven basket thrown on the high table in front of Trajan had erupted with the force of the imprisoned reptile within. Its long, black body struck out at the Emperor's head. Even as Trajan reeled back he watched Junilla leap from her couch like an athlete from the starting block. One hand down to Hadrian's knee, she hurdled across him to land between Similis and Trajan. Her hands snapped out and gripped the slender snake just below its flared head and halfway down its uncoiling length. The serpent wriggled furiously, but in a lightning move, she brought her fists together, making a loop in its body. And then she thrust them outward with great force and the creature snapped in two. Like a broken belt, the two halves curved in arcs in her grip and blood spurted left and right. The rain of gore elicited renewed screams of horror from the other women.

With a loud *Hah!* of triumph, Junilla hurled the two bits of serpent back into the basket from which it had stormed only a moment before.

And then Rufio was around the table. Heedless of the elite diners, he grabbed his mother's arm and swung her around. They hugged and looked down with disgust at the entwined halves of the snake convulsing in horrid arrhythmia as its brain refused to accept defeat. Rufio's mind was awhirl as he took in the carnage his mother's presence of mind had caused. Slashes of gore covered Plotina and Terentia while next to them the twins Aulus and Aufidius (or was it the other way around?) were more decorously adorned in a fine spray of red blots. The blood showed up spectacularly against their starched white kilts and their naked torsos looked as if they were suffering from an outbreak of the red-death fever.

To the other side Hadrian had escaped the worst of the bloodshed and Marcus, who had been reclining on the other side of Junilla, had missed being sprayed with gore altogether.

Remarkably, the intended victim appeared if not untroubled at least calm. He rose to his feet, glanced into the wicker basket at his would-be assassin, now stilled in death, and then parted Rufio and Junilla so he could look her in the face.

"My Lady Junilla, I am once again in your debt. You are indeed my own Hercules."

As Trajan continued to heap praise on his savior, Rufio tipped his head briefly at Similis, who appeared frozen in a rictus of shock, and then at Hadrian, who by contrast appeared mildly amused by the whole thing. Rufio sat in the space vacated by his mother's Herculean leap and patted a still-startled Marcus on the thigh as Quintus came to perch at the end of the couch on the other side of his brother. Over the way, slaves hurriedly ushered the Empress and Terentia away, and across the low table, still piled with food, two pairs of pale blue eyes stared back from white faces and from behind the twins two more pairs of dark eyes gazed from inscrutable black faces.

"My mother isn't fond of serpents," Rufio said blandly. He gazed frankly at Aulus and Aufidius, or perhaps it was Aufidius and Aulus. 'And her aim isn't always the best. I'm afraid your tunics look like those red-spotted mushrooms—"

"Amanita muscaria," Quintus provided helpfully.

"Your mother is—"

"Very brave," the twins said.

"I know," Rufio answered airily. "I inherited the quality from her. I also feel obliged to answer for her actions. I see your mother and the Empress have retired, no doubt to the women's bathhouse. May I suggest that we retire to the men's baths? And then I and my good friend Quintus here will make amends for her precipitate action by helping your slaves clean you up?"

Rufio looked sideways at Quintus and winked.

Flaccus watched Septimius examine the basket and its gruesome contents and shuddered.

"An asp." Septimius fixed the Legate's Greek major domus with a baleful glare. "How in the name of Hades did this reach Caesar's table? Who brought it?"

The man quailed at the barely suppressed fury and wrung his hands for the tenth time. Behind were stood several more slaves who had served Similis and his noble guests. All were blank with terror. "I told you, he– he is *tribunus laticlavius* from the fort," the major domus spluttered. "A broad-striper, sir. Who would question so senior an officer? He was most insistent the welcome gift from the officers and men of III Cyrenaica must be put before great Caesar immediately."

"You didn't think to check it first?"

"I– I never saw it arrive." He waved a hand behind him. "One of the slaves... but a tribune, a broad-striper?" He appealed to Septimius. "He handed it to one of them. Who would question a tribune?" The Greek spread his arms helplessly.

As a former frumentarius, Septimius had little time for juniors in the senatorial ranks flaunting their broad purple-striped togas. And he had even less time for an imposter, for so the man must have been. Look like an officer, act as haughty as an upper crust cunny with a broad stripe,   and what slave would question his orders? *A delivery to be made.* "What?"

"I said it is sometimes given as a gift, a pretty serpent."

"The wretch is trying to reassert his sense of importance," said Flaccus. Septimius had roped him in to help interrogate the slaves in spite of his protestations that his main function was the protection of Junilla.

"It seems from what I heard that the good lady can look after herself," Septimius said drily. "And her Emperor. Were there no Praetorians present as a guard?"

Flaccus shook his head. "It was to be very informal... well, as relaxed as such an event can be, and I was too far away to be of assistance."

"There are specialists who remove the poison sacs so the beast is harmless," the major domus pressed on. Are you not sure this was the case... just a gift?"

"You'd like that, wouldn't you? Get you off the hook I've no doubt Servius Sulpicius Similis has in mind for your neck." Septimius reached down into the basket and pulled out a length of torn snake with its diamond-shaped head at the end. Holding the reptile just under the head, he squeezed at the jaws, which yawned wide, baring two wickedly curved dagger teeth. He squeezed harder, ignoring the terrified gasps of the gathered slaves, and a squirt of clear liquid was ejected.

"This one would have killed." He threw the snake's remains back into the basket.

Flaccus shuddered again. He hated snakes. Spiders, even big hairy things with hundreds of legs he could cope with (just), but creepy-crawly serpents… He turned on the major domus. "Would you recognize this tribune again?"

"Please, I never saw the man."

"It's no good, Flaccus. For one they're too frightened to be of help and for two I'm pretty sure the fraudster is long gone and discarded his disguise." He smiled thinly. "You are a vigilis, are you not? So be vigilant. And I shall try to be so as well. There are strange things happening here in Egypt and if my informants are right, an age-old revenge is about to be played out. Isis beloved of Osiris dies and Seth rises to claim his own."

S·I·X | VI

"It was all gibberish to me," Flaccus informed Rufio and Quintus of the things Septimius had said.

"Though it fits what we heard up in the Subura at the counter of his thermopolium," Quintus replied.

They were speaking in low voices as the man in question was not far away on the bark. In a rare display of statesmanlike propriety, Trajan was seated with his wife on a double throne amidships. He and Plotina were arrayed in imperial splendor on the raised dais of the boat's "appearance kiosk" beneath its ornate covering. Four tall, slender columns supported this edifice, topped by a papyrus flower symbolizing Lower Egypt and a lotus flower for Upper Egypt.

"That thing he's having to wear is ridiculous," Quintus opined, referring to the exceedingly tall red and white headdress perched daintily on Trajan's neat crop.

"Don't let a real Egyptian hear you speaking ill of the *Pschent*," Septimius said, startling Quintus who hadn't heard the chef-turned-spy's approach. "It is the double crown of Upper and Lower Egypt, and symbolizes the unity of the land."

The canal banks hemmed in the boat so that in some spots there was barely space for the oars to make their broad sweep. Occasionally sporadic cheering was to be heard from villagers gathered on either side to witness the passing of the waterborne cavalcade of barges. Quintus suspected the enthusiasm was largely feigned, urged on by headmen anxious to keep their position as well as their heads. At each fresh outburst Trajan and Plotina raised languid hands in recognition.

"I thought it would all be sandy desert," Cato piped up, "but it's very green everywhere."

Septimius placed a big hand on the boy's shoulder and waved out at the scenery. "Alexandria sits at the edge of the Nile delta, attached to desert at one end and the great swathe of salt and freshwater swamp at the other. It is shaped like a tree reaching to Our Sea with spreading branches of the river, so many and all called the Nile by the Egyptians and Greeks who have dwelt here for eons. Their ancient forebears dug out numerous canals linking the branches so it's hard to tell if we're on river or canal, though as you see here the banks are most clearly made by the hand of man.

"However, there are two major outlets of the Nile. The great river as it flows from the south, from Upper Egypt, splits into two major branches of the delta just to the north of Heliopolis. The eastern arm meets Our Sea at a place called Tamiathis; the western meanders to flow out at Bolbitinus, which is close by Canopus and Alexandria. We are now being taken to join the Bolbitinus branch at the city of Sais and judging by the pace of our rowers we shall reach there shortly before dusk."

"You know such a lot," Cato said admiringly, gazing up with big round eyes and somewhat obviously fluttering eyelashes at Septimius.

Rufio leaned into Quintus. "D'you think I should warn Septimius about Cato?"

"Probably." Quintus choked off a guffaw. "I'm sure the brat's going to embarrass him... it's his way. At least Flaccus will be off the hook." He slapped at one of the infernal mosquitos plaguing the passengers. Rufio repeated the gesture at yet another buzzing pest.

"Everything here is as green as it is because of the annual inundation," Septimius was telling Cato, "which brings with it many biting insects, unfortunately." He smiled in sympathy at Rufio. "You see, every year between the months of July and September, the river floods, the season the old Egyptians called *akhet*. Then the delta region turns into a huge swamp, which is why the banks of river or canal have been raised so high, to protect the inhabited spots, but it will be another month before the water level reaches its peak here in Lower Egypt."

Cato pursed his rosebud lips thoughtfully. "Why does it flood?"

"The Egyptians believe that each year Khnemu, Anqet, and Satet— the guardians of the Nile's source at Philae—measure out the correct amount of life-bringing silt into the water to replenish the soil's fertility for the farmers. The silt needs the flood to distribute it fairly the length of the land. So when the three guardians see Sothis, the heavenly object we call Sirius, bright in the sky they know the ram-headed god Khnum is ready to release the flood into the care of Hapi."

"Is he called that because he makes the people happy?"

Septimius laughed. "No. Some call him Hep or Hapr, and he lives in a cavern under the Great Cataract, where the Nile springs forth from the ground at Philae. Hapi provides the extra water for the flood, which is why Egyptians throw offerings into the Nile at those places sacred to Hapi when the spirit appears with his retinue of crocodile gods and frog goddesses, although you must remember the chief crocodile god is Sobek."

"Crocodiles!" Cato said, jumping up and down. "Will we see any? I could use my sling on them."

"A stone would just bounce off and anger such a giant reptile," Septimius pointed out. "You'd be better off sticking your thumb in one's eye."

"Sobek! What barbaric names they all have," Quintus broke in.

"Hey, don't mind me!"

A look of chagrin briefly crossed Quintus's perspiring face. He hadn't meant any insult, but he'd grown so used to Rufio it was easy to forget his barbarian origins. On Junilla's side Rufio and Cato were descended from a line of Celtic warriors brought as slaves from Gaul one and a half centuries ago by the Divine Julius Caesar. Like his mother, Rufio exhibited the prominent physical attributes of his barbarian heritage: *Lofty in stature, of fair or ruddy complexion, terrible from the sternness of their eyes, very quarrelsome, and of great pride and insolence*, as the geographer Strabo wrote. With his untidy thatch of brown hair Cato followed his father in appearance (though his insolence must have come from his mother). An equestrian of lowly rank, Tulllius built up the family business through a canny eye for antiquities and a glib tongue. When Rufio was only thirteen, Tullius fell victim to an accident. In the Emporium's storage facility a poorly placed stone statue of Zeus raping Ganymede toppled over and killed him.

Septimius waited quietly a moment to let the boys settle down before continuing his narrative to a fascinated Cato. "It is customary for potent men to show respect by standing legs planted on the riverbank and there they manipulate their male parts, bring forth their seed, and spurt into the inundation. Hapi is Lord of fish, river fowls, and bees that inseminate the plants. He's also the god of fertility of both men and women, which is why he-she has female breasts and male genitals."

"Wow… you mean he can do *and* get done?"

Rufio stepped smartly in between Septimius and his brother and slapped hands over his ears. "I think that's enough about the birds and the bees." He raised exasperated eyebrows at Quintus's evident amusement. "Go and find Ma."

Cato waved a hand at the appearance kiosk, forward of where they stood. The backs of the imperial couple could be seen through two of the four slaves wafting massive feathered fans to provide a cooling breeze and drive off the insects. With their absurdly tall crowns, they appeared against the bright delta light as two silhouetted pharaoh figures planted before a temple pylon. "Ma's up there with the court." Cato made it sound like a prison sentence. "With Hadrian and his flunkies."

"Then go and flunk off with the best of them." Rufio gave him a shove.

"Knowing Hadrian's taste in boys, that might be a serious mistake," Quintus whispered.

"In spite of his high standing, Ma would brain him if he did anything," Rufio hissed back.

Cato scowled blackly, but did as he was told and stumped off along the deck that vibrated to the rhythm of the oarsmen below.

On the left a squadron of mounted praetorian guards kept pace with the several boats ferrying the imperial entourage toward distant Sais and the real Nile. The renewed cries of gathered spectators mingled with the calls of waterfowl, the buzz of myriad insects, the lowing of farm animals unseen over the raised banks, and above all the humid atmosphere coated everything in the fecund scent of fertility.

Fertility... Quintus, eyes fixed on the lean figure of beloved Rufio, his breeze-blown disarray of auburn hair glinting with highlights of gold under the relentless sun, cast his mind back over the Night of the Asp, as it had become known; or rather what had occurred in the immediate aftermath. *Sensuous, wanton, ethereal...*

Well, the fabulous twins proved the sad fact that ethereal beauty all too often masks a dim mind...

Lured on by the delectable twin white-wrapped bottoms of Aulus and Aufidius along with the equally enticing ebony buttocks of their fan-bearing slaves, Quintus and Rufio had negotiated long palace corridors to reach the boys' private apartments furnished with their own intimate baths.

"Nice set-up you have here. Luxury bathing, just for the two of you," Rufio murmured, openly admiring the spacious black marble pool with its own tinkling fountain set into warm-colored mosaic flooring, the amber sardonyx warm tub in the corner, onyx massage bench, and the comfortably cushioned reclining areas.

Quintus showed marvel at the golden walls with Egyptian-style painted panels of flora, fauna, and lithe young humans, intersected by slender onyx pillars. "Truly exquisite…" He transferred his hungry gaze to the glowing beauty of the ravishing twins… to be met with haughty blank looks of disdain from two pairs of icy blues.

"And who might—"

"You two… be?" sniffed Aulus and Aufidius, dainty nostrils on perfect noses flaring, pretty lips barely moving, delicate chins held high above long, slender necks.

Quintus squared up to them and adopted the haughty senatorial tone that so amused his plebby rascal lover. "I am Quintus Caecilius Alba, senator's son, and my companion here is Junius Tullius Rufio—"

"—trusted companions of Augustus Caesar Marcus Ulpius Nerva Traianus, lads, and here to give your handsome slaves a helping hand to rid you of the disgusting stains of battle."

Quintus didn't bat an eyelid at Rufio's wicked tone, or at the thought of what other stains might soon adorn their statuesque bodies, but he couldn't control the anticipatory twitch in his loincloth as Rufio took the initiative.

"I suggest your boys remove the precious—er…"

"Weshket collars," Quintus suggested.

"Right you are, my noble friend," Rufio guffawed, now in full theatrical swing and headed past the duo toward the hot tub in the corner.

All the beauteous twins managed were startled blinks and mute gapes of pretty mouths, while their Nubians fussed to unclasp the weshkets at the napes of their necks. Rufio bustled back with two dripping sponges and handed one to Quintus, winking. "Let's get to work."

The heavy collars lifted clear, Quintus followed Rufio's lead and began gently to rub Aufidius's (or maybe Aulus's) bared chest, paying loving attention to the dainty nipples. Rivulets of glistening water ran tantalisingly down the lean torso to pool along the top of the boy's skirt. The rough texture of the sponge and the sensuous swirling quickly transformed the nipples into buttons of arousal and Quintus worked his way lower, his free hand caressing the smooth flank while sponging the tightening abdominals and nub of belly button. His boy's lips twitched, but his eyes stared straight ahead. A sideways glance revealed a squatting Rufio already busy sponging, and fondling his way up Aulus's (or maybe Aufidius's) bare legs. *No time waster—he's already headed for the prize…* Hand and sponge disappeared beneath the hem of the skirt and the youth's eyes snapped wide open. At a quick signal his slave whisked off the youth's skirt to reveal Rufio's sponge working on plump wet balls beneath a rising erection.

"Back!"

The haughty beauty pushed Rufio away and his Nubian, in an obviously oft-rehearsed move, fell to his knees before him and set to adoring his master's manhood.

With an imperious grunt, Aufidius (or maybe it really was Aulus) brushed Quintus aside as his own Egyptian kilt hit the floor and the

Nubian twin slid into adoring position to begin his labial and lingual ministrations. Momentarily sidelined, Quintus and Rufio watched the hunky slaves work their impassive masters to full erection.

"If it weren't for the obvious, you wouldn't guess our beauties are enjoying this."

"Look at their faces: blank as statues…" muttered Rufio.

Just then twin taps on tightly curled heads triggered a seemingly choreographed shift of position by the young Nubians. They stood, dropping their skimpy loincloths, turned their backs toward their haughty masters and bent over with hands on their knees to present pert, dusky bottoms for use. As one, the twins stepped forward and impaled the proffered meaty targets and began fucking with elegant precision.

"By Jupiter's balls! It's a new sport: synchronized screwing," Rufio chortled. "This is what they call fun? Pathetic," he smirked sotto-voce. "Time to liven them up. C'mon, Quintus."

Unnoticed by the oblivious twins, whose eyes were shut in concentration, the boys silently circled behind them and quickly shed their clothing. Following Rufio's lead, Quintus slid up behind Aufidius (he was fairly certain it wasn't Aulus) and licked and nibbled a dainty earlobe while rubbing and pinching his perky little nipples. As the lad fucked his slave his firm ass bopped Quintus's erection rhythmically. The gentle splashing of the pool fountain and light, regular slapping of flesh upon flesh that filled the chamber, the absence of heavy breathing, nor grunting, betrayed the lack of passion in the proceedings—until to Quintus's left a shuddering gasp and slurping noises broke the spell. Rufio was on his knees, his face buried deep within the glorious ass cheeks that his thumbs

held prised wide as he feasted lustily on the intimate opening. Aulus (definitely) had his pretty lips parted in surprise, eyes wide, and his rutting rhythm faltered until Rufio's grip on his rump resumed it for him.

Encouraged, Quintus increased his licking and nibbling and set his spittle-wet fingers to work on Aufidius's bottom, swirling, probing, penetrating and soon felt the boy's smooth body shuddering. He heard sibilant hisses of arousal. "That's more like it, pretty boy…" he cooed. "Got you now."

With martial alacrity, he thumbed the lad's clutching rosebud open and rammed his drooling erection up into the steamy depth of the vulnerable channel. Relishing the squeak of alarm and pain, he snaked his hands around Aufidius to grip his Nubian's waist and began to vigorously screw his beauteous conquest.

Increasingly unbridled sounds of human carnal passion now stirred the calm of the room—grunts, groans, yelps, gasps, and sighs— and for his part Quintus lost himself in the visceral thrill of finally getting to fuck the aloofness out of cute Aufidius's rather vacant brain; to ignite his wonderful body to helpless ecstasy.

There were cries to his left and a scuffling commotion. He turned in time to see Rufio bring his boy and his impaled slave crashing to their knees with the force of his rutting. The view of Rufio's bunched buttocks continuing to thrust vigorously toward climax in his victim's delicate upturned butt sent Quintus over the edge. He pulled Aufidius deep onto his ramming cock and exploded in mighty gushes. The lad cried out in abandon. "Aufid-i-ous! Aagh! Ah!" Overlapping his brother's gasps of "Aulu-u-s!" (Not Aufidius, but Aulus after all… well, he'd get Aufidius next.)

Indeed, the fun and games continued. Not only did he skewer incoherently babbling Aufidius, but he and Rufio tumbled and thoroughly screwed the luscious twin Nubians out of their senses. The hot action propelled the tangle of slithery bodies into the shallow pool, spraying water all over the marble flooring.

By the end of the Night of the Asp they'd done the beautiful twins and their twin Nubians every which way and proved that dim wits need not spoil the enjoyment of gorgeously sexy bodies. They'd left the exhausted four sprawled limp on the floor, haughty disdain replaced by grateful puppy dog eyes acknowledging their exit.

The sun was low in the western sky when the imperial bark breasted the canal's surface coating of floating vegetation, the dipping oars rising again festooned with tendrils and leaves, and broke out into the main Nile. One moment a thicket of trees obscured the view and then the next open water spread away to either side like a shock to the system.

Quintus squinted at the far shore and gave a whistle of surprise. "It must be more than six hundred paces across at this point, and Septimius said this is the narrower of the two main branches, let alone the river after Heliopolis."

"Certainly makes the Tiber look like a stream of piss," Rufio concurred.

"Downriver of the Cloaca Maxima it is."

There was an immediate flurry of activity on the bark's deck as flunkies and servants scurried around in anticipation of their arrival at Sais. But no one was actually going onshore. Ahead against the opposite bank, glowing in the sun's long, dusky rays like a burning townscape, was a vessel many times greater than the conveyance that had brought the Emperor from Alexandria. A handful of small pleasure rowboats clustered at the boat's flat-sided stern like fussy unimportant relatives. "I'm not sure I'd enjoy bumping into a hippopotamus while paddling around in one of those."

"Hmm…too flimsy. You won't get me in one," Rufio agreed.

The bark's master expertly brought his craft alongside. The rowers shipped oars at the last instant with a precision that would, as Quintus observed, have turned Marcus green with envy. Ashur, who had been lazing about somewhere out of the beating sun, Quintus reckoned, trotted up with hands full of discarded cloaks (the early morning air had been chilly in an onshore breeze), wallets containing uneaten remains of snacks, and a second pair of Quintus's sandals.

"You and your elegant footwear," Rufio noted with the tone of one who had   no need of such excess.

The disembarkation took some time as everyone lined up to follow the imperial contingent into the massive Nile boat. Its numerous oar ports opened at a height just above their heads and from there on up the straight wooden sides seemed to go on forever. The length of the hull was broken at three points by what appeared to Quintus to be viewing balconies, perhaps from which passengers might while away hours fishing, or just observing the passing landscape.

There was much gilding in evidence amid the rich, deep reds, blues, and black. By craning his neck Quintus could just make out on the topmost deck the "appearance pavilion," foursquare on hefty closed-lotus columns. He pointed the structure out. "Compared to the one on this tub you could easily fit an entire cohort of legionaries in that."

Rufio frowned. "How many men make up a cohort?"

"Don't you know anything? Four hundred and eighty at full strength."

"I knew that, I was testing. Just because you're a patrician prick doesn't make you a military tribune… yet."

Quintus didn't deign a reply. Bit by bit, the mass of scribes, slaves, senior military and civilian personnel, and their servants disappeared through the gaping opening cut in the boat's hull. The doorway's edges were decorated in gilt-and-paint designs in the strange syncretic Egypto-Greek style and with a legend in the funny hieroglyphs over the top, of which the Latin *Cleopatra Regina in Flumine Nilus* underneath was presumably a translation. On the river behind them, four other barks of the fleet waited impatiently to discharge their passengers, while several large barges could be seen in the gathering dark.

Rufio peered at the boats. "What do you think they're up to?"

"Transporting our mounted praetorian guardsmen and their horses across?"

"Oh look, we're moving at long last."

They caught up with Junilla and Cato just inside the spacious vestibule. Eutychus was busy lecturing his charge on some matter while Flaccus argued with some oriental looking fellow dressed ostentatiously in a flowery Egyptian-style kilt and ornate short-sleeved jacket that did not reach down to his exposed belly button. Of the imperial family, retainers, Hadrian and his cohort of youthful followers, there was no sign.

"There you are my boys," Junilla greeted them. "Ah, good, Ashur, will you help Eutychus with his bits and pieces, thank you. Where's that Corbulo fellow hidden himself?"

It took two beats of the heart for the name to sink in and Rufio answered first. "Septimius, you mean? I've no idea, Ma. After filling Cato's head with nonsense about the Nile and the birds and bees and things he went forward. Haven't seen him since."

"Perhaps he's checking out this floating palace for agents of the evil Seth," Quintus said in a mock serious voice.

Had they been able to see the other side of the great vessel, Quintus and Rufio might have noticed a furtive meeting in progress. The towering hull blocked out the setting sun's last rays from the wooden wharf below. There, in deep shadow and lost amid crates and baskets of provisions being loaded by an army of slaves, a nondescript man in a shapeless dishdasha and head winding stood on the planking exchanging hushed words with a man whose bald head and shoulders were thrust out through an opened oar port.

"After Heliopolis will the boat put in at Memphis?"

"It will," baldy replied. "And better, I had sight of the Nomarch's planned excursions. He wants to show off the ancient tombs at each major necropolis. This much I know, but you will need to discover the exact itinerary and the dates…"

The clattering of a squirrel crane drowned out the hoarse voice. Septimius strained to hear, but dared not show a silhouette against the still-glowing western sky. When the crane ceased its groaning and rattling he caught the one on the wharf saying, "I'll pass on the word."

He shrank back from his hiding place on the upper deck behind the spider's web of cordage that supported the central sail and away from the rail. Infuriatingly all he'd been able to glimpse of the traitor on the boat was a pale glow from the top of his shaven head. The exchange took place in backwater Latin, not Greek or Demotic Egyptian. That went a long way to confirm his suspicions—first aroused by the dying words of Egnatius at his thermopolium back in Rome—that in spite of the terminology (*Isis, Seth rises...*) there was a home-grown aspect to whatever was happening here, borne out by the uncomfortable truth that someone had reached out all the way from Egypt to murder Egnatius in Rome.

So... we know in what region danger lies—and no surprise there, the lonely necropolis on the desert's edge—but the actual location, the intent, and the timing, these remain to be discovered. Gnaeus Septimius Corbulo knew that to persuade Caesar to forgo the visits would be impossible, not only because he wouldn't be the man he thought Trajan was to shrink from danger... *But really because he won't believe harm lies in wait in this accursed land.*

His first task in the two and a half days it would take to reach Memphis was to discover the identity of the traitor on board. For that he could do with some help and swiftly reviewed the options. There was Marcus Laevinius, a tribune of III Cyrenaica commanding the detachment accompanying the Emperor, but the young aristocrat was a typical inbred asshole more given to the airs and graces of a courtier. No, Laevinius would view the idea of snooping around as too unRoman for his delicate constitution and probably couldn't tell a spy apart from a colander.

Servilius Vata commanding the Praetorians, both foot and mounted, would have been a more promising prospect were it not for the fact that on several occasions he had taken loud exception to any member of the frumentarii and their intelligence-gathering activities. And Hadrian...? Septimius rejected that avenue too. The self-styled prince and heir may have distinguished himself militarily in his own book but Septimius gave little credence to the official record. The man spent more time in front of a mirror having his hair and poncy beard permed with heating tongs than in any strategic or tactical planning. The effete Athenian style might thrill his fashionable catamite friends but Septimius found it sadly wanting in a Roman.

Perhaps the two lovebirds, the Lady Junilla Tullia Rufia's son and the oh-so-serious patrician boy, they might prove useful allies. Likely lads, he thought, having heard from several sources of their resourcefulness in tight situations. And how could he not approve of a lad who loved to eat his sausages?

* * *

"Gentlemen, my name is Djed and may I take this opportunity to welcome you warmly aboard our cruise boat *Cleopatra of the Nile*, operated by the Khepri Corporation. Yes, this is indeed the royal transport of the fabled queen herself, though it has been much refurbished in the days since she graced the throne. It is the dearest wish of my staff and I to ensure your Nile Experience is a memorable one."

The florid flunky Flaccus had been arguing with when they came aboard turned out to be the boat company's second chamberlain (the first looked after the Emperor, Plotina, Hadrian, and their attendants in apartments on the topmost of the covered decks). He looked even more flowery because of the full-length wrap-around stole and dress of a gauzy transparent fabric he wore over the stiff, pleated kilt. On his feet he wore the most ornate, over-decorated sandals Rufio had ever seen. "I bet he can fly like Mercury with those galoshes," he whispered to Quintus.

"Shhh, this may be important."

"No expense has been spared to ensure your comfort on our trip to the source of the Nile," Djed continued in tones as floral as his perfume. "*Cleopatra of the Nile* is powered by sail and no less that four hundred rowers—we have twice that many working in two shifts per day—but sails alone will take us through the night when we are not moored so the noise of the oars won't disturb your beauty sleep." He simpered and motioned to the master of slaves to increase the wafting of feathered fans over his guests' heads. "We recommend you avoid drinking river water. Attendants will be happy to provide boiled water for internal consumption, but we are well stocked with a variety of fine local and imported wines as well as Egyptian beer for those with a taste for it." His pinched expression suggested anyone who drank the beer would be madder than a prodded hippopotamus.

"In the unlikely event that we are obliged to abandon *Cleopatra of the Nile*, I ask you to consult the information in your apartments as to the location of the ten crisis-craft. Should such an inconceivable catastrophe occur please refrain from dangling hands or feet overboard until you are safely ashore. The crocodiles can be pests. One final note: during onshore excursions please take care of your valuables and money. While we Egyptians are a law-abiding people, there are lowlifes from adjacent nations who prey on unsuspecting tourists.

"We shall shortly be departing for Memphis, so for the first hour the rowers will work hard before settling down for the night. The Khepri Corporation's augurs have taken the auspices and predict we shall have favorable weather for our sailing to Memphis where

Nomarch Sextus Agapetus eagerly awaits our arrival. The length of Egypt is divided into forty-two nomes, or districts, twenty in Lower Egypt, twenty-two in Upper Egypt," Djed explained. "Each is governed by a nomarch, who of course answers to the Roman governor in Alexandria. Now if—"

"Excuse me, but how does the boat sail against the river current? It's surely quite fast if it's flooding?" Flaccus looked apologetic for asking, but determined to get an answer.

"Fortunately, the swiftness of the river does not materially change with the inundation and the gods have blessed Egypt with a wind that nine days out of ten blows from north to south and so propels us against the current. On the way back we only use the oars and so move much faster with the current, or just the current alone at night. Any more questions?" Djed looked about expectantly, but no one else had any. "Good. An evening welcome-on-board feast will be served in an hour's time on the upper deck with local music and dancing. Thank you for listening."

S·E·V·E·N | VII

Memphis, 13th day of July, AD 108

Memphis lay about two miles from the Nile's western bank and extended for approximately six miles on either side of its great religious and administrative center. This was built on ground raised above the annual floods by eons of construction piled on more ancient foundations. Its walls shone a blinding white in the early morning sunshine. Beyond, coppery bright in the haze, could be seen the uneven line marking the escarpment of the desert plateau where the great necropolis of the pharaohs spread out for miles to the north and the south. Rich farmland lay between city and river, crisscrossed by dikes and irrigation canals. The lowest lying areas were already beginning to disappear under the Nile's rising water. Quintus gazed around with interest as he, Rufio, and Cato followed the train of imperial tourists and their Praetorian Guards to the city from the royal harbor. Ashur walked at his side, grumbling about the flies that seemed to find him the most attractive of the group.

Cleopatra of the Nile—or simply *Cleo*, as she had become known for simplicity—had pulled into the stone-built canal leading to the royal berth just as a huge sun lifted its bloody rim above the flat eastern horizon. It blazed a red swathe across the tranquil river's surface. Then, the air had been refreshingly cool, but an hour later the ever-present heat beat up off the pathway and every step made little dust storms, which did little to deter the flies.

"Some say its name is derived from Mennufer, the good place," Septimius the ever-ready encyclopedia informed them.

"He's as bad as you with the lectures," Rufio said to Quintus.

"Except you are so much more interesting," he added with a grin at the former frumentarius cum chef.

"Thank you. I must introduce you to some Egyptian cucumbers. They grow the finest and biggest specimens of anywhere in the world here."

Rufio stifled a laugh at Quintus's arched eyebrow.

"The ancient name was *Ineb-Hedj*, which means 'The White Wall,' as you see."

"Why are there no proper roads?" Cato stamped on the offending dried mud hard enough to raise a cloud of dust that surrounded him and brought forth a splutter of coughing.

"Serves you right," said Ashur as he waved a hand at the choking stuff.

"Egypt is a strange country," Septimius answered. "The desert presses in on both sides, so it's confined to the valley where the Nile waters the soil for more than seven hundred miles north to south and yet—apart from the delta, the Faiyum oasis, and a couple of spots in Upper Egypt—it's little more than six miles wide. What purpose would roads be? Everything goes by river transport. Besides, roads would eat up valuable growing space and they'd be under water for a quarter of the year."

In every direction men were busy erecting thin stones taller than themselves. "Lawful markers," Septimius offered. "They set them out to indicate the farmers' boundaries when the fields disappear under water so there can be no disputes over who owns what when the flood subsides. If a man is discovered cheating he can be severely punished. At its height, after the ides of the month named for Augustus, everything from here to the walls of the city will be under the deluge." A shout from up ahead alerted him. "It sounds like I'm needed. I will look for you later at the briefing."

Quintus squinted after Septimius as he quickened his pace to catch up to the front of the procession. "Is it me, or is the man on edge?"

101

"He has been jumpy ever since the business of the asp. Perhaps it's to do with that. Uh-oh, stand back!" Rufio jerked Quintus aside by his elbow. They all stood well back to let a train of elegant palanquins go by, each borne on the back of four dust-coated, panting slaves: a potpourri of Nubians, Libyans, Jews, Canaanites, and several paler-skinned men from northern climes. A hard slapping of bare feet on the impacted mud surface played a counterpoint to the clatter and jingle of accoutrements, and the flap and rattle of the swaying litters' flying curtains.

"Boys!" shouted Junilla as she approached and passed them in a blur of bright color and a brief glimpse of luxury. "This is fun, oh and Rufio, pet, I need you now to view some statues…" And she was gone, following the Empress and preceding several more conveyances bearing women of the court. In their wake they left behind an exuberance of perfume: camphor, nutmeg, sandalwood, rosewater, cloves; and less appealing scents of bare sweaty feet and dust.

A fuss of *Cleo*'s crew met them inside the gate closest to the government complex and split up the tourists to guide them to various accommodations. Dismounting her chair and dismissing the slaves with courteous thank yous, Junilla grabbed Cato and went with Flaccus and Rufio to look at whatever statuary the nomarch's staff had found for them.

Quintus had a sudden desire to explore on his own and he was aided in slipping away by the general confusion of ushering the imperial party off to the nomarch's residence where they were to be housed. Ashur insisted on accompanying his dominus, but Quintus ordered him to go with Junilla and Rufio to help in whatever it was they had to do.

The gubernatorial complex at the heart of Memphis had long ago lost its pre-eminence when the Ptolemaic dynasty made Alexandria the capital, yet the "good place" was still one of the world's busiest ports. It didn't take long for Quintus to discover that—while Legate Servius Sulpicius Similis might consider himself Trajan's vice-regent and Alexandria the beating heart of Egypt—the real governance of the province lived on here on the banks of the Nile.

After the close confinement of quinquereme, barge, and Nile boat, Quintus relished being detached for once. Not that he was really alone. A vast bureaucracy occupied a city within the city of administrative buildings. Diplomatic lodges for every nation within and without the Imperium stood opposite temples to gods of every conceivable persuasion. Priestly colleges stood shoulder to shoulder with mercantile colleges and tradesmen's guilds. There were treasuries, lines of barracks, counting houses, tax bureaux, and many grand edifices whose purposes Quintus was unable to determine, and a vast army of bureaucrats and their servants teemed in every street.

After Roman-dominated Greek Alexandria, Memphis was much more what Quintus had imagined Egypt to be like. Those he assumed to be natives predominated. Many wore Egyptian-style kilts and went bald-headed, their rounded pates glistening in the harsh desert light. Others dressed more conservatively in Greek chiton or Roman tunic. Everywhere young boys scampered around, some gainfully employed carrying messages or clutching amphoras, others simply at play under shade trees that graced the wider streets. Many young boys also sported shiny shaven heads but for a single tail of dark hair that fell from the crown down one side. He'd seen this strange style depicted on walls in the palace at Alexandria.

At every corner men and boys touted for custom, luring people into this emporium or that: carpet sellers, papyrus museums, brothels, ivory carvers, perfumers, and taverns selling the thick Egyptian beer. Hawkers with trays strung around their necks offered trinkets for sale, which struck an odd note since Quintus thought it unlikely any of the office-workers and professionals scurrying around would be interested in the tat he saw on display. In contrast, workers buzzed like the ever-present flies around the many food-stalls doing a brisk trade in late breakfasts.

There was time to idle away until he was due to join Rufio and everyone else of the party by the sixth hour. Before they had all left *Cleo* Djed explained that several tours of city and necropolis had been organized, but the actual arrangements for each day's excursions would be conveyed at a special briefing to be held in the nomarch's audience hall after the conclusion of imperial business. In the meantime it was best no one went off exploring on his own. *Bugger that for a laugh, as Rufio would say!*

As Quintus wondered whether the excursions would throw light on the more obscure mysteries of Egypt, a particularly persistent tout accosted him, a boy of no more then ten years, all eager brown eyes in a dusky face. "This one, sir, this one. Good bargain." The boy grabbed Quintus's hand and half dragged him toward a shop that looked more prosperous than many others he'd passed. A deep display table occupied the emporium's wide, arched frontage. Carved objects of what, in his limited knowledge of stoneware, he took to be onyx, fought for space on the table. (His father Lucius was always complaining that his youngest might at least try to learn something of the material used in construction and adornment of buildings, the Caecilii family's principal source of wealth .)

He was suddenly aware that the tout boy had vanished, but the wares took his attention. There were many figurines and traditional busts in evidence. In some the carver had used the rich, vari-hued-brown striations cleverly to make the figures come to life.

"It is Egyptian alabaster. Only the best alabaster comes from Egypt. Did you know that?"

A playful question. Quintus glanced up to see who was correcting his assumption and his questing gaze ran headlong into a pair of large irises as rich a nutty-brown as the stones arranged on the shop's counter. They were amused eyes, curious, limpid, almond-shaped, and set either side of a short snub nose of the kind that made Quintus want to reach out and gently pinch the flaring nostrils. He gazed from under brows arched in a perpetual question to which

Quintus could tell he already knew the answer, curves as black as his close cropped curly hair. The corners of his full lips, a pretty pink against the smooth tanned skin, disappeared into dimples that gave his smile a look of anticipatory amusement. The young man leaned provocatively against the doorpost in a careless stance. His expression could be described only as one of earnest naughtiness, though as Quintus straightened up to stare back he thought it more likely to be the look of a slick salesman ready to separate a fool from his denarii.

"You are new in Memphis."

It was a statement. "How do you know that?"

"The sun burns everyone dark here, yet your skin is pale though your hair is as dark as mine. Your bearing is noble. You are Roman, and Sekhemkhet Adonis—this is me—knows every noble Roman and noble Roman's son in Memphis because it is here they come to buy alabaster. My family are master-carvers. Not me. I am merely a humble seller. Besides, your accent gives you away... so refined."

The compliment, Quintus suspected, required a pinch of salt. It sounded like a flummery regularly employed to lure customers. On the other hand, the oddly named youth was attractively naked above his white kilt, but for the simple weskhet around his neck. Quintus was having trouble taking his eyes off the neat, dark coins of areolas surrounding delicate nipples that seemed to beckon with every slight movement the boy made. He sniffed at an exotic smell. "What is that... Sekhemkhet Adonis?" hesitating at the strange name combination.

"Call me Sek, it's easier. The scent? It is a peppermint infusion. We drink it hot and offer it always to passers-by. Come."

"Peppermint? I have had mint leaves in a cold sauce once and Plinius Secundus wrote of its use to flavor some wines, but hot...?" He was reluctant to fall for the obvious temptation, and yet... A handsome bronze medal fastened the weskhet at the back of Sek's elegant neck, visible to Quintus as he followed the young shopkeeper. He drew his brows together on entering the premises, wondering how wise such a move was but compelled by the spell Sek had cast over him. After the brilliant daylight, the interior draped gloom over more display cases. "How did you get your name?"

"My father is Greek merchant and my mother is Egyptian princess descended from the house of Nakhnebef, who the Greeks call Nectanebo, last pharaoh of Egypt before the Ptolemies made themselves kings." He turned and his eyes bored into Quintus again. Shards of reflected light from the entryway glinted in the dark orbs. "May I know your name?"

Quintus told him.

"The Plinius you mentioned, he is relative?"

"No, not at all. Pliny was a philosopher. His nephew is governor of Bithynia." He had no idea why he threw out that snippet of pointless information. In a perfectly smooth, polished bronze gong stood on a side table Quintus caught his reflection side by side with Sek's as he turned to look back at him and was startled by the closeness of their appearance.

"Do I make you nervous, Quintus?"

By the gaping maw of Orcus, he's got me in a dither. Not a state Quintus appreciated. His stammered negative was hardly a convincing denial.

Sek's seraphic smile preceded him as he resumed crossing the space crowded with stands and chests piled with sculpted alabaster. He took a small pot off a stand over glowing coals and poured steaming water into two stone beakers. He threw a handful of dried herbs into each. Immediately a pungent waft of mint struck Quintus's nasal passages. Sek added some other ingredient— "Honey to sweeten the infusion"—and handed Quintus a beaker. The stone was astonishingly thin and hot in his hand. Of course it was alabaster. With some suspicion he took a sip of the sweet-smelling drink and spluttered.

"You are not used to hot liquid." Sek sounded genuinely concerned. "You Romans do not take hot drinks, I think."

Quintus nodded as he recovered from his surprise. "Warmed mulsum, but never this hot."

Sek stepped up close. "Sip, just a little at a time. Savor it on the tongue for a breath, and then… swallow." He raised his own beaker and showed Quintus how to do it, the pools of his dark eyes fixed on Quintus over the rim, never blinking.

Quintus lifted the cup again to his lips. Suddenly the vapor filled his nose and mingled with the kick to his palate like a taste explosion. The room and its clutter of alabaster animal-gods, kraters, cups, carved game pieces, and trinketry seemed to sway. He staggered slightly to regain balance on a tipping floor. The sensations suddenly running through his mind reminded him of that Sinuessa night when deceitful Caprarius and his thugs Brutus and Tiro befuddled Rufio and himself with the Milk of Paradise. The drug sucked them into the arms of Lethe, buried them under the rapacity of their seducers. But Sek's sudden closeness felt different.

Quintus sensed his lips forming into a slow smile. He sipped the heady fragrance and found the nearness of Sek's cute nose as irresistible as his sphinx-smile. Quintus's index finger acted of its own accord, extended until he could draw it slowly down one side of Sek's nose to curve under a flaring nostril. He stroked softly down the delicate philtrum groove until his fingertip came to rest pressed gently against the middle of Sek's upper lip.

He wasn't sure how the beaker vanished from his slack hand, or where the bed came from; nor how they both ended up on it naked, entwined and exploring the planes, valley, nooks and crannies of each other's blazing anatomy. Pleasure mounted in clasped lips, handgrips, pressed fingers, bitten nipples, and hard cocks. Sek writhed like a captured eel and every wriggle inflamed Quintus to ever-higher planes of lust.

Squirming round onto his back, Sek invited Quintus to lift his legs and bend them back so his butt came up off the bed. Quintus gripped the proffered legs just above the ankles and pressed down so that Sek's knees tucked into his armpits. Rounded haunches framed the Egyptian-Greek's packed ball sac and the ridge of smooth flesh running down led Quintus into the valley between his ass cheeks. Knees spread wide, Quintus leaned his collarbone against the soles of Sek's upturned feet to gain more leverage. And then with an urgent pump of his hips, he slipped his swollen cock easily into Sek. They both gave vent to great breathy sighs. Quintus drove himself harder and faster, his whole body resonating with the pulse and pace of sexual desire.

In the midst of physical abandon Quintus thought he heard Sek speaking, questioning, wanting answers. But the words— if the utterances were even real and not a part of his inflamed imagination—they were surely of an erotic nature?

In the sweaty throes of Sek's ecstatic floundering he reached his right hand around the junction of bent thigh and lower leg to grasp

his own cock, and began a furious fisting rhythm that rapidly got him off. At the sight of copious streams of cum, Quintus arched his neck back so far that his trapezius muscles stood out like the roots of a thrusting tree. A deep groan rose up from the pit of his belly as he started coming in gut-wrenching spasms.

As quickly as his arousal had intensified, the sex-lust declined. He lowered Sek's legs and fell down beside him. "Wha– what did you put in that drink?"

Sek treated Quintus to a mischievous grin. "There were the dried peppermint leaves."

"Must have been something else? I— I felt it." The words wheezed in Quintus's constricted throat.

"Some say hot mint is an aphrodisiac, but I did add my special love potion."

"Ah…"

"Though it seems you needed it not, my Quintus. And now, may I show you some lovely pieces of alabaster? Nothing expensive. Something nice for your spouse, perhaps… or boyfriend?"

"Maybe another day." The look Quintus received spoke volumes about how often reluctant customers employed this cheap get out. "Really. I've no time now, dallying here with you. I– I have things to do. I must hurry."

Sekhemkhet Adonis pouted prettily. "I have just the thing for you, a beautiful bust of Ramesses the Great?"

"No!"

"Where did he come from?" Rufio gave the alabaster object a cursory once-over. It was no taller than his extended hand.

"Oh, just this place I passed." Quintus dismissed it with an airy wave of his hand.

"It's a piece of crap, you know." Rufio picked up the crude stone carving and ran a finger over the long obviously artificial beard jutting down from the figure's chin.

"He's a pharaoh," Quintus said helpfully.

"I gathered that from the scratched detail of odd-looking elongated eyes, the stupid fake beard, and the funny hooded-cobra draped over his head." Rufio traced the tails of the headdress, which fell down over the impression of a pectoral collar. "His smiling lips are cut slightly off center. Makes him look dodgy. Ramesses the Great, I suppose."

Quintus raised an eyebrow. "What makes you think that, clever clogs?"

The bust clunked down heavily on the chest from which Rufio had picked it up. "I've learned a bit since arriving in Egypt. I know he's the best-remembered king, and he's a bestseller with tourists who get all excited at the hundreds of wives it's said the pharaoh screwed in between knocking up temples all over the place and smiting all his enemies. Who conned you into buying the thing?" He grinned evilly at Quintus's uncomfortable shuffle.

"I stuck my head in and then it was… well, difficult to get out without buying something. I didn't like to be rude. He seemed like a nice stallholder…"

The Roman boy never saw the plume-thistle seller crouched under the shade of a spreading sycamore tree across the way from the alabaster shop. Sekhemkhet Adonis saw his squinty eyes follow Quintus and then swivel around to stare across the busy thoroughfare. Sek felt a stab of unease. The plume-thistle-seller wouldn't be pleased.

The fruit of the plume-thistle made a popular mid-morning snack, and the pyramids of cooked fruit piled on woven mats disappeared as fast as the man and his helper—a boy of no more then ten years, all eager brown eyes in a dusky face—could peel the spiny bulbs and drop the revealed fruit into a boiling kettle.

The moment Quintus disappeared in the throng the man left his assistant to watch over the process and ran across the street to burst in on Sek. "What did you learn?" he demanded in a rasping voice.

"Nothing." Sek glared defiantly, but he knew the penalty for failure.

The plume-thistle-seller glared from under shaggy brows. "*Nothing!* You stupid fool. Do you know how much time has gone into luring one of them Roman cretins into a shop and into your hands or those of Nefertari? And that cow charges just for her wasted time."

"There was nothing *to* learn, damn the double dugs of Hapi! How should I know that the idiot Roman hadn't attended the briefing yet? You were the one said it would have happened by now."

"They must have delayed it. Seth will not be pleased… to say the least. You must go to the old palace and exert that charm of yours again. I take it you had fun?"

"Seducing him was child's play—"

"Of course, thanks to our spies in Alexandria you already knew this one's sexual preference—"

"Then why engage *that cow* Nefertari if you knew he fucked with boys?"

"Insurance. You never know with blasted Romans, cunny on one hand, cock on the other. Now stop wasting my time, Get me details of the planned excursions to the necropolis." At the door he turned. "The time of Seth is at hand. The tyrant must perish."

E·I·G·H·T | VIII

Memphis Necropolis, 17th to 20th day of July, AD 108

Sextus Agapetus, the Nomarch of Memphis—a Greek freedman in Roman clothing—had a taskforce of slaves and supervisors gather together a jumble sale's worth of statuary in accordance with the prior instructions of Legate Similis, sent ahead from Alexandria. As he bowed to Junilla the Nomarch had smiled obsequiously but his voice took on an edge when he said, "One always obeys the words of the Legate's many-named praetor Lucius Junius Quintus Vibius Crispus when they are presented in hand-crafted form by the equally over-appelated notarius, Lucius Pomponius Bassus Cascus Scribonianus." Having delivered this barbed remark, Agapetus begged Junilla's pardon to return to the "burden of his great office," and left them to make their selection.

After the much-heralded briefing on what the following days would hold for the tourists—leaving Quintus concerned as to how he was to remember everything for the record, since he couldn't possibly take sheaves of papyrus, pens, and inks with him—he went to see what choices Junilla and Rufio had made from this collection while he'd been enjoying an unexpected tryst with Sexy Sek. (He felt a bit guilty about it, just a bit.) Flaccus and a clinging Cato showed him the way to an adjacent basilica where an army of slaves had set up many pieces where Rufio and Junilla waited. Standing apart from the rejects were sixteen fine copies of Greek marbles. These included a magnificent arms-spread-wide and gloriously naked Zeus ("after the famous Myron bronze," Rufio told Quintus), a discobolus, an Apollo missing an essential male part ("before it got damaged in the mists of time the original was equipped to bugger boys and beget

113

children, but the idiot copyist obviously lacked imagination in re-creating all of him intact"), and a reclining Dionysius, cup raised in tipsy greeting.

Because Trajan had declared an interest in colossal Egyptian statuary, Junilla had also picked out some good examples in red and gray granite, and others in hard sandstone. A Theban scribe sat cross-legged, his tautly stretched kilt making a tray for his writing implements. A twenty-foot- tall pharaoh stood in the classic stance of a Greek *kouroi*, left foot forward, fists firmly to the sides. He wore the tall conical crown of Upper Egypt ("called the *hedjet*," Rufio informed—"now who's lecturing?" Quintus retorted with smirk). Another colossal king, wearing the hooded-cobra headdress, stood with arms crossed over his chest. In one fist he gripped the royal flail ("a fly whisk really," Junilla quipped) and in the other a key-shaped object the nomarch's Egyptian assistant called an *ankh*.

"Ancient Egyptian women were very tiny." Cato pointed at the form of a woman carved from the same piece of stone who stood on the pharaoh's feet. In her ceremonial pose—one arm crossed over her breasts, the other pressed straight down at her side—she reached only to his knees, the back of her head against his stiff kilt's hem.

"I've seen this sort of thing in the Isis temple back home," Flaccus broke in. "It shows the relative status of women to men. His gender gives him the right to command and he is to be obeyed in all things."

" Dream on, my vigilant one." Junilla snorted contemptuously.

"Present company excepted," Flaccus stammered hastily.

Quintus peered up at the tons of stone gathered around them. "How is all this getting back to Rome?"

Rufio, every bit as curious, looked to his mother for the answer.

"Nomarch Agapetus has arranged several big barges to float the sculptures down river to Bolbitinus where a merchant fleet will be waiting to transport everything to Ostia. Mind, that won't happen now until next year's sailing season—Caesar won't want his collection ending up at the bottom of Our Sea."

"That's what happened to the Dictator Sulla," Quintus piped up. "He'd amassed a fortune's worth of booty after defeating King Mithridates of Pontus, you know."

Rufio put on his best long-suffering tone. "I didn't, but I'd hazard a guess we're about to find out."

Quintus plowed on undeterred. "Sulla wanted the finest objects in this huge art collection he had gathered in Rhodes to adorn his palace in Rome, but the vessel carrying the loot never arrived. It was thought it foundered during a great storm."

"His may have been *looted*, Quintus" Junilla said sharply. "What we do here is a different matter altogether."

"Oh, I– I didn't…" Quintus paled.

"That's it?" Rufio mopped his brow in the manner of someone relieved at being spared a torment.

"Yes."

"Well, I must applaud your unusual brevity."

Quintus struck an affronted pose. "Other than to add the caution that the ship's master would have done better to wait for good summer weather."

"Which is what we will do with our *officially sanctioned* collection," Junilla broke in. She landed a light cuff to the back of Rufio's head. "That's for mocking Quintus, pet. You should set your brother a good example, but I fear I shall be paying the Ferryman long before that comes to pass. Anyway," she continued to the others, "it means we have plenty of time to discover more wonderful objects to join those in store at Alexandria."

A dry cough heralded the scratchy voice of the nomarch's secretary. "I hope you won't think of robbing tombs up in the necropolis. I already had a deal of anger to quell from the priests in the Precinct of Ptah, where *he* came from." He waved a shaky hand at the *kouroi*-style pharaoh. "They're very attached to their Ramesses the Great. He has stood there for more than one thousand three hundred years."

"*Robbing!*" Junilla glared at the man. This on top of the slip Quintus made was too much. "I'll box your ears if you don't take that back. The Emperor will pay the priests handsomely for their Ramesses. Besides, I have no idea what we will see up at the necropolis and until that time I can't inform you what I might select to be brought down to the port. Should I decide on an object I trust you will have the details to hand of who is to be paid." She sniffed and tossed her head so her hair flew about in a scarlet storm to lash out at the secretary's face.

Rufio caught him as he fell back. "Don't mind her. You got off lightly. Others who crossed my Ma have lost that which is most important to them." He nodded at Quintus, who clearly chastised caught his cue.

"A terrine, my friend, a terrine."

The secretary had no idea what they were talking about, which only made him more terrified of these rapacious Romans.

"Isn't that the Nomarch's secretary?" Rufio nudged Quintus as they trailed Flaccus, Junilla, and Cato back to the residency where the Familia Tullii had been allocated lavish quarters. "Over there," he added, "talking to that Egyptian."

Quintus followed Rufio's indication and suddenly through the crowd saw the assistant Junilla had so alarmed. He appeared to be in deep conversation with… As the other man waved his arms in emphasis to whatever was being said, Quintus saw it was Sek parting company from the nomarch's secretary, and without thinking said, "In fact he's half-Greek."

"He walks like an Egyptian." Rufio thought for a moment, an interested expression materializing. "How do you know that?"

Quintus colored. "Well… you know. He was the one sold me that alabaster thing you called a piece of crap."

Rufio thought on this, regarding Quintus wonderingly. "You didn't? You did! That's why you look embarrassed."

"I'm not—"

"You are, too. How big is his cock?"

"No, yes, big enough. Now are you satisfied?"

Rufio chortled, clapped his hands, and gave Quintus a slap on the back. "No, but you obviously have been." He turned serious. "I wonder what they had to talk about so earnestly? Do you think your half-Greek puts it about a bit? I thought they were a bit thick, like they were arranging a tryst, don't you think?"

But Quintus didn't want to think about it at all.

Rufio and Quintus were standing at the base of a great piebald pyramid. For two-thirds of its enormous height red sandstone blocks predominated, jumbled a little by the passage of time. From there to the top the surface was smooth and shone a bright white under the sun. They watched the imperial caravan with its bodyguard of Praetorians under the command of Servilius Vata depart toward an oddly shaped pyramid some way to the south—its upper half had a much shallower angle than the lower half, which gave it a bent appearance. Quintus had difficulty correctly assessing distance in the desert but he thought the weird structure stood about a mile and a half away.

On the fourth day of visiting the tomb fields of Memphis the corps of guides hired by Agapetus to look after his guests had brought them to the southernmost part of the great necropolis. After a hot trek up the escarpment of the desert plateau, thankful for being mounted, and an ever hotter trudge on foot around several half-buried sites, wondering at the fresh colors of the ancient wall paintings revealed in flickering torchlight, the party was grateful to rest in the red-and-white pyramid's shade.

The women of the imperial company had declined to join the excursion: Plotina because she was weary of pyramids and the strange block-tombs of pharaonic nobles called *mastaba*s (and even the more recent mausoleums of Greeks and Romans buried in ethnic style); Junilla because she'd been assured by the nomarch's secretary that there were no statues at this site to "plunder." (He'd managed to escape with his manhood intact.) As they partook of snacks and cool drinks, Hadrian insisted on going to see the bent monument close up, "to determine, if we may why the architects chose to alter the shape of its construction half way up."

Rufio had other ideas. "I want to climb up this one," he'd said in an aside to Quintus of the pyramid Hadrian had declared to be of less interest than the badly formed one. Trajan and Hadrian's retinue, their assorted servants—carrying food, water, umbrellas against the sun, and all manner of paraphernalia—the guides, and a detachment of Praetorian Guards remounted after their brief refreshment stop. A hundred hooves—pony, horse, mule, and camel—raised a cloud of brown-colored dust, which settled slowly as the sounds of the imperial party faded into the desert's unnerving solitude.

"It's a pity Septimius couldn't come with us. He seems to know more about these Egyptian monuments than the guides, if you ask me. And I'm not happy that Vata insisted on taking our horses with them," Quintus grumbled. "He's wrong about them having to stick close to the animals' water supply. They won't be gone that long."

Rufio, who truth be told was still happier off a horse than on one, craned his head and raised a hand to shade his eyes from the sky's coppery glare. He peered at the high pyramid's summit. On completing an appraisal of its perfect triangular face he noticed the Egyptian guide assigned to them trying to catch his attention.

"Please young sir, I heard what you say."

Quintus glared at the old man, huffy at a minion taking exception to his earlier comment. But that wasn't what the man was concerned about.

"You cannot climb. It is too dangerous."

"The angle isn't even steep," Quintus argued. "It looks to be an easy climb to me."

The guide waved robed arms in puffs of dust. "No dangerous like that—"

"What do *you* think?" Rufio glanced aside at the handsome young servant allocated to them to carry wine skins, their as yet untouched pack-lunch wrapped in layers of exotic banana leaves, and two fleece blankets for sitting on. He just shrugged and treated his questioner to an adoring, open-mouthed smile of white teeth between full rosebud lips. Quintus thought the response indicated he didn't understand Latin.

"This boy is half-Libyan and knows nothing!" insisted the guide in a suddenly raised voice. "No one must disturb the pharaoh's tomb or incur the vengeance of his *ka*. Disturb the royal dead and be cursed a thousand times. He will send a plague upon your house for a thousand generations."

"I thought you told us in your execrable Latin on the way over here that all the Memphis tombs were looted ages ago?" Quintus protested. "Even before the Persians conquered Egypt, you said, and Alexander the Great had to throw them out."

The guide shook his head sorrowfully. "Anubis, god of the dead, prowls with the judges of good and evil, forty-two of them, to protect the tomb's sanctity and judge your soul. Even now Ammit, Devourer of the Wicked, waits to gobble up the sinful souls of those who disturb the king's peace in his eternal rest."

Rufio grinned broadly and grabbed the bulge in the front of his tunic, making sure the servant lad got an eyeful as he did so. "Well that counts me out. My conscience is as light as a feather."

"Don't mock," Quintus said with a severity that was almost genuine. It never did to make fun of others' religious beliefs, no matter how outlandish. There was always some dread beast lurking, waiting to snap its jaws and swallow the unsuspecting blasphemer wholesale. He squinted up at the rocky bulk. "But there's no way to get inside anyway."

The guide slapped at the many folds of his robe and wafted away the cloud of powdery dust that rose up in a cloud from the fabric. "In fact, sir, there is."

Both boys stared at him in surprise, registering the implication. They stared particularly at the grubby hand he held out, just like one of the beggars who skulked around the edges of the Roman Forum. Rufio snorted in understanding and fished out a few coins from the wallet fastened to his belt beside his sheathed pugio to drop in the outstretched palm. The man waved his other hand at the pyramid as the coins magically vanished into his robe with another explosion of dust. "Here the south side is easiest to climb, but once as high as you can go, move around to the north face and there you will find a small hole made by robbers long, long ago. But sirs, I implore you to not enter. The passage is steep, so steep, and airless, and there is no light."

"And Ammit, whatever it is, awaits." Rufio winked at the servant boy and dodged Quintus's kick at his ankle. "What is this pyramid called?"

"The one over yonder, the bent one your friends find so interesting, that is the first pyramid at this site of the great pharaoh Snoferu. But it was not used since it was not perfect, so then he builded this one."

"Snoferu? Another barbaric name." Quintus sniffed in derision. "He sounds more like a sneeze than a king."

The duotone colors of the structure piqued Rufio's professional curiosity. "Why is the bottom of stepped rough stone and then nearer the top it's a lovely smooth white?"

The guide shook a pointed finger as if what he as about to impart was Rufio's fault. "That, young sir, is because later generations of Egyptian kings removed the limestone facing to adorn their own tombs. But they did less damage than the Ptolemaic Greeks, and then you conquering Romans stole still more to beautify your public buildings until only the very top remains as Snoferu wished it to be." His baleful stare wandered across to include Quintus.

Rufio sniggered happily. "Ah well, he's the patrician, you know, so blame my conquering Roman friend."

"Amazing how you're a Roman when it suits and not when it would be a disadvantage," Quintus said snappily.

Cheerfully ignoring Quintus, Rufio turned to the boy. "What's your name, lad?"

"Hephaestion," came the shy answer, which overturned Quintus's impression that he lacked any Latin. A flash of defiance sparked in his dark eyes. "My mother she is Greek. My father is of Libya—he dead now—and he is half-Greek anyway." He glared at the guide as he spoke.

"Hephaestion, huh?" Rufio gave Quintus a wink as he took the young man's hand. "Name like that, you have lots to live up to… and a long climb ahead. You're not scared of Ammit and the avenging minions of Snifferus are you? Trust me, when you've faced down the Horror of Capri, a little old devourer of souls is nothing." He turned a bright smile on Quintus. "Just as well Ma refused to let Cato come on this jaunt, he'd have insisted on going with us and that would cramp our options a bit. Come on!"

Quintus breathed out a long-suffering sigh and followed the other two, Hephaestion—previously a silent companion—now chattering happily away answering Rufio's probing questions designed to lead to a particular outcome.

As Quintus had pointed out, the slope was not extremely steep but the sandstone blocks forming the pyramid's exposed underlying structure were each about waist-high and after scrambling up and over almost seventy of these the intrepid climbers were, as Rufio put it, "pretty pooped." It came as a relief that climbing the final third of the way to the top was out of the question. Eons of wind-borne sand had polished the blindingly white limestone facing to a smoothness that offered no grip.

"You're the military genius," Rufio said, a steadying hand against the shelf of hot limestone jutting out above his head. "How high are we, do you think?"

As he helped Hephaestion up the last ledge Quintus thought over the problem, calculating what he already knew of the base. "I paced it out to be about seven hundred and twenty feet and given that the angle looks to be less than forty-five degrees, I'd say we're some two hundred feet up."

"That's a lot of foots," Hephaestion grunted under his burdens.

A daunting view greeted the boys from their perch. To the right the featureless desert stretched to an uncertain horizon where distance-darkened yellow-gray sand merged with the brown haze of sky. To the left the river valley broke the gently undulating surface with a green-black slash of Nile vegetation. To the south the bent pyramid broke the monotony and it was just possible to make out the others milling around its skirts. It was too far, too hazy, to make out individuals, though the handful of Praetorian Guards glittering in their armor indicated the position of the Emperor and Hadrian.

"They must be hotter than Vulcan's forge in all that metal and pissing sweat worse than in the steamiest bathhouse laconicum," Rufio commented. "This heat really is something. Just as well all the women stayed down in the cool of the valley. Let's get out of their sight," he added, pointing at the distant band of tourists, "and see what's to see from the other side."

He led the precarious way around the ledge of sandstone just two below where the limestone facing began. On the north face they faced a spectacular sight. To the east a sharp escarpment framed the other side of the Nile's dark-green strip, which curved around to the north where the valley disappeared below the edge of the desert plateau. Commencing about a half mile to the north a crescent of funerary and burial monuments fringed along the plateau's edge. The closest looked like two giant slabs, the smaller sitting on top of the larger. The guide had described it as a mastaba for the nobility of the pharaohs Pepi and Ibi—more bizarre names. Quintus recollected the many smaller versions at the northernmost collection of pyramids. Just to its right another pyramid glowed a bright white under the sun. Farther off several humps marked more time-dissolved pyramids, ("the best preserved, sirs, was for Pepi, second of the name.") Farther to the west the extraordinary bulk and height of Djoser's pyramid dominated the skyline. Its six steps looked as if a giant had placed slabs of cake of decreasing size one atop the other. Beyond, beginning to merge into the haze could be seen another clump of three smaller pyramids and barely visible in the far distance the sharp edges of three pyramids at the northern extent of the great necropolis.

Rufio pointed at them. "Aren't those the ones we saw the other day?"

"The pharaohs Cheops, Chepren, and Mycerinus, you remember. Such barbaric names, even after Hellenization."

"There speaks my patrician poppet." Rufio turned to Hephaestion, who hovered close by. "Spread the blankets in this shade. Let's be comfortable." He gave Quintus another wink. "There's no one can see us up here."

Quintus had to agree. They were quite alone and in an airless day the silence was so complete that apart from the occasional mournful call of a kite only the blood whistling in their ears registered. If the guide's dire warnings had affected Hephaestion he didn't show any nervousness as he spread out the blankets to make a comfortable nest tucked in the shade cast by a block probably moved out of line when ancient tomb robbers discovered the burial shaft. Here several blocks had been dislodged to reveal the shaft and formed a shelter from the sun's unrelenting glare.

"Hides us from the ancient lemur as well," Rufio quipped after warily surveying the dark, square chute that sloped down at a steep angle into unwelcoming blackness.

In spite of being well watered, the wine hit the spot and when the pack lunch was finished they all felt drowsily aroused. Rufio's biceps were pressed sexily skin-to-skin against Quintus's on his right and

Hephaestion's slighter arm on the left, which is the direction he addressed his question even though gazing dreamily at Djoser's pyramid in the distance. "Do you want a fuck?" he asked in his best seductive voice.

Silence greeted this bald utterance, broken by Quintus's strangled choke. "I thought you'd never ask," he said as soon as he'd cleared his throat.

"Wasn't talking to you," Rufio murmured with a warm smile.

"I know."

The sheathed pugio dagger's hilt clattered against stone when Rufio tugged his belt free. He wormed a hand under Hephaestion's lightly clad bottom and pinched. "You like to put this to use, huh?"

"Hey!" The boy rolled away, but not far over and that only served to offer better access. Rufio ran hands over his pert buns and slid the blade of a hand into the vulnerable cleft between. Only the thin loincloth gathered in the crease protected the soft center Rufio found. His fingers digging into it elicited a burst of giggles. Hephaestion rolled back over the invading hand and trapped it, his face bright with laughing. "That's naughty."

Rufio turned back to Quintus. He knew him well enough to understand his lover's solemn expression disguised a grin. "Take off your belt and climb over the other side? We'll do him together." He switched back. "You do want a fuck, don't you? You wicked seducer of Alexander."

Hephaestion just laughed louder.

"So you do know some history?" Quintus muttered. "You irrepressible seducer of Hephaestion." But he did as Rufio asked, loosened the belt around his waist and set it aside, taking care not to poke anyone with the sharp point of his own pugio. He kneeled his way across to lie down on the other side of Hephaestion.

Rufio slapped his upturned ass as he passed overhead. "Everyone knows about Alexander the Great and his companion Hephaestion."

"Don't forget Bagoas."

"Who's ass?"

"Never mind. History with you goes only so deep… about this deep." He held his hands apart by a few inches.

"I think you'll find my friend is underestimating," Rufio retorted. With a boastful smirk he grabbed his crotch and made a clothed pyramid of his arousal, an echo of the gesture he'd made at the base of the monument.

Hephaestion's eyes went wide. "Ooh, you Roman men are all-conquering fuckers." He laughed again but rolled against Quintus with definite amorous intent. Rufio dug into the boy's bared ass again and watched him throw arms around Quintus, one hand forcing up his tunic and then dropping down to feel him up. "Nice…" he cooed.

With a slight shuffle, Rufio reached across Hephaestion and loosened the cincture around Quintus's waist, which freed the lower folds and allowed his cock to spring up into Hephaestion's questing hand.

Quintus joined the soft laughter. "I give in."

Into the boy's ear Rufio murmured quietly. "You want that, hey? Want to taste some big Roman patrician prick? That's quality cock, that is."

"You're sounding like Flaccus," Quintus warned.

"Put it in your mouth. Go on, Heph, taste it."

"Don't bully him, ahh…" Quintus let his head fall back and his torso arched up in pleasure at the ministrations of Hephaestion's evidently practiced mouth.

With their servant busily servicing Quintus, Rufio swiftly stripped away the interfering loincloth to reveal nicely sun-browned skin stretched tautly around a delightful pair of ass cheeks. Like an inverted pink volcano, the tight little hole winked, just waiting for Rufio's cock to press into it. Only that wasn't how matters went.

Quintus groaned loudly in protest. "Ooh, stop, Hephaestion, you'll make me come too soon." He struggled up, pushing the boy back upright and gazing lustily across at Rufio. "I want to fuck him, but not just that. I want you as well."

"Huh? How's that going to work?" But Rufio grinned happily and allowed Quintus to push his face down into Hephaestion's still upturned cleft.

"That's it," Quintus hissed. "Get him well slicked up for me... you're going to get fucked good and proper my lad... and so am I."

Hephaestion simply moaned a happy response as Rufio noisily lapped at his sweet pucker.

After some while Quintus knelt upright and took over in his best paterfamilias manner. "You stay down, lie back," he commanded Rufio. He turned to Hephaestion and dragged him over the top of Rufio and then spun him around to kneel again only this time facing Rufio astraddle his chest. Quintus pushed on Hephaestion's back so the boy's hands fell down beside Rufio's head. For a moment his dark forelock brushed Rufio's nose and forehead, and they stole a secret kiss.

"That's enough squishy stuff," Quintus said. Not so secret then. He shoved Hephaestion farther up against Rufio until the boy's cock slipped between his waiting lips and his fingers tangled in the mass of unruly red hair where its coils flowed out over the blanket.

"*Mmm*," Rufio murmured around the girth of the boy's solid-hard cock. "He's worked up all right, I can taste pre-cum seeping from his cock slit."

Hephaestion responded by leaning over harder to force more length into Rufio as Quintus knelt up behind him, fingering his ass cheeks and hole with one hand while stroking Rufio's exposed cock with the other, which was when he remembered the jar of honey Hephaestion used to sweeten their wine. Still pulling on Rufio's shaft he reached out behind him with his free hand. For a moment he fumbled among the discarded picnic items until encountering the unstoppered jar (no flies this high up). He scooped up a payload of honey, coated his throbbing cock, and greased up Hephaestion's asshole. With his aching cock in the crack but not yet penetrating, he leaned forward over Hephaestion's bent back and whispered in the boy's ear. "Bzzzz…"

And as if Quintus had announced his intentions, when he felt a cold coating of sticky honey enrobe his cock Rufio suddenly understood what Quintus wanted. He felt his lover position himself behind Hephaestion and then push his big cock up against the boy's hole. Hephaestion wriggled in anticipation, which forced his cock against the inside of Rufio's cheeks, this way and that. For his part, Rufio was sucking pre-cum as fast as it oozed out… "*Mmmm*, more sweet than bitter."

"Oh by Min's great foreskin…" Hephaestion was heard to breathe as Quintus grabbed him by the shoulders ready to force his way into the honey-sweetened asshole.

"Here I come… *ughn!*"

Hephaestion gasped, pressed hard against Rufio's face with the power of Quintus's thrust into him. As soon as Quintus had his cock right inside Hephaestion, he shuffled forward another inch, then reached down for Rufio's honey-slicked cock, positioned it against his own crack and slowly impaled himself, pulling Hephaestion slightly back in the process. That gave Rufio a little more room for movement, and he wasted no time in getting as much of Hephaestion's cock as he could, lipping the foreskin, then tonguing it back down the boy's shaft, then swallowing him whole all the way down to his packed balls.

Quintus fucked Hephaestion like a rabbit, though there was nothing cuddly about it. His haunches hollowed with the effort as the sexual heat between the three built up. With each withdrawal from Hephaestion to his cock tip, Quintus's head flew back from the shade so his neat little ears glowed redly and he fell back down on Rufio's shaft, crushing his balls, before rising up for the next stab into Hephaestion. The friction was intense, all the more for it being Quintus who was running the show and determining

how much he slammed down onto Rufio's cock and how much he shoved Hephaestion into the top of Rufio's throat. The savage rictus of his mouth showed how much Quintus enjoyed the dominant role.

"Aww, you're so lovely and tight." That was for Hephaestion. For Rufio, Quintus clenched his ass muscles and squeezed hard on his pulsating shaft.

Hephaestion only hummed *huh-huh-huh*.

Rufio burbled happily, gagging on the boy's cock, which seemed to swell with every three-way thrust. Suddenly, he knew he was entering the exalted state of swelling orgasm taking over all his body muscles and he submitted to the inevitable. "Ugh, fuck, I'm

coming…" he managed between mouthfuls of Hephaestion's cock.

Hephaestion beat Rufio to it by a matter of two heartbeats, a rapid blast of creamy cum filled his mouth on an outstroke and his throat on the next Quintus-forced assault. He strained forward to get his lips down to Hephaestion's tight-clamped balls so he could actually feel the writhing power there that drove the jizz into him. Rufio folded into an implosion, his mind receded from everything seen into a darkness that closed in from the periphery of his vision. All his energy compressed around his throbbing cock, held so tight in Quintus's ass.

Quintus whimpered as Rufio's cock head thumped against his prostate with every one of his back-thrusts. The weight of both boys made it hard to lift his butt off the blanket, but he tried, just in time for that energy contraction to reverse and explode. Rufio drove a gusher of spunk up into Quintus with deep grunts from the top of his convulsing larynx while coordinating the swallows of Hephaestion's cum before sagging back exhausted.

But Quintus wasn't quite finished with Hephaestion. Freed from the plug of his lover's cock, he knelt up higher and rammed the poor boy forward so hard that Hephaestion's stomach pressed down on Rufio's face. Rufio got hands under his shoulders and heaved him more upright and almost dislocated his neck in an effort to bite the nipple Hephaestion's twisted torso presented.

"Oh fuck, fuck, fuck!" Quintus yelled before disintegrating into a series of animal grunts that mingled with Hephaestion's breathy cries. Rufio was certain he heard the squish of Quintus's cum shooting into Hephaestion.

With an audible creak of bones and sinews, Hephaestion gingerly stretched himself out until was lying half-on and half-off prone and wracked Rufio. Some of the spilled seed glued them together. He felt Hephaestion's toes curl against his own. A moment later, Quintus plumped spoonwise against Hephaestion's side and locked gaze with Rufio above the mop of sweaty hair where the boy's head rested on Rufio's still heaving breast. "That was an unexpectedly hot-hot afternoon," Quintus said, trying to ape Rufio's shit-eating grin.

"Ooh, by the gods I needed that," Rufio murmured lazily.

"As I think did sweet Hephaestion. And he gets paid for getting laid."

Hephaestion raised his head, a hopeful glint in his eyes. "I do?"

N·I·N·E | IX

Memphis Southern Necropolis, 20th day of July, AD 108

"By the spurting marbles of Mithras, what in Hades is that?"

At Rufio's outburst Quintus shaded his eyes from the westering sun and squinted at a mysterious dust column rising far out in the western desert. They had made their way back around to the south face of Snoferu's pyramid and from that high vantage not only was the distant disturbance visible so was a similar swirl thrown up by the tourists returning from their examination of the bent pyramid. The one approaching from the desert began to resolve into indefinite shapes amidst the dust disturbed by many hooves. "Mounted men, some on camels. Quite a lot of them."

"Camels?" Rufio exclaimed. "Going that fast?"

"Racing camels are faster than horses for a bit," Hephaestion offered.

Quintus dropped his hand and stared at the approaching imperial party. The two were on a collision course. "I don't like the look of this. A force of men riding hard out of the desert can't be a common thing around here. Bandits… or rebels?"

"I don't think that idiot commanding the Praetorians—what's his name—?"

"Servilius Vata—"

"Has spotted them."

"The escort probably can't see the plume against the sun's glare," Quintus said, coming to the Praetorian prefect's defense with his cadet army training experience.

"I can see a standard bearer," Rufio said excitedly. "He… he carries a jackal's head with a long snout. The riders, they all look weird, like beasts. We have to warn Trajan!" Rufio hurriedly tugged the folds of his tunic free of the belt, held it high, and waved it vigorously from side to side. He and Quintus had only just dressed after the romp on the other side of the pyramid. A moment later Quintus copied his friend while Hephaestion jumped up and down. "There's enough of a hump in the ground over there to hide the ambushers from our people."

"We must get down, fast."

"We aren't armed," Rufio pointed out.

Quintus shouted back over his shoulder as he leaped down the first uneven step. "We've got our knives. They'll have to do. They were good enough for the Monster of Capri!"

"Typical," Rufio snapped at a terrified Hephaestion. "Damn patricians, always rushing to glory without any hint of tactical planning." And then he too was hurtling down the slope to glory. The floor of the desert looked a horrifyingly long way off and each jump from step to step jarred every bone. After a few drops, he noticed Quintus had taken to descending in sideways zigzags, which seemed to ease the effort and make it less likely he would lose his precarious footing. As he neared the bottom Rufio suddenly realized too late that the last block he'd aimed at was much taller than the others. His momentum carried him over its crumbling edge. Instinctively he bent his legs to lessen the impact. As luck would have it the depth of sand over the rocky ground at the foot of the pyramid helped to break his fall. It was still a hard landing. He rolled sideways and ended up on his side, struggling to regain breath knocked out of his lungs by the impact. A second later another heavy thump like a sack of vegetables thrown down announced Hephaestion's arrival.

Quintus marched over all martial and hands on hips. "This isn't the time to lie down!"

"Fuck off."

"Yes, fuck off," Hephaestion echoed weakly.

Rufio jerked his head back irritably at the over-tall sandstone structure behind them. "You, I suppose, just stepped off."

"You suppose correctly. Now, come on."

Back on the desert floor, the gently rising ground obscured the approaching enemy—for Quintus was certain that's what they were—from Trajan's party. "If we dash we can intercept," he cried out.

Rufio sprang to his feet, rubbing a pained hip and grumbling. "And attack them with what? We don't have swords, not even a hand slingshot. Oh, off he goes again." He gave Hephaestion a hand to his feet and then set off at a run after Quintus, who shouted back over his shoulder. The words were lost in the growing thunder of hooves, but the blade Quintus waved in his extended hand made the intention plain. "Oh great, knives against javelins and spathas no doubt."

The two plumes of dust converged like desert djinns, the one to the left partly obscuring the evilly twisted first pyramid of Snoferu, the one ahead now blotting out the low sun. Quintus must have become visible to the imperial column because Rufio saw the casually idling guards emerging from their brume spring alert. At the instant he drew level with Quintus and unsheathed his pugio—no sword but at least a long-bladed dagger—monstrous forms burst from the dust storm raised by galloping hooves. Apparitions of unearthly horror bearing weirdly shaped long-handled weapons rode at a slightly divergent angle to their own mad charge. In the swirling haze of desert dust the riders seemed hardly human, their snouts and long, squared ears adding to the sense of terror.

For a brief moment it seemed the enemy would ride right past as they bore away to intercept the imperial retinue. Camels, strangely elegant at full speed, roared, horses stamped the ground and reared as their riders wheeled them around to deliver killing blows. But just then a harsh cry from a rider at the head of the attackers caused the column to falter. Immediately, the front three camel riders wheeled away from their fellows and turned their mounts' heads toward the smaller clouds of dust Quintus, Rufio, and Hephaestion were throwing up. The rest continued on the line that would bring them broadside onto the hitherto unsuspecting Roman tourists.

But the boys' feint had some effect. That brief hesitation bought Trajan and his men a few precious moments to rally into a ragged defensive line. Seconds later, Romans and Rebels met and battle was joined.

A tremendous clamor abruptly tore apart the silence, which before had lain over the baking desert. Thundering hooves and barbarian bawling rose loud in the heat-stilled air, answered by shouts from the alarmed Praetorian Guard desperately mustering to meet the assault. Rufio's ears thrummed to the din of the camels' raucous trumpeting Their assailants shimmered and lost form to become a whirlwind of barely glimpsed legs in sand shot through with flickering shafts of sunlight, a torrent of revolving dust blaring at volume like faulty bass tubas as they bore down on the intrepid heroes.

"Shit a brick!" Rufio shouted. "What the fuck have we brought down on us?"

Quintus stopped running abruptly and Rufio narrowly avoided slamming into him.

"Seth smites his enemies!" bellowed the leading camel rider. As he emerged from his self-made sand cyclone he presented a ghastly vision masked in the headdress of a snarling beast, its long snout curled around bared teeth sharp enough to rip out a bullock's throat. Spade-shaped ears stuck up like a pair of clappers just above and behind its fiendish yellow eyes. An armored sheath of dark red overlapping scales protected the man-beast's chest and vitals. He gripped in one fist a short rope attached to the camel's halter, in his other he wielded a wicked, long-handled scythe. Rufio had never seen anything so barbaric as this flying monster and his baying steed.

Quintus yelled some command, but it went lost in the din, though at a sharp jab of his hand, Rufio swerved aside and copied Quintus in dropping to one knee, ready to rebut the charge, crazy as that seemed. In a blindingly fast movement, Quintus swayed sideways, came to both feet in a crouch just out of the scythe's killing sweep, and lashed out with his long dagger.

Quintus vanished in a swathe of dust as the Seth figure recovered. He came on like the ramming beak of a mighty war galley, towering above Rufio. The beast raised his alien weapon and swung it back to take aim. But the blow never fell. There came a mighty crashing sound, a tearing of flesh, a snapping of bones, and a shrill animal shriek. The camel stumbled, staggered, fell, and plowed like a crashing Circus Maximus chariot chin down onto the rocky sand beside Rufio, knocking him aside in the process. Broken hairy legs flew in all directions, the one Quintus had hamstrung with his pugio spewing blood amid the explosion of sand and small stones. The camel's beast-rider fell heavily over its stretched neck on the other side with an unearthly howl of anguish. He wriggled desperately to avoid his downed mount rolling over him in its bawling agony.

Quintus shouted again, mouth squared with the strain. Rufio understood. He shot up, took a step toward the downed camel, jumped, and rebounded off its ribcage to land boot first on Seth's neck. The force of his kick dislodged the monstrous jackal-beaked headdress and without waiting Rufio brought his knife down in a

powerful arc. With a primeval scream, he buried the pugio's blade to its hilt in his foeman's neck. The creature's demonic howl of pain was almost lost in the chaos of yelling men, whinnying horses, swirling dust, shrouded hooves, and flying apparitions of the battle raging behind. Breathing heavily, he made his way to where Quintus, still robed in a small dust storm, watched the battle develop. He nudged Quintus's shoulder. "The other two left us alone."

Quintus nodded. Through the haze they could see Servilius Vata and the twenty or so men of the imperial bodyguard engaging the horsemen and camel riders with swords and thrusting spears. "Tactics," he said briskly. "Destroy the larger group first and we will be an easy target. That's why only one of them came against us when they got near enough to see we posed no threat. But they might be wrong about that."

And so saying Quintus spun on his heel, dodged around a surprised Rufio and grabbed up Seth's cast aside weapon. "What an ugly thing, but deadly nevertheless. Come on!" He set off at a run across the compacted sand toward the melee, whooping a fearsome battle cry and swinging the scythe about his head in threatening arcs. At the same moment a figure rising up from behind the still mewling camel startled Rufio. He crouched instantly, pugio at the ready until he recognized a dust-covered Hephaestion.

"I found this. That thing must have dropped it when you deaded him," he exclaimed, waving a dangerous looking mace in his hands. He ran around the spitting camel, which was issuing oddly human groans, to join Rufio. "Let's go!"

The two of them dashed after Quintus and quickly caught him up, his waving of the scythe having slowed him. Rufio laughed at the top of his lungs and joined Quintus in yelling a bloodthirsty war cry, and the three covered the intervening ground in loping strides.

"Poseidon's pretty pink prick! They're running." Rufio yelled. They skidded to a halt in astonishment at the sight of the enemy in full flight. Two horses and a camel flew riderless in the wake of the fleeing enemy, their masters sprawled where they had fallen beneath the disciplined swords and spears of the Praetorians.

As the boys approached the milling retinue a cry of pain announced the questioning of a surviving rebel, but they found Trajan in high spirits. "By the warlike standards of Mars, my Mars rushes to the rescue again!"

Hadrian laughed in uncomfortable agreement and Quintus colored brightly. He avoided the indignant glare Vata threw true as a javelin in his direction. "I'm sure, Caesar, our paltry charge couldn't have frightened them off."

"It didn't," Vata snapped angrily.

"Not exactly," Hadrian said, slapping his bare thigh in some glee. "You see, according to that wretch Vata's men are playing with you killed the man in charge of those brigands."

Rufio pointed at himself. "We did? What, the bastard who chased us down was the leader?" And then Hadrian's words sunk in. "Bandits?" He looked outraged. "You mean it was robbery they had in mind?"

The prisoner let loose another flurry of sobs and a shout of agony."

"We lost one man, and two wounded," Vata said in a growl. "My men aren't inclined to gentleness."

Quintus nodded at this. Two of the Praetorians were showing how much nicer they could be than an aggravated vigilis questioning burglary suspects (Flaccus was on hand to advise). The man struggled half upright in their grip, bloody saliva flecking his purpled and swollen lips. "Bandits!" he gurgled in poor Latin. "No bandits! Seth rises... Rome comes to... Egypt... to die!"

The slap rang out across the sandy wastes. The man's head flew back, throwing blood and spittle to stain the sand, but he remained defiant.

"Seth rises to slaughter the sons of Isis." He pointed a shaky finger at Trajan. "The tyrant shall die—"

A wet, meaty crunch cut him off abruptly as one of the Praetorians stuck his gladius deep into the man's guts.

"We got what we needed." Vata snapped out orders for his men to remount and take up position around the Emperor and the other noncombatants, a phrase Rufio saw irritated Hadrian.

Trajan just smiled serenely. "Take your horses back, boys. A well-earned bath awaits back at the governor's palace. "Assassins, that's what the man claimed. Well they're going to have to try a lot harder than that… especially when my Mars is to hand." He broke out into another hearty guffaw and slapped Quintus hard on his back.

"I'm never going to live that down."

"Here, O God of War, take Hephaestion behind you," Rufio said with a wicked Celt's grin. "He's quite worn out, what with the both of us and then a dusty battle."

As he settled on the back of the saddle and slipped arms around Quintus's waist, Hephaestion said, "If I get laid again, do I get paid again?"

"Riders must hasten to Lykopolis and warn our lord and master that Menes is killed and the attack failed."

Desert Jackal—the name by which his band knew him—glowered at the wiry messenger standing before him. "Menes!" His mood blackened further at the news. "How is it possible? Did we not have advance knowledge of the strength of the bodyguard?"

"These Praetorian soldiers are not as the common legionary. We underestimated their skill and savagery. And we did not know that the guard would be doubled for the visit to the southern necropolis. Our master must be warned so that another attempt can be made.

I have a good man at Oxyrhynchus. I will get word to him to make the necessary arrangements."

"And if not there then at Lykopolis or at Thebes. By one way or by another we must succeed, for the time is right, the season is with us."

The messenger shook his head. "Best before they reach Thebes. The Roman garrison there is strong and well entrenched. Any attempt there would surely be too dangerous?"

Desert Jackal snarled his response. "For the cause—for Seth— nothing is too dangerous." A thin moonlight barely illuminated palms gathered thickly about a small pool, one of a string connecting the outlying oasis to the Faiyum swampland. Bubastos was out of the way but handy for the main Nile valley. A frog croaked, breaking the quiet and was immediately answered by more distant barking. Desert Jackal's ill-humor subsided and his voice resumed its more normal sibilant resonance. He sighed. "Better, though, that we preserve our forces for success than spend them in another failure. And we must abandon this place. Memphis will soon send troops to investigate. Take whatever you need and go to inform Pharaoh Caesarion what has happened here."

"I have a boat anchored—"

"Not the river. It's too risky now the Roman imperials are alerted. There will be a watch on everything at every post. Ride from the south of the Faiyum into the western desert. Use the oases to reach our Lord. I shall send the rest of our force into the desert to wait while I remain here at Bubastos until the enemy moves on south. That way we can maintain contact with our foes in case another opportunity arises." What he didn't tell the messenger was that he had a spy aboard *Cleopatra of the Nile* over whom he wished to maintain some control. The man had provided useful information, one piece in particular—

"I heard there were three warriors, separate from the main Roman body, who attacked our flank." The messenger interrupted

Desert Jackal's thought. Ready to take his leave he touched the knuckles of his clenched right fist to his forehead, the rebels' *salute of the cobra*. "Who were they?"

"Hah! One, nothing more than a guide's slave, but the other two? Boys by all accounts, Romans." He knew at least one was a full-blown aristocrat from both his on-board agent and an account furnished by the sniveling alabaster seller Sekhemkhet, the one who aggrandized his status by adding Adonis to his name, like some *sniveling* half-Greek. Thus he supposed the other, the redheaded spawn of hell, must be a Roman too. "When I saw them in Memphis I thought them of no account. A mistake."

A mistake that cost my brother his life…

The grinding of his teeth could be heard above the frog chorus. "They caused the death of Menes."

Desert Jackal answered the messenger's salute with his own—a fist clenched like the fangs of the serpent that drew a scrape of blood from his furrowed brow. "For that I shall ensure they meet a grisly fate. Their flesh shall be as carrion for desert predators and their bones left to bleach under Amun-Ra's burning rays. The deaths of those two are mine!"

The messenger hurried off on his mission, leaving Desert Jackal to his grim musing.

Yesss, I shall rip out their beating hearts and watch the light fade from their eyes. But first, the aristocrat's friend's little prick of a brother might be a way to neutralize the others… or set a trap for them. Anything to destabilize Trajan and his fawning retinue. Anything to raise my status with my men so that when Egypt is once again free of Roman savagery no man—not even he who thinks he leads us—will stand ahead of me. The spy gave me a name and now I call on our gods to give me the power… Enjoy your last breaths Cato, for your hours are numbered.

T·E·N | X

Oxyrhynchus, 27th day of July

A strong southerly following wind to belly out the great sail and the
added efforts of the rowing crew by day gave *Cleopatra of the Nile*
an average speed of just over seven miles covered for every mid-
summer hour. Four days after leaving Memphis the fleet arrived at
a large anchorage constructed above the usual flood level, but there
was nothing more than a hamlet nearby and a miserable looking
Roman fortress, no larger than would house half a century. Apart
from Junilla, Familia Tullii was gathered on deck and staring at the
forlorn grouping of hovels.

"Why are we stopping here?" Flaccus enquired of Septimius.

"Yes, why are we?" Cato wanted to know.

"There is a tributary of the Nile that runs parallel some miles to the west. It dies out in the Faiyum swamp. The ancients dredged it regularly so it often resembles a canal. Since it is at a higher level than the main river valley and the reach of the annual flood, the ancients built many towns along it. The Ptolemaic pharaohs expanded some like Herakleopolis, which we would have passed yesterday and which is now the important Roman town of Herculis Oppidum. You can't see it here through the vegetation, but about ten miles over there lies Oxyrhynchus."

"And how important is this…" Rufio stumbled over the strange name. "Oxyrhynchus?"

"It could be very important to our mission, Pet."

Everyone turned as Junilla emerged on deck.

"I've been picking the brains of the boat's captain and our purser, Djed. It's the capital of the 19th nome. The Greeks called it 'town of the sharp-snouted fish,' the elephantfish that apparently abound in the waters of the tributary. The old Egyptians apparently worshipped the fish because it ate the penis of Osiris."

"Was that before or after he jerked off over Seth's lettuce?"

"I have no idea, my priapic offspring," Junilla said to Rufio, "but the place was a major Greek center and according to Agapetus there should be some fine statues for us to examine."

"It's a prosperous and civilized city," Trajan said as he emerged from the imperial quarters after Junilla. "Since the time of Augustus many fine public buildings have been raised. There is even a large theater, a circus, a Greek-style gymnasium and several public baths. I am eager to inspect everything and present its magistrates a charter making Oxyrhinchus a *municipium* and giving citizenship to all its people."

Septimius bowed. "I'm also sure Hadrian, Servilius Vata, Marcus Laevinius, and yourself Caesar will be equally interested to inspect the sizeable garrison and the permanent barracks."

"That's as may be," Hadrian spoke up as he too came onto the deck, surrounded by his companions Titus Spurius and Cassius Quietus, eager for a day off the river. "But I'm after a sight of the temples. I understand there are many to syncretic gods here."

"What's that?" Cato whispered to Septimius.

"It's when divine beings from different religions are combined, or syncretized. We Romans are very good at absorbing foreign gods into the state religion. It helps keep the natives in check."

On leaving *Cleopatra of the Nile* the cumbersome procession first had to cross a long, wooden landing stage. Officers of the Khepri Corporation sent ahead had commanded a local workforce to erect this rickety construction, which spanned a lake of rising Nile water, so the disembarking passengers would not get their feet wet. From there it took almost three hours to reach the city, traipsing (or taken by wagon for the lucky) through verdant fields and orchards. With so much greenery amid numerous irrigation canals the heat was unexpectedly humid.

It was when an elderly slave sent to guide Familia Tullii led them to the spacious townhouse set out for them that Junilla took Rufio by the arm. "Where's Cato? Where's the little Samnite snake got to now?"

Rufio raised an eyebrow and shrugged, as did Quintus when Junilla pressed him. "I could swear he was here a moment ago. He was definitely with us when we crossed that tributary river back there."

"Don't worry, Ma. He'll find his way. He's more than capable of looking out for himself."

Junilla glared at her eldest's nonchalance. "How do you know that? It's a strange place, anything could happen to him."

Before they left the boat Cato tuned out the general buzz of interest as the cumbersome imperial retinue prepared to disembark. The endless parade of soggy riverbanks had numbed his lively and, according to his mother, over-inventive mind. As for the many monuments (too *many* crumbling mud-brick piles) they had viewed, been lectured on, clambered over or inside, well... as he'd said to Rufio on their leaving Memphis, "When you've seen one pyramid and masturbator, you've seen them all."

"Mastaba," Quintus corrected.

Cato ignored him. "Besides," he insisted, "the one sitting out on the Ostia road under the Aventine where we Foxes hang out is much better."

Rufio, who privately agreed with his brother, managed a scandalized expression. "You mean the one outside the Raudusculana gate? The tomb of Cestius? That's just a baby pyramid and a copy."

"It's in better condition than any we've so far seen."

"Because it's a fake built about a hundred years ago, whereas the ones here are the real thing," protested Quintus, in a stirring defense of history.

Cato remained unconvinced and bored. He had missed all that excitement on the desert plateau above Memphis and was aggrieved that he'd been left behind with "the flunkies and women." Back in Rome when he first heard about the Egyptian expedition Cato's heart almost burst with excitement, and the envy of his fellow roustabout youths of the Aventine Foxes, many of them much older, was most gratifying. Now, though, he missed the company of his run-wild friends. Trajan had said Oxyrhinchus was important, so Cato reckoned there must be some lads there to muck about with his own age, boys who could speak decent Latin as well.

In this anticipation he was proved correct. A slight bend in the road—well, track—revealed a jumble of one- and two-story buildings ahead across the river. Septimius had explained that the ancient Egyptians had a name for what the Greeks called elephantfish: *medjed*, so they named the town Per-Medjed because so many elephantfish lived in the river. Although it was not a patch on the Nile Cato estimated it was a good sixty *gradii* in width, crossed by a broad wooden bridge. A crowd of excited people lined the railings for much of its length, all cheering the imperial party and camp followers as they made their way toward the forum, or agora as the Greeks preferred. In the midst of this jollity Cato spotted a bunch of mixed-race boys jumping up and down, waving their arms, and making rude gestures at him to gales of laughter. One in particular caught his eye, with a mass of dark unruly curls, a swarthy skin, and wide-set dark eyes with brows above in a straight line. The lad's broad grin reminded Cato of his Little Aventine Foxes gang leader…and it promised mischief.

He glanced around to see Rufio in conversation with Flaccus— poor Flaccus, always hopeful of a grope—and Quintus. His mother was far ahead with Septimius and some of the imperial ladies of the court. Cato slipped out from the press of tourists and went to confront the boy who dared stare so directly at him as if in a challenge. "Roman?" he demanded.

The boy blinked, not expecting the question. "Yes, Roman of course. Do you think all Egypt is full of Egyptians?" The smile broadened in gentle mockery. "Who are you, so high and mighty in the middle of our Emperor's procession?"

Cato puffed up his chest. "I am of the Tullius Emporium of Artistic Excellence, son of Lord Caesar's master of imperial ceremonies and statuary—that's my mother. I am important in the Aventine Foxes, western vexillation." He thought dropping *Little* sounded grander.

A hasty exchange of Latin, Greek, and native Egyptian in translation greeted this pronouncement and the gaggle of urchins looked suitably impressed. However, the cocky boy who had confronted Cato gave him a gap-toothed smile that suggested he didn't much care what all that meant. "But you must have a name. How am I to lead you astray and show you all the enjoyable things there are to do in our great city without a name? I suppose you are called Tullius, but that sounds boring—"

"Boring! So what did your parents name their foul spawn?"

"Hah! I asked first, mewling whelp of a fox."

The boy doubled up over Cato's fist and in a heartbeat they were rolling around in the dust at the edge of the bridge, encouraged by yells of the other boys. After a ferocious wrestle, Cato ended up on top, astraddle his opponent, both of them breathing heavily and grinning like madmen. He couldn't put his finger on it, but Cato thought he'd won rather too easily, like the boy enjoyed being dominated. "I am Matius Calvena."

They disentangled and Cato offered Calvena a hand to his feet. When he reciprocated Cato was sure he saw a glimmer of recognition in his new friend's eyes at hearing his cognomen, but put it down to a natural curiosity. This was borne out by the torrent of questions that followed: was Rome truly as big as people claimed; were there really seven hills; how many races had he seen in the Circus Maximus; was the Roman Forum more magnificent that anywhere in the world; how many animals and criminals slaughtered in the arena; did generals celebrate Ovations often... and so on. As Calvena led him across the rest of the bridge and into a warren of streets clustering the river front Cato answered as best he could, while making much all the battles he'd been involved in. Irritatingly, though these boasts were largely true (with a pinch of salt), Calvena obviously didn't believe him.

"I bet I can show you something you've never seen before," he boasted.

"Such as?" Sounding like that was very unlikely.

Calvena made an O of his left hand and wiggled his right index finger in the ring. "The Brothel at the sign of Sobek."

"Oh, really…?" Cato sneered. "I could show you any number of brothels in Rome."

"Inside? Yes? In the rooms where you can see the whores actually doing it?"

That threw Cato. He certainly hadn't been inside a lupanar, even though his mother's best friend Lucretia owned one in the Subura. Rufio frequented it and he knew Flaccus did. He was unwilling to let Calvena win out on such an important point, and then he brightened. "I can tell you something I bet you've never seen?"

"Such as?" his new friend mocked.

Cato drew in a deep breath, paused in walking, and drew Calvena close. In a conspirator's whisper he said, "I've seen my older brother and his friend Quintus fucking." He drew back with a match-that smirk.

Calvena had the grace to look impressed, and nodded his head sagely. "Were they any good at it?"

The sniff said that in his qualified opinion Cato had seen better.

"Well, I can't pretend to beat that, but I can promise you something almost as exciting. It involves… swallowing." Calvena's straight brows waggled up and down suggestively. "Come with me Cato and let me show you. It's down by a canal running into the river. This way…

* * *

Rufio was horny. Hardly an unusual state of affairs, but he was reflecting on the little opportunity he and Quintus had aboard *Cleo* to provide each other relief, when he heard what he took to be the soft sound of footfalls out in the hall beyond his door. He frowned. As far as he knew the allotted apartment should be deserted since Trajan had pressganged the entire company to support his appearance at some ceremony arranged in their honor by the civic dignitaries. He listened carefully but when no other sound followed, he returned to musing about shipboard life.

It was no wonder there hadn't been sex of any kind for days, what with all the coming and going on the overcrowded boat. Their quarters were never secure from others of Familia Tullii. And whenever he and Quintus had a quiet moment to themselves Cato or Flaccus or even Septimius might pass through the uncomfortably communal quarters they had been allocated. Only Junilla enjoyed the true privacy of a cabin with a door. Even the bathing arrangements were overcrowded, of necessity: space on the upper deck was limited for the makeshift wooden tubs—one for men and one for women—with most time given over to the imperial court and the Empress's ladies and slave girls.

By welcome contrast the accommodation provided to Familia Tullii at Oxyrhinchus comprised several spacious rooms, more than enough for everyone to have their own private space. Rufio—stretched out comfortably on his soft bed, only his loosened loincloth draped with unusual modesty across his midriff—was considering some hand relief when the noise outside came again, This time he spied movement on the other side of his pushed-to but not closed door, a shadow crossing the gap with stealthy intent.

Rufio sat up abruptly. He strained his ears, but whoever lurked on the other side had become still. *It must be my missing cunny of a brother sneaking in from wherever he's been.* "Cato?" he called out. "Cato, is that you? So you found your way, you annoying brat."

E·L·E·V·E·N | XI

Oxyrhynchus, 27th day of July

It was difficult to hear Flaccus above the music. He had been restless since they took their seats. "I hope this is the last cultural presentation of charming ancient Egyptian customs we have to endure on this expedition."

Quintus knew exactly how he felt and his continuous fidgeting communicated a desire to flee. A sideways glance confirmed that Flaccus wore the look of someone about to risk ire by slipping away. They were perched uncomfortably on benches under a striped awning that while it kept the worst of the sun's rays at bay also accentuated the afternoon's stuffiness beneath the canopy. Heat rising from the captive tourists cloaked everyone in a perfumed fug. Quintus wiped aside an irritating trickle of grease, one of several running down his nose and cheeks. They came from the dissolving perfume cone perched on top of his head. Its melted drops ran down brow and neck, making Quintus even more miserable. He thought the strange custom perfectly revolting. Nomarch Mitrius (surprisingly for the sizeable Roman presence in this nome, a real Egyptian) insisted on his imperial guests wearing them. "The heat from our heads melts the cones and so cools the body and makes us smell beautiful at the same time," he'd assured them. "We Egyptians have worn perfume cones since time before imagining."

For Quintus, the ancient practice wasn't working—he still sweated in spite of a less than formal tunic (Trajan's faint scowl of disapproval on seeing him thus attired informed Quintus he was letting the side down). *How by his lucky brass balls did Rufio get out of this?* At least the elite wore cones of beeswax; he hated to think how those topped by the cheaper kind made from animal fat must be coping. He leaned closer to Septimius seated on his other side. "It's really rather gross. I feel I'm going to need a bath just to rid me of the grease."

"And it's all quite unnecessary, if you read a few geographers." Septimius spoke from the side of his mouth, but his eyes never left the snake charmer who had just appeared on the orchestra floor. "Many wall paintings in the ancient tombs depict men and women at banquets with cones on their heads. It's popularly supposed they were a form of perfume. Perhaps, but there are authorities on the old Egyptians who argue that the cones were not supposed to be physical but symbolized happiness, wellbeing, and goodwill at enjoying the feast. And now because of a misinterpretation by fanciful Greeks we must endure these gloppy things and listen to modern Egyptian aristocrats perpetuating the myth."

"I'm concerned about Cato," Flaccus hissed in Quintus's other ear. "I'm going to go find him."

The flimsy excuse to escape further artistic torture hardly stood up. The likelihood of Flaccus locating Cato in this sprawling metropolis was near to nonexistent, but Quintus just tipped his head in mute approval. He wished he could do the same but Trajan had dismissed polite protest that many of the entourage would prefer to rest rather than endure a local event of "great social and cultural significance," that being the presence in the citizens' midst of their God-Emperor who was about to present them with full citizenship of the Imperium.

Flaccus sidled off between the rows of benches, keeping his head down and nodding apologies to those whose feet he trod on and had to sit back to let him through. Quintus thought their frowns more likely indicated a level of envy at his getting away than any irritation at his shoving past them.

Quintus and Septimius, being relatively low in the imperial pecking order, had a side-on view of the orchestra. Under its own florid canopy in the shape of a giant *nemes* headdress topped by the *uraeus*—the rearing cobra Wadjet of Lower Egypt-—and the vulture Nekhbet of Upper Egypt, the imperial thrones were raised on a platform set at right angles to where Quintus was seated. Naturally, the troupe of exotic dancers weaving their terpsichorean magic on the orchestra floor addressed their performance at the Emperor and Empress. Their gyrating surrounded the preparing snake charmer as they executed complex sinuous patterns of movement in what was advertised as an ancient religious rite celebrating the rising of Ra-Horakhty. Quintus was hazy about the relation between the various forms of ancient Egypt's senior deity, representative of the Sun, but he had understood some of the carnal story of Osiris, Isis, and Seth accompanied by the exotic, erotic, and definitely oriental sounding music.

The rippling strings of a *sambuca* evoked the Nile's lapping at its reedy shores and merged with the *tintinna'bulum*'s tinkling bells, the wailing atonal flute, *lituus* horn, and *aulos*. These instruments played with and against a *cithara*, the bass blare of *cornu* and tuba, the unfamiliar rhythms of *sistrum*, *cymbalum*, beaten *tympanum*, and a droning bagpipe; Quintus shuddered at its barbaric sound. The curved cornu and straight bronze tuba were nods at the extensive Roman military presence in Oxyrhinchus. In his cadet training, he was more accustomed to hearing the cornu issuing battle signals than accompanying dancers on an orchestra floor.

The whirlers gradually made individual exits and the musicians quieted, players dropping out one by one until only the cymbalum and tympanum player remained to beat a slow, hypnotic cadence. The charmer—sun shining blindingly off the dome of his shaven head—remained crouched in a cross-legged position as he shuffled in a strange manner across the orchestra floor toward where Trajan dominated the throne at the forward edge of the low dais. In keeping with the event, the Emperor had ordered his bodyguard to adopt informal attire and the men blended into the deep shade behind the imperial thrones. From his position it seemed to Quintus that the snake charmer floated just above the tiles like magic. At the same time he ushered three woven baskets housing his snakes forward with only perfunctory aid from a young grinning assistant. Once arranged a few paces short of the Emperor, he unslung an aulos from around his neck, put the mouthpiece to his lips, and began a plaintive tune. Behind, the cymbalum and tympanum players faded away.

At every juncture the audience leaned forward in fascinated anticipation, Quintus among them, for a moment the dripping perfumed wax forgotten. He had a passing knowledge of Marsi snake charmers, who were often to be seen entertaining bystanders in the forums of Rome. Commoners, equestrians, and patricians alike held the itinerant mountain tribe of central Italy in some regard as snake hunters and charmers, and for those healing drugs they sold that contained snake venom. Marsi snake charming performances were designed to attract potential customers to fork out money for the medicines with their marvellous healing powers. Twice Quintus had stopped while crossing the Forum with his father to watch from a distance, and he knew his sisters swore by the efficacy of the potions, though he'd always shied away from taking any.

One after another the assistant whipped away the basket coverings and from each in turn a hooded king cobra slowly emerged, swaying to the eerie notes of the aulos. The humming of interested voices stilled when the charmer handed the instrument to the assistant to continue playing, while he slowly lifted the biggest of the serpents from its snug home. For several minutes he held it aloft in one hand while making slow passes before its rearing head with the other. In a movement as sinuous as the big snake's he slowly stood, stretched out his arms as if offering the reptile's swaying head to the Emperor. And then with another wave of his free hand, he made a hissing noise and instantly the cobra's hood flared out in a spectacular display. Its forked tongue flickered out evilly from between exposed curved fangs. The spectators gasped with one voice.

A second lad slipped out onto the orchestra helped by a third to carry an obviously heavy clay bowl toward the charmer. They placed it just behind him and, when one retired, the other carefully picked up one of the smaller snakes from its basket and began to use it obscenely, allowing its coils to wind around his thighs so its diamond-shaped head protruded like a tongue-licking phallus between the fork of his crotch. Quintus saw he was a little older than the assistant playing the mesmerizing tune.

As this went on, the charmer leaned down, stretched his cobra out, pressed it to the ground, and rapped the snake on the head. To everyone's astonishment the snake turned instantly into a staff of wood, which the charmer slowly rotated about his head several times until pointing at Trajan. The Emperor politely led a smattering of applause for the trick. The man bowed and handed the stiff branch to his assistant, who appeared to be performing anal penetration on himself with his snake's straining tail. The boy extricated the snake, dropped the cobra back in its basket, and carried off the serpent-turned-staff. The other boy increased the volume of his aulos playing as the charmer delved into the clay bowl to bring forth a fistful of wriggling, entwined black eels.

Quintus squirmed inside. He'd never acquired the popular Roman taste for the slimy creatures, which the trickster held in a writhing bunch above his head—a revolting Medusa come to life. He wished he could be off out searching for Cato, anything but to witness whatever was next planned.

Cato glowered at Matius Calvena sourly. The little charmer was a deceiving cheat, it turned out. It was now painfully obvious that he had befriended Cato only to bring him to this dire pass. He cast his mind back over the events of only a few weeks ago when the minions of deranged Malpensa, the butthole who fancied himself

as the Satyr of Capri, had seized him for ransom. They threatened to treat his poor defenseless body to all kinds of indignities, emasculation being the least of them. Now it seemed he was fated to suffer a similarly terrifying situation.

Calvena only grinned broadly and rubbed his hands together with discomforting glee. Even if he'd wanted to do the same Cato couldn't because of the thug who had pinioned both arms agonizingly behind his back. "Don't take it personally, Tullius Cato, this goes beyond your concerns or mine to a much greater purpose."

Suddenly, Cato didn't think his new—former—friend was as

young as he'd seemed back at the bridge. There was a more adult, more corrupted glint to his eyes. They had been ambling along a narrow alley amiably enough toward the surprise Calvena had promised to show him when they reached its end. The street debouched onto a cobbled frontage of the river at its confluence with a wide, brown canal. The surrounding buildings looked run down, shabby dwellings and deserted warehouses.

"So where's the surprise?" Cato asked.

"Here it is," Calvena answered with an expansive wave of his arms.

Cato spun around and straight into the arms of a huge fellow. There was a brief glimpse of mountainous oiled flesh before massively bulging arms covered in hieroglyphic tattoos enfolded him. Cato saw a face round as the moon surrounding a gaping mouth stuffed with jaggedy, snaggle teeth. And then he was clasped in a fleshy vise, face squashed up against the hairless chest. Body odor and the stale oil lathered on iron pectorals made Cato gag. He struggled as fiercely as a freshly caught eel, but to little effect. With a shudder of revulsion he bit down hard on the unyielding chest muscle of his captor, but the giant only gave vent to a hollow explosion of laughter. The cuff to his head left Cato dizzy.

Then he was bent around, arms behind him to confront Calvena and the other stranger who had materialized from a nearby hovel. This one had the slender and upright posture of the old Egyptians Cato had seen in some wall paintings, accentuated by a long hooked honker of a nose on his narrow canny head. "We know who you are," he said in a flat inflection.

That sounded ominous. When Cato wriggled against the giant's constrictor arms he only pulled them up higher. "Wh… what does that mean?"

"My leader is unhappy with your brother and with your brother's catamite friend. They have overstepped the mark of guests in our country and must pay the price. When they hear that we hold you, they will come. And Jackal of the Desert will take great pleasure in eliminating them."

"Hah, Beaky! You have no idea who you're taking on... *ow!*" Another jerk on his arms and a good-natured guffaw from behind.

"Don't be absurd, child."

"Who you fucking calling a chil— *aargh!*"

"Quiet," came the gruff voice from behind, hard on the slap across Cato's ear.

"Their deserved destruction is but a lever in the sand-box of greater purpose, but the Desert Jackal demands revenge for the death of Menes."

"I don't know what you're talking about. Menes? Purpose? What greater purpose? I've eaten more greater purposes before breakfast than you've hot dinners— *ouch!*"

"Quiet." More of a growl with the second hefty slap.

"That hurt, you great big walking wall painting!"

The embodiment of old Egypt stepped forward with a congratulatory pat to Calvena's shoulder. His beak of a nose closed in. Unblinking eyes like gimlets bored into Cato. "The Sacred Seal of Khnum, he who creates us all from Nile clay, bespeaks us of cycles holy to Ra and his son Shu, who stands on his own son, Geb of the Earth, and holds aloft his daughter, Nut of the starry heaven. This cycle of destruction and rebirth is renewed every one hundred years and thirty-eight.

Cato regarded Beaky-Honker with insolent incomprehension.

"Yes, I see it means nothing to you, Roman scab—"

"I'm a half-Celt from Gaul—"

"Silence! Count backwards one hundred years and thirty-eight to reach the day when your cursed Augustus enslaved the sacred land of the Pharaohs. He was a mortal then, with none of the divine power to usurp our land. Yes, one hundred years and thirty-eight, so this is the year Seth rises, Lord of Chaos and Destruction, to right the wrong." Beaky sighed, as if deeply saddened, his eyes never leaving Cato. "There are few granted the vision to see this momentous time, so far have you Romans debased our noble people. You have blinded many to our greatness, but not all. What celestial irony that it should be the green shoot formed of Roman seed planted in Egypt's soil that has never forgotten how Egypt's kings smote their enemies, even through six generations. Now Great Pharaoh is reborn in the seed of Seth and he will see the end of the Whore of Italy, the end of Rome. As Rome stands at the side of weak Osiris, Isis, and Horus so shall all Romans perish when the forces of Seth bend you to his divine lust and his fertile weapon penetrates you."

"What gibberish," Cato said through teeth gritted in pain. "Anyway, when it comes to bending people over and forcing them to submit to the penetration of his 'fertile weapon,' my brother Rufio could knock your Seth into the smallest piss pot."

Few things unnerved Rufio, but being all on his own in strange accommodations with something lurking outside his bedroom door played uncertainly on the imagination Quintus insisted he lacked.

"Who's there?" He was about to snatch up his pugio from a small bedside table where he'd put it when there came a shy scratch on the door's timbers.

"Dominus… Quintus is that you in there?"

Ashur! Rufio dropped the knife. A faint smile curled the corners of his lips. He lay back again, began to stroke himself, and cleared his throat. The voice came out a touch deeper than his usual light baritone, "Yes. You may enter."

The Syrian slave pushed the door wide and stepped in, saw Rufio on his back, idly massaging the rising mound of cloth and what it barely hid. A hand flew to his mouth. "Oh, I– I thought it was my dominus in this chamber. I…" He trailed off and stood there, round eyes firmly riveted to the tumescent column poking up underneath Rufio's underwear.

Oh-ho, who's a little fibber? He must know that Quintus isn't here...

"Quintus got roped into this civic ceremonial thing, whatever it is, a local food tasting event or something."

"It's a cultural presentation, Tullius Rufio," Ashur blurted out before realizing his mistake.

"Ah yes. So you know." Rufio smiled. "Unfortunately the dreadful headache I developed made it sadly impossible for me to attend the native dances, and snake charmers and that sort of thing." He yawned in a bored manner, and continued slow strokes up and down his cock, aware that the action was pulling the cloth aside to allow Ashur a view of his full balls.

"I suppose I'd better find the correct room and tidy up his things." Ashur didn't move.

"I bet you ten sesterces you can't swallow every last inch of what you're staring at." A red eyebrow canted an upward challenge.

Ashur gulped audibly. "I– I don't know. You are bigger than Quintus, fatter around the base as I recall... from Rome, I mean," he stammered shyly.

"I'm sure he'd like to know you said that."

An expression of horror filled Ashur's face. "Oh no, please don't say anything. He would thrash me to within an inch of my life—"

"That I'd like to see, but you can always make me forget you said it. Oh stop putting it on. Quintus would never take a rod to your delicate backside. Come here and shut the door first."

"A slave does need firm commands." He closed the door with a backward kick of his heel, pressed until its latch clicked into place, then crossed the floor to kneel smartly beside the bed. Rufio lay back with a sigh of gratification, hands tucked behind his head, and watched languidly through lowered lashes as Ashur pulled the loincloth aside. He gripped Rufio's cock firmly around the base and immediately began to lick all around the foreskin, wetting everything nicely before easing the sheath back to reveal the purple plum-shaped cock head. And then it disappeared between slick

lips. Ashur took a deep breath and lowered his head, slowly, firmly, down and down. Rufio murmured his pleasure at the sensation as the ring of Ashur's mouth tightened around the girth of his shaft. Saliva trickled down over ribbed veins pulsing strongly just beneath the taut skin as more blood stiffened Rufio's erection. Then the lips reached right down to caress the base of his pubis, buried in the fiery pubic hair above the shaft, titillating the stretch of ball sac below.

Rufio raised his legs and splayed them wide, thrilling to the tickling of Ashur's silky hair brushing his inner thighs. Rufio extended a hand to grip his head, marveling at its smallness in his hands, Ashur's tight throat and stretched mouth stuffed with urgent cock. Ashur barely gagged when Rufio shot his copious load straight down the slave's willing throat as he bobbed up and down vigorously under Rufio's relentless hands, urging on the orgasm.

"Ooh, that's so good. Gods above and below but Quintus is a lucky fucker to have had you looking after him all these years."

As he finished coming, Rufio idly wondered whether Cato had found his way to their apartments and what the silly bugger was up to.

Cohort III Vigiles Urbanae, who kept watch over Rome's Viminal district, were better at fighting fires than acting as policemen, and certainly none would claim the skills of an informer, those rarities who sniffed out criminal mysteries. Nonetheless, Flaccus and his mate Libo reckoned themselves pretty handy when it came to detection. "Just logic, really," Libo always boasted, and so in the spirit of logic Flaccus made his way back to the wide bridge where they had crossed the canal-river.

He had the vague intention of asking anyone hanging about if they had seen Cato and was gratified to find several youngsters leaning on the balustrade, idly wasting their day. When he questioned them, thankful that two lads had at least some Latin, none could remember seeing Cato.

"This boy you seek is your bum boy?" the eldest of the crew asked with a hopeful smile.

"Not at all!" Flaccus shot back… and then took a longer look at his interlocutor.

The hesitation was all it took. All flashing dark eyes, flushed cheeks, and smiling white teeth, the boy sidled closer and pinched the hem of Flaccus's tunic at the arm possessively. "Why look for him?" the boy pouted prettily.

Flaccus sniffed and considered his options: willing boy; himself an escapee from those stupid cultural antics; bit of time on his hands; hardly a willing floozy in sight, so why not a boy? A fuck would be good, He was about to enquire whether the prospective screw had a place to go, when he heard Libo's disapproving voice in his head.

Cato!

That's when he caught a glint of something in the dirt. Reaching down, Flaccus scooped up a small glittery object. A winged phallus of silver, broken free from a chain in some struggle. Cato's good-fortune travel charm given him by Felix, son of the Aventine Crossroads boss. He showed it to the young grifter and saw the look of recognition in his eyes.

Medusa became bald again. He dumped all the eels but one huge specimen back into the bowl of water. This one wound its arm-thick body around his neck, thrashing violently so that the snake charmer staggered a pace closer to the imperial dais under its weight. His assistant increased the hypnotic pace of his aulos wailing. And then the man ducked his head out from under the coils and with hands parted, pulled the beast out straight as he'd done earlier with the cobra. And in the same manner, he pressed the eel to the ground and then slapped the side of its head sharply.

The spellbound audience sighed in unison. Quintus found he was perched on the edge of the bench.

Very slowly the charmer raised up the stiffened eel. Even though he held it in one straining fist close to its tail, the creature's body remained straight as a staff. With his free hand, the charmer softly stroked the eel from mid-body to its swollen head—stroke, stroke, stroke...

The music welled up louder, grew more frenetic. The stroking speeded up. The eel's great jaws slowly yawned wide as the charmer began swaying forward, back, forward. The movement reminded Quintus of a legionary preparing the hurl his heavy javelin, the same preparatory swaying, adjusting feet and hips ready for the command to throw. He saw the unhappy looks exchanged between some of the guards standing to the rear of the imperial enclosure. The man kept up the stroking, now much faster than before. The aulos squealed like a goat having its throat slit for the sacrifice.

* * *

Flaccus burst from the alley like a sacrificial bullock escaped from the hands of its priests. "What in the name of Hades is this!" he bellowed.

The giant imprisoning Cato, whirled around in surprise. Cato didn't wait. He leaped up to ease the pressure on his arms, and then dropped down through his captor's greasy arms. The man stumbled as Flaccus tore into him and Cato slipped free.

Calvena screamed out a warning and Beaky made to grab Cato, who ducked easily under his arms. But lacking balance from the movement, he was unable to avoid Calvena's outstretched leg. Even as Flaccus delivered a mighty blow to the tattooed giant's cauliflower head and yelled a warning, Cato teetered on the cobbled edge of the riverbank.

Arms flailing, he gave a cry and fell backward the few feet into the river with a great splash.

At that moment two Roman soldiers ran along the bank, alerted by the commotion and the familiar call of a vigilis requesting backup. The giant, still woozy from the blow to his head, stumbled off up an alley, hastily followed by Calvena and the Egyptian.

Flaccus caught his breath and ran to the edge. Cato's fall had carried him several feet out into the murky river, which merged into a tangle of reeds and mangrove-type foliage on the other side. And from there came a disturbance on the river's surface, a V-shape of ripples, heading straight for where Cato spluttered and doggy-paddled to keep his head above water.

Flaccus pointed in horror and shouted out: "Crocodile!"

As Quintus later wrote, the sound of the aulos squealing like a goat at the slaughter set my teeth on edge. The atmosphere crackled as if a thunderstorm was imminent and raised the hair at the nape of my neck. My whole body was pricked with tension. Suddenly, the same sense of dread that robbed me of rational thought and filled me with terrible fear in that Capri sea cave overcame my senses.

But this was a different feeling to that generated by the Witch of Cumae's appearance.

The snake charmer's stroking of the rigid eel became a blur.

Adrenaline coursed through me, shocked my system. I knew not why, but I was ready, ready for something momentous…

For the first time we all heard the snake charmer's voice. He declaimed some incomprehensible words like an incantation in a loud, hoarse voice. Something in its tenor churned my innards. I quailed at the words' evil impact.

And then they grew clearer, rendered in Latin. "Rome comes to Egypt. The cycle is complete. Seth rises to smite his enemies!"

To a universal howl of astonished terror from everyone around me—and my own voice raised loud among them—a pale blue glow encompassed the eel's head, And then a great blast of energy flew from its gaping maw, crackling, flailing, with licks of blue flame spitting off the main thrust like Jupiter's lightning bolts. Its swelling head was aimed straight at Trajan.

At time of extreme stress the human body can make impossible things happen. The building dread must in some inexplicable way have prepared me for action. Even as I now write I cannot imagine how I achieved what I did. The only explanation is that Jupiter's all-seeing eye guided me and Vulcan's strength propelled me. All I can recall is the feeling of my hand on the man's shoulder who sat in the row in front of me as I hurdled his body; of my feet meeting the hard pavement; of covering the *gradii* separating me from the assassin snake charmer. I know I slammed into him.

By the time Septimius recovered from his surprise, he was hemmed in by panicking people blocking his path to aid Quintus. He was, for seconds, forced into the role of spectator. The body blow Quintus delivered knocked the assassin off balance and deflected the eel's blindingly bright blast from its intended target. Instead, crackling like spiteful fat frying, a burst of raw energy struck one of the thick

poles supporting a corner of the imperial canopy and instantly exploded into an inferno. Screams filled the temporary arena as local dignitaries and foreign guests alike scattered in a frenzy of terror from the rapidly spreading blaze.

Clenching his fists in impotent fury, Septimius saw Quintus pick himself up from the agora's hard tiles apparently dazed from his effort, surrounded by squirming eels and overturned snakes. The fire-breathing eel, hurled from the charmer's senseless grip, flew in an arc of spitting blue fire to land among a group of fleeing dignitaries, where it detonated. Shrieks of agony filled the air and added to the chaos of the conflagration. As Quintus recovered he found the charmer's assistant towering over him. The boy struck down with the sharp mouthpiece of his aulos, but he was no match for a Roman military cadet. Quintus dodged and grabbed his arm, tore the musical weapon from his grasp, and threw him bodily to the floor. He would have followed up but at that moment the enraged snake charmer attacked, hands stretched forward, fingers like claws, mouth in a gaping grimace of spitting fury. "Seth rises to smite his enemies," he kept shouting.

Quintus lashed out with the aulos. As an instrument it might have been fine, but its qualities as a weapon were sadly lacking. He flung it aside in disgust and almost tripped over a hissing cobra. Terror lent strength to his unbidden vision of Junilla tearing asunder the asp intended to strike down Trajan. He snatched up the serpent just below its swelling head. The hood flared out, jaws almost splitting as it struggled to turn itself on the arm grasping it. Pure instinct took over. He spun around, sensing movement behind him, and thrust the cobra's head at the bawling snake charmer's face.

Maddened by the unaccustomed noise of the crackling fire now consuming all the imperial enclosure, mercifully emptied of spectators, the big snake closed its terrible jaws around its master's bald head. Quintus heard the dreadful tearing of flesh and bone as the powerful fangs drove venom deep though his skull into the man's brain. The charmer's body went as rigid as the snake and eel he had turned into staffs. His arms flew out, hands shuddering, fingers curling. And then he collapsed. Quintus loosed his grip on the cobra, which fell with the man, jaws almost entirely enclosing the assassin's head.

"Let's get out of here."

It took seconds for Septimius to get through to him, but then Quintus let the frumentarius lead him away from the carnage.

* * *

The water was too muddy to see far through it, but Cato saw the terrible scaly head of the big crocodile rushing through the murk toward him. He could vaguely hear the cries of Flaccus intermittently as his ears cleared the surface and then went under. The leviathan came up speedily, rolling sideways, jaws agape, ready to take him. Cato fought the water with arms and legs and felt the side of its rasping head brush him. The violent disturbance of the water caused by the beast's thrashing almost thrust Cato away, but he managed to grasp the sharp armor plating with one hand and hung on grimly. As the crocodile bucked back against him, Cato brought his other arm up and, finding its nearest eye, wasted no time in shoving his thumb into the glutinous orb.

In an instant the creature turned, almost swiping Cato with its lethal tail, and made off. He turned topsy-turvy in the powerful backlash of tail and rear legs as it powered away into the murk. Terrified the monster would quickly return, Cato flailed about and found an arm. He seized Flaccus and swam desperately with him toward the bank. There, several men had gathered and kept up a furious racket, splashing hands on the water surface to scare the crocodile away.

When they came in, a satiated Rufio lay languidly on his bed nibbling at some dates Ashur had left him when he went finally to tidy up Quintus's room. "Hail and well met," he greeted Quintus and Flaccus. "I see you found the prodigal Cato. I don't know what Eutychus will have to say when he sees you all dripping wet like that. Or Ma, for that matter… why, Flaccus you are dripping as well. No, don't tell me. I've no wish to know what sexual antics you've been up to. And how was the great cultural show, Quintus? I am really sorry my headache prevented me from attending."

It would be a while before Rufio discovered what it was he said that resulted in his scragging.

T·W·E·L·V·E | XII

On the Nile to Abydos, 31st day of July to 9th day of August

Writing up his account of their journeying, Quintus gave thanks to Hermes, patron of scribes and poets, for the plentiful supply of cheap papyrus and inks. (He preferred the Greek deity because he associated his Roman counterpart Mercury more with messengers, a rather lowly role.) Egypt, after all, was the source of almost all the Imperium's paper. He thanked the fleet-footed god also because the idea of scribbling on an endless chain of wax tablets was unappealing as well as being completely impractical. Calculation indicated that what he had so far recorded added up to a weight in tablets that would exceed what twenty slaves could carry. By contrast the Egyptian paper was lightweight and durable—and you could doodle, which wasn't as easy with a stylus on wax. On the other hand, an inadvertent doodle could be scrubbed out in wax. Quintus regarded with some alarm the lewd margin drawing he'd been unconsciously doing of Rufio in flagrante. A blot covered it up.

The recounting of events at Oxyrhynchus had taken some time to record. He was uncomfortable at giving his own part much coverage. In fact he was still unsure quite what happened that fateful afternoon apart from the growing feeling of dread he experienced and the few bruises he collected, some of which needed simple medical attention. Mercifully, Trajan restricted his praise to a passing pat on the shoulder and a murmured wish for an assignation at the first opportunity. When it came to Cato, however, Quintus was fulsome in his written praise of Cato's quick thinking and bravery, and he waxed lyrical about the enormous size of the scaly predator the boy had vanquished with no more than a thumb.

The six days aboard *Cleopatra of the Nile* that took the fleet to the large city known to the ancients as Abedju and to the Greeks as Abydos provided Quintus with plenty of time to catch up on his observations, mostly held in memory or in the form of cryptic notes on a binding codex of wax tablets, which were in need of scraping clean to take fresh notes.

While Quintus exercised his "colorful muse," Cato passed the time bent over work as well. He did not enjoy doing this as much as Quintus. Indeed, after putting to flight the Emperor's enemies (yes, Flaccus did have a little hand in the matter) and his heroic dispatch of the giant man-eating reptile it wounded him to the core of his being to be trapped in a small room with Eutychus and an abacus. "You learn your numbers, my little lotus flower," Junilla had commanded. "And then put him to his words," she ordered the tutor.

"Yes, domina," Eutychus said crisply.

"Yes, domina," Cato mimicked in a prissy voice the instant Junilla left them alone. It wasn't fair that Ashur got to do all sorts of interesting stuff and his brother slopped around the boat without a care in the world while he slaved away at his numbers and letters. Cato accepted that the manner of Trajan's saving by Quintus was pretty sharp, but really... what was an eel compared to a killer croc?

Thoughts of eels exercised Septimius as well. As a fine cook who handled all kinds of sea creature he was aware of the extraordinary ability of some kinds of eel to cause great shock (some fishermen argued that kind of eel was really a fish). But eel or fish Septimius never heard of one manifesting the power as a visible and deadly force across such a distance and out of the water it seemed was required for the lightning shock effect to work. The snake charmer— the former snake charmer—had been a man of evident skill at the dark arts. He had also been in the pay or under the sway of the rebel forces opposed to their Roman masters.

He cursed under his breath. The traitor on board had so far evaded his cautious questioning of crew and staff, many with shaven heads. Was the spy the go-between who arranged the snake charmer or was that yet another agent's handiwork? From what Cato said of his near capture someone on *Cleo* had passed on information that let the thugs in Oxyrhynchus know the boy's relation to Rufio. The sigh was one of frustration. His hands were tied, and there was no sensible help coming from the military geniuses on board. It was a waiting game in which Trajan seemed blissfully unaware of what danger was afoot. He had put the Oxyrhynchus affair down to an unfortunate accident!

It is a strange quirk of this land that far more occurs on the western bank than the eastern, *Quintus wrote*. To the west the land is fertile and green; to the east more barren and the desert reaches to the shore of the Nile. So it was with some surprise that we drew into the eastern bank for a change. Here we witnessed the Cave of Artemis, an ancient temple hewn from naked rock. The great Queen Pharaoh Hatshepsut dedicated it to a local lion-goddess called Pakhet, but the Greeks later identified this creature with Bast, the cat-goddess. One of the Khepri Corporation's experts conversant with the weird pictographic language of the ancients managed a translation of the symbols carved above the temple's entrance. He said it was a tirade the Queen aimed at the Hyksos who invaded and brought the country to its knees before her time. Legend has it that these wild people introduced the horse to the Egyptians who had never known such creatures before. Rufio wanted to know, "Were the Egyptians' camels no match for horses?" to be told that camels were unknown in those far-off times. "Camels are desert creatures," the expert explained, "and our forbears hated the desert, never left the valley, and so never needed camels. Old writings tell us that camels came to Egypt only during the Persian and Ptolemaic periods." And now they are everywhere, horrid beasts.

On the western shore we briefly visited Hermopolis Magna, which boasts several basilicas, a small theater, and baths to serve the Greek and Roman population. The inhabitants lined the streets and there was much cheering, but the Praetorian Guards had no intention of a repeat "accident" such as happened at Oxyrhynchus. Very little of old Egypt is visible here since generations of Greeks and Romans have covered over whatever existed before, but many mastaba tombs are located farther out beyond the cultivated valley. (The inundation is becoming very noticeable now and small boats are needed to get us ashore, since the floodwater isn't deep enough to take *Cleo*'s draft.)

I must note Lykopolis. This large town is the cult center of jackal-headed god Anubis. Not a pleasant being. His domain is the mortuary temple where priest-embalmers process the deceased, a peculiar and messy sounding business. Anubis has an alternate form called Wepwawt, a dreadful barbarian sound meaning "Opener of the Ways." Under his watchful eyes the priests cut open the corpse to draw out all the viscera, which they then pack into four small containers with natron taken from the oasis of Siwa to preserve the offal for the time when the dead man will need the organs again on the "other side." I shudder as I write of these appalling and no doubt very odorous rites.

Hunting hippopotamus is said to have been a great sport at Lykopolis, which may explain why there are so many gewgaws in blue faience of the creatures and so few of the real thing in the river's waters. We made no stop at this place but only endured a long lecture from the boat's experts and professional guides.

"They did not put in!"

Desert Jackal cursed loudly enough to cause the runner to fall to his knees. Messengers bearing bad news didn't always survive its delivery. "Leave us," he said finally and watched the tent flap fall back in place as the relieved runner fled.

"It is a setback, not a disaster."

The Jackal dipped his head slightly at the young man seated

calmly on a folding stool such as Roman magistrates used to dispense judgments. "As you say, Lord Caesarion."

"The intelligence that the boat would stop here at Lykopolis for at least a night was faulty. Check back down the chain to ascertain who passed it on and have them punished. Fortunately, while you were on your way here I received confirmation from your man on board that Trajan will stay several days at Abydos. If we leave immediately and take the desert tracks we will be there before the Emperor. Ours is a straight line while *Cleopatra of the Nile* must navigate the river's many twists and turns between here and Abydos. There will be plenty of time to prepare." His smile, thin-lipped and grim did not reach his brooding eyes. "I have in mind some more twists and turns to entertain Trajan, a tumbling that none can help him avoid.

"Must we move again, father?"

Both men turned to look at the child of about seven years who had pushed through drapes closing off the rear of the tent. His sturdy, upright stance spoke of great pride.

"You should be sleeping, my little Caesar," his father admonished, but with an indulgent smile.

"The shouting woke me up." The boy gave Desert Jackal a reproving look.

"My apologies, Prince."

"We go to Abydos, my son, and then if needs must return to the Great Valley. But I promise you by all the gods of this land and those of the usurper that soon you shall be enthroned in your rightful place at my side in Alexandria, the seventh of your name and, one day when my task is done, you will be Pharaoh in truth. Our tribesmen stand to arms ready to do my bidding the instant the tyrant and his minions are no more. Seth will not be denied. Neither will the true Caesar of Egypt." He stood.

As Desert Jackal bowed his head he swore the light of the single candle cast a shadow across the tent wall of a great beaked snout, jaws parted to reveal a jagged row of cruel teeth.

* * *

The imperial progress reached Abydos, capital of the 8th nome of Upper Egypt—six miles from the drowning western bank of the Nile—by way of a wide canal and a long line of decorated barks. The Khepri Corporation's expert guides were all agog with information they were eager to impart about the fabulous monuments built by two of old Egypt's greatest kings, Seti, first of his name, and his son Ramesses the Great, second of his name, in the "world's oldest city of all," cult center of "Osiris for all time."

"In that case we should be safe from old Seth," Rufio said with a bounce to his step, happy on terra firma again.

"Hmm." Quintus was less sure. He took his cue from the dour expression that Septimius seemed to wear all the time now whenever he thought he wasn't being observed. He knew the spy knew—or suspected—things they did not.

"Oh that's just because he's sulking over not being able to create any fabulous dishes when we're surrounded by hundreds of cooks."

"Hmm."

The first days were spent traipsing out to the desert's fringe to ogle the many buildings of Ramesses and the great temple of Seti where voices echoed among the fat, bulging stone columns. The tourists marveled at far, far older tombs of the earliest Egyptian rulers including the first, called King Scorpion. Quintus found the numerous burial places for mummified animals—dogs, cats, apes, and crocodiles—very bizarre. The temples closest to the city were equipped with Nileometers because in a few weeks at the height of the inundation the water would lap at their foundations. On the other hand, constructed on older foundations the modern city stood above the flood level and raised causeways linked it to higher land in several directions.

Within the party the mood was upbeat. The final night at Abydos promised a fine oriental banquet laid on by Nomarch Eusebius Antipater, with various entertainments ranging from theatrical performances to a troupe of acrobats he boasted were the finest anywhere in the world. "Sounds like he took their advertising blather too much to heart," reckoned a cynical Rufio.

Orders laid down by Servilius Vata forbade the entertainers anything that might be used as weapons, including creatures large, small, or wriggly, and sent Marcus Laevinius to vet the participants. The tribune honked nasal orders at a detachment of III Cyrenaica and set about searching the players and athletes with commendable thoroughness and many loudly voiced complaints. "We perform our magic naked," the head of the acrobats said indignantly. "How we conceal anything, heh?"

Antipater's venue for the feast was extraordinary, no less than the first court of Seti's great temple situated between the first and second pylons. Carved reliefs depicting Ramesses celebrating his victory over the Hittites at Qadesh covered the great angled slabs of the first pylon. Quintus explained at some length to Rufio that this famous battle of antiquity marked the greatest northern extent of the Egyptian empire.

"When did it take place?"

"A long time ago."

"About when you started to tell me about it?"

For once the cuff landed home. "I should grab you by your hair, lift your chin, and smite you like the Pharaoh smote his enemies." Quintus pointed at the massive carving of the oversized king hauling a handful of much smaller Hittites by their long hair, his killing club raised on high ready to strike them down.

A raised platform about the height of a man ran the width of the huge court and on this, set well back from the edge, sat the second pylon, in effect a covered hall supported on two rows of twelve colossal square columns. In front of this portico were arranged many tables and couches. Those in the center, just above the narrow ramp rising from the floor of the court, were for Nomarch Antipater and his imperial guests. Trajan had insisted that Junilla, Rufio, and Quintus join them. The most august Roman and Greek citizens of Abydos filled the tables to either side along with the senior military personnel, Flaccus, Septimius, Eutychus, and Cato (pissed at being sidelined "yet again"). Many more tables lined the sides of the lower court, leaving the central space with its two wells clear for the entertainers.

A thousand braziers illuminated the area and their flames threw the intricately carved sidewalls into writhing life. The underside of the second pylon's portico roof glowed in reds, greens, blues, and yellows through the ingenious use of powdered minerals thrown by slaves continuously into strategically placed fire-pits.

More slaves—a veritable army of slaves—served an endless array of delicacies. There were loaves stuffed with beans, round flat breads with raised edges filled with baked egg and vegetables, fish in abundance cooked in many different ways, Nile wildfowl—goose, duck, quail, baked crane, and domestic poultry. Meat courses boiled and baked and broiled followed of beef, antelope, ibex, gazelle, and deer. These dishes were seasoned with many spices: aniseed, cinnamon, coriander, cumin, dill, fennel, fenugreek, marjoram, mustard, thyme, and parsley.

"Still no nice juicy, crackly pork," Rufio grumbled. He was disappointed at the lack of pork, a perennial complaint since setting out from Alexandria.

"I don't know why you go on about it," Quintus retorted, not for the first time. "You know Egyptians say the pig is the beast of Seth, so its flesh is unclean and cannot be eaten."

"The idiots don't know what they're missing. Besides, a scraping of pig fat is the ideal thing for lubricating a tight—"

Whatever Rufio considered pork fat ideal for was lost under the clatter of servants delivering mountains of legumes and vegetables. All kinds of beans were served as accompaniments, as well as chickpeas, lentils, peas, onions, garlic, celery, leeks, lettuce, big bright radishes, and cucumbers. As he picked one up, Rufio couldn't resist waving it gaily at Septimius, several tables away. For the visiting Romans two common ingredients were missing—the Egyptians disliked olives, which didn't grow well in the climate anyway, and while they enjoyed dried fish, the fermented fish guts Romans loved as garum or liquamen held no appeal to the Egyptian palate. It seemed that the local Greeks and Romans had accustomed themselves to not missing olives or fish sauce.

As slaves toiled under the weight of massive bowls piled high with grapes, fresh and dried dates, pomegranates, dôm palm fruit, watermelons, and figs smothered in honey, the evening's entertainment began. The guests chewed fruit, slaves wiped their running chins and refilled empty wine or beer cups, musicians having provided background diversion now speeded up and increased the volume of their playing, dancers pirouetted and mimes told the story of the Ramessid conquest of Israel and the great victory at Qadesh—though brandishing imaginary weapons the play lost some of its excitement.

Quintus ran a hand over his short hair. "Thank the gods Nomarch Antipater hasn't provided us with those dreadful perfume cones to chill our heads like the idiot at Oxyrhynchus did."

"Mmmm, I'm happy I missed out on that delightful sounding custom," Rufio mumbled around a mouthful of watermelon. He spat out a stream of seeds. "Anyway, what would be the point?" He waved a hand vaguely at the sky above, now awash with stars. It was true that the night air of the desert was starting to cool. He patted his lean stomach and blew it up to show how full he was. He followed the nod Quintus aimed at the dark portal of the first pylon and saw the famed acrobatic troupe running in, bouncing, jumping, and somersaulting until some score of them were tumbling about each other in marvellously intricate combinations.

On three sides, faces shiny with the sweat of overindulgence in food and drink leered at the lithe girls clad only in a brief covering of their pudenda, bared breasts bouncing, or the completely naked boys and young men, their genitals every bit as briskly animated.

As the music swelled and increased in beat, the gymnasts formed in combinations of ever more complex and dangerous looking figures. Eventually, seven tumblers took up positions near the foot of the ramp leading up to the elevated section of the court before the second pylon. The rest of the troupe continued their elastic contortions around them.

Applause rang out when the bulkiest of the group bent over backward, slowly bending his torso until his hands touched ground behind his head. With hands and feet firmly anchored, he arched his body into a bridge. Two of the team nipped up lightly to stand on his bulging abdominal muscles. They bowed toward the imperial party and waved at the crowds lining the sides of the court before linking hands. Thus secured, they swayed outward while bending until their touching knees made a second platform. Now a fourth acrobat climbed nimbly up to balance on their knees. He too made much of his precarious position, pretending to almost fall from his perch and generally fooling about as the audience alternated between jovial catcalls and loud cheers at his every recovery.

Finally, the smallest of the troupe, no more than an adolescent, made theatrical gestures to indicate the sixth and seventh of his fellows. They bowed to the Emperor, then faced each other, arms stretched out, and locked hands together. At this juncture the boy ran across the court and jumped up onto their locked hands. The two men bent low under the weight until the backs of their hands almost touched the floor with the boy maintaining his balance. As this maneuver took place the tympanum players began a drum roll, which gradually faded away. The great court fell silent with the tension. The three acrobats remained frozen. And then the two supporting the boy suddenly straightened up, their arms snapping taut like the torsion sinews of a ballista, and shot their burden impossibly high. The boy made an aerial somersault to land squarely on the shoulders of the highest man in the pyramid.

Applause broke out all around. The drummers hammered out a triumphant rhythm, which fell in a repeated diminuendo to a second expectant hush. To general astonishment, the boy gathered himself and jumped up off the fourth man's shoulders to flip over into a single handstand on the lower acrobat's upraised hand. There, with his free arm held out horizontal to the floor for balance, the youngster slowly spread his legs outward until his genitals resembled a bunch of fat grapes clustered in the center of his cantilevered limbs.

As if this feat were not enough to earn the rapturous applause that greeted his effort, the man at the human pyramid's base began to make crab-like movements—left hand-right foot, right hand-left foot—while the human edifice above him swayed like a tree in the breeze. The effect was comic, and laughter rippled around the court. Trajan almost rolled off his couch he was laughing so much. He swung his legs to the floor to free his hands for clapping.

Quintus wasn't joining in the merriment. "What's wrong, misery face?" Rufio wanted to know.

He received a haughty sniff in response. "I don't appreciate bawdy gymnastics."

That just made Rufio laugh all the harder. "Do you think another one will leap even higher and land on his balls?"

The remaining males of the troupe formed a square between the court's two sacred wells, gyrating and stamping their feet in time to the insistent drumming rhythm. The girl acrobats performed handstands, their legs flipped so far forward over their heads they could see the back of their heels. In this position they hand-walked in circles around the human pyramid. The athlete acting as the bridge for this edifice kept up his crablike motion and when he approached the ramp leading to the second pylon the rest of the troupe broke formation to fan out either side of the swaying pyramid. A chant grew in volume, urging him on. It seemed an impossible stunt to navigate the incline on hands and feet with all that weight resting on his stomach, but that is what he started to do. Halfway up the ramp, the topmost acrobat lowered the arm he'd stretched out parallel to the ground to join its fellow, gripped by both hands of the man below. He closed his legs so that he and his support formed a tall spire.

Rufio had to shout at Quintus to be heard above the noise of the rapturous audience. "Look, the top one's got a stiffy harder than a centurion's vine rod... and his cock's almost as long too."

"Trust you to notice a thing like that."

The man at the base shuffled around in a semicircle and the others compensated for the wildly shifting angle on the ramp until the fully erect lad on top of the figure faced the imperial couch. In a move of unbelievable swiftness, he let himself down from the upside down hand-to-hand hold and maneuvered until he was stood upright on the lower man's upraised hands. He acknowledged the roar of approval with a casual wave, but when he started cheekily to stroke himself Hadrian's loud shouts of encouragement were clearly heard over even that clamor. Plotina's face turned into an expressionless mask. In contrast Junilla grinned and mouthed something at Rufio. He chortled gleefully when he interpreted the lip movements: "His isn't as big as yours, Pet!"

The acrobat left off masturbating so he could carefully balance himself on his lower partner's palms. Everyone stilled to see what on earth he could do to top what had already been accomplished. For a moment he stood poised. Beneath him his support's arms shook under the strain, which communicated to the two below him so that their knees shuddered visibly. Above them all, the boy slowly bent his own knees. It was the signal. Tendons bulging, his support lowered his arms and the boy with them and then, as if firing a stone ball from a catapult, he thrust up and forward to launch his fellow acrobat like a missile high into the air over the tables.

Heads craned, turned to follow the arching trajectory aimed perfectly at…

Trajan.

The Emperor instinctively lifted a hand in front of his face.

The young acrobat twisted around in mid-flight to come down feet first. He hurtled into Trajan, powerful legs neatly scissoring to either side of the Emperor's neck. He thrust his hands out like buffers against the imperial head to arrest his momentum. Before anyone could believe what they were seeing, the acrobat interlocked his legs. In the manner of a python, between his flexing thighs he began throttling the life from his victim.

It was the oddest thing but from his position Rufio had an uninterrupted view of the boy's rock-solid cock over the nearest strangling thigh. Most of it had disappeared in Trajan's mouth, still open in shock.

Laughter and applause at the gymnastic antics instantly turned to shrieks of alarm and horror. Men of III Cyrenaica held outside the temple rushed in through the first pylon, swords drawn, seeking anything to use them on. They began closing in on the acrobatic troupe. Laevinius could be heard shouting orders to take them alive.

Trajan fell back on his couch under the acrobat's weight. The legs continued their furious scissoring action. And then the boy let out a high-pitched scream, though it was hard to see the cause. The reason for his second yell was perfectly obvious. Vata, with unusual presence of mind ran around in front of the imperial couch with the sword he must have concealed for decorum's sake under his cloak. He paused barely a heartbeat before thrusting it straight up into the boy's exposed anus as far as it would go.

The young acrobat convulsed violently. Blood spurted from his mouth with his third cry and his thighs went flabby as his life ran out. Released from the killing pressure, Trajan fell back one way on his dining couch against Plotina. The dying gymnast, his cock still pointing stiffly at the night sky, fell the other way against Hadrian. Vata struggled to free his sword and did so by putting one booted foot on the nearest rump and jerking the blade out. More blood flowed out over the table to pool among the discarded dessert dishes.

Rufio was a hand's breadth behind Quintus in reaching the Emperor. To his amazement, Trajan appeared to be laughing, although the way he shoved the corpse off his lap showed no humor for the formerly frolicking acrobat.

"Are you all right, Caesar?" Rufio gasped.

"All the better for seeing your blazing head." He seemed unable to quell another bubble of laughter. "Do you think he wanted to kill me by strangulation of the neck or asphyxiation by thrusting his prick down my throat. Or perhaps both?" He swung his legs around, away from where two Praetorian Guards wearing nervous expressions (as well they might for not having protected their Emperor) were dragging the corpse away. The lower court was a confusion of soldiery, defiant performers, and frightened guests milling about. Trajan shook his head and looked at the fist of his right hand. "It saved me, getting it up between his legs before he landed on me. Made it a little harder to choke me to death. And…"

He flexed the fist, made a grabbing motion with it, "…I was able to grab and squeeze his balls."

"Mashed them up into a terrine, I hope," Junilla spat out. She had left her place on the other side of the Empress so that Plotina's women could surround and comfort her. A goodly splash of assassin's blood had splattered her gown, which hardly left her disposed to calmness, though in fact Plotina was made of sterner stuff than many.

"What a terrible waste," Hadrian murmured. "I had a good look at the poor boy before they took his corpse off me. A fine specimen and an exceedingly pretty face.

"Poor boy!" Junilla glowered at Hadrian. "He just tried to kill Caesar."

"I know." Hadrian squeezed his cousin's shoulder. "You know, Marcus, for a moment there—just the tiniest god-space of a moment—I was rather envious of the way he speared you with that handsome weapon. Obviously the strangling bit wasn't very nice, of course."

"But he can't have imagined he could get away with it," Trajan said wonderingly. "Not with all the guards around, and Vata, and my very own Mars," he added with a nod at Quintus.

"It was a suicide attack, Caesar," Vata offered. "They're getting desperate… whoever 'they' are."

This time Trajan seemed to accept the threat. He moved to reassure Antipater that the event would not reflect badly on him or his administrators. "After all," he told him, "we did bring our own security with us."

Antipater looked relieved, but still concerned. "There are rumors, Caesar. Many rumors. They come from the desert reaches. There are some who claim to know…" He looked uncomfortable.

"Know what?" Vata demanded. "If you know of something, why haven't you mentioned it before?"

Rufio saw Septimius give a shake of his head in a resigned manner. I tell him but he won't listen, the gesture said. Rufio tended to agree with the frumentarius about the Praetorian Prefect's military boneheadedness. He gave Septimius a sympathetic smile.

Antipater shuffled and looked as if he'd rather be anywhere else, riding the back of a hippopotamus perhaps. "Gossip is not fact, Prefect. But the buzz in the agora is that there is a line of descent from a long time ago and its leader claims…"

"Come, tell me," Trajan urged Antipater.

"Egypt. He claims Egypt for his own. Behind the banner of chaos, of Seth's all encompassing darkness, this figurehead will rid Egypt of Roman rule…" He stammered into silence.

"Who is this figurehead… this scion of a long line?"

Antipater shook his head. "I have only heard it said that the beast claims descent from the last rightful pharaoh, but others say he is the embodiment of the god, of Seth himself."

Trajan dipped his noble head thoughtfully. "I see." When he looked up again he seemed perfectly calm. "And to fulfil his claims Augustus must perish. They wish to cut off the head and then divide up the body." A smile creased his lips but his eyes narrowed. "Or squeeze the head. Not very good at it, are they? They will have to do a lot better than they have so far to rid Egypt of our Imperium or its administrators or indeed of Imperator Caesar Marcus Ulpius Nerva Traianus Augustus."

A murmur of approval greeted this assertion.

"You know," Rufio spoke privately in Quintus's ear, "Trajan has more names even than those pompous Alexandrian pricks Lucius Junius Quintus Vibius Crispus and Lucius Pomponius Bassus Cascus Scribonianus."

Quintus gave Rufio a tight smile. "You ought put that to music. The Roman mob would love it."

T·H·I·R·T·E·E·N | XIII

To Thebes, 10th to 14th day of August

If it were in his philosophical temperament to hang his head, Eutychus might have done so when Junilla confronted him that fateful afternoon. Cato, a secret witness to the dressing down, was torn between an unusual sense of guilt and chuckling gleefully at being the cause of his tutor's discomfort.

Junilla's glowering expression took in the wax tablet in her hand. She looked like a discobolus working up to hurl her discus at poor Eutychus. Cato suspected the tablet's contents were unfavorable to both pupil and paedagogue. "What do you mean," she began, "by the statement 'the improvement in his handwriting has uncovered his inability to spell'?"

Cato thrust a fist against his mouth to stop a fit of giggles giving him away. He lay sprawled on his belly above the room that had been his school prison for weeks on board *Cleopatra of the Nile*. It hadn't taken a member of the Aventine Foxes long to discover the gigantic floating resort's many secrets: hiding places; little used passages; forgotten closets; and best of all the crawl space he was now squeezed into. If it ever had served a purpose its function escaped Cato. A crack in the boards forming the ceiling of the room below afforded the spy a perfect—if vertically foreshortened—view of his mother and Eutychus.

His wonderful secret empire extended from bow to stern, side to side between two of the main accommodation decks and so afforded him endless possibilities hidden from annoying adults. Aside from spiders, cockroaches, and the odd scorpion he had it to himself. This was not surprising considering only a small, agile person could make any way through its dark expanses. Here and there, usually where narrow staircases passed through from the lower deck to the one above, were placed small hatches that allowed Cato ingress and exit. In his anxiousness to overhear what Eutychus had written and what his mother had to say about his tutor's report, Cato was somewhat incautiously half-in and half-out of one such opening. He didn't risk scrabbling farther into the security of the crawl space for fear of any inevitable noise alerting those he spied on.

Junilla's voice rang out again. "Don't you think, 'the stick and apple must be waved in the face of this particular donkey before he decides to exert himself' is extremely rude, not to say uninformative?"

"Domina, my apologies for the indelicate phrasing, but I felt it necessary to make plain my concerns. He makes some progress but could try harder. You see, there is far too much to distract attention on this vessel, too many destructive emotions for an easily led boy—"

"Easily led? You stated in your curriculum vitae, Eutychus, that you are a stoic, so why can't you just instil some of your philosophical fortitude and self-control into my son?"

The tutor dipped his head in acknowledgment. "I would that I could, domina, but your youngest son has given me a new definition of stoicism: he grins and I bear it."

Cato jumped, almost banged his head on the low roof at the sudden tug on his protruding ankle. "Wha—?" he hissed as a second jerk shook him. He twisted around sufficiently to see a face peering at him with curiosity and grinning impishly. "Ashur," he whispered.

"What are you doing in there?"

"Keep your voice down! None of your beeswax."

"You're spying, I know. I've watched and seen you vanish all over the place."

"Sshhh!"

"I will, but only if you let me come along."

"Why should I do that?"

Ashur looked thoughtful in a demure, considering kind of way.

"Because I'll tell on you otherwise… or maybe," he hurried on sotto voce on seeing Cato's building outrage, "because I can save you from being eaten by another crocodile?"

"At least his education hasn't gone to his head," they both heard Eutychus say. What Junilla replied went lost under the sharp slap she must have delivered.

"Ooh, I bet that hurt," Ashur murmured. "Let me come along and I will tell you secrets about Quintus."

Cato eased himself around to glare out at the slave. "You never would."

"No, probably not," Ashur admitted amiably. "He'd thrash me to within an inch of my poor life if he ever found out."

A scowl of disbelief crossed Cato's face. "You mean he'd fuck you to within an inch of your miserable life, but I'll bet he's never laid a hand on you with a birch."

"So, am I coming with you?"

After a reluctant nod, Cato slid out onto the stairs, pushed closed the concealing hatch behind him and, passing Ashur, pulled open one opposite. He climbed up and into the dark space beyond. Ashur eased his slight form through the aperture after Cato—which is how they came to solve the mystery that had vexed Septimius for an age and enjoyed a stirring experience at the same time.

"This is amazing," Ashur breathed after their sixth, seventh, maybe eighth pause (he'd lost count) to peer down into rooms below or with eyes pressed to gaps at floor level into chambers on the deck above. "You can spy almost everywhere."

"I haven't been this far forward before, though."

"Isn't it where some of the crew are quartered? I wonder how they live. Let's check it out." Ashur brushed past Cato to take the lead and as he did so something sharp hurt his hip. "Ouch! Is that your sling?" A mumble came as answer. "For the love of the gods why have it stuck in your belt crawling around in here?"

"I never know when it might come in handy."

"Stupid," Ashur muttered in an aggrieved tone, rubbing where the short staff sling had jabbed him. "A hand catapult would be more use. You can't even get a swing up with that thing in here." He crawled on, grumbling under his breath, carefully shuffling on splayed elbows and knees. Ahead a shaft of dusty light spewed up from a gap in the boards. He wriggled the last few feet, lowered his head to the crack, and gazed down on…

"Oh!"

"Huh?" Cato grunted with swelling interest. The sounds rising through the boards sounded like a small herd of snorting cattle.

Ashur twisted his head around as Cato slid alongside and winked at him in a distinctly salacious way. "Here, get an eyeful of this."

Cato put face to crack and with difficulty prevented a gasp bursting from between lips parted suddenly in visceral shock. "By Vesta's velvety vulva," he muttered, one of Rufio's favorite exclamations. Ashur's head joined his, and cheek-to-cheek they stared down into a cramped cabin.

A poor palliasse almost filled the space, not that much of the ticking could be seen underneath two writhing, naked bodies. "They're both men," Cato whispered. Not much of the man underneath was visible. He was a man evidently from what the boys could see of his beard. Stomach pressed into the mattress, he bucked up and down against the man straddling his back. A shaved-bald head, long neck and back, and a pair of white buttocks humping up and down at a furious pace, supported by splayed limbs, was undeniably that of a male figure.

Ashur's breath came hot against Cato's cheek. "They're fucking." His tone suggested his companion would not know the word's meaning or understand what he was seeing.

"Not bad, either," Cato said with the sneer of an expert on the subject. "This is my third time this voyage. I can't tell you about the first or I'd be crucified," he confided in Ashur's ear (not that he risked being overheard over all the grunting from below), "The second was in Alexandria when I caught my brother and Quintus making the beast with two backs."

Ashur gave him an amused but admiring glance. "And there was me offering to let you in on some things about my dominus and Rufio. So you're quite the voyeur. Oh look… I think the one on top's about to come."

Beneath them the pair were clearly reaching a climax. The man fucking growled like a dog fox in heat, the one underneath moaned in unison. "I'm shooting!" the fucker ground out between gritted teeth. He spasmed as if he was being racked and at the same time rolled sideways so he could reach around. Spooned together, still screwing hard, the position treated the voyeurs to the sight of the bottom man's spurting cock gripped in the fucker's fist.

"Wow…" Cato exhaled quietly.

"Wow, yes. That's what I call a proper fuck."

They would have squirmed away, both privately intent on finding some relief from what they had just observed, except as the two post-coital men rolled onto their backs the faces of both showed up

well in the side light coming from an open window out of sight to the boys.

"I know him," Cato whispered.

"Of course. He's one of the rope crew works the sail," Ashur said dismissively.

"I know *that*. I mean the other one, the bottom one. I've seen him at that Oxymithing-place. He's not one of *Cleo*'s crew, and yet here he is on board while we're rowing up the river. I guess he got on before we left Abydos. You know what this means?" Cato whispered urgently.

Ashur shook his head.

"I bet you anything the other one, the rope or sails man, or whatever he does, is the spy. He's the one who's been telling the rebels everything, the snakes who took me."

"What do we do?"

"Tell Septimius and Flaccus."

"Good. You do that. For me I'm off to find my dominus. I hope he's feeling randy as Mercury. If I'm lucky he might even give me one of those lovely, sloppy mouth jobs.

* * *

Aboard this floating palace, *Quintus wrote*, the banks and islands gliding by our decks give little hint as to the Nile's tortured course. It seems like a watery highway straight as a military road, yet in truth it bends left and right all the while at the will of the land… just slowly so the twists are not apparent.

Some miles after our departure from Abydos (and the upheaval of yet another attempt on the Emperor's life), the Nile takes the shape of a back-to-front letter C, a great bend to the east. If we took to camels and crossed the desert from the small settlement we just passed—Diospolis Parva I think it's called—to our next major destination, the great Roman fort at Diospolis Major (which we prefer to call Thebes), it would be a third the distance of the river route. It would, however, be an uncomfortable journey for the land in between is barren, wild, mountainous, without any water or respite, and hotter than Vulcan's forge.

Feeling virtuous for catching up on his record, Quintus pushed aside the scroll, charged his pen, and started writing on a smaller length of papyrus, its ends weighted down by the maligned alabaster bust of Ramesses and an interestingly colored rock he'd picked up after the battle of the Red Pyramid. The tip of his tongue peeked between pursed lips as he concentrated on the meter. It was a reworking of the poem that began: *I'll fuck you and bugger you...* "Needs more impact," he muttered, chewing the end of the pen. How about, sodomize you and fuck your fa—"

"Ho there, Quintus. Still at it?"

The quick shuffle of papers did not escape Rufio's sharp wits. His last three words hit Quintus hard with the (probably) unintended double meaning.

"What is that?"

"What *that*?"

"The *that* you just hid away under that pile of scrolls."

"Oh... that. Nothing"

"So why are you blushing?" Rufio placed both hands on the table and leaned down threateningly. "What is it?"

"I said, nothing," Quintus answered irritably.

Cobra-fast, Rufio struck and whipped out the paper and had it unrolled before Quintus could prevent him reading anything. He slumped back on his stool in resignation and regarded Rufio sourly from under lowered lashes as his lover's expression underwent a transformation from curious to puzzled and then to beaming incredulity.

"This is... hot stuff, hotter than Etna blowing its stack. My, my, I didn't know you had such a wild imagination. It's strange but you put it in such a way that reading about it feels even more exciting than actually doing it." He tweaked his cock through the light tunic, unconscious of the action. "It's the lead up to the action as well..."

he started reading aloud: "*Kissing and glancing, soothing, all make way but to the acting of this private play.*" He waggled his eyebrows, "*Name it I would, but being*—as you are—*blushing red, the rest I will speak when next we meet in bed.*"

Quintus passed a weary hand across his fevered brow.

"And then you really get down to the sex action... well, what can I say? It's hot stuff. By the dripping prick of Bacchus you are the King of *Pop-eye-rus* Porn, Quintus Caecilius Alba. We could make a fortune with this!"

Quintus looked up. "We?" he said faintly.

"With your words and my drawings to bring them to licentious life on the scroll. Just imagine how many dirty old men will cream their loincloths to get hands on stuff like this, with illuminations in glowing color." He shrugged. "Dirty young men too. Probably dirty maidens as well."

"You are a competent draftsman of columns and busts and the like to show prospective customers what tat they might purchase," Quintus pointed out with a touch of recovering defiance.

"Tertulla's tits, I'm better than that. Give me the pen." He didn't wait but snatched it up, slapped the ink well down on one corner of the scroll to hold it down, and leaned an elbow on the other end. With rapid strokes—and to a look of abject horror on the poet's face at the desecration of his manuscript—Rufio scratched away for a minute. Before Quintus's eyes grew an astonishingly lifelike rendition of a bearded man taking the fat, hard cock of a young man in his mouth, full balls banging against his chin. In Rufio's fertile imagination and—to Quintus's surprise—fluent artistry, both participants were clearly enjoying the experience.

"I think adding ejaculate squirting between his lips is an unnecessary addition—"

"No, no, it adds veri... very—"

"—similitude. You are really very talented after all."

"I'm not just an incredibly attractive face, you know." Rufio grinned broadly. "You versify the lines and I'll tickle the jaded palate with my palette, hahaha! I tell you Quintus, a fortune in our hands."

"We could never publish a work like that. Who would copy it for distribution?"

An airy wave of the pen. "Oh leave that to me. Ma knows this bookseller and publisher Sosius who does odd jobs on the side for senators with a lurid taste in literature. The biggest problem is keeping up production when his army of copyist slaves, bored stiff with Cicero, Virgil, and Horace, masturbate themselves silly instead of penning the words."

"And how will they copy your... your visual actuations in 'glowing color'?"

Rufio began work on a second drawing. "They carve wooden blocks to impress on the papyrus for the mass production." He glanced up. "Don't you know this, O Author?"

Quintus went red in the cheeks again. "I haven't reached that far, to have a proper publication, only a few copies to hand around at a reading. I don't know how a publisher works."

"The books made with reproduction drawings are cruder than an original, of course, but that only makes the five or maybe six copies executed in my own hand fabulously rare... and expensive. We both personally sign those and Sosius will make a fortune. I can get Ma to ensure we receive our fair portion—he's terrified of her. The other beauty of illuminated scrolls is that other bastard booksellers won't be able to make pirate copies and cheat us so easily. There... how does that look?"

Quintus peered at the visualization of his lines: *I speak not of the mob from who I have nothing to fear—truly the fear's of you and your cock dangerous to both good and bad boys. Shake it about as you please, and place with as much force as you please in whichever ass takes your fancy, but keep this boy of mine modestly safe.* The modest boy Rufio had drawn was most immodestly pleasuring himself in a crouching position on the upstanding cock of an older patrician (obvious for his broad-stripe toga rucked up about his waist).

"Amazing. Rufio you have been hiding your talent under a fig leaf." Quintus sighed heavily. "But this couldn't go out under my name. I know you don't care, but my family. And what would Trajan think?"

"I should think he'd say, 'Whoopee!' Still, I suppose you're right. It's easy to say 'to Hades with what people think' when you're young and foolish, but once it's out there in the public's face, we'll have to live with the impetuous folly of our youthful actions for the rest of our lives, branded forever as the Kings of *Pop-eye-rus* Porn."

"So... no?"

"Certainly not! We'll sign off as Anonymous."

"I learned that this morning. Means Mr. No-Name. So who's anonymous?"

Rufio hurriedly rolled up the libidinous scroll and threw it at Quintus, who fumbled it and then threw it down with his journey notes, and then they both confronted Cato standing in the doorway.

"What is that?"

"What *that*?" in unison.

"The *that* Quintus just hid away under that pile of scrolls."

"Oh... that. Nothing"

"So why are you blushing?"

Rufio looked aghast. "Me, blush?"

Cato strode over to the table and before either could stop him, uncovered the scroll and unwound enough of it to make his eyes goggle. He slapped a hand across his mouth and the scroll snapped shut. A grin split his face from ear to ear. "I've just seen that for real."

Rufio exchanged looks with Quintus. Both raised querying eyebrows. "What do you mean?"

"You should do one with Circus jockeys for Hadrian. Ashur told me he likes to give it to young charioteers up the—"

"What do you mean?" Rufio repeated insistently.

Cato dropped the rude scroll on the table. "I know who the spy is. The one Septimius has been trying to uncover. Red and black eyebrows arched even higher. Cato regaled them with what he had seen with Ashur—"who is looking for you, by the way Quintus, and hoping for... well, I'll let him tell you that."

Rufio broke in. "So the one who was getting it up the ass is not a member of the crew?"

"No, but I saw him before, even in Alexandria in the market come to think of it, and at Oxythingummybob and he must have come on board at Abydos to pick up information from the man who works with the sail crew, who is the rotten spy."

"And pick up something else as well," Rufio added with a snort.

"It's no laughing matter," Quintus said in a severe tone.

"It isn't," Cato agreed. "He must be the one who told the brigands who grabbed me who we all are... and that rat who tackled me said his 'leader' was out to nail you two, the one he called a jackal of the desert or something."

"Have you told Septimius?" Quintus asked.

Cato shook his brown curls. "I was trying to find him when I heard you two chortling over..." he pointed at the offending scroll, "...that. Anonymously."

Angry shouting swelled until a loud slap brought quiet. Septimius and Laevinius watched dispassionately as four of Vata's Praetorian Guards pinned the two spies to the deck. "Get them down into the following barge quickly. I don't want the Emperor or Empress disturbed." Vata took a salute from the centurion in charge of the detail. "Find out everything."

The officer gave the Prefect a grim nod and slapped fist to breast. "Yes, Sir, your command is my will. Everything," he repeated ominously.

As the spies were bundled away, cries stifled by gags, Flaccus fussed a protesting Cato away from the scene. He had identified both men when the soldiers hauled the miscreants from the crew quarters, but Flaccus knew Junilla would not want her youngest to witness the questioning, even if from afar over the stern of the boat. A brazier was already blazing on the first of the following barges that housed some of the legionaries. Irons were heated and pincers readied. As fortune had it, the Nile's northeasterly curve at this point here meant the prevailing southerly wind now blew across the vessels' bows so the prisoners' screams did not reach ears on *Cleo*.

"Their corpses will make a fine meal for a lucky crocodile or two." Gnaeus Septimius Corbulo looked unconcerned at the fate of the two spies. He turned to Laevinius. "With respect, Tribune Pinius, as the Praetorians are reserved for the protection of Caesar and the imperial party, I recommend that from this moment on no one leaves the boat without having a bodyguard of at least four of your men to accompany them."

"Agreed." Laevinius showed only slight resentment at being told his job by a civilian, but he was aware of the role Septimius played.

"That includes you two," Septimius added sternly for the benefit of Quintus and Rufio.

It transpired that the next time Quintus disembarked he was accompanied by a detachment of Praetorian Guards because he agreed to visit the temple of Hathor at Tentyris with Hadrian and a handful of his youthful catamite-followers. The rest of the imperial tourists decided against another hot, dusty trek to yet another monument, even one in fine condition, as Djed had informed. Instead *Cleopatra of the Nile* anchored off the northern shore of the river (as it was at this point on the great bend) adjacent to the modern Greek-Roman settlement of Kaine.

"Your friend Tullius Rufio," Hadrian addressed Quintus as they approached the vast blocky edifice dedicated to the cow-goddess Hathor inside its massive compound of mud-brick walls.

"Yes, Father?" Quintus responded cautiously, using the honorific Hadrian was entitled to as one of the consuls for the year.

"His brother, Cato, isn't it?"

Quintus confirmed the name, still wondering where this was going and remembering Cato's suggestion of presenting Hadrian with a poetic scroll featuring drawings of chariot jockeys in the Circus Maximus having it off in all sorts of unlikely positions.

"He strikes me as a lively and precocious youngster. I sense his concupiscence, a yearning to know more of life, wouldn't you say so Cassius?"

Quietus, the young companion so addressed, fawned and agreed with enthusiasm. "Quite the ephebe, Publius."

They walked side by side within a cordon of ten Praetorians and followed by two of the Corporation's experts. Hadrian turned his head to look directly at Quintus. "Does Cato share any carnal thoughts with you?"

Fortunately, at that awkward moment a gaggle of priests rushed up to pester Hadrian with petitions begging for his intercession in this, that, or the other, and gave Quintus a merciful release from concocting a suitable response. The retinue processed though the entryway in the stone screen that shut off the hypostyle hall from the court, guarded by six giant Hathor columns. Immediately the interior's deep gloom enfolded the party, a darkness oppressed by a forest of heavy stone piers. Quintus made a note to tell Rufio to keep his brother as far as possible out of Hadrian and his boy-greedy companions' sight in future.

They wandered around the elaborately carved monumental masonry, entered the crypts dedicated to several arcane deities cut into the massive walls, climbed one of the stairwells in the thickness of the wall leading to the roof. From up there the Nile glittered brightly in the distance and the walls of Kaine stood behind the bulk of *Cleopatra of the Nile*.

Hadrian expressed a desire to view the relief carvings on the temple's exterior and it was on the towering rear wall Quintus was confronted by a shock of history, a history much closer to home than he would have imagined. The guides stumbled over each other to present the gigantic depictions of a queen and, Quintus presumed by the double crown of Upper and Lower Egypt on his head, a pharaoh. Both figures faced in the same direction (that of the sun's rising) and their arms were raised in the Egyptian style of reverence. The queen wore a clinging sheath from headdress to ankle; the male figure wore a huge collar but was otherwise bare above the waist, below which he wore a stiff Egyptian kilt.

"Who are they supposed to be?" Hadrian demanded of the guides.

"Sire, this is Queen Cleopatra—" said one.

"And her son the Pharaoh—" butted in the other.

"—Ptolemy Philopater Caesarion."

"Caesarion!"

Quintus blanched. He stood transfixed by the image of the story he'd told Rufio on *Fortuna* as they approached Alexandria.

Titus Spurius, the other of Hadrian's *comites*, pointed up. "Is his kilt always so sticky-out stiff at the front, or is he pleased to see us, do you think?" He nudged Quietus.

The resulting fit of giggle annoyed Quintus. It was oddly moving to see writ large on this wall a grown-up version of the adolescent denied by the Fates his right to rule Egypt, killed at the command of Augustus in the annexation of Egypt. At the back of this temple he still lived, grown up, King of Egypt. Hieroglyphic writing filled the wall around the figures but Quintus spotted one close to the base where wall and ground met. It appeared different to the others: newer, brighter scratches. "What does that mean?" he asked one of the guides.

The man leaned over and peered at it with a puzzled expression. "It is… not of the time, sir. It is not of this temple."

"What does it say?"

He straightened up. "It says 'Isis dies as Seth rises and I'—it is a crude cartouche meaning the 'king above'—'I rise again to secure the land.' That's all." The guide frowned in perplexity.

"Come!" Hadrian called. "I've seen enough. There is nothing here of interest as I hoped. This is a recent Greekly-Roman monument, not historical at all."

With a bemused look, Quintus watched the consul stalk off.

F·O·U·R·T·E·E·N | XIV

East Thebes, 17th day of August

"Our accommodations are simple, Caesar." Attius Clemens, prefect of the important Roman fort at Thebes, possessed the hoarse voice of a career soldier, a man long used to projecting drill words across a parade ground at his soldiers. His words were aimed squarely at the two young patricians Cassisus Quietus and Titus Spurius Hadrian had insisted on bringing along with him for "the jaunt."

These two effete fun-lovers and Hadrian were the only other members of the imperial party to accompany the Emperor. Hadrian nodded affably at the grizzled equestrian prefect and grinned boyishly at his imperial cousin. "Like old times on campaign, hey Marcus? Roughing it with army lads." He added the last with a wink for the benefit of Spurius and Quietus.

They were all traveling light: only four slaves carried the few items of baggage and no Praetorian Guards accompanied them because Attius Clemens feared their undiplomatic presence would create friction with the regular legionaries stationed in the camp (jealousies over pay differentials often led to off-duty fisticuffs).

"I have ordered some carpeting for your room, Caesar," Clemens growled, turning his back on the others. "The bare floor can be very cold in the mornings."

In almost every respect the permanent camp for the six cohorts on detachment from XXII Deiotariana was best described as dusty-spartan, Trajan thought. The fort buildings of sandy-colored mud bricks clustered like a drab skirt around the ancient stones of the great temple of Amun-Opet at the southern extent of Thebes. Its long walls of brightly painted intricate relief carvings enclosed courtyards, a processional colonnade leading to a large porticoed forecourt, hypostyle hall, chambers for officiates, and increasingly darker and lower sacred shrines. The great monument with its two obelisks and two colossal statues of Ramesses the Great enthroned before the entrance pylon rose up like some great riverboat cresting through the dross of Roman occupation.

Due to the increasingly waterlogged nature of the land everyone else of the imperial party had remained aboard the boat; but also in part because of a ceremonial aspect to Trajan's visit, a consequence of his being head of the state religion. The numerous Theban priests, having pronounced the timing of the imperial visit to be auspicious, had petitioned him to carry out Pharaoh's ancient rites in celebrating the annual festival of *Opet*. Of this mystery, all Trajan knew came somewhat hazily from Hadrian's hasty reading of Greek and Roman historians. "It's basically the New Year and takes place at the peak of the annual flood. Like now," he'd said.

Helpfully, the dour Clemens was a surprising mine of information. In spite of his manner, which hardly suggested the scholar, Prefect Attius Clemens was unusually knowledgeable for a Roman soldier about the customs and cults of the region he governed. "We may call this place Thebes, Caesar," he informed his imperial visitors as they toured the long temple's exterior. "But to the locals it's Waset, or city of the royal scepter. The ancients also referred to the great northern temple as *Ta-pe*, which became in Greek Thebes, though because they associated the local god Amun with Zeus, they also named it Diospolis Major, Great City of Zeus. Confusing bunch, the Greeks, if you ask me."

"*Cleopatra of the Nile* is moored by a great pile of masonry to the north of here," Trajan said, waving Hadrian down, the young consul eager to boast of his scanty knowledge. "Is that the *Ta-pe* you mentioned?"

"It is, Caesar. That too is a part of Waset. Known to the priests as *Ipet-isut* or the Most Select of Places. It's a complex of temples and temples within temples, center of the triad cult of Amun-Ra, his consort Mut, and their son Khonsu. The three gods dwell there but at this time of year the priests carry them here to this temple of *Ipet-reyst*, the Southern Place or Amun-Opet. Between the two precincts Thebes was the most powerful city of the ancients even eclipsing Memphis and Heliopolis as the major political, religious, and military capital of Egypt."

Hadrian kept nodding enthusiastically at the explanation in a manner that to Trajan indicated his colleague's eagerness to butt in, but as they returned to stand before the great pylon, Clemens pointed along a wide avenue of human-headed sphinxes and kept up his monologue.

"You see the great way. It connects the temples for the procession of the triad to attend Opet—the festival of the Egyptian New Year—in this sacred place. Its significance lies in the renewal of the pharaoh's divine powers through the bestowal of Amun-Ra's beneficence on his subjects through the medium of the pharaoh." Clemens dipped his head slightly. "In this instance, that is you, Caesar. Associated with the benefits of the annual flood, the pharaoh demonstrates his power in bringing fertility and a new growing season to his people." A hint of a blush tinged the prefect's cheeks. "In effect, you will be bestowing your godlike seed on the soil and the people through the power of Amun-Ra."

Before Hadrian could open his mouth Trajan asked, "Why did we commandeer this temple and build a permanent army camp around it? It's not the usual Roman way to tread on people's religious beliefs, rites, or sacred places. Are there not better sites in the locale?"

Clemens glared for a moment as if his commander had accused him of blasphemy, but he quickly remembered his manners. "Before my time, Caesar. The records indicate that the first Romans to reach here spotted its usefulness as a defensible position. As you see, when the river rises each year, the surrounding land is submerged, but here we're on a low hill and so protected. This monument is sound and solid, whereas the precinct to the north is far more widespread and so vulnerable to attack. It's also quite decrepit."

"From where we are moored I saw its ramparts. They look solid enough."

"The pylons are massive, but behind there is little coherent left. I myself attended to the construction of new drainage there and my predecessor erected a series of storage magazines outside the great pylons, but the natives caused us so much trouble we abandoned it and leave it well alone. Here, we're secure behind our own stout walls. Nevertheless, your imperial presence here at this time in the role of Pharaoh will go some way to smoothing relations with the priests and the local people. There are many who deeply resent our being here. Perhaps that's not surprising. My predecessors commandeered this temple without awareness of its religious importance. In there…" he jabbed a thumb back over his shoulder, "…some inner halls were converted into a club and bathhouse for the officers and for any Greek and Roman merchants passing through, or who have settled here."

"Sirs! Kind sirs!"

The party stopped at the loud cry.

A tall man garbed from shoulder to ankle in a dirty brown-gray robe strode forward. He bowed so obsequiously it was a miracle his head winding didn't unravel. "I am temple guardian," he announced with great gravity, holding out a beckoning hand full of wiggling digits in the universal gesture of come with me but cover my palm with silver first. "Come, come, I show you secrets and marvels of Amun-Opet. I show you where Amun-Ra, Mut, and Khonsu reside in the *Heb-Ipet*, the innermost chamber; the holy of holies."

"Shoo! Get away." Clemens waved the scrappy figure off. "Take no notice, Caesar. His kind are not temple officials, the scoundrels are interested only in relieving you of money on the pretense of telling you interesting facts about the temple, when the only fact to be sure of is that they know nothing."

Then Hadrian suddenly got in. "Who raised this temple?" he demanded of the persistent self-styled guardian. Quietus and Spurius simpered.

The man smiled wisely. "It is written on the walls, kind sir. Please, come, let me show you."

"You see, I know," Hadrian announced triumphantly. "And I know because I have read the works of Herodotus, Diodorus Siculus, of Manetho and of Strabo in his *Geographica*." He turned on the Egyptian, who wriggled like a puppy in hope of a treat. "Does the name Userma'atre'setepenre' mean anything?"

"Means fuck-all to me," Quietus muttered to Spurius.

Trajan's brows rose as far as the old man's drooped.

"That's how the ancients named the man commemorated on those pylons behind you. Ramesses. The temple of Hathor at Tentyris, do you know anything about that?"

Hooded eyes looked up more eagerly. "Oh yes, Lord, a most ancient place of wonder—"

"Hadrian snapped triumphant fingers. "Eyewash! It's a piece of modern rubbish."

"Come, come, I show you everything. *Hssst*, it is most of interest—"

"Attius Clemens is correct, Marcus," Hadrian announced to Trajan, making the gesture of washing his hands. "This fellow knows nothing."

"I'm impressed," Trajan said with a quiet smile of amusement.

"I show you the shrine and sacred sun-boat of X'ander."

Hadrian grimaced as one of the honor guard soldiers dragged the man off, still protesting that his fee for a tour was reasonable.

"X'ander?" asked Hadrian's companions together.

"He means Alexander the Great," Clemens answered tersely.

"Of course," Hadrian quickly broke in. "The innermost shrine was apparently built at his command, but according to Manetho there's no sun-boat. Long ago looted no doubt. Why do you regard me like that, Marcus? Architecture is in my blood, cousin, as you know. Why, Augustus voted funds for the restoration of many such monuments throughout the land, especially farther up the river. Should we do less?" He set his head back and stared at the blue dome overhead at a vision granted only him. "One day, I know it in my bones, I shall found a great city on the banks of the Nile."

"Aside from the presumption, won't that be a piece of modern eyewash?" Trajan said drily. "And aren't you getting a bit ahead of yourself?"

Hadrian colored at his gaffe. "As you say, Caesar." Such unguarded comments could easily be construed as prophesying the Emperor's death, predicting the succession, and therefore treasonous. Trajan smiled in a conciliatory manner. He liked to keep Hadrian off balance.

Attius Clemens interceded, putting on his most gracious air, clearly a great strain. He extended an arm toward the main barracks. "And now, please allow me to show you to your quarters."

At least inside the mud-brick barracks the walls were plastered, painted a warm off-white. Italian countryside scenes of grassy knolls under the shade of linden trees, with brushing willows framing distant farm animals, adorned the larger walls, an ornamentation designed to refresh Roman minds worn sore at the glare and grit of the Egyptian desert. The unexpectedly damp heat rising from the expanding river oppressed Trajan so he was happy to retire to one of few modest rooms set aside for visiting dignitaries. The scarcity of guest accommodation was another reason for having left the others back aboard *Cleopatra of the Nile*. Having agreed to meet Hadrian and his two companions at sundown, Trajan dismissed the two slaves who brought in his things, happy for once to be left to his own devices. He planned on a refreshing siesta and contemplation of what Clemens had said about his role as pharaoh and intercessor between Amun-Ra and his subjects. With the door closed on the outside world, he took in his simple surroundings.

The room was surprisingly spacious, but he suspected from the smell of new paint that his coming had precipitated a speedy renovation to knock together two chambers. Each must have originally had a single window, but now there were two, the harsh outside light moderated by angled louver slats. Crude tiles covered the floor on which sat a truckle bed, a clothes chest pushed against one wall, and a single stool. On top of the chest an unlit three-stick candelabra, a pitcher of water, and bowl juggled for space.

He read aloud the note scratched onto a wax tablet propped against the jug. "Call for wine if thirsty. Under no circumstances drink the water, it is for washing only." *Better that Plotina and the other women remained aboard in luxury.* The better part of a decade spent in the luxury of Domus Augusti had worn Plotina's famed humility thin. He recalled a time in their earlier marriage that she was happy living among soldiers. That was when appearances counted for much and he needed to be seen with a wife at his side, but he doubted she would enjoy being incarcerated in a rough-and-ready military camp these days.

Trajan didn't miss the boat's hurly-burly. He was in fact happy to exchange the continuous social whirl for simple food and contemplative solitude for a day or so before the rigors of ceremony. On the other hand he could do with some male company. Hadrian had his two *pedicabo sociis*, his fuck companions Quietus and Spurius, who no doubt would also go hunting among the boys hanging about on the small temple dockside for fresh young meat to tickle their jaded palates. Yes, he found himself missing the company of Quintus or his brother Marcus or scallywag Rufio.

So when the diversion came, he welcomed it.

It occurred to him that there was no sign of the promised floor covering to warm his feet in the night chill. Which is when he noticed a rolled up rug in the far corner, mocking with its harsh woven underside. He strode across and bent to shuffle it nearer the room's middle, grunting at its unexpected weight. He straightened and assessed the angle. With his left boot placed firmly on the rug's visible edge, Trajan gave the bulk a mighty shove with the sole of his right boot. The mat unrolled briskly across the floor, the cylinder growing narrower with each rotation, until finally the inner edge flipped over and slapped against the tiles. Its momentum also rolled out a man. Over and over he went and then sprang up to kneel in submission on one knee, thick black hair falling over his forehead to brush the floor.

Trajan recovered from the surprise in an eyeblink. By instinct the pugio was in his hand, the point of its razor-sharp blade aimed at the intruder, but he relaxed a fraction at the sight before him. Wariness gave way to a stirring of interest. He saw a slender young man clad only in the briefest of glittery loincloths. Lithe, oiled muscles glinted in bars of sunlight thrown as sharp, angled slashes across the floor from the slatted windows. And then the head came up. A pleased

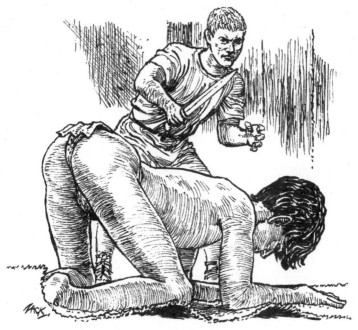

grin widened the handsome lad's generous lips so the smile seemed to stretch from one side of his square face to the other. Above it, the aquiline nose rose to separate a pair a black, slightly arched brows. His was a masculine and yet beguiling appearance, in some ways similar to Quintus, but in others—particularly the sinful grin and come-hither eyes—like wicked Rufio.

Isn't that just what I wished for a moment ago?

"How dare you hide away in Caesar's private apartment."

The boy stood to reveal an enticing outthrust package tucked inside his cloth-of-gold underwear, and his cheeky, self-satisfied stance only served to offer it up. "Great Lord Caesar, I am a gift from your soldiers." He cast his eyes down under long lashes, suddenly submissive and coy. "For you I am your Little Caesar… your Caesarion."

The words carried a threat concealed inside enticement, but he couldn't put a finger on why. *He wears hardly anything…* Trajan sheathed the dagger after assessing that his intruder could have no weapon concealed about his person, other than the one hidden under the flimsy cincture wrapped around his loins. He paced the room to confront the youth. Immediately the eyes snapped up in a frank engagement that brought Trajan to a halt a pace away. He stared back. "A gift from what soldiers?"

"The Roman men of Thebes, Caesar. The horseman officer, he thought they should clothe me more, so more you have to unwrap of your gift." He gave a shrug of eloquent seduction. "But I think you are man of action who do not enjoy delay…?"

The boy was truly exquisite. Whoever set this up knew Trajan's taste with rather alarming accuracy: young but not callow; a figure well-built though not overdone; iron-hard, flat belly, lightly muscled, rising to adorable pectoral shelves, each boasting volcanic cones of nipples; torso hairless without seeming in any way effeminate and similarly smooth, sturdy legs. His expression of naked lust alternated between demure submissiveness and jaw-jutting aggression.

Eyes still fixed unwaveringly on those dark pools, Trajan unbuckled his belt, shucked free of the ornate tunic he'd been obliged to wear for the visit, and with one hand on his own, the other on the boy's, he ripped off their loincloths. "My *Caesarion*, you say." He lifted a hand to Caesarion—this oriental Egyptian Little Caesar— and gripped his chin. At a lower level two hardening cocks kissed at the tips. The boy sighed and tilted his head back to receive the kiss he anticipated… and then he turned away abruptly and threw himself onto the bed, which creaked in protest. He knelt on all fours and peered coquettishly over his shoulder, ass thrust up in outrageous invitation like a cat on heat.

Trajan wasted no further time. He reached across to the chest and yanked one of the sweet-smelling beeswax candles from its sconce. Stepping up behind Caesarion, he grasped one buttock on its flank and with his other hand played the wick end of the candle up and down the boy's ass cleft. Caesarion gave a purr of pleasure and thrust back against the tallow rod.

"You like that, do you?"

"Mmmmm, but great Caesar's own candle surely delivers more flame."

A flick of the wrist twisted the fat taper inward. Caesarion gasped at the entry, but wiggled his butt even more. Trajan rotated his wrist, worked the candle in deeper, moved it back and forth a few times, while his cock thickened. The heat of his palm melted a thin skein of wax and switching hands he used the tallow to grease himself. And then, discarding the candle, he gripped Caesarion's hips and with a hard flick of his pelvis, slipped into the lubricated hole with a waft of honeyed beeswax.

Caesarion's carrion-black head reared back at the sudden intrusion, mouth deliciously agape as he squirmed under the vigorous thrusting and strained to see over his shoulder at the man fucking him. "Do me harder, great Caesar, harder, faster, oh, oh…"

Trajan reached out to knock away one supporting arm and

forced the youth down flat on the bed, following him down to fuck him even harder. He wormed his left hand beneath the slim body to grasp the unsheathed and slippery cock pressed against the roughspun covering so that with every thrust deep into the boy, Caesarion fucked Trajan's fist, grunting with each effort.

The pace increased. Trajan rode the boy harder and faster as requested. He felt like a charioteer in the Circus Maximus, flogging his team on to victory, the uproar of the mighty crowd urging him on. Sweat flew from his flesh in such quantity that in fact it was like slithering up and down a lathering horse. He felt Caesarion's cock thicken even more and begin to fill the cavern of his fist. The flowing orgasm brought Trajan to his own climax. His balls clenched and emptied in eight huge spurts of exquisite pleasure… and then a few lesser jerks and aftershots.

When he rolled off the boy Trajan lay back, an arm flung across his eyes to shut out the persistent sunlight shafting through the

shuttered windows. His body still heaved with recent exertion, a reminder he wasn't quite the young buck who rode the Dacian plains and fucked two or three times a day. For a while his mind sideslipped into a daydream review of some past conquests—of young men, not countries: slaves, junior tribunes seeking advancement, sons of prominent municipal citizens—so he didn't at first understand what was happening when Caesarion slipped a foot under his neck. The smile on his face dimmed when the other leg came across his throat, and he gasped as the fleshy scissors tightened suddenly and drastically.

By all the horrors of Hades, not again!

It was as if the Abydos acrobats had dispatched yet another gymnastic assassin to eliminate him. Screwing his head sideways to relieve the pressure proved impossible, but from the corner of his eyes he could just see the boy's face blackened with concentration, his entire body shuddering with the effort. Trajan could not believe the enormous power the killer was exerting on his larynx. Where had this constrictor's power come from? He could feel his own strength failing with the lack of air. His hands scrabbled frantically at the squeezing thighs, but to little avail. Nails raked up skin and flesh, but with inhuman strength and silence, the asphyxiation continued.

Black pools began to swim before his eyes. He flailed about with hands and useless legs, struggling desperately to find some purchase. And then he felt something hard against his slapping hand on the floor. What was it? Leather... *My belt!* His hand dithered and slapped at the leather, and then he felt cold metal. *It must be my pugio! Jupiter, Greatest and Best, please...*

Trajan felt the dagger slip from his weakening grasp as his heart convulsed, and still the assassin applied excruciating pressure. He was sure the cartilage of his larynx must collapse . This was no way for the ruler of the Roman Imperium to die, in ignominy, in the thighs of a dirty native whore...

His hand groped and closed around the pugio's cool ivory hilt. He tugged at it frantically, cursing the workmanlike tight fit. And then the bolster came free. He lifted it up, carefully adjusting the grip.

The blow shattered Caesarion's unearthly silence. He screamed, the high-pitched exhalation of animal pain as Trajan drove the blade as hard as his remaining strength allowed into the thick meat of the assassin's uppermost thigh. But he wasn't content to leave it there. In the quarter of the blade adjacent to the quillon were a row of serrated teeth and Trajan yanked the knife back and forth savagely. At the ripping of flesh, Caesarion squealed again. The pressure on Trajan's throat eased and he wriggled free of the killing thighs.

The boy was doubled up clutching his ruined leg, sobbing but spitting fury. "Isis dies," he hissed. "Seth will avenge me."

"Cousin!"

Hadrian burst into the chamber. The playboy prince was gone. In an instant he took in the scene and the young soldier-courtier jumped across the room to take the dagger from Trajan's carmined hand and thrust it at Caesarion's throat.

"Hold! Don't kill him. Publius we need to find out who sent him. He wasn't acting on his own, I'm convinced."

"Isis dies! Seth rises, and I will tell you nothing, Roman pigs. This Caesarion will die rather than loosen his tongue."

"Oh, I wouldn't worry about your tongue, you lion-fodder. We'll see it loosened soon enough." With calm efficiency Hadrian held the blade threateningly at the young assassin while sweeping up Trajan's tunic. He held it for him to slip over his head while concealing the Emperor from the centurion and legionary who rushed into the bedroom, alerted by the fanatic's ranting. Attius Clemens followed his men and looked suitably horrified at the carnage.

"You certainly did make a mess of his leg," Hadrian said with imperturbable calm. He offered Trajan an arm and helped him to the stool.

"I'll be fine in a minute, once I can get my breath back." He rubbed at his sore throat and stared at his would-be killer, shouting incoherently and spitting at his captors as they dragged him off.

The expression on the camp prefect's face was one of dark fury. "Caesar, I swear by the sacred Bulls of Apis and Mithras that I will drag the truth from the wretch. How in Hades did he get in here? He goes on about Seth... it isn't the first time the name has been associated with a terrorist attack. But what is puzzling is that the other incidents also involved a man or a youth calling himself the Little Caesar, as though they were a part of a rebellious movement."

Trajan simply nodded his head and with a croaky voice said, "I shall be in your debt, good Attius Clemens, if you can get to the bottom of the mystery the boy poses, but I should look closer to home as well. Someone in this fort brought him in... hidden inside that mat. It was rolled up as if the men ordered to bring it in dumped the roll down and forgot about it. When I unrolled it... he... he sprang out and attacked me."

If Clemens thought it strange that a mere lad, and unclothed at that, could have overpowered the Emperor, he wisely kept the thought to himself. Hadrian, however, raised a carefully primped sardonic eyebrow, but he too kept silent on the matter. On the other hand he had his own plans for the late afternoon and—if his young friends scored—a very entertaining evening.

East Thebes, evening 17th day of August

Like burnished copper, the Nile resembled a lake of liquid fire under the westering sun. Palms on the other bank were stark black spiders silhouetted against the glare. Many days of watching the Egyptian sunset inured sight to its beauty. Rufio and Quintus had more interest in the curves, contours, and hard-muscled planes of their own geography. Air stale and stuffy from a day's heat made the Familia Tullii quarters below deck unappealing, which is why they preferred to tangle on a duck-down mattress tucked out of sight under the gunwale near *Cleo*'s stern. The light breeze blowing along the river cooled overheated flesh under fingers trailing delicious tickles over smooth skin. Theirs was a secluded spot at the busiest of times, but close to dusk they were the only ones abroad.

Or so they thought.

A rare moment for contemplation. Quintus ran fingers through Rufio's abundant locks, a color match for the flame-red sun kissing the trees of the western bank. Rufio sighed and waggled Quintus's semi-hard cock to and fro, slapping the top of one thigh with it, then the other. In the realms of tumescent love-lust, neither heard the faint bump of a small hull, the slithering and scuffling, suddenly suppressed; nor its resumption.

Or felt the blows.

Cato and Ashur had discovered the viewpoint three days before, a small air vent in the crawl space that looked down on the general deck near the stern. Ashur couldn't see much for the low sun's blaze in his eyes as they jostled each other for the best position to spy through the small opening. "Are they there?" He could barely suppress his eagerness.

"Ssshh… they'll hear."

"Oh yes, I see them. Just." Ashur couldn't quite choke down the giggle that bubbled up in his throat at the indistinct sight of his master in Rufio's arms, still in their tunics but rucked up. The light made it hard to see what they were up to, but in a funny way that made it all the more sexually thrilling… imagining it.

And then suddenly the quiet nook below exploded.

Dark figures leaped up over the gunwale. Cato gasped. Ashur felt the tremor run through Cato's body where they were pressed together. He heard two meaty thunks and then the shadowy creatures—three, four, five, more, hard to tell in the dusk light— swarmed over Quintus and Rufio. Fists rose and fell in a flurry flailing of arms.

Cato gasped, dug Ashur in the ribs. "We must help!"

Septimius sat back, a sense of degradation filling his soul. The occasional movements of legionaries on the barge caused its timbers to creak. Overhead a clatter of wings announced a flock of ibis taking to the sultry evening air mingled with the shingly rattle of shackles, blocks, and ropes of the small flotilla of feluccas drawn up beside the military barges. Insistent voices—soldiers and salesboys—bargained to and fro over this trinket or that.

Septimius reined in a sigh. A frumentarius was never far from the less savory aspects of military life, but he'd been a quiet chef minding his own business (literally) for some time. He'd hoped to avoid having his nose rubbed in the shit again. But then he should have refused the gentle but persuasive pressure of imperial bureaucrats to at least keep up controlling his former knot of agents in the field.

He despised the men who took pleasure in torturing their prisoners for information. He disliked the suffering while at the same time accepting its necessity. And though it sat badly, Septimius had to hand it to the two carnifexes of III Cyrenaica who accompanied the military detachment: they knew their job. The butchers had dragged out the process of questioning the former crewman and his accomplice for days but in the process obtained valuable intelligence. Everything was at last clear and the ripples of half-imagined fears that reached him at his Suburan thermopolium were now confirmed as an uncomfortable reality. The two unfortunates believed in an impossibility, or their brains—perhaps not their best feature—had been craftily taken over, filled with conviction of a cause by a clever manipulator; by that worst of all things—a deranged idealist Hades-bent on revenge.

Now he knew the truth it concerned him that Trajan was a distance away at the southern temple complex in pursuit of some religious nonsense, unaware of what they faced. After the murderous attempts on Trajan's life so far, it didn't reassure as it should that he was ensconced in an armed military camp.

The north temple's pylons glowed in the dying sun's rays, busy with priestly comings and goings in spite of the dilapidated state of the precinct. Time to return along the jetty to *Cleo* and report his findings to Servilius Vata. He was moving toward the gangway when he heard the disturbance. Long light obscured detail but he could swear several men were dragging something over the side of *Cleo*'s tall wooden walls to lower it into a felucca drawn up alongside… something, or someone. His first thought—that some felucca boys were pestering one of the tourists—vanished at the muffled cry of distress.

Had no one on board seen anything amiss? Heart hammering in his chest, Septimius bounded down the bouncing gangplank, thumped onto the jetty's stone paving, and ran at full speed toward the huge imperial bark.

A careless stomp on his ankle and a curse from the oaf who almost tripped over him shook Rufio to his senses. Something was terribly wrong. Vulcan hammered on an anvil inside his head, but he managed to haul himself up to peer over the rail. In the last glimmer of sunlight through distant foliage speckling the hull he made out the terrified face of the Empress looking back up at him. Two thugs—one with his hand gagging her—dumped Plotina unceremoniously into the bottom of a waiting felucca.

Where was Quintus? *Oh gods, they must've taken Quintus as well! And there's never a Flaccus or a cucumber-bearing Septimius around when you need one…*

Rufio staggered upright, cursed the needle being drawn through his skull and rubbed the sore spot above his left ear where whichever cursed piece of lamprey-fodder had struck him, and hauled ass toward *Cleo*'s stern. His thoughts weren't coherent, otherwise he might have considered raising the alarm, but in his addled state all he thought of were the little pleasure boats moored at the stern. Get one and chase the kidnappers.

If the blow hadn't dazed him, he might also have heard furtive movement behind. At the squared stern of the vessel an inset stairway led down to a small dock to which three small rowing boats were secured. The tourists could use them for pleasure excursions (not that anyone had—Rufio made a mental note: complain to Khepri Corporation about use of their flimsy boats in predator-infested waters). They were part of the complement of what Chamberlain Djed called crisis-craft. Well, this definitely smacked of crisis.

He unhooked the nearest boat's bow line, and leaped in. Fortunately, his momentum didn't shove the craft far enough from the dock to stop him grabbing the edge. No oars aboard. A frantic visual search located six sweeps stacked upright against the back wall just beyond the stairway. Cursing, he took two. Into the boat they went, followed by Rufio. As he pushed off a dark shape hurtled through the air at him. Rufio stifled a scream…

Cato was first out of the crawl space. He slid through the narrow hatch like an elver desperate to be born and landed on a lower step in time to catch Ashur who emerged as fast but less elegantly. From the wooden depths a rising hubbub could be heard. Cato wondered what was the cause, the attackers or the finally aroused guards, but Rufio who he'd last seen clubbed about the head must come first.

Ashur followed down the stairs and along a companionway a short distance before grasping Cato's arm.

"What!"

"Cato, we aren't armed. Don't go out there. Let's go and rouse the guard and bring them to help my master and your brother."

"No! I'm going to Rufio. You get help, but keep your eyes wide for any raiders."

"I heard men running. I hope they've gone. I'll find someone."

Cato hesitated a moment, then nodded curtly and ran on toward a doorway leading to the outer deck, feeling suddenly alone. It didn't take long to find the little love nest, but of Quintus or Rufio there was no sign. A splash out on the river caused him to peer into the dusk where he saw the triangular sail of a felucca.

The craft pulled away from the lee of *Cleo* toward the western bank. And then he discerned the pounding of feet on hollow steps, caught sight of a last flash of red hair disappearing down at the stern. Without any further thought, Cato flung himself after Rufio. He was sure he'd never make it. It was obvious: Rufio was taking one of the sport boats after the pirates, although Cato had no idea why his brother would be so foolhardy. What could they have worth the risk? His own feet pounded the deck, skidded around the corner, and virtually fell down the back steps. A boat shape edged away from the dock. He jumped the last four steps, caught balance, and leaped out across the water. As he covered the gap, he saw Rufio look up in alarm and loose a shocked cry.

"You stupid little fucker!" Rufio recovered in time to drop the oars, spread arms, and catch Cato, staggering only a little under his slight weight. "What in the wet vulva of Venus do you think you're doing!"

"What are you up to?" Cato snapped back breathlessly after his sudden sprint. "Can't let you have all the fun."

Rufio glowered. "No fun. Those bastard bandits took the Empress *and* Quintus."

"Then there's no time to argue. Let's go."

"You are not coming."

Cato gestured at the sail growing smaller in the dusk. "They're getting away."

"Shit a mud brick. All right cunny-face, sit at the back and guide me." Rufio set the oars between the thole pins on either gunwale, sat on the midway cross bench, flexed his biceps, and pulled on the oarlocks to dig the blades into the water.

"Where'd you learn to row?" Cato settled himself on the narrow transom and strained up to see over Rufio's bobbing head.

"Cassander. A Greek lad in Surrentum showed me how."

"I suppose you showed him how as well. Was he handsome?"

"Is... and mind your own business."

"Did you enjoy carnal relations—that's what Eutychus calls it."

Rufio almost lost his rhythm. "Eutychus!"

"When he's describing how Greek paedagogues lose sight of their Platonic responsibility toward their youthful charges."

"Oh. For a moment there I thought... Never mind. Where are the kidnappers?"

"Still there, but their sail's flapping."

"The wind's against them. Good. We shouldn't be too far behind. Keep an eye out for any basking crocs."

"It's getting to be night-time, Rufio, I don't think they bask in the dark."

"No, but I bet they lurk in the dark."

"Are you armed, by the way?"

"Got an eating knife—"

"Well that will be just excellent, if we're intending to eat them."

"—and my pugio, you cloth-eared twit. What about you?"

Cato tugged at the handle sticking up from his belt. "Short staff-sling." He patted a small leather wallet attached to the belt. "And some ammo."

"Clever *caligae*," Rufio sneered between pulling on the oars. "That should put terror in the bad guys' hearts."

Cato just sniffed. "I did well against that Malpensa and his gladiators in Trajan's new forum. Or have you forgotten? It was... let me see... um, eighty-one days ago, which I know is a long time. Ashur told me people tend to lose their memory when they get old."

"I thought you were supposed to be crap with numbers? And besides that fight was in daylight, this is night. How are we doing?"

The sail was a black shape against the fading orange sky. "I think they're nearly across. Hard to say. Row harder."

"Can't," Rufio gasped. "And the current's taking us north."

"They're going that way too, a bit anyway."

Rufio saved his breath for rowing. From *Cleo* the west bank didn't look so far off but out here on the water the distance seemed endless—and with the flood the river didn't end at the tree line that marked the normal bank.

"I suppose they'll want a ransom from the Emperor."

"Or worse… the Emperor's life in return. Just hope… we can do something… fuck up the plan."

Cato thought about this for a moment. His eyes were playing tricks as the sail they followed merged with the dark vegetation lining the shore, which drew closer with every oar pull. And then he lost sight of it altogether. A bleak thought sprang unhelpfully into his mind. "You know, don't you, that the people of Thebes stay well clear of the west side?"

Rufio looked up, face drawn with effort. "And why is that?"

"Quintus told me. The west bank is the Land of the Dead."

Rufio groaned. "Oh wonderful."

Behind thickets of reeds and then woods clustering along the river the verdant mile or less on the west bank threw the stars' reflection back at the heavens, for it now lay beneath a covering of floodwater. When dry it would be fine arable land to feed the populace, were it properly cultivated, but only food offerings for the dead were ever grown here. Neither Greeks nor Romans after them found any reason to interfere with ancient and powerful lemures or revenants—in Egypt the dead inhabited the land in all too corporeal form.

The inundation lapped at the desert's edge, where stood the Castles of Millions of Years, the great mortuary temples of the dynastic pharaohs. Behind these commemorative shrines lesser but still monumental tombs were cut in the cliffs of the Theban heights. The scale of the temples ensured the funeral cult of Egypt's deceased kings, their mummified remains enclosed in ornate coffins and secured inside stone sarcophagi. Only attendants enslaved to serve and perform rituals required to preserve the afterlife of their royal masters lived there; pointless rituals though, for few of the dead remained undisturbed. Even in antiquity looters robbed the tombs for the valuable grave goods. But ritual brings its own comfort, and so the slaves and lowly mortuary priests pursued the time-honored traditions of appeasing the royal dead.

There were, however, intruders in the disturbed terrain. Hidden away in a deep wadi that cut into the barren desert heights, beyond the hulking Theban Mount, many more pharaohs, their consorts, sons, daughters, their wives and husbands, viziers and nobles lay entombed in many rock-cut tombs. Here, in this desolate place devoid of even the slightest plant life, the rebels were hidden away in the longest, deepest corridor-tomb.

Its walls, pillars, and low sloping roofs adorned with an endless frieze of painted reliefs, it descended deep under the mountain. In a subterranean hall were gathered several men warming their hands around a small blaze, lit to keep the afterlife's chill at bay. Untold eons ago the tomb builders who hewed out the chamber left uncut six monumental square pillars to support the roof. These sentinels made it a cramped and oppressive space. Some men sharpened weapons, others exercised muscles grown stiff with the cold. The fire and a few smoky torches threw inhumanly elongated shadows across the painted faces of gods and kings on the walls, animating those who should be left at peace.

Some of the living were recent arrivals. Their leader stood apart, listening to the tall young man with thinning hair who called himself Caesarion.

"So here we find our cause in the Great Valley once more." The softly spoken words carried a dry sense of irony.

Desert Jackal (though no longer dressed for the part) dipped his head in regretful admission. "But we so nearly succeeded at Abydos, Lord Caesar. The boy's sacrifice would have been worth it."

"He had no misgivings?"

"None. He believed in the cause."

"A conviction no doubt helped along with healthy doses of that narcotic you advocate. We will need more than somnambulant clay in our hands to rebuild our land."

"As you say, but it helps in some cases. The devotee to our cause we smuggled into the fort, who even now brings an end to the tyrant, needed no such stimulus."

"I am the sixth of my line. I want my son to be the first of a new dynasty, one such as the Theban kings who ruled the Egyptian Empire for half a thousand years enjoyed." He paused and fixed Jackal with a steely gaze. "That is why I have too have put in hand an action to bring results."

Desert Jackal waited expectantly, though irritated. This indicated Caesarion's lack of trust in his skills. Jackal had served him for years with unswerving devotion, himself descended from a long line of men who had served the cause, but Desert Jackal was the true Egyptian here; the man he faced was tainted by his Roman bloodline.

"The Empress will be brought here shortly."

The ramifications took several seconds to sink in. "You think Trajan will cross the river to rescue his wife?"

"He is bound to. I have many mounts readied in the valley above, lookouts watching the route from opposite the fort, more in the valley to inform me of the men bringing the Empress. Trajan, will come and I have sufficient forces to prevail."

"Unless the hand of my assassin has already succeeded in removing him."

Caesarion's lips tightened to a narrow line before he spoke. "Let us call my plan an insurance in case yours fails. I still win if both succeed."

In certainty one of us will win. Jackal's expression gave nothing away."Everything is in place at Memphis and Alexandria. The Roman administration will collapse in chaos when news of the Emperor's death reaches them."

"What of that arch-spy?"

"Septimius Corbulo is with the main party, Lord. His connections in Alexandria have been taken care of. Permanently. I have severed his tendons so his legs are of no use."

"You rely too much on metaphor." A hand raked through a strand of hair, put it back in its place. "Then we are ready to act."

I am. Finally. After so many years of scraping and bowing and organizing. I am ready. "We are, Caesar. My only regret is that I have so far failed to get my hands on the two Romans who killed my brother Menes."

"Do not allow personal revenge to cloud your judgment at this crucial moment." A narrowing of the pale eyes. "Still, satisfaction can sharpen a man's appetite for victory. Is that why you display the instruments of Osiris? A divinity I'd have thought alien to your soul, but perhaps appropriate to the moment?"

A white, full-length shroud-like garment with a fabric *wesehk* collar woven around the neck clung to Desert Jackal's wiry body. On his chest, picked out in colorfully dyed woolen embroidery were the *atef*—the white crown of Upper Egypt flanked by red ostrich feathers—and below the *heka* and *nekhakha*, the shepherd's crook and flail held in disembodied green hands, the symbols of Osiris, god of the Afterlife. In this form he judged the deceased's fitness for a fruitful afterlife or an eternity of misery. The Jackal's smile more resembled that of a pleased crocodile. "I intend to judge them unfit and help them on their way to the devourer's jaws."

Caesarion stared, as if for the first time unsure of his lieutenant. "Do with them as you will… but only after we have killed Trajan and his camp followers, after we have taken the vessel that desecrates my ancestor Cleopatra's name, after we have taken these wretched tourists who would treat our sacred land as a playground. Strike off the head and the rotting corpse will fall as Egypt rises again."

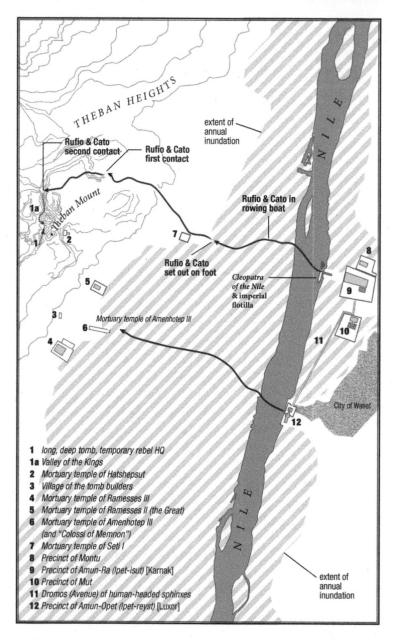

THEBAN HEIGHTS

extent of
annual
inundation

Rufio & Cato
second contact

Rufio & Cato
first contact

Theban Mount

Rufio & Cato in
rowing boat

1a

1   **2**

7

Rufio & Cato
set out on foot

*Cleopatra
of the Nile*
& imperial
flotilla

8

5

9

3

6

Mortuary temple of Amenhotep III

10

4

11

City of Waset

12

1   *long, deep tomb, temporary rebel HQ*
1a *Valley of the Kings*
2   *Mortuary temple of Hatshepsut*
3   *Village of the tomb builders*
4   *Mortuary temple of Ramesses III*
5   *Mortuary temple of Ramesses II (the Great)*
6   *Mortuary temple of Amenhotep III*
    (and "Colossi of Memnon")
7   *Mortuary temple of Seti I*
8   *Precinct of Montu*
9   *Precinct of Amun-Ra (Ipet-isut) [Karnak]*
10 *Precinct of Mut*
11 *Dromos (Avenue) of human-headed sphinxes*
12 *Precinct of Amun-Opet (Ipet-reyst) [Luxor]*

NILE

extent of
annual
inundation

East and West Thebes, night 17th day of August

Papyrus might make an excellent material on which to record the written word, Rufio reflected, but in thick sedges the reeds made a ripping sound along the small craft's hull that would alert anyone within hearing. Not helped by the family of ducks that detonated into flight, alarmed at the boat's sudden appearance in their flooded habitat. Rufio yanked the oars inboard before they were snatched from his grip by frondy plants growing as much as twelve feet above his head. One, caught on a retreating oar, swished back with sufficient force to almost topple Cato from his transom perch.

It took them an age to haul the boat through the jungle of reeds, gripping clumps of the sharp triangular stems and pulling hand over hand. Afterward, Rufio could never explain where river ended and land began, because when the boat eventually emerged into a clearer channel, moonlight revealed a wide expanse of lake stretching as far as he could see. Here and there scattered low humps of ground broke the monotony. In the far distance several flat, obviously man-made structures stood above the swamp.

"They must have come this way," Rufio whispered.

"They did."

Rufio glanced over his shoulder to where Cato pointed at a dark shape against the distant moonlit mountains, drifting slowly between drowned fruit trees. "It's heading a bit to the north." He dipped the oars again, trying to row as quietly as he could manage while still propelling them onward. The blades often found solid ground just beneath the surface. Night creatures made plopping noises among the reeds, insects chirruped and some of them bit. A more mechanical sound came across the swamp, the rattle of ropes in crude pulleys. After another while Cato hissed a low warning. Craning his neck over the boat's prow Rufio saw the felucca, its sail lowered, apparently stationary, its raised bow seen above a low hillock where grew the last of the trees and scrub before the desert. He shipped oars and used one to pole them into the muddy edge on the side of the ground away from the pirates' felucca.

The brothers stepped out into a sticky morass, which sucked at their naked feet. Rufio stifled a yelp when a slimy something wriggled up between his toes. It plopped down and squirmed off through the ooze—a mudskipper off to a safer haven.

Crouching down, he led the way to drier ground and secured the bow line to a stub of tree in the hope of needing the dinghy again. They approached through the thin copse toward the felucca with a caution that proved unnecessary. The pirates and their prisoners were gone, the felucca deserted. Rufio walked around the vessel and after only a few paces ahead of its bow the channel of water dried up altogether. On the left the ragged walls of a large temple stood out as a formless black shape against a star-strewn sky. Moonlight painted the desert floor a bone-white, against which upstanding features stood out in stark relief, as did the thin spiral of dust ahead. The quarry!

Cato cast around, gave a low whistle, and pointed at the ground where Rufio saw a disturbance of fresh footsteps and hoof marks.

"Just one animal," Rufio muttered. "A donkey for the Empress to ride on? Must have had it tied up here ready. Quintus and those dog turds are on foot, so they won't be moving fast. Come on."

"On bare feet? Stones will cut us to shreds."

"Why aren't you wearing shoes?"

"I couldn't wear anything where I was when you got clobbered and…" Cato trailed off, evidently unwilling to reveal some secret. He covered the hesitation by attacking. "And why aren't you wearing any?"

"I didn't have time to think where I'd left them."

"Of course not. You were too busy having it off with Quin—"

"Shut it! Here." Rufio removed the loincloth he'd hastily retied under his tunic before dashing off down *Cleo*'s deck and tore it into two lengths, which he wrapped around each foot.

Cato scowled and then followed suit.

Experimentally, Rufio put weight on one foot and then the other. "That should do the trick for a bit. After all, we go barefoot often enough in the summer and it can't be worse than running around the Palatine at Lupercalia."

"Last time you did that you ended up with Quintus."

Rufio gave a low chuckle. "It wasn't quite like that."

Cato's second mention of Quintus raised unhappy thoughts that he'd suppressed while struggling across the river. Quintus must have succumbed to the vicious assault as well. *Oh Quintus, I'm coming for you.*

The commandeered Praetorian mounts flew across the moon-bright plain skirting the edges of the flood between the two great Theban temples. Septimius and Quintus kept up with the Decurion in the lead. This dash to reach Trajan had been very hurriedly organized. Quintus was still in a bit of a blur as to the events that preceded it.

He remembered the love nest, the foreplay he'd been enjoying with Rufio, and then not much until…

A hard slap. His cheek burned. The force with which it was delivered threw him to the floor but had the effect of rousing him. He shook his head, groaned painfully. He looked up at the stool and the villain who had been holding him on it. An unprepossessing individual with tombstone teeth, a false grin in pockmarked skin, Quintus took an instant dislike to him. The thug reached down and dragged him back to his feet in rough hands, slammed him back down on the unyielding stool. Quintus made a mental note to complain to the Khepri Corporation: better upholstery needed on the utility seating.

A spread palm threatened another slap. "Where is she?"

"Who?" He had no idea what the idiot was asking.

"The Empress," in a guttural accented voice.

Quintus shook his head. He tried taking stock. *A throbbing head but no broken bones.* Thank the gods Rufio—*where is he?*—hadn't actually stripped him of his tunic (clothes always bolster confidence), but loincloth, sandals, and belt were missing, and with the belt his dagger. A quick glance around showed he was in the main vestibule that divided the general quarters from the imperial apartments.

"Where is she, Roman cunt-boy? Speak or watch the blood spurt from the hole where your dick used to be."

"How should I know where she is?" Quintus glared up at the ugly invader.

The pirate grabbed him by the hair, or tried to. Quintus thanked the Caecilii household gods for his military crop. Not much to hold onto. Instead the man snatched a nasty curved dagger from the sash around his waist and pressed its point to Quintus's throat. Determined to die fighting rather than be slaughtered like a farmyard hog, Quintus prepared to make his fuzzy brain work sufficiently to do something when there came a loud scrabbling behind, accompanied by curses in Latin, Egyptian, and something in gibberish.

The drapes closing off access to the imperial apartments were thrust aside. Three pirates emerged with a struggling Plotina between them. A fourth dragged along one of her terrified attendants. The Empress was scantily clothed in a long underskirt as if she'd been snatched in the middle of preparing herself for the evening's entertainment. Her attitude, as far as Quintus could see, was defiant. At least her eyes flashed dangerously and she moaned forcefully under the great paw clamped hard over her mouth.

The man standing over Quintus gave a snort of relief. "You found the bitch then Harkhaf? 'Bout time—"

"No names, Baaco, you stupid baboon," the man gagging Plotina growled. "We have to get out fast. Neb," he grunted at the third man holding Plotina, who didn't seem to be of much help. "You go help Baaco get that prick to the boat. Me and Tiy can handle this cow." He nodded his shaven head at the thug restraining Quintus. "Be like an overturned hornets' nest back there any moment."

Quintus smiled. No names… Baaco, Neb, Tiy, Harkhaf, the man in charge. I will remember… but by Jupiter where is everyone? Where are you Rufio? Got to get away. He kept eyes glued to the hilt of the weapon held to his throat. For a brief space of time its point wavered as the snatcher called Neb nipped nimbly around his fellows, ready to bind him. Quintus tracked Tiy and Harkhaf's scuffling progress with Plotina toward the Nile-side exit and the as-yet unnamed fifth pirate who followed them, the hysterical attendant gripped in his arms. Just for an eyeblink everyone's attention was distracted as they tried getting through the door without letting the struggling Empress loose. Quintus acted. He sprang up and sideways from the stool under Baaco's knife hand. Grabbed Baaco's wrist. Brought the man's arm down sharply over a raised knee. At the nasty cracking sound the kidnapper let out a howl of pain. The knife clattered to the deck.

Should I go for the blade or escape? But in the time it took Quintus to think that, Neb had swerved around Baaco to cover the escape route either into the general apartments or the dockside exit. Quintus chose a third option. He lurched forward, head-butted Baaco in the abdomen, tried wrestling his adversary to the boards. But the battering he'd taken disadvantaged him, slowed down his reflexes. Baaco swung his good fist, caught Quintus a painful blow to the side of his already woozy head. But Quintus still held onto the shattered wrist, twisted the two bones as hard as he could. Baaco howled. Quintus pushed him at Neb. As the two collided Quintus kicked the knife away with his bare foot, barely aware of the risk of cutting his toes. It skittered away from both kidnappers…

Right into the hands of Septimius. The frumentarius-turned-chef had crashed through the double swing doors from the dockside and barely paused to take in the scene. He swept up the still spinning dagger.

Seeing his danger, Neb dashed after the other kidnappers, in his haste running into No-Name trying to get through the doorway with the girl slave.

Baaco uttered an obscene oath, torn between retribution and following his comrades. The abrupt, breathless appearance of Septimius in the vestibule decided the injured kidnapper. He cursed again and took to his heels, nursing his broken wrist. No-name solved the traffic jam in the exit by twisting around oncoming Baaco and throwing the Empress's slave down. The poor girl screamed as she struck the deck. Blood spurted from a wound inflicted on her upper arm. It was a diversionary tactic, and Septimius hesitated as if to help her, but realized his first and foremost duty was to the Empress. He went to chase after the retreating brigands.

"No, Septimius," Quintus shouted, and then, "Corbulo," he yelled louder. "They'll surely kill her if you try to stop them." He didn't add that he feared for Rufio, lying out there somewhere helpless from the blow he'd taken before Quintus fell. If Septimius didn't cause a delay the raiders would surely ignore him in their haste to get away. "There has to be a better way to get her back," Quintus said, catching his breath.

Septimius paused to comfort the fallen slave girl, and they both turned at the sudden commotion made by arriving soldiery and Praetorian Guards.

The rest went in a blur. Quintus rushed out to find his loincloth, belt, and pugio, but no sign of Rufio. Aghast at his lover's possible fate, he returned to the vestibule swearing all kinds of bloody vengeance and ran into Ashur.

"We saw it, dominus, and Cato went to help you, but…

"Where is he?" Ashur shook his head miserably.

Alerted by the commotion Flaccus hurried out from the general apartments. He was horrified to hear about Rufio—he clearly didn't give a toss about Plotina's fate.

After fruitlessly berating Vata and Laevinius for leaving only a skeleton guard aboard (the rest were constructing a camp to provide some comfort after weeks cramped on barges), Septimius ordered mounts for himself and Quintus to ride with a small escort to inform Trajan and Hadrian of the desperate development.

"I'm coming too," Flaccus insisted.

"You're a flat-footed fireman," Quintus snapped back. "You've never ridden a horse."

"I can try—"

"Don't be daft."

"Stay with Lady Junilla," Septimius suggested.

"That's right. "Quintus ducked his chin forcefully; patrician taking command. "Who's going to look after Junilla when she hears about Rufio and Cato?"

Flaccus conceded the point. And they were off.

The encroaching flood meant detouring, doubling the distance between the great temples. Quintus was anxious, worried about Rufio, the Empress, and what might have happened to young Cato. What would Junilla say? What would Trajan say? A fine Mars he'd made this time. And then they were galloping down the long avenue of human-headed sphinxes. Torches inside the Roman fort cast a strange glow across Amun-Opet's tall pylons, which towered still higher into the night sky. The two obelisks were bright orange blades pointed accusingly at the moon. Seen over the fort's battlements, in the eerie underlighting the paired colossal heads of Ramesses the Great stared into Quintus's unhappy soul with serene judgment.

The town of Thebes was built close beside the southern temple of Amun-Opet. The landward side of the processional avenue of human-headed sphinxes remained above the annual flood level. A few streets extended to the river's edge beside the fort's northern wall, taking advantage of the raised bedrock on which the temple stood. At Hadrian's pressing, Cassius Quietus had been busy extracting useful information from a grizzled centurion called Nepos and Paetus, a young tribune. Both men shared similar interests to Hadrian and his companions. Now he, Titus Spurius, and Hadrian were strolling dryshod along the wider of the streets into town.

The three were in high spirits in spite of the afternoon's dramatic events. "But we were not the target of the idiot boy's murderous attack," Hadrian pointed out. "Pity he died under questioning, we might have learned something useful. Anyway, exalted rulers always run the risk of malcontents having a go now and then, while mere courtiers go unnoticed through life."

"I hardly count you as being 'mere', Publius, though hopefully not stuck up enough to disapprove of the establishment to which we're headed... or its unsubtle name," Quietus said with a giggle. "It's known as the Two Cocks.

"What's in a name, Cassius?" Hadrian said. "But I hope the boys are a touch more fragrant than the bunch you brought in from the banks of the Nile this afternoon."

Spurius gave a delicate snort of amusement. "Oh Publius, and there was me thinking you liked a bit of rough now and then."

"Indeed, Titus, and especially after saving Caesar's life, but preferably not smelling of river fish."

"Worry not." Quietus gave a jaunty hop and went on in the voice of one advertising quality wares. "Nepos and Paetus assure that in Accommodation Commodious are Boys Accommodating."

"I don't like that tribune of yours, Cassius."

Quietus screwed the corner of his mouth up and snapped his teeth snarkily. "He's not *mine*, much as I wish he would. I adore Paetus."

"After two minutes' interrogation?" Hadrian looked skeptical.

"Too effeminate," Spurius added primly.

"Only in front of you, Titus. To the men he's a blade of steel."

Spurius snickered. "And knows where to stick it, I'll bet."

"Enough, children," Hadrian admonished with a smile. "I think we may have found our love arbor." He pointed up at two large phalluses attached above an inset doorway. The extended plaster penises, painted in life-like colors, were crossed shaft-to-shaft as though sword fighting.

It turned out that grizzled Nepos and dreamboat Paetus were fairly accurate in their review of the Two Cocks. To Hadrian it was evident that the brothel's patron knew exactly who his noble customers were (Thebes wasn't so big that those who mattered wouldn't be kept informed as to the identity of Attius Clemens' guests). As a happy consequence service was swift and efficient, while diplomatically the man bowed to the convention of false names. Once he understood that his three clients were happy to share space, in fact demanded it, a well-appointed chamber was made available, furnished with many cushions and bolsters. Around three walls ran a shelf on which several phallic oil lamps burned with a pleasing perfume. Above, lewd paintings filled the walls with every manner of interesting contortions to awaken lust. Not that the three men needed such aid when the lads selected by the patron came tumbling into the chamber like three overheated puppies.

Before Quietus could say *told you so* boys and clients were naked and coiled in a bundle of limbs on the cushions. Mouths eagerly sought nipples to tongue and arouse, lithe muscle to squeeze, pert bottoms to part and lick, cocks to tease with busy fingers and hot mouths, even as servants brought pitchers of wine and goblets.

"Here's to a delightful evening of appreciation of Egypt's beauty," drawled Quietus, taking a sip. "At least these pets don't smell of the Nile," Spurius snorted.

"Eager to please and quite docile. Come, taste the wine, you yummy thing." Quietus held his goblet to his boy's lips. "Nothing like a little drink to induce full compliance…"

Hadrian smirked at his companions while absent-mindedly caressing the lad he languidly hugged against him. "This should prove a less tumultuous entertainment than our Imperator's experience this afternoon..."

Spurius spluttered and giggled in his plaything's ear. "You're going to love my tumultuous attention, aren't you, pet?" He fed glistening parted lips a little wine, then resumed his toying with the lithe limbs in his possession.

"Come here, let me devour every juicy bit of you..." Quietus enfolded his catch and eagerly proceeded to do just that.

As the older partner, Hadrian eventually ended up stretched out part on his side, shoulders propped on a cushion against the wall, his legs comfortably spread wide. A beauteous boy lay cradled in his arms, back pressed to his chest. His left arm curled around under the boy's armpit, Hadrian pinched a nipple, appreciating its wild arousal. With his other hand he walked fingers lightly down over the boy's raised hip. He toyed for a long moment with the long curving saddle of his pelvis before sliding on over the slight swell of abdomen, down to slip through crisp pubic hair. And there he found the boy's bone-hard prick. A light grip upward, he rubbed the thumb over its crown, worried gently at the knob, wet with mounting excitement and savored the lad's gasp. He gripped, fondled, and pressed its length against the boy's tummy. Hadrian's eyes, though, were soaking up the slow, languorous action working a little lower down.

The second lad, his ass raised and legs splayed sideways, was sprawled belly down between Hadrian's spread thighs. His cute head bobbed up and down as he sucked Hadrian from tip to balls. Spurius, lounging part upright, secured the young cocksucker in this position with his arms encircling the boy's waist. One set of fingers were buried deep in the boy's spread cleft, rubbing at the tight little sphincter ring, the other hand he had tucked underneath the boy's light body where he stroked the stiff cock trapped in soft cushions.

"Well done, Titus. You certainly know how to ply a youthful, peachy ass…"

"You know I can't resist boy flesh… give me a young thing and I'll make him mine—mindless with lust. After all, that's what they're for."

Quietus, crouched somewhere behind Spurius, had his boy on his knees, face to face, kissing him ardently, stroking his pretty head with one hand, the other working his cock hard, the youth completely in his thrall.

From outside the chamber came faint strains of music, a lyre player with plaintive voice singing love songs. Inside, passions swelled as blood heated up. Fingers, eager, hungry, caressed skin damp with lust-sweat, pinched nubs of nipple, mouths lapped at cocks vibrating with erotic urgency, suckled tender balls, explored the valley of Venus, licked, tongue-speared, and prepared. The rhythm of breathy moans and slurps of sexual excitement drowned out the distant chant as helpless nubile flesh gave way to demanding penetration.

Hadrian rolled his boy sideways and fucked him spoonwise. Spurius and Quietus (who frequently competed to see who of them

was the quickest to come or the last to come, the first to bring off whatever boy they were screwing or to give him the most orgasms) had their lads flank to flank, one on his knees, the other legs up on his back, kneeling with hands clutching hips and thighs, fucking like mindless dogs.

And then another sound intruded, alien in the circumstance, but sadly all too familiar. Hadrian grunted, sped up his rhythm and shot deep into his boy. He had expended his aftershots before the distant cornu finished its call of alarm.

"What the fuck…?" Quietus cocked an ear in the direction of the fort. He pulled out of his boy's asshole and rapidly stroked himself to shoot over his back.

Spurius followed suit, but fell between his lad's splayed legs and thrust three times into the boy's gaping mouth, shot a good load of cum into the waiting throat. "Something's up," he croaked.

Hands, so busy with peachy flesh moments before, raked through sweaty hair, a quick tidying up before donning wildly discarded clothes.

"What in the name of Cybele's cunt is going on?" Hadrian wondered. "Not another assassination attempt I hope to the gods. I better get back fast. You two settle up."

And with that he was gone.

"Did you bring any coins?" Spurius asked.

Quietus shook his head. "I thought you had."

"You arranged this, you piece of turtle turd."

The two youths glared daggers, and then Quietus broke into laughter. "Turtle turd… that the best you can come up with? Come on. The man will have to take an IOU."

S·E·V·E·N·T·E·E·N | XVII

East and West Thebes, 17th and 18th days of August

The sharply delineated landscape lay still. No sand stirred in the breathless night. Even nocturnal creatures hunkered down as if aware of danger abroad. Small discontinuities in the monochrome world shifted and then coalesced. Two figures materialized. Treading carefully for silence and to preserve his makeshift footwear, already fraying, Rufio led the way. Had he known of Hadrian's humping frolics across the river, he would undoubtedly have preferred to be there than where he was. Providentially, since he didn't know, he could concentrate on rescuing the Empress Plotina and Quintus from the raiders who had snatched them.

The lighter sand freshly churned by the kidnappers made tracking them easy until the trail petered out at a well-worn path. Rufio shrugged at Cato. "Must have taken this way up into the hills."

They both peered up at the jagged terrain ahead, stark in the moon's silvery radiance. The track climbed steadily into a shallow wadi between rocky outcrops and mysterious heaps of smaller stones scattered randomly across the desert. Rufio hitched his right shoulder in a wagons-roll gesture and they set out. He began to feel itchy as the walls of the valley narrowed and the way grew more precipitous. They were exposed to watchers in the bright light. He reckoned they had walked the better part of two miles since leaving the boat when from ahead something dislodged a small rock. Its rattle echoed off the cliffs.

Both boys froze. Rufio signaled Cato to get behind him. He eased his pugio slowly so it wouldn't hiss as the blade pulled through the scabbard's throat. When no other noise disturbed the night he pressed on cautiously toward the first twist in the trail, a sharp bend to the right in what was now a steep-sided V of rugged cliffs. Cato's padded footfalls following barely registered. A promontory of rock larger than a Roman townhouse jutted out ahead. Deep shadow hid much detail of the facing side. When Rufio reached the rock's moon-cast shadow an apparition sprang up, suddenly limned by the moon's light but its face in shadow. A human growl assured Rufio this was no desert djin.

Instinct took over. He went into a crouch, blade held out in front. The man confronting him waved a dagger. A longer weapon would have given Rufio pause, but to a graduate of the school of Aventine Foxes sorting a man armed with a short blade should be no problem. The bastard was left-handed, which meant they were point-to-point. He'd have to watch out for feints aimed at his left.

His opponent gave a hollow laugh, shuffled feet in preparation, but Rufio sensed reluctance; was it that he was uncomfortable as a left-handed fighter? Rufio suddenly darted forward two steps, went into a low threatening crouch, face tipped up. His adversary gasped.

"You! You was on the boat. Thought I'd a-killed you."

The man held slightly higher ground and before Rufio could make any response, he advanced, knife held high.

"Duck!" Cato cried out, startling Rufio and their enemy who couldn't have seen the smaller adversary hidden in Rufio's shadow.

Obedient, Rufio dropped to the ground, heard the whirr low over his head, heard a sickening thump as the pebble connected with the kidnapper's temple. At the shock of the impact his arms shuddered, his legs wobbled, and in a disconnected way down he went, poleaxed. The slingshot stone ricocheted with a sharp zing off the rocky outcrop behind.

"I had him. Easy," Rufio complained, straightening up, arms spread wide in annoyance.

"Why didn't you take him, then?" Cato calmly rewound the cords of his sling around the short staff and tucked it back in his belt.

"I would have, if you hadn't yelled out. Anyway…" He went to examine the fallen man. "Hello, what's this?" He bent over the prone form and picked up the man's right hand. "Wrist's broken. Serves him right. He must be the one who struck me. Must have thought he killed me."

"Is he dead?" Cato sounded uncertain, though it wasn't the first time his sling skills carried a man to the banks of the River Styx.

"Is the pontifex maximus religious?" Rufio pointed to the caved in cranium. "Not bad at such short range."

"It's the staff. Adds a lot of velocity. Not much good at distant targets though. Ma wouldn't let me bring my long sling."

"I'm sure there are many innocent winged creatures of the Nile will thank her. Well, that's one less to deal with. They can't be far ahead with two prisoners to slow them down. I'm guessing the valley swings right around to our left farther up. I reckon if we take to the cliffs we could cut across the bend and get ahead."

"How do you know it goes that way?"

Rufio shrugged. "I just feel it does. Septimius said that above the temples on the plain there is a valley where many ancient rulers are buried. And something Quintus said about the pharaohs wanting to be buried under pyramids, but the stone here is all wrong for building such monuments, so there aren't any… except that one." He pointed over his left shoulder at the mountain rearing up.

Cato looked up at its worn triangular face painted black and white by the moon. He nodded. "It *is* shaped like a pyramid."

"So let's get going." He replaced the pugio in its scabbard and stripped the fallen brute of his blade, which he tucked in his belt, adjusting the point to avoid it stabbing him. Then they set off up a narrow, stony path that he hoped would cut across the shoulder of the mountain.

"By the blood of Jesus, it's Boudica to the life!" Primus Pilus Centurion Aurelius Verecundinus gave away not only his age (sixty-three), but also his adherence to the troublesome Christian sect. In any other circumstances the hardened career soldier would have kept his faith strictly to himself for fear of persecution (the heretics denied the Emperor's divinity, which was treasonable), but the astonishing sight of Lady Junilla Rufia in full military armor shocked the veteran to the core. As any who would listen knew, as an unkind present for his sixteenth birthday Verecundinus was drafted and whisked to Britain to help refill the ranks of Legio IX Hispana, decimated by Boudica's rebellious Iceni tribesmen. He saw service immediately in the final battle against the terrifying warrior-queen. "Dressed for the occasion as a Roman officer, she was, exhorting her troops from her war chariot, daughters at her side…"

On receiving the news that raiders had abducted her eldest son along with the Empress, and a search of *Cleo* had so far failed to locate her youngest ("Up to no good somewhere, no doubt. Eutychus better know or I'll serve his balls up to him…"), Flaccus

expected Junilla to dissolve into distressed tears. Which revealed a shocking lapse in judgment. In less time than Flaccus could say *Jumping Janus takes it both ways* his part-time boss annexed a complete set of centurion's *lorica segmenta* body armor, leggings, tunic, greaves, shoulder belt, gladius, and transverse-plume helmet. In less time than Flaccus could say *Julius Caesar buggered Mark Antony* she marched into the pursers' offices, took command of *Cleopatra of the Nile*, ordered the few Praetorian Guards on duty to draw weapons and prepare to repel any further raids, bellowed for Servilius Vata and "Pinny" (as she knew Septimius called Pinius Laevinius) to attend her, and got them sorted.

Vata was to take all his men except those Junilla had deputed to the boat's protection and follow Quintus and Septimius to join the Emperor. "And make sure whatever is decided, Caesar does not cross the river in pursuit and put himself in danger. Understood!"

Quite abashed by Junilla's force, Vata acquiesced immediately and rushed off to prepare his men. She turned on Laevinius. "Pinny, I want one of the barges, with a cavalry detachment readied immediately to cross the river here. We'll pick up the kidnappers' trail and chase them down."

Laevinius frowned, either at her use of the unfortunate diminutive or at her as dominatrix, perhaps at both. "But my Lady, the barges are not powered—"

"Then, my dear Pinny," she said with dangerous calm, "grab some of *Cleo*'s oarsmen."

It was Flaccus who dared point out that the barges were not designed for rowing. Laevinus gave him a grateful smile, which he turned back on Junilla. Big mistake.

"My very dearest *Pinniest. We* won't row, then. Get some of your men off their fat asses and 'persuade' all those useless fornicating felucca fellows down there to get rowing and tow us over. Now!"

Attius Clemens held a hurriedly whispered conference with his senior officers and then returned to where Trajan paced up and down between the two great obelisks standing before the temple pylon as if the tall stone spires marked the limit of his marching.

When Quintus and Septimius had ridden in with their small escort, Trajan was ensconced with the camp prefect and three of Thebes' most senior priests of Amun-Ra finalizing details for the Opet ceremonies as though there wasn't a care in the world—which astonished him on learning of the foiled assassination. The religious preparations went out the window, however, at the news of Plotina's kidnap.

Now Quintus watched anxiously, attempting to gauge the Emperor's temper. Other than the walking up and down he seemed outwardly calm in spite of the earlier attempt on his life—which on hearing of it only convinced Septimius that matters were coming to a head. Even as Septimius began expounding to Trajan the unfortunate events on *Cleopatra of the Nile* and what he had learned from the two captured spies, the fort came alive. Many more torches flared into life, centurions and optios strode about yelling orders, cornicerns sounded the call to arms.

"From what we gleaned, the man on board *Cleo* infiltrated the Khepri Corporation's operations at some point as we progressed from Alexandria toward Sais, Caesar," Septimius explained. "That means he was established well before we all came on board."

"To what purpose?"

"To pass on at every halt any Intelligence about the composition of the court and our military force he could gather. This he communicated to contacts on dry land when he was able. One such agent came on board at Abydos. With the previous failures of the rebels' plans the stowaway spy was ordered to liaise with the boarders who attacked us. Sadly, his previous detention did not prevent the primary objective of the raid, the kidnap of the Empress. The better news is that it prevented the raiders killing anyone, since without inside help from their man they wasted too much time in finding the Empress to do any more damage."

"But who in the name of all the gods is behind this?"

Quintus took a deep breath. He had gathered most of the amazing plot from Septimius on the way over, but a headlong gallop wasn't the best time to take it all in or analyze the consequences.

Septimius bowed his head a fraction. "Hard to believe, Caesar, but the name I have is…Ptolemy Caesarion."

In the sudden astonished silence, Hadrian burst in through the fort's gates. "I heard the alarm. Are we under attack?"

Trajan turned to his cousin, face expressionless. "In a manner of speaking, Publius. Caesarion?" he muttered, turning back to Septimius. "Whoever he is, he uses the name as some kind of rally cry, a name from the past."

"Caesar, it seems not," Quintus broke in. "From what Septimius gathered—"

"Once the spy cracked he told us everything," Septimius finished. "He so firmly believed in his lord's victory, he actually boasted of it." Septimius nodded at Quintus to continue.

"They claim that—contrary to the record and everything we

have held to be the truth—Divine Augustus did not have the boy Caesarion executed. He escaped the conqueror's clutches, fled to the desert, and eventually founded a movement devoted to ridding Egypt of Roman rule. For scores of years and several generations, from father to son, the movement has swelled, grown in power and reach until today. It is Caesarion, the sixth of his name, and Ptolemy the twenty-first of his name, who we face now."

Trajan looked perplexed for a moment. "Then what was all that nonsense about Isis dying and Seth rising?"

"A smokescreen," Septimius assured. "Seth represents the Egyptian desert, where this so-called Caesarion dwells. Seth also commands storms, and we are certainly embroiled in a storm of unrest."

"Seth is also god of chaos, Caesar," Quintus added.

"And that is what this upstart wants." Septimius spread his arms wide. "In our disarray he seeks to seize whatever advantage he can. The spies said he claims direct descent from the Divine Julius Caesar, and as such is the rightful ruler of Egypt, Libya, Canaan, Palestine, and Syria—all Alexander's oriental conquests... so he claims, Imperator."

Quintus noted the shift of title. Septimius evidently felt it tactless to call Trajan Caesar and gave him the much higher honorific. It wasn't lost on Trajan, who managed the tiniest of tight smiles. His eyes, however, dark in the low light, took on a grim definition. He swung around to Clemens.

"How quickly can we mount an expedition across the river?"

The prefect grunted. "Some hours yet, Caesar. It will take time to muster sufficient transport, and then get men and mounts aboard. Besides, the damned flood makes navigation difficult, almost impossible in the dark."

"Do what you can. I shall lead a small force across at once... what is this?"

In a clattering of hooves on stone, Servilius Vata arrived with a body of mounted Praetorian Guards. Vata slid from his horse before it had fully halted. "Caesar! We are here to aid in any way we can." He glanced at Hadrian, as if surprised to see him there, standing idly by.

"Good Vata, well met. Bring ten men, their horses, and come with me. Clemens, find us two boats. In a small force we can be across and chasing before this fake pretender to Egypt knows we're on his trail. Hadrian, get our horses—where are those damned fornicating friends of yours?"

Quintus thought Hadrian looked a bit shifty.

"Er... busy, Marcus... Caesar. We won't need them."

Vata intervened, placing himself between Trajan and Hadrian. "Caesar, I must beg you not to go across the river. Leave that to us. You must not risk putting yourself into danger."

When Trajan made to argue, the Praetorian Prefect raised a peremptory hand. "Caesar, I beg you. The Lady Junilla ordered me to say to you that she knows how you must feel for she herself suffered the abduction of her youngest son by the criminal Malpensa. Now she faces the dreadful fact that her son Rufio and perhaps Cato, for we can't find him, have almost certainly been taken by the pirates along with your wife. Yet Lady Junilla commands me to make you stay here and wait until we are certain of the enemy's intentions.

Quintus was sure he caught a twitch of Trajan's lip at hearing of Junilla ordering about the Prefect.

Vata squared his shoulder. "I will take ten of the Guard across now, that we may be ready to act in any capacity the situation demands."

"I wasn't told of Tullius Cato's kidnap in Rome," Trajan said, turning an enquiring glance on Quintus.

"It is so, Caesar. Cato was taken then, but we got him back unharmed. Now I fear for his and Rufio's lives."

"Junilla is never wrong," Trajan said quietly to Hadrian. "We shall wait here, at least until daybreak, by which time," he added with a raised voice, "I expect to see the western bank swarming with Guards and legionaries." He nodded curtly and then leaned close to

Quintus and spoke in a low voice. "I can see you are disturbed about Rufio. You're already mounted. Will you go with Vata?"

"Oh yes, please, Caes—"

"Go then."

"I'm coming too." Septimius took Quintus by the upper arm and led him away to where their horses, painting misty torchlit breaths in the night air, waited under blankets thrown over them. "We can cross with Vata and then split off. The Guards will trample around and scare any sentries to ground. They'll still be riding in circles when the sun comes up. Stick with me. I know this ground from my time stationed here. We'll find out what's really going on."

It was a half-mile of tortuous walking to cut across the elbow of the wadi. They came down a series of twisting paths no wider than a footstep, worn into the steep sloping cliff by thousands of laborers' feet a hundred-hundred years ago. The moon was now lower in the starry sky and longer shadows made a confused jumble of the unforgiving and barren landscape. Sound carried well at night in the desert so Rufio heard footfalls and hooves long before the caravan hove into view, carefully following the winding track along the still rising valley.

Rufio crouched behind a boulder, Cato at his side. "As I thought, they have the Empress on a mule. But I can't see Quintus." He turned an anxious face to Cato. "Gods, the bastards must have killed him."

"You don't know that. Perhaps he got away."

"They will pay." Rufio gritted his teeth. His eyes flashed in bitter anger.

"I can see better now. Definitely no Quintus. There are four."

"Not too many."

"Cocky! What do we do?"

"The man they left behind hasn't caught up with them—"

"Since I brained him."

"—so they haven't a clue we're here ahead of them. Surprise is on our side." Rufio considered options as the pirates and their captive slowly drew near. They would pass right below. "Can you hit the fucker in front with that thing? The one leading the mule."

"Is Jupiter greatest and best?"

Rufio almost felt his brother's grin. "Now who's being cocky? Just try and knock him out. The second he's down, we both charge and jump two of them. I'll take the one this side of the mule, you go for the one at the back. And Cato…" He turned to face his brother squarely. "Whatever happens, get the Empress away, fast as you can, back down to the boat. Got that?"

"What if you need a hand?"

"No, get the Empress away. Don't worry about me. Ready?" Cato bit his lip, but nodded briskly. He hefted his sling and carefully selected a big river-smoothed pebble from his pouch. Rufio silently drew the sword he'd taken from the pirate. In his left fist he brandished his pugio. "I'll get down lower. You stay here to take your shot. Wait for my signal. Loose and then join me as quick as you can." He crawled down the gritty incline toward where it ended in an abrupt line above a ten-foot straight drop to the pathway. The enemy approached, not seemingly bothered about the noise they were making.

He waited.

They came closer. Thirty paces away. Twenty. He could hear the mule's snorting. Plotina looked bowed over. "Horned Cernunnos," he prayed under his breath to the Celtic god, "make her alert enough to escape with us."

Ten feet.

The man leading the mule must surely spot him in an instant, even in his shadowed position. He circled a hand above his head, made a let-fly gesture. In answer, a low whirring buzz filled the air. He felt the missile's breath almost part his hair. A heartbeat later the stone struck the front man. It made a sickeningly wet thunk. Rufio saw bits of his head fly apart from the impact, shards of splintered bone silhouetted against the moon-drenched cliff rising on the other side of the wadi. Rufio didn't wait. He hopped the last two feet to the edge and hurled himself at the man walking on the nearside of the mule, sword held at the thrust, pugio at port. He landed square, knees bent to absorb the shock, four paces from his target.

The unintended consequence of this sudden assault was that Plotina put the man walking on the other side of the mule out of action. The pirates had seated her sidesaddle, legs over the mule's left flank, with hands bound in her lap. At the sudden commotion she reared up, lost her balance, and fell backward off the animal just as Rufio recovered from his leap. As she went over with a muffled cry of outrage, her legs flew up in counterpoint and the heel of one sandal smacked Rufio's man a sharp blow to the head. Then she fell flat on the third man, who went down under the unexpected weight and broke her fall.

The man struck by Plotina's heel staggered right onto Rufio's sword thrust. He doubled up, went down with a pained shout. Not waiting for any recovery, Rufio buried the pugio hilt in his shoulder. The blade plunged deep under the collarbone.

In the next instant a flying dervish hurtled down the final slope and jumped on the rearguard. Cato used his sling as a short-arm cosh, its pouch loaded with a big stone. The rearmost kidnapper had the slight advantage of seeing two of his fellows go down and the third disappear under a flurry of Plotina's billowing palla. He was quick to react and ducked under Cato's swing. Seeing his brother's danger, Rufio wrenched his dagger free of his opponent and pulled the sword blade from the man's side, kicked him hard under the chin for good measure (with a yelp of pain—he'd forgotten he wore no footwear other than the ragged loincloth), and swung around to assault the fourth man. The pirate had managed to throw lightweight Cato to the ground and was about to stomp on him when Rufio slammed into him.

They both fell to the hard ground, rolling round and round each other, grappling to avoid blades and gain advantage. The wrestlers fetched up against Plotina and the blackguard she had pinned beneath her. The mule stepped daintily over the human tangle and trotted to the side where it stood patiently waiting the outcome.

Rufio and his opponent struggled, hot breaths blowing up puffs of gritty sand from the wadi floor. Rufio cracked the other's knife hand down and used the leverage he gained to try and pull him upright. This worked only in part, but it presented Plotina with an opportunity to use her wrist-bound arms as a cudgel and she smashed her curled fists in a mighty roundhouse to the side of the kidnapper's head. He slumped back, half-senseless.

Before she could pull back, Rufio reached over the dazed enemy and grabbed her hands. "My lady, let me..." He used the pugio's razor-sharp blade to sever the binding.

The moment her hands were loose Plotina pulled the dirty cloth they'd used to gag her away. Her earnest eyes went wide. "Who?"

"Tullius Rufio, Junilla's son. Go, Lady! Go now with my brother, there. I'll be right behind." He pointed the dagger at Cato.

Plotina frowned in perplexity. "He's a child," she hissed.

From somewhere Rufio dragged up a pale grin. "Actually, he's a brat."

She watched Cato rise from his knees to a wary stance, then glanced back at Rufio and nodded her understanding. She stood and gathered the underskirt about her in some haste. She jumped over Rufio and the downed kidnapper. Rufio watched anxiously to see them get away, Cato bounding down the slope, the Empress, palla gathered to her waist, close behind.

A sudden weight bore him to the ground again in a flurry of blows. The pirate who had fortuitously broken Plotina's fall, freed of her weight when she attacked the man wrestling Rufio, had recovered his wind. He was a big, heavy fellow and laid about Rufio with meaty fists, who fought back with every ounce of ferocity he could summon up to give his brother and the Empress the best chance of escape. The last he saw of Cato was a disembodied face, painted white by the low moon, glancing back fearfully as he disappeared over the slope of the valley. Rufio urged him on.

The man the Empress had momentarily stunned shook his head and joined his fellow in subduing Rufio. Three more rebels appeared as if from nowhere. The fight was over. In a trice they had Rufio pinioned tightly and were dragging him farther up the valley. The mule followed obediently, leaving two pirates dying or probably dead behind them.

"Oh ho you hellhound, you're going to pay dearly for this," one of the newcomers spat in Rufio's ear. The valley widened out under the towering pyramid of the Theban Mount into a natural flat arena. To see that he'd been correct about the angle of the wadi and its geographical relationship to the mountain above offered little comfort. To left and right subsidiary wadis led off into dead-ends under sharply rising cliffs. His captors hauled him off into one that led away up a slope to the left. At a hundred hard-fought paces the two thugs restraining him hauled Rufio toward a dark jagged hole opened up at the base of the right-hand cliff face. As he was frogmarched down some rough steps that looked to have been recently hacked out of the scree, he saw horses milling around a picket line farther up the slope.

What at first sight looked like a cave turned out to be something quite different. On reaching the base of the crude steps Rufio passed piles of fresh rubble, small and larger rocks that must have covered up the entrance of a man-made entrance, its sides and top cut to form a monumental doorway...

...a doorway to what?

Faint glimmers of torchlight revealed a rock-cut corridor descending at a shallow angle. They passed under the intricately carved lintel and down six steps into an antechamber with a rising roof. Brightly colored paintings covered everything except the floor. Serried ranks of pictures executed in minute detail and brilliant colors marched along the walls depicting numerous male figures hauling ropes interspersed by weird half-human, half-animal figures seated on thrones. The two men gripping his arms shoved him to the edge of a giant stairway. Rufio shuddered at the sight. It descended steeply into a dimness that the torches burning at the top could not dispel, a stairway surely passing through the throat of Hades itself.

"Seth waits," growled one of the thugs. "He doesn't like irrumating discards of trash who get in the way of his plans, and he eats Roman rubbish like you for breakfast."

"Yum, yum," said another.

E·I·G·H·T·E·E·N | XVIII

East and West Thebes, 18th day of August

"I feel like a boy tonight."

Ashur felt Flaccus growl hotly in his ear, felt the bulk of the man press against his back. Anxious and frustrated at being left behind on *Cleo* while others mounted rescue attempts on the other bank of the Nile, they were holed up in master Quintus's cabin. Flaccus had exhausted the stream of filthy swear words with which he'd vented his impotent anger, and Ashur had swallowed his choking anxiety over Cato and Rufio and the Empress and Quintus and… well, everything. He was quieted enough to take in the vigilis's intent. The man's hot breath on his ear was oddly soothing. Flaccus had a rough charm, quite unlike Quintus… or cheeky Rufio. He was uncouth but also dependable in a sort of bumbling, bungling way— which was not to say that the man was uncomely, Ashur thought. He'd heard Flaccus boast before that his regular regimen of exercise at the baths gave him a figure that frequently drew admiring glances from women in the street. Indeed, he was a well-built hunk in his twenty-eighth year, somewhat older than Ashur was accustomed to but…

When the big hands came to rest on his backside and gently caressed, Ashur allowed himself to slump against the comforting bulk of Flaccus's strong torso. When callused fingers probed inside his loincloth to lightly tease his cleft he couldn't stifle a gasp of guilty surrender.

"Oh, master…" a whisper, "…forgive me—"

Flaccus wasn't quite sure when it happened, this gradual awakening of interest, but he had taken a liking to Quintus's body slave. Sexy, boyish, likeable, totally fuckable, and patently utterly devoted to his master. Now, thrown together by circumstance, he couldn't help himself: he needed the Syrian boy's smooth body, craved hot sex to soothe his pent-up rage, wanted the simple comfort of pleasuring a naked lad, and the release it promised. "You delicious thing… let me make passionate love to you. I'll arouse you, make you wriggle and squirm…"

A little gasp rewarded his gentle nibble of an ear. An expert tug, and the lightweight loincloth dropped to the slave boy's naked feet.

The firm grip of his hands pulled the tunic up past the belt to bare the boy to his nipples and then gently eased it over the head to girdle upper back and shoulders.

"Little Ashur…" He felt like kissing the inviting mouth, so he did, the rapt face cupped in his palm upturned against his broad shoulder. His tongue probed deep, and while he ravished the lad he eased the tunic down and free of his trapped upper arms. Ashur was his.

He scooped the boy up and, cradled in his arms, lowered him onto Quintus's bed. Drinking in the enticing nude beauty lying there vulnerable with inviting bobbing erection, Flaccus quickly stripped and eased himself down next to his prize. Ashur's big brown eyes begged for tenderness, so his caressing fingers on the lad's face were considerate, his lips and tongue on his nipples delicate. He was rewarded with a sob of arousal and youthful fingers tentative on his shoulder inviting him in.

He couldn't help himself… he leaned up and resumed kissing the gorgeous mouth… *an unmanly thing to do to a boy, but so arousing!* He felt ripples of passion course through Ashur's flesh, fingers in his hair pulling him in, the responsive tongue playing with his, the two of them melding into ardent coupling. He enfolded the pliant body, stroked smooth flank, thigh, firm buttock, savored the boy's gasps hot in his mouth.

When his fingers brushed the tender balls in a teasing circular motion, Ashur convulsed and loosed an audible gasp of abandon, opened his thigh to further touch—and Flaccus was unleashed. He rolled onto the slight body and set about devouring all that was on offer with eager mouth and fingers. He licked and nibbled erect nipples, lean tummy, twitching belly button, even as he caressed and probed every warm intimate delight with his fingers. His lips and tongue finally reached the boy's rigid cock, licked and gobbled it to pleasing effect: a shuddering thigh enfolded his head, a salty squirt of pre-cum flavored his palate to set his own hard-on quivering for action. He growled pleasure in a thrilling bass tone…

…which set every youthful sinew in Ashur vibrating.

"Uhhh! Ahhh!" He moaned, awhirl with quivering, floundering abandon… helplessly in Flaccus's power as the vigilis exquisitely tormented his squirming body. Burly hands manipulated his limbs and he gasped when he felt his balls mouthed and sucked, his vulnerable hole tickled and rubbed. He barely took in being flipped on his tummy until slick lips and cruel tongue opened him up to liquid fire. He was barely aware of his rump being hoisted up, all was just swirling arousal deep inside his—

"Eeehh!" He spasmed as hot, solid meat invaded him, remorselessly stretched him, filled him. He nearly fainted at the searing surge of pleasure, heard himself groan and blubber as the intruder began pumping in and out. His waist was in Flaccus's grip and his back and shoulders were kissed and nipped while he melted into being fucked silly, all his senses lost to carnal abandon…

And then, a big thump in his guts, a hard gush and another, grunting, and fingers twisting his aching hard-on back and up and mashing his balls, a slithery voiding of his insides—and a mouth gobbling him as he shuddered to painful orgasm, again and again!

O Domine, Quintus, sorry, sorry... I betrayed you! Do you realize what it is to be a slave... what's a boy supposed to do? On the other hand...

Flaccus was whispering in his ear. "Cutie pie. You're quite the fuck..."

Yes, he was feeling much less anxious now...

A nibble on his earlobe. "I'm still pent-up, angry, though..."

Calloused hands gripped his shoulders and flipped him over, and Ashur saw the glint in Flaccus's eyes as he moved in for a kiss.

Sorry, dominus...

The moon dipped close to the serrated black knife-edge of the Theban highlands. Cato had to admit to some admiration for his charge. Empress Pompeia Plotina was proving to be a tougher bird than he'd have imagined possible. When her long skirt held her back, clambering around rocks and dropping down sharp ledges, she gathered up the hem and tugged, tugged again, and shredded a seam. Quickly, she ripped the fabric all around and then wrapped the torn off excess about her neck.

"Waste not, want not, my mother always said. You never know when it might come in useful. What?" she demanded imperiously at Cato's surprised stare. "You think because of my station I can't be practical."

"I— I thought you might be a bit shook up, and all, after, you know."

"Huh! It takes a bit more than a bunch of lumpen thugs to frighten a citizen of Nemausus. That's my home city," she added on seeing his incomprehension. "What's your name, child?"

Cato sniffed at the diminutive and straightened his shoulders. "Junius Tullius Cato, at your service."

"Ah, Lady Junilla's. Yes."

Cato had no clue as to how to address an Empress, so he ducked his head, and then jerked it sideways. "We must make haste, er… Lady."

He set off at a fair pace, at least as fast as his improvised footwear allowed, and Plotina managed to keep up. In the fading moonlight he saw the bend in the track where the turd with the broken wrist had jumped out, the large outcrop above still bathed in a weak silvery radiance. As they approached, now almost slithering down the slope, a thrill of sheer terror coursed through Cato's veins.

As it came into sight the man's corpse moved in the shadows and rose up. To her credit, the Empress's shriek was a thin indrawn breath; to his, Cato slammed a hand across his mouth. "A lemur," he croaked in horror and his blood ran like ice. The humped shade stood like a weird Egyptian man-beast. "R-r-run lady! It's the pirate we killed come to take his revenge."

And then the dreadful wraith roared, took steps forward on four legs, and a desert lion came into the open moonlight and roared again. Cato saw blood mixed with saliva dripping from its maw and he shuddered on realization that the terrible beast had been feasting.

The lion crouched, tail flicking.

Cato came alive. He'd promised Rufio to get the Empress to safety, and that's what he would do. By instinct he fitted a stone in the pouch of his sling and began whirling it around his head. The light was against him and made the aim difficult. The beast crouched lower on powerful front paws, lashed its tail, and sprang. Cato loosed. The missile flew true but with a feline fluidity, the creature's action moved against the trajectory so the stone only glanced off its shoulder and did nothing to halt the attack.

A thumb in its eye isn't going to work here…

Cato prayed to whichever god would listen. Sinew, thew, and monstrous muscle bunched behind slavering jaws lined with teeth glistening in the fading light powered toward him. He closed his eyes.

He heard the dreadful crushing sound, flesh, blood, and bone; an agonized howl, followed by the noise of a heavy carpet crashing to the dusty ground.

Cato opened his eyes.

As Mistress Moon sank below the mountainous distance it cast a slight glint in the lion's dulling eye; the other was part of the mess that had been its head. Cato blinked, shook his head, looked up. High above, he could just make out the form of the Empress, standing legs akimbo on top of the outcrop of rock. She held the torn off hem of her dress stretched between her hands.

"Told you it might come in useful. That boulder would have torn my nails to bits without it."

Cato said nothing as he glanced back at the dead lion, its head a pulpy mess, and the great rock that had been dropped on it, now rolled slightly to one side. Behind, the part-eaten corpse of the pirate remained unmoving—no lemur, just dead, as he and Rufio had left him.

A rattle of small stones announced the Empress's return to the track. Cato watched in silent amazement as she strode to the leonine corpse and gave its long flank a kick with a court shoe that, Cato thought, probably looked very elegant when she slipped it on. Now it more resembled a legionary's battered *caliga*. She turned to him. "Well then, we'd better get on. Which way?"

Cato recovered himself, swallowed, and made to pass her by to lead, but she arrested him with an imperious hand. For a moment Cato stood in puzzled indecision. Then a slow smile crept across his face—something he tried to avoid because his habitual scowl looked so much more grown up—and they gripped arms in the traditional male greeting.

"That was a fine shot, not your fault the beast wobbled out of line at the last. So, Cato, my young hero, we make a good team. I see you inherit your mother's fiery personality. I find her... *attitude* inspiring. The way she tackled that wretched asp in Alexandria; I have since aspired to be as direct. You must call me Plotina... though perhaps best not when we are in formal company. But in future I shall make a point of greeting you whenever our paths cross, which I think will be often. Lead on."

It was too late for recriminations. "You could not have done a thing to save us when disaster struck," Quintus whispered to Septimius as he tried to ease the rasp of the coarse rope cutting at his wrists. For one thing, the frumentarius had been correct about the few mounted Praetorian Guards Vata transported over, blundering around in the dark. Their torches cast no useful light in the vast, waterlogged open plain and served only to give away their position to anyone watching. Which as it turned out the enemy had been.

At the first opportunity after landing from the transport and walking the horses through the marshy flood edging the desert plain, Septimius had told Quintus to slip away with him into the night. "My contact in Alexandria told me to find a certain man in Abydos, a Roman who plies his trade across the desert between there and Hermonthis, a few miles south of us here. He's lived in this land all his life and is unafraid of the dangerous crossing, which takes him close by this ancient necropolis. He told me of a valley in the hills up there where many pharaohs were entombed in vast caverns. The entrances have been lost over the ages, but he'd heard rumors that one of these tombs is in use. Few he knew would speak of it. Too frightened.

"I myself have been there once. In the valley I mean, I never saw any tombs, it was an investigation to see whether it would be worthwhile constructing a fort to give succour to the passing caravans. We decided not. But it is there I believe this Caesarion and his forces are hiding. The way that winds up from the plain opposite where *Cleo* is moored will be heavily guarded. But there is another route, a tiny path across the shoulder of that pyramid-shaped mountain ahead."

They slipped into the night away from the muffled confusion of the Praetorians, relying on the knowledge Septimius claimed and the light of the moon. Two vast shadows loomed in the night, edges rimmed in silvery light and reflecting from the pools of stagnant water. "The Colossi of Memnon," Septimius said of the weather-melted stone. "The first guardians of the ancient necropolis of Thebes. I think they are the only remnants of the great temple they guarded, dismantled by later kings to glorify temples on the other bank."

They walked the horses, keeping sounds to a minimum. The land began to climb. After a few minutes Septimius spoke quietly again. "Ahead are the ruins of a once-town."

"I thought no one dared live on this side of the river, the Land of the Dead?"

"That's so, Quintus. A historian has written that here dwelt slaves and artisans who were made to build the great kings' tombs. Perhaps their rulers considered them to be dead. But who knows. No one has lived here for a long time. On the other side of these streets the land climbs steeply. We'll leave the horses tethered and take to our feet."

The eerie ruins contributed to the feeling Quintus could not shake off that baleful eyes watched their every move. Under the moon's contrast the walls glowed brightly in the sharp light and cast inky shadows across rooms of untold purpose.

After passing through the remains of an outer wall that must once have protected those who worked and toiled there, or imprisoned them, the ground rose even more steeply in a series of sharp zigzagging ledges. Where the path met a gully too steep for safe riding, they dismounted.

And that was when the rebels fell on them.

"What is the meaning of this?" The voice thundered and rebounded from the illustrated walls. Five men tumbled down the last steps into the pillared hall. Two threw down their burden. A medusa head of coppery locks lashed back as Rufio looked up, spitting fury. His gaze locked with the angriest expression he had ever seen...

And that includes Aunty Velabria on a bad day.

He saw a man in his late twenties, yet with thinning hair, hooded eyes in a strong-boned face looking gaunt in the low light, lips compressed into a thin distempered line. Rufio recalled busts he'd seen of the Divine Julius Caesar; from the resemblance this man could be a descendant. His simple purple-bordered tunic looked Roman, but the bestial device embroidered on the breast was an Egyptian design depicting... Seth!

"Harkhaf, I won't ask again. What does this mean? I sent you to fetch me the Empress Pompeia Plotina and you bring me... this..."

"This filthy rat, Lord Caesarion, murdered Menes my brother, now delivered into *my* hands. When I, Desert Jackal, get through with you, you will wish you'd never been born."

Rufio cocked his head as he reeled up to all fours and spat with cobra-accuracy.

"You will learn the meaning of—"

The gobbet of saliva struck the weird-looking Jackal on the cheek.

"Wait!" The word rebounded from the close walls. Caesarion restrained his subordinate. "Harkhaf...?"

The man the Empress flattened when she fell off the mule hung his head and wrung his hands. "Lord, we... we boarded the boat and seized the Empress. I left Baaco behind in hiding to warn us if any should pursue us and he never came. Then... then this one who should be lying dead on the boat, he flew down on us from nowhere with a terrible desert sprite. And the sprite spat stones at us and killed Tiy and Intef and—"

"Where is the Empress?"

"Let me torture this fellating brat," Jackal spat out. "I'll prise the information from his vile, cock-sucking mouth."

Rufio, halfway to his feet, wiggled a little finger. "Something that size isn't worth tickling." The vicious backhand rocked him on his heels.

"Leave him be," Caesarion commanded. "But get him out of my sight." Two men took his arms and hauled him over to a side of the chamber. Jackal seethed but stood back to let them pass. "Harkhaf, where is my prize?"

The man shuffled wretchedly. "The desert sprite bewitched us, great Lord, and spirited the woman away.

"Caesarion," Jackal almost pleaded. "Let me start on this cack-eating excuse for a man."

Rufio fixed the Jackal with his best sneering expression. Inwardly, he was beginning to feel truly frightened. No one knew where he was. Only Cato could help—if he made it back safely. His knife and the sword he'd taken from the raider had been thrown down in a far corner. *I would rather die by my own hand than let this disgusting... what is he? Dressed so stupidly like an Egyptian mummy or something. Die by my own hand? I'm sounding like Quintus... oh, Quintus.*

Caesarion gave Jackal a look of irritation, but when he again addressed Harkhaf he missed the expression of deep disdain Jackal aimed at his back. Rufio hoped it indicated a difference of opinion that might be exploited. Something truly evil lurked behind the Jackal's twisted façade.

"You lost her to a 'desert sprite,'" a statement in a resigned tone. He turned to the Jackal. "Then we must wait to see the outcome of your plan and hope to Amun-Ra and Jupiter Best and Greatest that your fanatic acolyte will succeed in ridding me of Trajan."

What the fuck! Rufio quailed inwardly. *Kill Trajan. By whose hand this time?*

The weirdo was salivating worse than a Molossian forced to wait before its bowl of dog-food, so Caesarion's next words offered at least a reprieve. "You will have to wait for your... fun with this one. He isn't the prize I asked for, but in case matters across the river do not go as you have promised me they will, this boy will have to do in place of the Empress. Your spies have been efficient at least, so we know his and his mother's relationship to the powers."

A low drumming sound reverberated through the hall. It grew in volume and became clearer as the hollow echoing of several shod feet. A dozen men came thumping down the last sloping chamber off the corridor and into the hall.

All eyes turned on the newcomers, none more so than Rufio's.

With no ceremony, two figures were thrown down on the hewn stone floor to land at Caesarion's feet.

Rufio stared with a mix of horror and relief at Quintus and Septimius.

N·I·N·E·T·E·E·N | XIX

West Thebes, 18th day of August

Amphibious Boudica made landfall at the head of her army when the pressganged felucca boys could row no farther across the shallow lake of Nile floodwater. Peering into the gloom, thankful for at least a modicum of light from the setting moon, Junilla thought she could see what might be the furled sail and mast of another boat ahead under the thinning trees. And then as it lost way the barge scraped against another craft—one of *Cleo*'s sports dinghies she realized.

What does this mean? Oh Bona Dea, could it be Rufio?

But surely the pirates had taken him as well as Plotina? The thought made her anxious and she turned around to see that Pinny was using his noddle for once. Before she could command him to action, Laevinius ordered soldiers over the side to help haul the barge to a hummock of dry land.

Primus Pilus Centurion Aurelius Verecundinus, belying his advanced years, was one of the first overboard. He lashed out with his vine cane at any sluggard. "Get on with it, lads. Put some of that famous legionary spunk to good use. We've a load of revolting Gyppos to teach a lesson! That's the spirit. Get the nags off quickly and form up by those trees."

Two other centurions and their optios marshaled the force with asperity. In no time Junilla set the pace, riding at the head of the small column. She rode with less caution than was wise in the near dark, desperate to find Plotina and unravel the mystery of what had happened to her darling Rufio... *and when I find out where Cato got to at a terrible time like this I swear I'll kill the little brat.* She passed by the enemy's abandoned felucca—no clues there—and a little way after she saw the looming walls of some great monument on the left; one of the pharaonic mortuary temples no doubt. *But what in the name of Cernunnos is that?*

From the murk of night a shape emerged, darker than the desert floor. Junilla squinted to focus, aware just behind of Pinny's sudden apprehension. The shape moved and solidified into two figures. They halted and a reedy voice cried out, "Stay where you are. I have a sling and I can kill at a hundred paces!"

Junilla's heart stopped beating, and then she gulped air in relief.

"I will flay you alive when we get back to the boat."

Cato was in no position to answer back, enfolded against his mother's heaving bosom as he was, her cold armor-plated breast. When she finally let him go it was obvious from her expression that his mother didn't immediately realize she was in the presence of the Empress. And in truth, battered, clothes shredded, footwear falling apart, Plotina lacked an imperial appearance. And to balance the books it was clear she didn't recognize Junilla at first either. He'd had a moment's fright as well on seeing his mother as a centurion.

"Lady Junilla, I must protest. Cato has done me a great service in freeing me from the hands of kidnapping murderers." Before he could quite escape her clutches, Cato found himself embraced again and his chin squeezed in a manner uncomfortably familiar: aunts Antonia and Velabria still chucked him under the chin like he was a toddling infant. "He's a hero, is your son."

Cato squirmed back, looking abashed for once, and listened quietly as Plotina described the events that had overtaken them while he pondered the mystery of when on earth his mother had learned to ride.

"So they have Rufio after all." Junilla sounded dull. "We thought you had both been snatched from the boat, but you say he went after you."

"He made me escape with Plot— the Empress I mean. Oh, and Rufio hoped to find Quintus also taken captive, but… but he wasn't with them. It seems the worst must have—"

"No, pet, Quintus is well, apart from a bump on his head. He went with Septimius to inform Trajan of developments, so you needn't worry on that score. Quintus is fine and free."

Cato nodded, a little comforted, but then his face crumpled. "Ma, I— I just hope they won't hurt Rufio any more than when I saw him being struck down."

Junilla seemed to increase in stature and the segments of her armor creaked a different tune to all the leather fastenings. "Verecundinus, you're with me and ten of your men. Pinny, escort the Empress to the barge and across to *Cleopatra of the Nile*." Cato watched in some amusement at affronted Laevinius drawing himself up to his full height to match Junilla's, but before he could remonstrate, she slapped him down. "She is your Empress, tribune, and requires an appropriate honor guard, whereas I require a toughened soldier and a fast-moving unit."

The gladius keened loudly as she whipped it from its scabbard. The blade's point stabbed at the stars. "A mother's love knows no bounds, and these felons should know her wrath knows no limit when her children are threatened."

"Wow…" Cato murmured, deciding that applying himself to his school lessons might be a sensible idea in future. "I'll show you the way, Ma."

"You will not. Find him some proper footwear," she ordered Laevinius. "You will go with the tribune and soldiers guarding the Empress."

"But—"

"Go!"

Well, she did look a bit terrifying. Cato conceded. "All right. Just get him back. They'll be like angry hornets after losing their real captive." He watched Junilla remount with a skill he had no idea she possessed. Plotina mistook his puzzled expression for worry. He barely reacted to the hand she placed on his shoulder.

"Come, dear Cato. When we reach *Cleo* we will both go to the shrine and offer prayers to Jupiter for your brave brother's safe return."

She meant well, of course, but he'd far rather go the other way, back up the valley, armed with stones and sling to crack some heads.

Deep in the bowels of the tomb something stirred in a rough chute of a corridor. It led away from the burial chamber to nowhere; a long, plunging appendix that might have had a purpose long ago, one lost in the mists of time. The passage commenced immediately under the great sarcophagus, long emptied of its treasures and its immortal inhabitant by tomb robbers of antiquity.

A faint mystic glimmer surrounding the being dispelled the Stygian darkness and outlined its bestial form: a monstrous snout preceded the hulking animal head topped by preternaturally tall, spatulate ears. The being moved slowly and its queer ears twitched at the vibration of distant voices. No mortal could hear through the immense weight of rock bearing down on the corridor, but the beast heard everything, knew everything… and it was angry. Those responsible for awakening the force would rue the day that their evil desires had done so.

The rebel leader seemed more interested in Septimius. "Separate them," he commanded. The two rebels holding Quintus marched him smartly over to join Rufio, also held between two pairs of beefy arms. Before either could utter a word, they were pushed down the avenue of six columns, through an ornate opening, and into an adjacent transverse hall. The men flung them down like sacks of refuse and then returned to the antechamber to join in the hoped-for fun of taunting Septimius.

An encrustation of painted figures covered the vaulted roof, which stood much higher than that of the antechamber. A deep gloom obscured the alien symbology and several freshly lit torches did little to dispel it. The vast roughly hewn sarcophagus they had fetched up against stood at the center of this burial chamber, supported on two stone supports, their ends carved into grotesque animal shapes. Its side reached to just below his chin and, as there was no lid, Quintus got a glimpse of the empty interior before he was forced to the floor.

Rufio shuffled his butt about in a forlorn attempt to get comfortable, but there they were, on the cold unyielding floor, shoulder to shoulder, backs pressed up against the last resting place of whichever pharaoh once occupied this terrible tomb. "Only it wasn't," Quintus said, as if he had read Rufio's thoughts and put them into words. "Someone took the mummy away long ago, so gods know where he rests now."

At least their limbs remained unbound—clearly none of the rebels thought they had a chance of escape, and Quintus gloomily agreed with that opinion. They had a good view of proceedings in the antechamber along the avenue of columns but no one could overhear anything they said if they spoke quietly.

"I'm so happy to see you alive, Quintus, but unhappy to see you captured." Rufio clutched Quintus's hand. He squeezed back. "We were certain those slug-eaters must have taken you along with the Empress."

"And I was sure of the same, that they had grabbed you. You were nowhere in sight. You said 'we,' who was the other?"

In a few sentences Rufio told his tale. Quintus expressed admiration for Rufio and Cato's bravery in tracking down the kidnappers and rescuing Plotina, and he was about to tell his own side of things when Rufio interrupted anxiously.

"I heard them talking before you turned up. There's some plan in train to kill Trajan, Quintus. The fucker who's responsible for all the attacks on this trip—the asshole calls himself Desert Jackal—he cooked it up."

Quintus shook his head, and squeezed Rufio's hand more tightly. "Don't worry. Trajan's fine. The attempt failed. The assassin is already dog meat." He spoke behind a raised hand lest anyone might read his lips. "Trajan himself dealt with it."

"What happened?"

"Boy rolled up in a carpet."

"What?"

"Long story. Later. They mustn't know they failed. It's our only hope of staying alive long enough. As soon as it's daylight all the legionaries will be on this side of the river searching for us, but..." His face fell. "They'll never find this place, I fear."

They peered into the distance at raised voices. "You have been a thorn in our side—my side—for too long, Corbulo." Framed in the avenue of six massive columns Septimius gazed into Caesarion's implacable eyes with a serenity Quintus did not believe he could feel. "When I was younger, absorbing lessons at my father's side, I saw your meddlesome hand at work, interfering in our affairs. You think I am ignorant of your role as a frumentarius? Sniffing here, there, everywhere, as a hyena hunts down the discards of others, you and your spying friends. And then... nothing until now. Why are you back?"

Septimius twisted the corner of his mouth into a mocking grin. "To see that Seth does not rise." The slap rang out and snapped his head back. He rocked on his feet even in the grip of two rebels.

Rufio hissed in frustrated anger. "The one slapped him, that's the rat-turd calls himself Desert Jackal, the one in funny garb who keeps looking daggers at us."

Quintus's brow furrowed. The man's apparel seemed wrong, but he couldn't work out why he felt that. He certainly didn't like the look of those hooded stares thrown their way.

Septimius jerked his head sideways to flick a drop of blood from his lip. He held his chin up defiantly. "Tell me, why the nonsense with this 'Isis dies, Seth rises' business?"

"That's what I want to know," Quintus muttered.

Septimius's voice echoed through the halls in a goading tone. "Do you imagine invoking ancient Egyptian deities will cause Caesar Augustus to tremble?"

Caesarion prevented the Jackal lashing out again. Even at a distance Quintus could almost see the vibrations emanating from the oddly dressed madman.

"The day Octavian died my forebears noted the date with joy."

"As you say, your forebears, but why should I or anyone believe Caesarion survived and begat a family?"

Rufio nudged Quintus's shoulder with his own. "I thought Augustus executed him. You said he wasn't even a man full-grown."

"That's what the histories tell us."

Rufio pressed his head close. "You have to admit, he has the likeness of Julius Caesar."

Quintus frowned thoughtfully, then nodded slightly in reluctant agreement.

"I don't care what you believe. It is what I believe that matters." Caesarion shrugged eloquently.

More rebels gathered around, hopeful looks on faces smudged by torch soot, in anticipation of torture to come. Yet Septimius remained unruffled. "But if what you claim, that Ptolemy Caesarion escaped death and begat a family, is true surely you have no reason to bear a grudge… and for *six* generations?"

The question underlined his incredulity at such a misplaced long-lived bitterness. Caesarion ignored the taunt. He turned his attention briefly toward a distant corner hidden from Quintus's sight behind the line of columns. "Come here boy! Grudge? It is no grudge, but the restatement of justice."

Quintus and Rufio watched a sturdy young boy of perhaps seven or eight years walk out from behind the farthest column to stand by Caesarion's side.

"My son. Why should he suffer an exile's life, as each of us has,

right back to my great-great-great-great grandfather? My son is descended from the Divine Julius Caesar, undisputed ruler of Rome, and Queen Cleopatra, the legitimate ruler of all Egypt and its possessions of the Orient."

Quintus closed out the argument. Its outcome, one way or the other, would have no bearing on their imminent doom. He returned the shoulder nudge. "How is it that whenever I'm with you I end up forced to sit against a cold stone wall awaiting a dreadful fate?"

Rufio sniffed dismissively, flicked hair from his eyes. "I seem to recall the last time we both got sucked off… twice."

"And look where that got us." Quintus supplied his own sniff.

"We escaped."

"Thanks to Cassander and his steering oar." Quintus cast his gaze left and right. "I don't know about you, but I can't see too many Greek fisherboys around here. What I do see is the maniac out there you tell me can't wait to turn us inside out, no doubt to read his future in the coils of our intestines, and he's in some sort of fancy dress pretending to be… that's it! Look at the device on his breast. He's dressed as Osiris. Why?"

Rufio lifted his eyebrows.

Quintus sighed in exasperation. "All the Isis dies, Seth rises crap? Isis and Osiris? Osiris and Seth are like day and night, good and evil, so why is an adherent of this Caesarion, who represents himself as Seth, dressed like his bitterest enemy Osiris? Doesn't make sense. Oh, what does in this crazy country? Anyway, as you say he appears to dislike us a lot, quite enough to be planning any number of vile deaths for us. In fact if looks could kill we'd already be arguing the price with the Ferryman."

"You can't really blame him. We did kill his brother that day above Memphis."

It was the turn of Quintus to arch an eyebrow. "So *he* says, and it worries me when you sound reasonable."

"You shouldn't worry so much, my Little Mars," Rufio said, imitating Junilla's voice. "Something will turn up. It always does. I mean Cato escaped with the Empress. They'll bring the cavalry."

"Across the flooded river?"

"Now *you're* sounding reasonable, but we don't need reason now… we need magic and horses *can* swim."

"Don't be daft. Anyway, what do you know about horses?"

"Trajan won't leave us to suffer at the hands of these bastards. They'll all be arena-fodder before you can say feed the lions."

"You make it sound possible." Quintus sighed softly and shook his head. "I think we should prepare ourselves as Romans have ever done, ready to face death with a steadfast mind and noble heart. It's only a pity we're both disarmed or we might fall on our blades even now."

Rufio glanced up from under lowered lashes. "Fuck that for a laugh."

T·W·E·N·T·Y | XX

West Thebes, 18th day of August

The power built, fed by inchoate anger at the blasphemy coiling like oily smoke in the world above. The beast scented evil, forces in conflict, the overpowering stench of treachery rising. Osiris, his forty-two scattered body parts creeping together, coming to coalescence as it was written, as it was to be, as Ra demanded the cycle and recyle. His son, falcon-headed Horus, walked abroad, again seeking the unification of Upper and Lower Egypt, Lotus and Papyrus… yet treachery was present. The blasphemy must be ended lest utter chaos come to reign.

Rufio tapped the back of his head on the sarcophagus. "Do you think tomb robbers took the mummy away?"

"Was that a subtle change of conversation designed to take our minds of the inevitable?"

"Surely they wanted only the valuables buried with the pharaoh, but as far as I could see, this damned thing's empty. So where do mummies end up?"

"Probably stumbling around in the dark in a stew of dark thoughts like our dread lemures." The quip did little to ease Quintus's glumness, but he waved a hand at a square hole in the side of the burial chamber about large enough to allow a man on all fours to crawl through. "Perhaps he wandered off in there, or maybe the identical one on the other side." In the dim light and through the choking smoke of the torches it was possible to see solid wall in the shallow depth of each mysterious declivity. "Doesn't look as if they go anywhere, though. Like the hole you can just make out under this thing, just behind us on the other side." As Rufio had done, he tapped the back of his head against the sarcophagus. "I wonder where that goes… if anywhere."

"I thought I heard a noise when they made us squat here and it wasn't me farting. I think it might have come from that hole."

"What noise?"

"A sort of shuffle… no, not quite. More of a snuffle, like a dog sniffing something interesting. Only it didn't sound so friendly. Like a deep-throated growl."

"Overactive imagination."

Rufio waved a hand in an arc, looking up at the intricate wall and ceiling paintings. "We're sitting in the burial chamber of a long-dead king, whose mortal remains are walking about somewhere, probably as bitter as your Uncle Livy at the loss of his earthly wealth, and desperate to wreak bloody vengeance on whoever disturbed his rest—like we're doing right now—surrounded by arcane imagery devoted to the cult of the dead, at the mercy of a bunch of crazed, fanatical insurgents who hate Romans… Overactive?"

Quintus didn't have much to say to that.

More slaps and bodily thumps echoed from the antechamber.

Rufio suddenly drew his knees up and sat forward like a hound that had just caught an interesting scent. Quintus nudged him. "What?"

"You're wrong about keeping quiet about the failed attempt to kill Trajan. We need to shake them up, put them off their stride."

"No—!"

"Yes! It will change the balance, throw that Caesarion." And before Quintus could restrain him, Rufio shot to his feet. In the confines of the burial vault his voice burst forth as a hollow boom. "Trajan lives. Your assassin is dead."

As the reverberation of his voice died away, only the faint guttering of the torches broke the silence. Caesarion stepped into the center of the avenue. "What do you know?"

"My friend here came from the fort. He knows I'm telling you the truth. Trajan is marshaling his forces even now."

Caesarion turned abruptly to Septimius. "You were with him. Is it so?"

It was hard to see, but Septimius appeared reluctant before he nodded his head.

"This is arrant nonsense," Jackal burst out. "They cannot know."

"You wrapped the assassin in a roll of carpet and hid him—" Rufio didn't need to go on, which was as well since that was as much as he knew.

Caesarion leapt at Jackal. "I see by your face he is right. He knows the plan. The spy Corbulo knows it too."

Still seated, knees drawn up, Quintus felt the floor shift as if some large pile driver had struck upward from underneath.

"It cannot be. They cannot know," Jackal spluttered.

Caesarion advanced another step. "You assured me your plan could not fail—"

"Your reserve plan to snatch the Empress failed." A look of intense hatred creased Desert Jackal's narrow face and made his oddly elongated profile seem almost alien.

The solid rock floor bucked violently. Quintus rolled sideways in alarm, got halfway to his feet. Rufio, a pace in front, seemed to feel nothing untoward as he watched the effect of his words on the unfolding dispute.

I am the embodiment of pure evil in the eyes of mortals; Seth of the desert storm, Lord of Chaos, so in their ignorance they say. But I am Protector of Upper Egypt and adopted by the Hyksos as ruler of all Egypt. The blasphemy now boiling above must be ended lest utter chaos come to reign, for Seth is in truth a unifying principle. There is one who claims my name to disguise his purpose, yet he is of little consequence, and another who in his treacherous heart plans to thwart that purpose. His is the worst blasphemy for he claims the form

*of my nemesis Osiris to resurrect the cult. All is blasphemy... Yet...
there is also innocence, curiosity... acquiescence?*

For many hundreds of paces the rough corridor connected the
lair left by the tomb builders to house the shade of Seth to the burial
chamber in which lay Pharaoh Seti, beloved of Seth. To the beast
now aroused down there it was but a blink of time since robbers
stole the mummy and all the valuables left to serve Seti. The blink
ended, blasphemers gathered, Seth rumbled, and moved, and saw
through the Stygian darkness a glimmer of light far away up the
steep incline. He gathered unimaginable power...

"For too long have I served you, *Lord* Caesarion. For generations
my family has subordinated itself to your purpose like slaves under
the yoke of your bitter ambition."

"As was commanded by the first Caesarion, as was given under
oath by your forbear—"

"No longer!" Jackal spat out. "Roman blood flows in your veins.
You are arrogant in your self-appointed right to rule everything
you touch and call it *your* Imperium. You think you are giants
who stride the world in your segmented armor, insects worse than
devouring locusts. It is time to face your destiny Caesarion of the
blood of Caesar who came first to exploit, then the others who came
to conquer and even now steal our ancient treasures—*ach!*"

"They're really losing it," Rufio cried excitedly, and then stumbled
as if a weakness had taken hold of his legs.

The Jackal reeled back from the slap Caesarion delivered. "You
are mad." Caesarion spat. "The stress of all your failures has driven
sense from you, you cur." He swiveled around to face his two men
holding Septimius. "My ancestor never faltered, but he knew the
golden rule of politics, that sometimes discretion is the better part
of valor. We will retire to the deep desert oasis and plan again. Wait
for a better opportunity... perhaps at Philae, perhaps later yet."

"Did you hear that?" Quintus hissed at Rufio.

Nothing. Nature, cosmos, creation held the same breath. And then Quintus felt the world come apart. A dust storm issued with a sudden shriek from under the sarcophagus. In a heartbeat the coffer resembled a cauldron consumed by its own steam and fire, and Quintus was caught up in it.

The moon touched the rim of the surrounding mountains. Primus Pilus Centurion Aurelius Verecundinus rubbed his hands in satisfaction at a job well done. They had burst into the circular hollow at the dead end of the gully and there found a small squadron of horses at two picket lines, and overcome the few men left to guard them. As he came up, Junilla gave him a hard grin from under her imposing helmet that barely constrained the torrent of hair glinting red highlights when one of the men turned his torch in her direction. She jerked her head at the dark, gaping maw in the cliff. "Let's find out where this goes. You see people have passed here recently."

Verecundinus peered at the windblown sand on the steps leading down, scuffed by many boots. "These are very fresh," he agreed. "This breeze would soon smooth them out."

He ordered two of the ten legionaries ahead, carrying brands brought with them from *Cleopatra of the Nile* and newly lit. They proceeded cautiously into the tomb, staring in wonder at the murals of ancient Egyptian life, death, gods, and of kings who believed in their own godhead.

"What was that?" the leading soldier cried out.

It came again, a deep groaning of the earth, a grating of rock against rock and a shudder that ran through walls, ceiling, and floor.

The blast sundered Seti's mighty sarcophagus. Seth erupted like an earthquake.

Only halfway to his feet, the god's hand caught Quintus up like a doll and hurled him through the thickening air. An impression of painted images on walls and columns coming to life filled his

rotating vision, blood thrummed, men screamed, the antechamber's rocky floor rushed up, a fleeting impression—a man, mouth agape in a rictus of horror, arms outstretched. He broke Quintus's fall.

The crump shook everything. Dust showered down from the ceiling. A crack widened across the vault from one corner to the other as though a giant hand had skewed the chamber. Two paces to the left of where Quintus was crouched, Rufio was barely aware of his lover's sudden flight—the force the other half of the sarcophagus created as it hurtled past somersaulted him aside. He saw its bulk thrown past him to crash into the burial chamber's end wall where it split into two chunks. One part rebounded, narrowly missing flying Quintus, to come to a halt half blocking the opening to the antechamber. The other slammed into a corner of the mysterious declivity on that side of the chamber.

Seth rose amid a dust cumulus that eddied in the torchlight and stood over Rufio where he lay part-stunned on the floor. He looked up at the giant figure looming over him. Preternaturally elongated

jaws gaped to reveal serried ranks of sharp fangs. The monstrous form exhaled a scalding desert breath over him. Flaring nostrils tipped its uplifted snout, sniffing, sniffing as if for... *Innocence? Acquiescence?* Rufio sensed the questions but scrabbled back as the beast-headed figure stepped up fully into the burial vault. Eyes flashing with an immaculate intelligence took him in. Dust flew from the beast's gorgeous neck collar. Rufio slipped into a dreamscape, that he couldn't afterward define as reality or the result of so many knocks to the head. Sharp prehensile claws scraped his bare flesh, yet with a gentleness that spoke of a caress, a torso of extraordinary toned beauty glowed an ethereal blue against the flaring orange of torchlight. He was aware of a short Egyptian kilt barely concealing an erection of enormous proportion; aware of being cuddled, of being encompassed and entered; aware of internal muscles he never knew he possessed gripping the monstrous prick of godhead.

* * *

"Earthquake!" shouted one voice after another. The corridor shook, trembled, and then settled. Junilla picked herself up from the edge of the gaping pit in the sloping tomb floor that had opened up. Verecundinus peered over the edge into a bottomless depth. "An old trap, Lady. Cunning buggers those old Gyppos. We can get around the side if we are careful." And he led the way. Junilla followed, waving encouragement to the soldiers behind. Once past the deathtrap, she took the lead again, striding with renewed urgency, the clanking and creaking of her armor echoing hollowly to mingle with the chinking of the others.

Suddenly, the slope increased and she came to the top of a long downward flight of steps. The first torchbearer followed some paces behind, so the void was still in darkness when Junilla started down, only to come to a shocked halt at the apparition that emerged from a niche in the wall.

Ankhesenamun... it moaned. Tendril hands wandered forward, reaching for the hem of Junilla's tunic. *Ankhesenamun and Tuya...*

An ice-shock chilled Junilla to the bone. Her breathing hitched at the jolt of seeing the horror waving its fragmented hands and arms, unbound from the cerements of mummification. As the thing groped at her, she backed up the first steps she had descended. Her small army stood rooted to the spot, unable to believe their eyes, moaning in superstitious awe. The embalmers' wrappings trailed like lengths of moldy seaweed into the lower darkness. Blind eyes stared sightlessly either side of an aquiline nose and gaping, yet blocked mouth.

A vision of her beloved Rufio buried somewhere below in these ghastly depths, trapped by detestable villains, shattered the paralysis seeing this abominable revenant had precipitated. Her sense of disbelief fractured and out snapped her armored arms. Mailed hands encircled the disgustingly dry neck and with a Celtic warrior's bellowed warcry—one that Vercingetorix would have applauded— she used every ounce of her considerable strength and simply tore the desiccated mummy apart as easily as she had ripped asunder the snake in Alexandria. "Damned forever, you filthy creature!"

A rushing sound like a distant wagon rumbling over cobbles at great speed shook the walls, followed by two sharp cracks, not quite simultaneous. And then a deep grinding sound rattled the floor.

As his vision cleared, Quintus saw Caesarion's young son kneeling on the floor only an arm's reach away. The former cocky bluster was gone, replaced by terror. Quintus looked around, still dizzy from his impact with the unfortunate rebel he'd landed on, but there was no sight of the boy's father in the dust and panic. More muck fell from cracks above, some lustrous with paint. Seeing the child biting his white knuckles hit Quintus deep inside. Any thought of whose son he was became irrelevant. He scrabbled crabwise over and flung protective arms around the boy. "It will be all right. We will get out." *Fuck knows how, though.*

Behind a pillar Septimius was taking advantage of the confusion. He punched one of his captors hard enough in the gut to put him down. The other had turned around to see what was happening and Septimius kicked his legs out from under him. At that moment— over the rumbling ground, the weird animal howling coming from the burial chamber, and the cries of terrified men, a much deeper grinding set up. He glanced at the wide opening that connected the antechamber to the small hall beyond, where a single torch cast a glow over the steps leading up to the next corridor level. For an instant Septimius couldn't relate to what he was seeing. The opening was changing shape, becoming lower. Then he understood and his heart hammered in his chest.

Years ago a historian who prided his knowledge of the ancient tomb builders' skills had given him an understanding of their tricks. "The cleverest," the historian explained, "is the use of dammed reservoirs of sand, which hold up slabs of stone above vertical guide grooves. To either side of the tomb corridor a square chute at an acute angle is constructed. At the highest point a precisely cut block is poised, held secure by trigger wedges of stone. At intervals corresponding with as many doors as the builders deem necessary to secure the tomb from intruders, clay stoppers that hold back the sand in the reservoirs protrude into the chutes. Once the king is buried with his servants and goods for his use in the afterlife, the triggers are knocked out, the great blocks rush down the chutes, smashing the clay stoppers and thus releasing the sand. As the sand escapes under pressure of the weighty slabs, one by one the doors are lowered into place, entombing the deceased king and his living servants... though obviously not alive for very long."

Septimius was looking at one such door! And it was sliding inexorably down in its grooves. Something must have occurred eons ago to prevent the closure of this tomb, but there was no more time left to ponder the mystery of it. No time left to find the boys either. He ran for the dropping door, rolled under it. As he pounded up the stairs the door shut with a bone-crunching thump. He snatched the torch from a wall holder and begged Jupiter to look after his friends. In the light he saw another opening vanishing. He went through at a crouch. Along the upward sloping long corridor. Ahead, a third door, already more than half shut. More stairs. Another small hall. In time he remembered a pit just off-center and swerved around it. Stifling air choked the breath from his aching lungs. One more doorway. Almost closed, the gap narrowing even as he strained for more speed. He wasn't going to make it. The thought of a lonely death in this awful place sent a last surge of energy to his pumping legs.

The gap narrowed, narrowed, narrowed...

...narrowed.

T·W·E·N·T·Y-O·N·E | XXI

West Thebes, 18th and 19th days of August

In a triumphant gesture designed to calm the soldiers quaking behind her, Junilla held aloft the grisly mummified head in one fist. This was one lemur that would not stand in her way. With the other hand she shoved the torso out into the void. Still joined to its head by wisps of unwinding cloth strip, it fell down the wide stairway, unraveling as it bounced from step to step. An infestation of scarab beetles secreted among the dusty folds scattered in every direction. "Never come between a mother and her son," Junilla bellowed in a stentorian voice, and then she hurled the head after the desiccated corpse. It too bounded down the steps. At the same time she narrowed her eyes to see what seemed impossible. At the foot of the stairs the roof of what appeared to be another corridor marching away into the distance seemed to be lowering itself—as if a portal was sliding down to close off the way to where Rufio must be held captive.

Panic clutched at her breast. Junilla started down the stairway, calling on Verecundinus to follow.

Septimius threw his body at the vanishing gap, fell to his side, rolled in desperation over, over, over…over the grooved sill. The sharp lower edge of the door grazed his spine. The thunderous *whump* as hundreds of talents of solid rock met unyielding rock sounded like Jupiter's thunderbolt striking him. He gasped for air, made to roll away, but something held him back. In closing, the great slab of rock had trapped part of his tunic between it and the floor slot. He shuddered at the thought of how close he'd come to being cut in two. He raised his head, opened gritty eyes and…

Yelped in fear.

Something painted a dirty yellow by the dying brand's flame bounced down the last of the steps rising from the floor in front of where he lay. Bounced twice like a raggedy harpustum ball and struck him full in the face. A dry, dusty, musty smell assailed his nostrils. In a gasp of horrified disgust he slapped at the object. It rolled and turned up dead eyes, mouth gaping as if the dead thing wished to congratulate him on escaping. He flapped a hand ineffectually only to discover that he lay sprawled beside more saggy, gritty, parched cloth and there was something more solid under it, bony and that crunched unpleasantly under his hand as if he had slapped down on a mound of beetle carcasses.

The grating of boots on gritty stone broke through his daze. Someone descending the steps. A hand gripped his firmly.

"Well, well." He heard Junilla's familiar though gruff voice. She helped haul him to his feet with a ripping sound as the fabric of his tattered tunic tore away. She gazed at him in the flickering light and wished she hadn't. There was no message of hope in his eyes.

More footsteps. Verecundinus took her elbow gently. "Lady Junilla, there is nothing more we can do here."

Not since the loss of her husband had Junilla felt so deeply chilled. She knew the real distress, the deepest grief at the loss of her eldest son, would set in later when she was reunited with Cato on the boat. And there was Quintus to consider too. In the few months she had known him, the patrician boy had become almost like a third son—well, a son-in-law in a way. The tears would come, but for now they still had to return to safety. Vengeance could wait for daylight. Then whatever was left of the rats' nest of rebels would be satisfactorily wiped out.

When Quintus saw Septimius's heel vanish and saw the slab crash down into the floor groove he knew true despair. They were trapped and it was no consolation that the Jackal, Caesarion, and his men were also doomed to a slow, exhausting death. Even so, he pulled little Caesarion to his feet and drew him along between the six columns. He thought the lad would resist, wanting his father, but he followed meekly enough. They navigated passage around the chunk of sarcophagus and into the funerary chamber. To one side of the gaping hole that had once been almost hidden beneath the sarcophagus lay Rufio, begrimed tunic hoiked up around his waist.

Quintus dropped the child's hand and rushed over, careless of the rubble lying underfoot. He knelt and grabbed Rufio's wrist, felt there a strong pulse. Pale lids parted, blue orbs blinked. "Oh gods, Rufio, you're alive." He pulled him up into a hug, felt his tears soak Rufio's shoulder. "But for what? A lingering death in this stinking hole."

Rufio sat up, a bit groggy but otherwise unhurt. "I— I don't think so. But we have to be quick. Help me up. Over this way. He showed me how to get out. But we have to beat the sand."

"Sand?"

"Yes. Look." Rufio pointed to where the other part of the smashed sarcophagus had struck the chamber's end wall. Dark sand flowed out like water from the declivity Quintus had pointed out earlier.

"*Who* showed you?"

Rufio shrugged. "I— I'm not sure. Seth, I suppose, or… something. A force of nature, like Aunty Velabria only a hundred times more powerful and… vengeful. Yet not for me, not for us—" His eyes widened. "You have Caesarion's son."

"We can't leave him. That is if there really is a way out."

"Come on, grab that brand and I'll get this one. Quickly!"

Quintus grabbed little Caesarion's hand and followed Rufio. They ducked into the low, cramped space from which the sand now spewed at a greater rate. A sizeable block of finely dressed granite was wedged against the lower end of the declivity. It looked as if it had been thrown down and the force had smashed the corner of the lacuna. It left just enough space for a single person to squeeze through and when Quintus could see around Caesarion he realized how the block had ended up where it did. For the first time since his capture a glimmer of hope brightened his soul. He saw Rufio, torch in hand, climbing on all fours up a steeply angled shaft, the chute down which the block must have traveled.

Their troubles were far from over, however, for the sand streaming down the channel would very soon fill it up. If they couldn't keep ahead of the rising level they would drown as surely as rats in a barrel. In the lead, Rufio gasped, blew out mouthfuls of grit, and scrambled on over the liquid effluvium. Quintus pushed Caesarion ahead of him. The boy remained silent. *Probably in shock, and no wonder.* Then he too was floundering knee-deep against the mounting pressure of slippery grains, struggling to keep his torch from being snuffed out.

After climbing some distance the source of so much sand became apparent. He drew level with a round hole the size of his head cut into the tomb side of the shaft. From this drain leaked a constant flow of the stuff. Quintus felt a strong vibration of rock grinding on rock through the stone. It struck him then that what he was feeling and hearing was a door lowering like the one he'd seen Septimius disappear through just before it slammed down.

They climbed and crawled and banged incautious heads on the low roof, struggling to keep ahead of the rising sand level. At one point Quintus ceased his crabbing to glance back, astonished to see a head and then shoulders and arms heave up from the billowing surface. *Caesarion! He got away.* He called ahead. Rufio simply grunted and blew out another mouthful of grit, but Quintus received a tight little smile from the boy ahead of him. He felt vulnerable having their enemy behind him—and armed, he saw— but calmed himself with the thought that the madman wasn't likely to do anything until they were at least out of this predicament. And anyway, he was between Caesarion father and Caesarion son and there was no way past him in this claustrophobic pipe.

It felt like an entire month of strain on knee and elbow joints, constantly fighting the pressure of yet more sand raining down, until finally they passed what appeared to be the last drain hole, because the chute was clear above it. Soon after that, Rufio let out a huff of relief. Little Caesarion crawled over the lip of the slope onto a flat surface. Quintus joined him and found he could just stand without banging his head. They appeared to be a in a small chamber with no way out. Caesarion climbed up. No one said anything. The torches guttered.

"Quintus, there is air coming in. I can feel a breeze," Rufio said. "Here. There are gaps between some of the stone blocks."

"Let me." Caesarion wormed past Quintus and ruffled his son's head. The child flung arms around his father's waist and went to where to Rufio was prising at one block with a dagger-like blade of crudely cut rock he had picked up. "You called your friend Quintus, so according to my agents you must be Tullius Rufio?"

Rufio paused in his jabbing to look at Caesarion. He didn't answer, just resumed working at the gap.

Two more shards lay discarded on the floor. Caesarion picked up one, Quintus the other, and they all went to work with a will, eager to get out of their prison. In a few minutes a block about a foot-square pushed loose, fell away, and made a dull thud as it landed outside. Several others followed in quick succession. Blessed fresh air poured in through the opening. It was still dark outside.

Quintus expressed surprise. "I feel as if we were stuck down there for longer than half a night."

Rufio slipped over the lip of the opening and helped little Caesarion over when his father held him up, then followed. Quintus was last out. They were on a ledge that dropped gently down in both directions. To the right the path jinked up again and seemed to rise over a shoulder of the Theban Mount, clearly outlined as a darker shape against the myriad stars. To the left, it dipped down and around a bend, presumably toward the entrance of the tomb in the gully.

"No one else got out," Quintus said grimly. It was aimed at Caesarion.

The great leader looked much diminished and it wasn't the grime of climbing out through cascading sand. The set of his face was slack in resignation, the expression of one whose cherished ambition has crumbled to dust. He shook his head. "Any the monster left alive will soon run out of air to breathe."

"Monster?"

"I only caught a brief glimpse in the whirlwind of dust and eviscerated bodies. The face of a monstrous jackal."

"Seth…?" Quintus breathed.

Caesarion gave a deep sigh. "I don't know. How can such a thing be real? Our gods—our Roman gods—are a useful adjunct to governance. We respect them, but never expect to see them manifest in physical form. I suspect the hand of magic is more likely. A black force brought to bear by that treacherous excuse for a human who was the lieutenant I trusted."

"Desert Jackal?"

Caesarion nodded.

"I can hear voices," Rufio said, his voice tinged with excitement. "Coming from around the corner. I'm sure I hear my mother. Yes, no one else I know has that carrying voice when she's ordering people about. There's the clank of legionary armor as well. And swearing." he looked round and grinned. "We must get down there. She is sure to be in a terrible state thinking we're all dead."

"I *will* be dead, if I go with you." Caesarion held his son hard to his side. "I knew it was over when the bastard turned his coat. He'd planned all along to wait for the appropriate moment. A knife in my back one night. A rousing charade for the men in his thrall, embracing ancient Osiris, Isis, and their son Horus. Egypt and all its possessions in his hands with the might of Rome thrown… or at least suffering a major setback. That would buy time for Pharaoh Desert Jackal to raise new armies. All madness, of course."

"Your madness, though," Quintus said firmly. "It was what you wanted."

Caesarion straightened his shoulders. "I am what I say, descended from Julius Caesar and Cleopatra. We had a right."

"But time passes. The patriciate and equestrian order had rights. The people of Rome had the right of self-government and then by slow and steady means, Augustus removed it. Time passes, things change, it is the nature of life. We cannot go back to the Republic any more than Egypt can return to being her own mistress."

Caesarion nodded slowly.

"Go the other way. Take your son. You'll have a chance if you get away from the immediate vicinity before the sun is up." Quintus looked to the east where a pale gray was now outlining the Theban Mount. "Not so long now. We won't say anything. They'll think you perished with the rest down there." He shuddered at the thought. "Rufio, what do you say?"

The silence stretched out. Rufio sighed. "I'm not at all sure why we should let you get away, but..." he threw an eloquent look of resignation at Quintus, "...but I'm a pleb, he's the patrician. They always know best. Anyway, you're the one with the sword. You could have used it, but you didn't." A smile lit his grimy, blood-smeared face. "Good luck." And with that he began to make his way carefully down the narrow ledge.

Quintus nodded curtly at Caesarion. "Will you give up your cause?"

Caesarion gazed back squarely. "You are a good man, Quintus. You took care of my son. I am only twenty-eight. Many years left to me. Who knows what the future holds? May you fare well."

The boy gave Quintus a shy wave and followed his father along the other arm of the ledge and then out of sight over the lip in the ground. By the time they reappeared climbing the side of the hill, diminished by distance, the two figures, tall and short, were no more than vague shadows. Quintus turned to follow Rufio, pondering on the nature of the "monster" that had accosted Rufio and left him unharmed while taking apart Caesarion's men... or were those victims adherents to the evil Desert Jackal's cause? And what happened to him? Quintus shrugged his shoulders and realized that he ached in every quarter. Desert Jackal was surely dead and buried in a very fine tomb, which he did not deserve. *Doubtless a day will come when future historians will be mystified by what took place here. How in the name of Hades am I going to write this up?*

He raised a hand to the rock face to steady himself on legs that still felt wobbly from the frantic climb to safety and began to make his way carefully along the ledge toward the corner, where it met rising ground and became more of a pathway. As he rounded the jutting corner, he saw the flare of several torches below in the gully. Shadowy figures milled about. And then he heard Junilla's cry rise to the starry heavens. Such relief and joy.

Quintus wondered sadly whether his own parents would ever show such unfettered emotion at discovering their youngest son alive and well when they had feared him dead.

T·W·E·N·T·Y-T·W·O | XXII

The reunion with Junilla at the mouth of the dread tomb might well have finished us off after our escapades, *Quintus wrote.* She certainly didn't seem to want to stop suffocating Rufio in her unforgiving metallic and leathery grip until she'd throttled the life from him. I was only a little less crushed in an armory hug for not actually being a sibling. Even Cato showed a welter of emotion at our return, as did Ashur (who seems to be harboring a deep sense of guilt, though I assured him I did not hold him responsible for his absence at the moment of the attack or the events of that long, long night).

After all the excitement at Thebes (including the flummery of New Year ritual at the temple of Amun-Opet, to which thankfully we were not expected to attend), everyone aboard *Cleo* is happy to travel serenely on up the river toward our final destination smothered in the scent of cut flowers in every cabin—recompense for the terrible affront of a kidnap: "Those awful, awful locals," Djed said with eloquent shudders of theatrical revulsion.

We are due in one hour at Elephantine. This Roman fort is situated on an island in the Nile adjacent to the ancient town of Syene. Just upriver, where sits the island of Philae amid the lower reaches of the great cataract that prevents further navigation, is the source of the Nile according to the lore of ancient Egypt. Rufio objected to this. "How could the silly things think the Nile starts here? Didn't jolly old Ramesses the Great build temples much farther down south? And the expert at Memphis when he was talking about the sneezy pharaoh—"

"Snoferu," I told him.

"Yes, that one. Didn't he tell us Snoffy built a great fort deep in southern Nubia? So why imagine this was the source, when the Nile obviously goes on from Syene and Philae?"

It was Septimius (apparently recovered from his ordeal at the hands of closing doorways and harpustum-playing mummies) who supplied the answer. "The earliest inhabitants of Egypt believed that the great torrent of water pouring over the high rocks of the cataract *was* the start, the source of the great life-giving Nile."

"Ah, so it was a *ritual* source." Rufio's smugness would have received a stinging response had he aimed it at me. "Everything in this land is ritual—priests to the left, priests to the right, always with a taking hand stretched out. I shall be happy to return home." He's bored with journeying. He and Junilla have marked for collection enough statuary to fill the Colosseum to its topmost tier. At every halt, a veritable navy of transports has set off for the north, laden to the gunwales with limestone, basalt, and granite of every hue. Rome will think it's turning Egyptian.

So we are due to visit the island of Philae where Trajan will dedicate in his name the new kiosk supposed to house the bark of Isis—a *ritual* thing, of course. We are then to make haste back to Alexandria. According to Djed the journey up river without any stops takes thirteen days, but the return—rowing and with the current in our favour—will take only nine days with the briefest of resupply stops. And this we must accomplish if we are not to be stranded in Alexandria over winter. As September passes into October the weather's temper becomes uncertain and Our Sea is closed to navigation but for the most urgent of reasons. And Trajan is anxious to return to Rome well before the winter storms threaten to attend to those problems that arise when the Emperor is absent from the center of government. The trip has given him much to think about, with particular emphasis on strengthening garrisons all along the Nile.

Quintus put down his pen, sanded the last entry, and let the scroll curl up on itself. *I wonder what will become of Caesarion, the sixth and seventh of the name?*

Khnum, who made people from Nile clay, had his temple on the island-fortress of Elephantine. The tourists dutifully trouped around its precincts, took feluccas to Syene on the river's eastern shore, where numerous more temples stood to this deity and that, and where many quarries had been mined by the ancients for the great monuments to the north. They sampled perfumes made from local flowers and herbs that flourished on the banks of the Nile there and pleased the inhabitants by leaving much money behind.

Nothing, however, prepared the ambling party, joyous at the imminent dedication of Trajan's Kiosk, for what happened at Philae.

"As you know, I'm not a great one for the gods, but at least I know Isis," Rufio began as they clambered off the barge that had brought them from Syene up the lower part of the cataract with much hauling of ropes and splashing of water. "We have her back home."

"Well this is her temple," Quintus agreed, casting his eyes over the monumental piles of stone that made up a great colonnade leading to the first pylon of the temple Hadrian called another "pile of Ptolemaic fakery." But it was to the east edge of the sacred island that everyone was heading, where the rectangular kiosk's unweathered yellow columns made it stand out as new from the other monuments.

A century of Praetorian Guardsmen had secured the island in the early hours before sun-up... at least, that's what Vata thought. He had men stationed at the three access points and otherwise had been ordered to keep the Praetorian presence to a visual minimum. The eager crowd gathering in the open space between the temple of Isis and the new kiosk comprised the imperial family, the administrators of Upper Egypt's first nome, and the senior management of the Khepri Corporation, together with all the majesty of the Philae priesthood—Greek, Egyptian, and Roman colleges.

The kiosk, which measured fifty paces on its west and east ends and sixty-five paces on the north and south faces, stood on a great

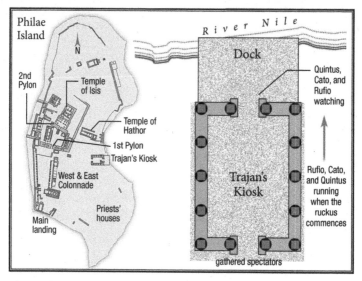

Philae Island

2nd Pylon

Temple of Isis

Temple of Hathor

1st Pylon

Trajan's Kiosk

West & East Colonnade

Main landing

Priests' houses

N

River Nile

Dock

Quintus, Cato, and Rufio watching

Trajan's Kiosk

Rufio, Cato, and Quintus running when the ruckus commences

gathered spectators

plaza of stone flags. Entrances to the west and east pierced walls twenty feet high, on which stood fourteen columns, each supporting a curiously blocky pier above the lotus capitals. The unornamented architrave ran all the way around the building at over fifty feet above the podium. Timbers for a shallow roof were in position but as yet uncovered.

"It's uncompromising," Quintus said mildly. He and Rufio were looking after Cato ("I don't need looking after." "Yes you do. I am invited to be among the select allowed inside the monument, pet," said Junilla, "and I can't trust that you won't dash off on some half-assed attempt to rescue another damsel in distress"). Given the overbearing desert-dusty heat they were happy to be standing some way back from the unfolding event.

"I think it's ugly. It's not Roman and it only looks partly Egyptian." Rufio tossed his wild mane about in the hot breeze blowing up the Nile cataract but doing nothing to cool the stifling air. "To think, we came all this way to see that monstrosity. It's an oversized box to put a boat in."

"A sacred bark."

"Oh, woof, then. Oh shit..."

Quintus froze at the unearthly moan that issued from the heart of the kiosk. The high wall hid everything of the interior space and from their angle it wasn't possible to see in through the western entryway, which was anyway blocked from view by the crowd standing in between, impatiently waiting to be summoned within for the rituals to commence. The worthies crammed together there seemed to shudder as if a sudden blast of wind had torn at them, a collective backward stagger.

"By Luna's loving loins, what's going on?" Rufio cried out.

"You can see in from the other end," Cato said excitedly as the commotion increased.

Quintus saw several distant Guardsmen grabbing shields and spears and start running across the plaza from the colonnade where they had been keeping out of view. When he swung back he was startled to see that Rufio and Cato were already running along the southern side of the huge kiosk in the direction of the shore. "I'm supposed to be the one on the front line," he called after them, and broke into a sprint to catch up.

The eastern end of the monument backed onto a deep parapet that protruded out onto the river. Quintus assumed it represented a dock for the solar bark of Isis to pull up too; symbolic, obviously because it stood some fifty feet above the water level. He matched pace with Rufio and Cato as all three skidded around the corner of the kiosk and onto the hardstand of the dock... and came to a jumbled halt. Clustered around the east entrance were several heavily armed insurrectionists, at least Quintus assumed them to be so by the way they had two Praetorian Guards trussed up.

"Who are the other men?"

Cato's question was partly answered when a harsh voice rose up over the hubbub of tourist-spectators. Quintus and Rufio flinched at the familiar shrill cadence.

"Osiris claims his right! My sister and bride Isis will return to her homeland, away from the festering influence of Rome."

"Desert Jackal," Rufio exclaimed.

"He's really got his Egyptian mythology in a right old muddle."

Rufio snorted derisively. "At a time like this, Quintus, you can complain about his education! How the fuck did he survive?"

The voice rang out louder, infected with madness. "Egypt's true castles of the millions of years will prosper and survive. Not like this Roman abomination, born of your overweening arrogance. I tell you this! The waters of Sacred Nile will rise up and swallow all your sacrilegious monstrosities, those of Rome and of Ptolemy…"

"Why don't the other soldiers get in there and do him over?" Cato snapped. "The Aventine Foxes wouldn't stand around like a bunch of wet pederasts, we'd be in there in a flash, biffing and bashing and—"

Seeing that the attention of those men holding the two Guards was entirely concentrated on whatever was taking place inside the kiosk, Quintus crept forward, keeping close to the wall. He was halfway to the entrance, the other two close behind, none of them with a thought of any plan but determined not to let Desert Jackal get away with whatever he thought he was doing when…

At Philae, the Nile was very wide, more the appearance of a lake than a flowing river, and far away a disturbance broke its tranquil surface. In the rear and thus looking outward more than Cato and Quintus in front, Rufio saw it first. Even as he noticed, the ripples formed into a wake, as if an invisible boat was heading toward the island. "But a very fast one," he said aloud.

"There is evil magic at work here," Quintus called back softly. "It's why the soldiers can't do anything. Some power holds them back, I can feel it."

"So can I," Cato agreed. "I hope Ma isn't in any danger. She's had enough to cope with, with what you've put her through."

"Me?" an aggrieved Rufio hissed. "You leapt into that damned dinghy with me as well—"

"Shhh…" Quintus reached the sides of the great doorway attached to the innermost lotus column, abandoned by the rebels who had all packed inside with their two prisoners. He peered around the edge. Backs confronted his sight, men enclosing the figure of Jackal-as-Osiris somehow standing high above his followers. No, not standing… levitating. And shrieking with the voice of a demon.

"Quintus."

"Hush, will you!"

Rufio pressed around Cato and tapped his shoulder. "Quintus. Something is coming. Something big, coming this way."

"What?" Quintus didn't look around, transfixed by the vision of Desert Jackal glowing ethereally, holding his audience in thrall by some means Quintus could only imagine as truly evil.

"It's coming. Really big. This way, right at us—"

Cato's gasp of fright dragged Quintus back from the astonishing, unhinging sight inside the kiosk. He turned to see... "By all the gods of the pantheon, in Jupiter's name what is that?"

In a great wave of surging water and the roar of a wind from Hades, a spout was forming, spiraling high into the air, growing fatter and taller as it rushed at the shore. Around the column the surface domed as if an underwater volcano was about to erupt, spewing up gaseous bubbles. A ferocious wind tore a tight circle around the spout causing it to rotate as it crashed into the dock wall. A storm of immense strength flattened the three boys against the kiosk wall, soaking them. The base of the waterspout swelled outward, pregnant with arcane power.

They all cowered back, but there was nowhere to go. And then from within the bulging wall of water something formed. First a snarling snout of prodigious size, slavering jaws, flaring nostrils scenting prey, and then glaring eyes, orbs dark at the rims, burning with infernal fire at the centers. Tall bestial ears emerged from the waterspout and the huge head came clear. Mighty claws reached out. Quintus felt an inchoate force accumulating with the rapidity of a summer squall. Blue-tinged, muscular arms thrust him aside and gargantuan Seth, impatient to be inside the kiosk, stepped into the entryway.

Three faces, dripping and white with apprehension, gazed up at the embodiment of chaos, half the height of the kiosk, as the being barked words in an incomprehensible tongue. The insurgents who had been guarding the east door made a dash for safety, dodging between the great beast's legs. Several ran straight to the dock's parapet edge and dived over, others fell over backward, to slam into its sloping sides before dropping senseless into the water. In seconds the entryway was cleared. Quintus couldn't help himself, drawn by a force more demanding than curiosity to peer around the edge of the door, compelled to witness an event he knew in his bones to be transcendent. The press of Cato and Rufio at his side, equally curious, comforted him.

The bulk of Seth obscured much of the opposite doorway, but it was just possible to see Trajan and Hadrian frozen in place, gazing up in wonder.

Do they see it too? They must, it's not just a chimera of my imagination. Quintus shook his head. In his great paws, Seth held Desert Jackal about the waist high in the air and shook him as a child in a rage shakes a rag doll, though there was nothing childish in this assault. All the while the giant creature issued more ancient curses in the guttural tongue of a desert dog and with such violence that the very walls and columns of the kiosk trembled. Abruptly, Seth turned to face the river.

"Back!" Quintus cried out. Cato and Rufio retreated hastily, hard up against the kiosk's outer wall. Quintus barely made it back to their side before Seth strode onto the dock, still shaking the Jackal. And then before their horrified gaze the god began taking the treacherous rebel apart. Limb by limb and part of limb, he ripped Jackal into forty-two precise pieces: "One for each of Egypt's nomes," Quintus spoke unwittingly from his memory of the scrolls he'd studied in Alexandria.

Amazement, fear, awe, gut-wrenching terror, the boys watched Seth cast each piece of Desert Jackal far out into the river.

When he was finished, the water rose up again in a massive, frothy wave into which Seth stepped, to be borne away, slowly sliding beneath the surface until only a trace of a ripple marked the spot where he merged with the essence of Egypt. A profound silence followed the final sound of lapping water.

An ibis cried out. Ducks began squabbling. Suddenly the air came alive with the buzzing of insects, the click of scarabs on the paving, the bark of a distant hippopotamus, and the babble of hundreds of people swelled up from the other side of the kiosk. Quintus, Rufio, and Cato put cautious heads around the doorway. A few Praetorian Guards with Servilius Vata and his centurions were entering from the other side. In minutes military, spectators, priests, and members of the imperial court flooded in, ogling in surprise at the few battered and groaning men lying about.

Junilla pushed through the bewildered throng. "Oh, there you are! But what are you doing out here? I thought I left you up by the colonnade. I sent Flaccus looking for you."

Rufio stepped forward. "It was the..." he trailed off, unsure how to describe what they had just witnessed.

"I know. That's why I was concerned for you when that silly business kicked off in there." she said. "We were so shocked to see those swine had invaded the island to occupy this sacred site, and on dedication day as well."

Rufio and Quintus exchanged looks of puzzlement, which said: she seems to be taking it well.

"I'm sure Caesar will be annoyed with the Praetorians for letting a bunch of protestors in."

"Is that what you saw?" Rufio asked carefully. "A bunch of people protesting? About what, by the way?"

"Well you wouldn't have seen it from this side, but for some obscure reason of their own they were peasants opposed to the ceremony and this." She waved a hand around at the open-topped rectangle of the kiosk. "Still, it was hardly necessary of Vata's men to go beating them up. Right, better be off with you. After the delay I think we're about to start and you boys were not invited to witness the dedication."

"Are we going mad?" Quintus stared off at the dusty-orange haze that marked the desert line of the eastern bank of the river a mile or more distant.

Rufio flung an arm around his shoulder and squeezed. "Perhaps, but you saw it too, didn't you, squirt?"

Unusually, Cato seemed lost for words. He nodded.

Quintus lifted a hand to place over Rufio's where it lay on his shoulder. "That's what you saw—think you saw—in the tomb?"

"Yes. Fucked me… I think."

That woke Cato's interest. "You only think! Wouldn't you know? Big thing like that?"

Quintus started back along the dock to the corner they first rounded. Rufio and Cato followed. As they walked along the length of the bark shrine that would bear Trajan's name for all time to come, the chanting of priests commencing the rituals inside wafted melodiously over the high wall.

Coming from the opposite direction, Flaccus hailed them. "Oh, there you are! But why are you all wet? And what are you doing out here?"

"You sound just like my mother," Rufio said with a flat expression on his face, but a grin dimpling the corners of his mouth.

Flaccus looked nonplussed. "Really?" He shook his head as if a fly was bothering him. "She sent me to see where you'd got to when she couldn't see you and that ruckus started in that... er, that whatever it is."

"Kiosk," three voices chimed.

Flaccus shook his head again and this time swatted a fly flitting around his forehead. "Our poor Imperator. He's really had enough to put up with on this journey without a load of local yobs making a fuss. You'd think the priests would keep them off the island. Anyway, you're all fine—"

"We are," three voices confirmed. "And thank you for bothering, Flaccus," Cato added with a simper saved up especially for his favorite vigilis.

"Hmm." Flaccus shuffled uncomfortably, eyes barely leaving Rufio until he dragged them down to Cato. "Well, yes. I was told by Eutychus to tell you that he's pleased we won't be putting in anywhere on the way down to Alexandria, at least not for trips off the boat. That way, he says, he and you can concentrate on your lessons."

"Oh joy!" Cato cried with a clap of his hands. Flaccus didn't see the way he slipped a forefinger through the ring of his other fist and pumped it because Flaccus as usual only had eyes for his brother.

"You look as if you'd seen a ghost, Rufio. Not white about the gills exactly, in fact definitely a bit flushed...and damp. As do you Quintus Caecilius Alba. Have you been swimming in the river? You know how dangerous that can—"

"It's the sun," Rufio intervened rather illogically. "We require some shade."

"Ah, well I can help there." Flaccus pointed back at the hulking length of the temple. "You see those palms over there. Bench beneath them, and the sun's in the right position to give it shade. I'd better go find Junilla and tell her you're all alive."

None of them bothered to let Flaccus know she already knew of their continued existence, and he left with a brief wave. They started across the sun-emblazed plaza in the direction Flaccus had given.

"So that's it," Quintus said eventually. "An irritating local incident for the Guards to tidy up."

"And we're the only one's who saw what really happened. After all, not even Septimius really saw that thing in the tomb, did he?"

"No, he wouldn't have, though he did encounter something horrible on his way out."

"I overheard him saying he ran into a live mummy," Cato piped up.

"Mummies are dead, dummy," Rufio replied.

"This one was talking, I heard Ma say so."

Rufio shot Quintus another communicative look, and grinned. "Talking mummies? Likely story. Whatever next."

They reached the marble bench parked under a clump of palms close to an entrance to the outer court and first pylon of the temple, and fell down gratefully on the cool stone. Rufio scooped up a handful of small stones and began shying them at a couple of basking lizards. Quintus pondered what they had witnessed… surely they had been witnesses? Could three sane young men share the identical dream? He thought not. So the rest of the gathering had been induced as a mass to see something much lesser, just an annoyance.

Rufio broke into his musing. "Did you feel anything, I mean more than plain terror?"

Quintus frowned. "I'm not sure, but come to think of it I did have this sense that it had no intention of harming me. Don't ask me why."

Rufio nodded his head slowly. "I felt the same in the tomb as well… more, that it was concerned, at least a tiny little bit, that it almost wanted to comfort me." He gave Quintus a warm smile. "I was terrified for you, not of it. It… no, *He* felt my love for you and terror that you were hurting."

"Oh, love, love, love," Cato said, blowing raspberries.

"You'll learn one day, brat." Rufio tossed another stone at the bobbing reptiles.

"That Jackal bastard must have found a way out like we did."

The lizards, hissing annoyance at being disturbed, skittered off. Rufio looked up and blew out a long breath between pursed lips that Quintus would have liked to kiss (but not in front of Cato). "I wouldn't be surprised he engineered the whole thing, had men loyal to him and not Caesarion prepare the tomb. Dig the entrance out, make it an ideal hideaway, knew all about the mechanism for shutting it that hadn't worked whenever whoever was buried there originally. It's logical that the sand traps had to be both sides of the tomb itself or the system would be off balance and jam. He got out the other side is my bet."

"Well, he's not around any more," Quintus murmured.

"That's not true," said Cato brightly. "In point of fact, as Eutychus would pedantically tell me, after what that thing did to him I'd say he's *all* around."

And Cato burst into a fit of giggles. Quintus and Rufio looked at each other over the boy's shaking head, cracked smiles (of relief and gratitude for being alive?), and joined in with gales of laughter.

Elephantine Island, 28th day of August

No side trips to visit temples, no more statues to collect, no assassins rushing about brandishing swords and carpets, the whole company settled into a languorous holiday spirit in comfortable accommodations for the remaining days on land before returning to Alexandria. To make a change from the often over-exotic fare served up on *Cleo*, Septimius announced one evening he would create a repast simple and virtuously Roman. That meant men only, but included honorary centurion Junilla. In addition to the Familia Tullii, Trajan, Hadrian, Spurius, and Quietus attended.

"In the market I found these magnificent cucumbers, Caesar."

Septimius showed one in its whole state. "I have prepared them in a variety of ways—in oils, soured wine, garum, with herbs—and accompanied them with hardboiled eggs and a fine flat bread baked on the outside of clay ovens in traditional Egyptian style."

"Splendid," Trajan declared. "I love simplicity in eating, but I want you to help me hold a magnificent spread once we get back to Rome, a thank you to you, Junilla, and to you Quintus and Rufio... and of course young Cato."

"I shall commence work on a menu, Caesar," Septimius assured.

The conversation turned to several topics, none to do with the weird and frightening recent events. For no apparent reason Rufio suddenly said with some glee to Trajan, "Did you know, Caesar, that Quintus is one of the Rhyming Caecilii?"

"You make him sound like a family of performing acrobats who entertain in the circus between the races."

The word *acrobats* came close to a subject the company was avoiding. Trajan coughed politely, squeezed Quintus's shoulder. "I am grateful that there has been such a fine crop of poets this past year." He gave Rufio a stern look. "I am glad to see—unlike you—that literature flourishes and that we have budding talent like Quintus to enlighten us."

"Th– thank you, Caesar." Quintus turned a shade of Rufio's hair.

"We shall have a reading arranged on our return to Rome."

"Count me out."

"Tease as you will, Rufio" Trajan said firmly, "but your well-rounded ass will be flattened on a seat in the front row." He turned back to Quintus. "You have read your work in public before?"

"He's had it read *back* to him before. I seem to remember these two old coves in the library—"

"Silence!" Trajan commanded, but unable entirely to conceal a twitch of a smile.

Quintus nodded reluctantly. "I have, Caesar, on a few occasions in spite of the fact that people are slow to form an audience when a reading is announced. Most sit around outside gossiping and wasting their time when they could be giving me their attention."

Rufio placed a hand in front of his mouth in a theatrical yawn.

"And when they do come in some don't stay very long, trying to slip out unobserved. Some even march out boldly."

"I doubt anyone will try doing that if I am present at the reading. Perhaps I should remind the selected audience of how the tyrant Nero treated any who had the temerity to doze off during one of his music recitals?"

"How did he?" said Rufio, never strong on Roman history.

Hadrian piped up. "He had them executed on the spot by a handy Praetorian."

Trajan gave Quintus another squeeze. "But I'm sure we won't have to resort to such drastic measures."

Amid the polite laughter Septimius said he was praying for a calm sea on the way home because of Rufio's tendency to seasickness. He turned aside to fix Quintus with a naughty glint. "That Rufio of yours, he needs licking into shape."

Quintus covered up another blush with his napkin and avoided Rufio's mischievous, grinning eyes—Septimius's lighthearted remark had hit closer to home than he could possibly have imagined. For only that very afternoon…

For that afternoon, the first time in what seemed like an age, Rufio and Quintus had time to themselves, tucked snugly away from prying eyes. Rufio gave a long shuddering sigh. The touch of Quintus' hands on the bare flesh of his thigh was almost more than Rufio could stand. So sensuous, it made him burn all over. *Can this really be the dark-browed, sanctimonious patrician prick who used to call me a guttersnipe?*

Barely aware that he had leaned back, Rufio felt Quintus incline with him, press against him. He relished the tease of fingertips drawn lightly over his tunic-covered abdomen. A low groan grated

unstoppably from deep down in Rufio's throat and he actually
felt the smile that doing so brought to Quintus's lips. He reached
around to cup Quintus and smiled as well at the swell of cock in his
grip through tunic and loincloth.

"Oh, Rufio."

So softly he thought he might have imagined it.

With a slight sideways pressure on Rufio's crotch, Quintus turned
so they faced each other, noses almost touching. Misted eyes, lidded
with desire, big dark lashes fluttering slightly. The tip of his tongue
slipped out, licked his upper lip, and their mouths met. Rufio tasted
the wine, an ambrosia they had both taken. Tongue against tongue,
so beautifully slick, so sexy, so…

… and they were ripping away the interfering tunics. They sat up
to help, arms brushing up and down tanned backs, over the ripple
of spines, hovering above the widening valley between ass cheeks as
bronzed as the rest. Then they were writhing in each other's arms,
competing bump to bulge. They fought each other for supremacy
and more by luck than strength Rufio scrabbled down Quintus, all
the way south until his lips closed over the length of the thickened
shaft flexing under flaxen cloth, felt it strain against his mouth.

Hands clamped on his skull, pushing him down hard. Then Quintus reached out and bodily dragged Rufio up and off him, rolled him onto his back, and pinned him to the protesting bed.

Oh no, Roo-feee-o. Not all your own way. Quintus pressed him underneath and then spun around to grab a foot. The pedes were not a part of human anatomy Quintus had ever considered much before, but some inner instinct had planted the seed and it grew and sprouted. Now was the time to turn thought to deed.

Quintus licked the stubby tip of Rufio's big toe, slipped it between his lips and sucked. He heard the gasp as if Rufio found the sensation strange. Quintus bent farther so he could wipe his tongue up and down the foot, sole to heel and back to the curling toes. A soft giggle broke from Rufio's mouth but he lay quietly as Quintus worked his way up and over the instep. Then he pulled the other foot close, leaned in, and repeated the action.

"Oh, Bacchus bless me, Quintus…"

Rufio blurted the words with a gasp and then Quintus felt both Rufio's hands wandering lightly around his cock and balls, plucking at him through the restraining loincloth. *No, no, it's too soon!* He wriggled out of Rufio's reach to kneel at his feet so, by leaning forward, he could stroke his tongue the length of Rufio's legs, from foot to knee to thigh to… not quite to the twitching length of cock still tightly wrapped, but as far as the compacted lump of his beautiful balls.

I love him. I want him to know I love him. Every taut muscle under the lightly haired length of his amazing legs. Quintus loved the taste of his calf flesh, the moist secrets under his knees when he rolled him slightly sideways, the sharpness of shin, and the bursting sinews of his thighs on the flank. And astonishingly for Rufio, he remained happily supine under the busy tongue. Quintus tasted the silky flesh of inner thigh, and again back to the underside of those big balls. He relished already the taste of what they held.

* * *

The tongue painted hot trails across his skin that cooled and pulled as they did so—and suddenly Rufio could no longer bear to lie still under the maddening licking. So he sat up, swiveled around, and took Quintus's nearest foot in his grip. *Time for some of your own liquamen, my lovely patrician.* He swallowed the big toe, as Quintus had done to him. Quintus reciprocated even more vehemently and they were sucking each other's toes while their still-clothed cocks pressed and bumped against each other in a frenzy of anticipation.

Quintus tucked his head in and started licking up Rufio's legs again. Rufio did the same, and they slowly wriggled until their tongues reached the nexus of limbs. Rufio reached the tucked waist of Quintus's loincloth and forced his tongue under until he could lick the tip of his cock. *Damned thing's in the way!* He tugged the loincloth loose and his lover's long cock bobbed free and into Rufio's eager mouth. *Oh, the taste, the cock taste, the Quintus Caecilius Alba flavor, like a hot mushroom round between my lips.*

And Quintus got to target as well. The feel of his lips around Rufio's

cock, up and down and around his naked balls, was incredible, like they'd never done it before. He wanted the same. A deep breath and then he took in the entire length of the rigid shaft, exhaling as his stretched mouth dropped down, relishing the pulse of blood in Quintus's vessels under the smooth skin, so soft over so hard, he went all the way down until his throat bulged with his lover's hard-on.

"Aaah, Rufio! What you doing to me…?"

He relinquished cock meat and looked up. Their eyes met: cornflower blue under lashings of flame-colored Celtic hair; raging black but burning with fire and lust. Quintus raised Rufio's cock so he could see the flicks of pointed tongue tip running over the slit and then down under the exposed lobes to that sensitive spot, round and around… and back up again.

The sensation thrilled somewhere between pain and tickle, yet so addictive that Rufio wanted him to keep doing it. That oh-so virtuous patrician innocence combined with wanton lust only served to fire Rufio higher into sexual abandon. He yanked

Quintus's cock up and did the same, tasting a sudden flowering of pre-cum juice. He licked at the neat slit again and lipped another pearl of lubricant, a heady ambrosia that went straight to his brain like a shot of that Egyptian fire-liquor Septimius had pressured them into trying in Alexandria.

Rufio was making pre-cum so fast Quintus thought it was like he was taking a piss, the taste of passion. He wanted to do so much more, but somewhere at the back of his mind a voice told him a fuck would come later. Right then neither wanted to change what they were doing to each other. Quintus started to rub Rufio's cock head with his lips, tongue, cheeks, and throated the full length, faster and faster. He felt and could see from under his lashes Rufio doing the same in return, and his mouth with the tongue protruding under the cock head made Quintus shivery with anticipation.

Quintus felt his balls contracting uncontrollably. They hurt with the urgency of impending climax, and like two farmhands milking cows, only using their mouths, they moved in communion toward the pinnacle of orgasm. Quintus was dizzy with desire and from ramming his head up and down at this pace.

The natural lube Quintus was producing in a continuous flow was driving Rufio crazy. He could hardly wait for him to begin coming, ready to cease the frantic head movement, ready to mouth-grip the pulsing shaft firmly but gently to let Quintus's whole load erupt naturally and pour down his gulping throat. *And I'm going to feed him my cream any instant. The way he's sucking me I just know he wants it. He wants it he wants it he wants it…*
The release was enormous, exhausting, fulfilling.

"Absolutely exhausting," Cassius Quietus was telling everyone. "The longest and bloodiest fight in the Colosseum I ever saw."
Quintus shook his head to clear the dregs of daydream arousal.

"Oh yawn, gladiators," Rufio said quietly next to him. With unusual politeness, he covered up a cucumber burp with the back of his hand. "I really don't know what you Romans see in the sport."

"Ah, I see you have reverted to being a barbarian Celt when it comes to something you don't approve of."

"You told me you don't care for the noble sport."

"It's true I'm not keen on the profligate shedding of blood for entertainment, but I don't sneer at what others find enjoyable."

Quintus was searching for a response when Trajan spoke up. "If all goes well on our way back we should reach Rome in time for the Ludi Plebeii. It's important for me to host the Senators and Magistrates' feast on the penultimate day."

"I suppose the festival goes some way to cement relations between the plebs and the upper classes," Hadrian drawled.

"Oh I love the Plebeian Games." Spurius beamed happily, wiping cucumber oil from his lips. "I do hope you will have a fine haul of beasts from Egypt, Caesar. But best will be the prisoners. I'm sure they will give our beginner gladiators some fine sport." He turned a slightly wine-bleared gaze on Rufio and Quintus. "You lads should get your bookings in for the best seats in the Colosseum. And you know where they are." He winked and dipped his head in the Emperor's direction.

Spurius failed to see Hadrian's warning signal, that he might be about to go a step too far, even in an informal gathering such as this.

"I'm sure a grateful Caesar will grant you seats in the imperial box," he added airily. "You can really see blades tearing flesh from there."

Hadrian coughed, but Trajan waved the presumption aside. "I would rather listen to Quintus reciting his poetry than have him crying for blood in the sand. However, we will see." And with that the general buzz of conversation took over again.

Rufio leaned in close. "Rather than watch grown men prance about with mismatched weapons giving each other a licking, I know

I'd rather give you a good licking, like this afternoon." Rufio caught Junilla watching them, smiling privately. She liked to know "her boys" were getting on. He tipped her a wink.

"That so, my wicked Celt?" Quintus murmured, his daydream broken.

"Mmmm, give me a *mmmm*-murmillo hot from victory." Spurius squinched his lips in a salacious smack.

"Oh you're so cheap," Quietus mocked. "I'll take retiarius ass any day."

"The gods spare us," Rufio whispered. He rolled his eyes in unusually well-mannered despair. "I tell you this, Quintus, after what we went through with Malpensa's fighting beauties in Rome, I swear by the colossal cock of Cernunnos I'll never have another thing to do with gladiators."

But… erm—
Rufio and Quintus will return in…
*Boys of Imperial Rome: **Twisted Blade in the Arena***

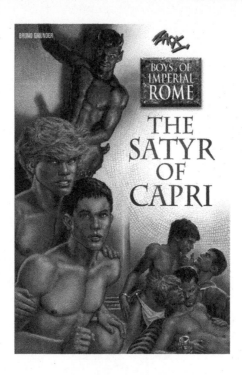

Zack: THE SATYR OF CAPRI
Boys of Imperial Rome

320 pages, soft cover
5¼ x 7½" / 13 x 19 cm
978-3-86787-854-8
US$ 16.99 / £ 10.99 / € 14,99

Rome, AD 108. What, or who is the mysterious Satyr of
Capri? Rare statue, man, or monster? Why do danger and
death stalk all who are connected with the elusive secret?
New friends and lovers Quintus and Rufio are unwittingly
embroiled in the quest for the truth. From the mansions of
the rich to the teeming underbelly of the world's mightiest
city, braving the violence and tasting the sensuous pleasures
thrown at them, the boys risk all to unravel the secret of the
Satyr. Plunge into the world of imperial Rome—debauchery
and cruelty, envy and greed, grisly legends and disaster
beneath the cliffs of Capri, undercover deals and urban gang
warfare—for a roller coaster ride bursting with sex and action.